LILAC INK

THE KNOCKNASHEE STORY - BOOK 1

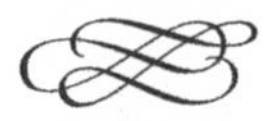

JEAN GRAINGER

❀ Created with Vellum

To my mother, who won't read this book in this life, but will somewhere, I hope.

AUTHOR'S NOTE

This book is partially set in West Kerry in Ireland, an area known as a Gaeltacht, where the Irish language is still the first language of the people, and so this book contains some Irish words and phrases. These words are, for the most part, either self-explanatory or explained in the narrative, but there is also a glossary at the end of the book, should you want more clarification.

You will also notice that the American sections use American spelling and punctuation where the Irish ones use Hiberno-English.

It is often pointed out to me that I have 'misspelled' words, such as honour, favour, travelling, kerb etc, but these are just spelling variations between Ireland and the USA, so I'll stick to what I know because to be honest, I am more afraid of being haunted by the ghost of the scary Sister Margaret who taught me to spell, than of my lovely readers.

CHAPTER 1

KNOCKNASHEE, DINGLE PENINSULA, CO KERRY

pril 1938

Grace Fitzgerald studiously applied a modest scrape of butter to her morning toast as her older sister, Agnes, while spreading a lot more butter on her own toast and marmalade as well, grumbled on and on about all the immoral shenanigans in the sleepy town of Knocknashee.

Today's diatribe was mostly to do with Peggy Donnelly, and the new range of pink and mauve cardigans and scandalously short skirts – barely reaching the knee – she'd put in the window of her shop, the wearing of which was bound to lead to dreadful behaviour among the young people of the town.

'So we won't be shopping in Peggy's until they're taken down. I don't know what's come over her. Grace, are you listening to me?' Agnes leaned in and pointed with her knife.

'Yes, Agnes,' Grace replied gazing down at her plate. Secretly, she thought Peggy's new display brightened the place up and doubted very much it would lead to naked dancing and satanic rituals on the strand. But she couldn't say that sort of thing to Agnes, not even as a joke.

Anyway, she didn't want to be cheeky to her sister. She was entirely dependent on Agnes, who had been like a mother to her – as she was often reminded – since their parents died.

It had been horrible, and so sudden; it still upset Grace to think of it. Eddie and Kathleen Fitzgerald had served as the master and mistress of the school attached to this big stone house. They were on their way back from one of the islands dotted off the coast, where they'd set up a school for the island children and visited twice a year to bring more resources for the only teacher, a past pupil of theirs who had married an islander. On the way back to Knocknashee, their little boat was caught in a squall and capsized, and they drowned.

Grace had just turned eleven when it happened. The Fitzgeralds' only son, Father Maurice, had been away on the missions in the Philippines and couldn't come home. So it was Agnes, the second oldest at twenty-six, who had to take over the running of the household and the school. Grace had been a surprise baby, arriving many years after her parents were sure their family was complete.

Together she and Agnes ran the school now, though her sister had no desire to be a teacher. Unlike their parents, who had been much loved, Agnes had no vocation for it. But she did it anyway, she said, to put food on the table for Grace. It was a big sacrifice for her, because it had meant giving up on her plans to marry Cyril Clifford, the son of the local hotelier.

Before Mammy and Daddy drowned, Agnes had been sure of a proposal from Cyril. They'd been doing a strong line together for years, and he was considered a fine catch; it was just a matter of time before he put a ring on her finger. But after the accident, everything changed.

If Agnes married, the law required her to give up teaching, and Cyril could hardly be expected to take over responsibility for Grace as well as a new wife and any future children they might have, so until Grace was old enough to look after herself, the marriage was put on hold.

Grace knew to be very grateful, because Agnes could have solved the problem in a second by putting her into an orphanage, the same way Charlie McKenna's children had been sent away when the postman was left unable to cope after his wife died in childbirth.

To make matters even worse for Agnes, a year after their parents died, Grace contracted polio and was rushed to the hospital in Cork.

Agnes tried desperately to keep it quiet – people were so frightened of the disease – but of course it got out. And Cyril wrote to Agnes, saying his parents were afraid of him catching polio from the furnishings in her house, and then guests would be put off coming to their hotel, and that it would be best all round to discontinue what he referred to as 'their friendship'. Poor Agnes was humiliated and disgraced in front of the whole place when he married a woman from Limerick not a wet week after he'd finished it with her.

For the next four years, Grace was in hospital. Agnes was unable to visit because the school board forbade it on account of the risk to the schoolchildren in her charge. Agnes had to manage everything all alone, with a broken heart. No wonder she'd become so unhappy and saw badness everywhere.

Grace had been lucky by comparison. She'd had to have a lot of painful operations and therapies, but at least she'd been well looked-after in Cork. The consultant, Dr Warrington, had such a bright, kind face; just the memory of him cheered her up. He went so far and beyond for his patients. His wife was a wonderful woman too; she'd put Grace through her school exams, as she did all the children. The couple had no family of their own, and all their loving energy seemed to go into nurturing the suffering youngsters in their care whose lives had been devastated by the terrible disease.

One of Grace's happiest memories was when Mrs Warrington told her she was so clever that she should train as a teacher at one of the new colleges instead of learning on the job as lots of rural teachers did. Though it turned out the doctor's wife had overestimated Grace's abilities.

The summer of Grace's leaving cert, when she was sixteen, she'd finally been allowed home from the hospital. Dr Warrington had driven her to Knocknashee from Cork himself so she didn't have to take the train and bus alone, and like his wife, he'd told her he was sure she'd do very well in her exams. But when the results arrived, she'd failed so badly that Agnes was too kind to even show them to her; she'd put the letter into the fire instead.

It was probably for the best, as Agnes said. Even if her marks had been good enough, Grace would never have been able to go to teacher training college in Limerick or Dublin; she'd never manage alone, not with a twisted leg in a calliper. And though that door was closed, a window opened. Agnes persuaded Canon Rafferty, the chairman of the school board, to appoint Grace as her teaching assistant. For a small wage from the Department of Education, she could take the four- to eight-year-olds off Agnes's hands.

Grace knew this was good of Agnes, and it was also kind of her sister not to take a penny of her wages for her bed and board. The polio meant she could never be married, not now that she was a cripple, so Agnes insisted that every penny Grace earned went into a savings account in the post office so she could pay someone to look after her when she was left alone in the world.

Unfortunately this meant Agnes had to pay for everything out of her one wage, and a lot of scrimping and saving went on in their house as a result, hence the tiny scrape of butter Grace allowed herself for her toast. At times she felt guilty for even existing.

Agnes had moved on to another topic now. 'And as for that Tilly O'Hare girl, walking off the bus from Tralee into the square wearing a shirt and tie over her skirt, and her hair short like a man's. Bad enough she wears her dead father's overalls around the farm, but *a shirt and tie*! I don't think she's right in the head. Every seed, breed and generation of the O'Hares were…peculiar. So you'd better stay away from her, Grace.'

Grace took a bite of her toast as a way to hide her grin. She rather wished she'd been there to see it when Tilly got off the bus and caused such a scandal in the town. Agnes was a firm believer in always looking respectable. Today she was wearing a long black skirt, though almost everyone wore knee-length now, and a buttoned-up black cardigan with a white blouse underneath. With her fair hair set in waves, light-blue eyes and heavy tortoiseshell glasses, she looked forbidding, but Grace assumed that was her intention.

'I mean,' her sister continued, with a deep sigh, 'that brother of hers, Alfie, going off to Russia. In all honesty, what would take a Christian God-fearing man to that cradle of sin? And her older sister, Marion, shacked up with a married man above in Dublin? Did you ever hear the likes? No shame.'

Agnes pursed her lips in such a way when she said that last bit that Grace nearly laughed, because it put her in mind of Flossie the tabby cat's bum; she had to bite her lip to keep a serious face. It was a shame, because it wasn't as if Agnes was ugly. She would be pretty if she only smiled a bit more.

'So I have your word? You'll have no more to do with her?' Agnes's china-blue eyes were fixed on hers.

Grace hesitated. She usually went along with whatever Agnes said she should or shouldn't do, or who she should or shouldn't talk to. But Grace was very fond of Tilly, who had written to her a lot while she was in hospital. Those letters had been a lifeline for her. Agnes had been far too busy with her work to write; by the time she'd marked the books of the whole school, because she had no assistant, the most she had time for was a card at birthdays and at Christmas.

'Tilly was my best friend from school, Agnes,' she reminded her sister carefully.

'Maybe she was,' said Agnes, looking very put out. 'But that was when you were twelve years old. You didn't see her at all while you were in hospital, and you've barely seen her in the year since you've been back. It won't be any trial to you not to see her at all.'

Grace remained silent. She hadn't told Agnes about Tilly's letters so as not to sound like she was criticising her sister for not having written more herself. And she tended not to mention the times she and Tilly got together for a walk on the beach, because she knew Agnes might not approve.

'I don't ask for much, Grace,' said Agnes, with another deep sigh. 'God knows you are a worry to me with your flighty ways, but I care for you and ask for nothing in return. I don't mind one bit having to pay for everything in this house out of my own wages while yours go into a savings account. And all I want in return for all my sacrifices is a commitment to stay away from the likes of Tilly O'Hare, and if you can't grant me that one small request, well, 'tis a sorry state of affairs, I must say...'

Grace shrunk inside. She knew she was a burden to Agnes. Being so young when their parents died; then catching polio and driving Cyril Clifford away; coming home from the hospital with her right leg all twisted and shorter than the other, thus ensuring no man would ever look at her, let alone marry her; failing all her exams; being too soft on the bold children in her care because she didn't understand how to teach properly. How could she go against her sister, who was only trying her best to keep her respectable, in the way a schoolteacher had to be?

'Grace? Are you paying attention?'

'I am, Agnes.'

'Then promise me you'll –'

At that moment their late father's brass carriage clock on the kitchen mantel struck the half hour. It had been given by the Irish National Teachers' Organisation for services to the profession, and it kept excellent time. Grace stood up as quickly as she could, a clumsy, noisy, clattering effort because she couldn't bend her bad right leg in the calliper.

'It's half past eight, Agnes. I'd better be going over.' She hoped her sister wouldn't notice that she'd managed not to give a commitment to cut Tilly off.

Agnes nodded, satisfied, as she helped herself to another cup of tea and a second slice of thickly buttered toast with more marmalade. Because Grace was only the assistant, she was the one who made sure all the children were in and accounted for, the fires lit and the two classrooms ready for the day. 'Make sure the blackboard in my room is fully clean, Grace – you left chalk on it yesterday. And tell young Mikey O'Shea I want to see him before school is over – he was trick-acting in the back of Mass on Sunday with his wastrel of a father.'

Grace's soft heart sank. Poor Mikey was only six, but she knew if she sent him to see Agnes, he'd get the leather, the poor misfortune.

Agnes took being headmistress very seriously. She felt responsible for all the souls in her care, and that meant beating any child who showed a tendency towards sin.

In fact her readiness with the leather strap was the first reason she'd fallen out with the O'Hares, because Mary O'Hare was the only one who had ever dared challenge her.

Grace would never forget it. Agnes had slapped Tilly so hard one day, she made her hand bleed. It was in the year Grace's parents had died, and she and Tilly were still only eleven. Agnes had taken over the school and was finding it difficult because she was having to fill in for both her parents and teach forty children instead of twenty, so it was hard for her to keep order, particularly with children like Tilly, who was always encouraging the others to laugh.

The next day Mary O'Hare appeared in the classroom, walking stick in hand, the *tap, tap* of the metal tip on the floorboards heralding her arrival before they saw her. Mrs O'Hare was a small, stocky woman, with a slow gait and a dark moustache of hair on her upper lip. She was a martyr to the rheumatism, but she marched right into the classroom, no knock or a bit, and raised her walking stick at Agnes.

'You're only a long string of misery, Agnes Fitzgerald, and no wonder your man Clifford has been trying to escape you for years.'

'Get out of my classroom!' gasped poor Agnes, white with shock.

'I will when I'm finished, but listen carefully to me now.' Mrs O'Hare punctuated each word with a point of the stick in Agnes's bony chest. 'You lay a scrawny finger of yours on my Tilly ever again, and I swear 'tis the last thing you'll ever do.'

'You can't threaten me with violence,' Agnes had protested, her brow furrowed and her shoulders back. 'You'll be sent to prison.'

'I will not, because I won't lay a hand on you. But I've fairies on my land, remember that, and I've been good to them and they've been good to me.'

Agnes's face went red. She opened her mouth, probably to say only ignorant people believed in the fairies, but then clearly thought better of it and closed it again.

'And don't ye take a tack of notice of this auld *cailleach*,' Mary told the class, looking around at them all.

Little Grace knew that everyone called Agnes a *cailleach* behind her back, the Irish word for a witch, but this was the first time someone had said it to her face; this would surely go down in the history books as a day no child present would ever forget. She remembered thinking she should speak up in defence of her older sister, but she'd just sat there in silence, feeling a guilty mixture of delight and terror.

Remembering about Mary O'Hare gave Grace an idea that might save Mikey. 'If only John O'Shea wasn't so fierce bad-tempered,' she said softly as she left the room. 'I've been told he's a history of cursing anyone who crosses him.' She hoped against hope that Agnes would believe her, even though John O'Shea was the nicest little man you could ever meet.

His father, Seánie O'Shea, had been a *seanchaí*, a storyteller of renown all over the peninsula for his wonderful stories of *púcas* and the *bean sidhe* and the fairies. He told tales of curses that spanned generations, of thwarted love and wicked people, as well as of great passions and things that happened long ago that were so funny, you'd cry laughing at him.

The *seanchaí* were an ancient role in Irish life, the descendants of the bards of old, and very well respected. A family would never refuse hospitality to a *seanchaí* for fear of being cursed, so she hoped Agnes might have the same concerns about John O'Shea. Agnes said she had no time for the old ways, the mythology and the old *piseógs* – silly superstitions of ignorant people, she called them – but she was wary of Mary O'Hare for that reason, and she would never go outside the door on the feast of Samhain for fear of the dead.

Six-year-old Mikey O'Shea had the same sweet nature as his

father, but he was a lively boy with a cheeky grin, and last Sunday he'd been hopping around a bit. The canon had been giving a particularly long sermon, but he expected full and complete attention from everyone.

He had scowled down from the altar at John and Catherine O'Shea, who were standing at the back with their tribe of small children, and made some pointed remarks about people lacking true devotion.

Grace didn't think that was true. The O'Sheas would give a beggar their last bite, even though like many in Knocknashee, they had real problems raising a large family while working a small farm. Catherine was expecting another baby any day now, and Grace couldn't help feeling that if the O'Sheas didn't look entirely engaged with keeping Mikey in order, maybe they were trying to figure more important things out.

She left the kitchen and limped to the hallstand. The leather and metal splint that went from the top of her thigh to her foot, where it slotted into a built-up shoe, was uncomfortable. She managed, but there were times when she longed to walk upright and straight.

Then she would remind herself of all the other children she'd known in the Victoria Hospital in Cork, struck down by the horrible infection. The little ones who had to go into the terrifying iron lung because their chests were affected, or those who died. And some children had both arms and legs paralysed. She was very lucky; she was spared the worst. All she had was one discoloured and twisted leg that was permanently cold and a calliper to strengthen the muscles weakened from the disease. Dr Ryan, the local GP, had checked her over when she came home and told her she had Dr Warrington to thank for being as mobile as she was. The Cork consultant was a great man and someone Dr Ryan much admired.

Standing at the mirror in the small hallway, she brushed her thick auburn hair, frustratingly curly, and pinned her hat on. She had Daddy's hair and also his eyes – large and green and flecked with amber. She didn't have his height; he had been over six feet, but Grace had never been tall, and the polio had shortened her even more, so she was only four foot eleven. Sometimes she thought she looked like one of those collectable china dolls with her pert little nose and curved, slightly pouting lips.

'I'm right quare looking and no mistake.' She sighed as she fixed a stray curl under her hat, but then she mentally shook herself and told herself to count her blessings, as she did every night when she said her prayers before bed. She might never marry or have her own children, but she had the children of the town to look after, and it was a wonderful job and she loved it. She had a roof over her head and a way of earning her living. She had her books to comfort her; she was currently reading *The Count of Monte Cristo*. And at least she wasn't a prisoner in a dungeon like Edmond Dantès. She was alive and free.

Come on, Grace, she ordered. *You've so much to be grateful for. So put your best foot forward – isn't that what Dr Warrington used to say?* A little in-joke since she only had one good foot. She often wished she could see the good doctor and his wife again, but they had other little girls and boys to care for, and they could hardly be expected to keep in touch with every child who had passed through their hands.

CHAPTER 2

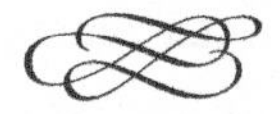

Grace walked awkwardly down the front path and turned next door to the two-room Knocknashee National School. The school and her parents' house shared a wall, so she didn't even have to go out on the street, just through a little gate, to enter the schoolyard.

There were sixty-five children enrolled and taught in two rooms. The building was bright and sunny, as their parents had built it to be thirty-five years ago, and the two long classrooms were of equal size, but there the similarity ended.

Grace tried to have the juniors' room looking the way she remembered her mother keeping it before Agnes took over: lots of pictures of the baby Jesus, showing donkeys and cows and shepherds and kings, all worshipping the tiny, smiling child, and some of her mother's paintings of flowers and meadows and the ocean. It would have been nice to get the children painting a few pictures to peg up on a line across the room, the way her mother had done, but Agnes said the school funds wouldn't run to paint, and besides, paint made a terrible mess, so Grace had to give up on that idea.

The only thing Agnes allowed as decoration in the seniors' room where she taught the older children was an enormous brown and beige replica of the Shroud of Turin, the length of linen in which Jesus was wrapped for burial and which bore the miraculous imprint of his face, complete with crown of thorns. It was a very holy reminder of the suffering of Jesus, but Grace thought it was a scary image to show children; it used to make her sad and frightened when she was a child in that classroom.

Crossing the yard, she saw a few of the older children were ready for the day and were kicking a real leather football.

'Did you get that for your birthday, Patrick?' she asked a red-haired lad with freckles and ears that stuck out like a toby jug.

'I did, miss.' He was clearly delighted with his gift.

Paddy and Eileen O'Flynn wouldn't have much going spare with eleven children, so she was glad they'd been able to get him something so nice. 'Ten is a big age – it should have a fine present.' She smiled at him. 'But maybe you should let me put that in my bag for now?'

He nodded that he understood and ran in alarm to get the ball and bring it back to her. 'Yes, could you mind it, Miss Fitz? I'd be afraid…'

'Of course I will.' She took it from him. 'Come to my room after school and I'll have it for you.'

It would be nice if Patrick and his friends could play with the ball at breaktime, but it was too risky. Two months ago Agnes confiscated a football from the Murphy boys for fear of them breaking a window, she said, and it was never seen again. It was as well not to run the risk of another such incident.

With the ball safely hidden in her big cloth bag, she went in to light the fires, then she rang the bell and the day began, all the children running in to take their seats before Agnes arrived through the gate into the yard.

Once everyone was settled, Grace closed the door that separated her room from the corridor and told the little children to get out their books.

Mrs Warrington might have been wrong about Grace being bright, but she tried her best to be a good teacher. The children came to her without the ability to read or write or do any arithmetic, and they left her for her sister's room with a neat cursive, all the classics in their little heads and able to add, subtract, divide, multiply and make a percentage. They wrote stories as well as essays, and she'd found a set of tin whistles in the spare room among her parents' things and taught them a few simple tunes. Every evening before they went home, she played the school piano for them, their joyful young voices ringing out; it would do your heart good to hear them. But most importantly she wanted them to leave with a love of learning. She suspected that love would dwindle under Agnes's sterner methods, which were more focussed on saving children's souls than teaching them about the wider world beyond Knocknashee, but she hoped some of the joy would remain and come back to them later.

Today she did their letters and numbers with them, but then she moved on to history and geography, telling them about the world in simple ways.

At the moment they were learning all about the explorers, so the children of Knocknashee who went to sleep to the sound of the Atlantic in their ears dreamt they were on that very ocean on board the *Santa María*, or with Cortés as he burnt his ships in the New World to further encourage his men to seek their fortune. She showed them pictures of Montezuma, the Aztec emperor, and told them where the gold and silver taken from Mexico was used. They gazed in amazement at the picture she showed them in a book of the ceiling of Santa Maria Maggiore church in Rome, where the gold leaf came from gold that the conquistadores sent back to King Ferdinand of Spain, who in turn gifted it to the pope.

People from this little town didn't go far, many being born, marrying and dying in the parish. For some of them, Dingle, the town six miles east of them, was an every-five-years excursion and Killarney might as well be Kathmandu. So many of Grace's pupils might never see Rome – most were unlikely to go beyond the county bounds their whole lives – but Grace had learnt through her illness that the only boundaries to the exploration any person could do was imagined. There were books, there were paintings, and now there were film reels – the world was there for all to see without ever setting foot outside the parish.

The morning flew by. She supervised the children playing in the yard at lunchtime, after they'd all eaten a small snack and had a glass of milk. She paid attention to those who had no lunch – times were hard – and she discreetly gave them some bread and jam. Mrs O'Donoghue from the grocer's supplied her with a loaf and a pot of jam for free as she needed it, and she stored them in a cupboard where Agnes wouldn't find them. For a reason Grace couldn't specify, she just knew Agnes wouldn't approve of handouts.

Lunch duty was always left to Grace, because Agnes didn't want to be exposed to the sun and the wind. It was Agnes who had inherited their mother's delicate complexion, along with Kathleen's long narrow nose and fine fair hair. Daddy's and Grace's skin tone was different; he said there must have been a bit of a Spanish sailor in him since he went so brown in the summer.

In the afternoon, Grace read her children the next bit of the tale 'Tóraíocht Dhiarmada agus Gráinne', a mythological story of a beautiful girl and the man she bewitched to fall in love with her as they were chased all over Ireland by the old warrior Fionn mac Cumhaill – Fionn wanted the young girl, Gráinne, for himself. Grace read it in English, as all the children spoke Irish at home and their English needed work. They hung on her every word as she sat on the desk, her right leg stretched out in its calliper and the children gathered around her. She did the voices of the different characters, and if she got confused and mixed up one character's voice with another, the children were quick to point it out.

Then they translated the list of local townlands from Irish to English, and they used the map to go all over the peninsula, learning why places were called the names they were.

Knocknashee, where they were from, meant 'the hill of the fairies'. The high mound that gave the village its name was gentle and green, with some scree at the top. The legend said that the fairies danced up there, and that it was a portal to the underworld. On certain nights of the year, one had to be careful; people around here still believed in fairies – the *bean sidhe*, or banshee in English – and would never interfere with their ways. Oíche Shamhna, the pagan festival of the dead, what people called Halloween now in English, was the most dangerous. It was widely believed that on that night, the worlds of the living and the dead were closest. There was a risk a fairy would steal a baby and leave a changeling, a fairy child, in its place.

Before she knew it, it was less than an hour to home time, and she was beginning to feel confident that Agnes had heeded her words about the fierce curses of John O'Shea. But then came a knock on the door. One of the older girls stuck her head into the room and, looking a bit nervous and sheepish, said the mistress had asked to see Mikey O'Shea at once.

The little boy looked terrified, his eyes filling with tears. As he got up from his seat, his legs trembling, Grace felt a burst of rebellion. She gestured to him to sit down again and followed the senior girl back into her sister's classroom. Agnes, who had the strap already waiting on her desk, looked confused and annoyed when Grace appeared instead.

'Can I have a quick word with you, Mistress Fitzgerald, in the corridor?' asked Grace. In front of the children, she was not allowed to call her sister Agnes.

Agnes didn't look at all happy, but she followed Grace out into the passageway. 'What's the matter, Grace?' she snapped as soon as the door was closed behind them. 'Didn't Sinead tell you to send Mikey in to me?'

Grace stood facing her, determined not to back down but shaking inside. 'She did, Agnes. But I don't think you should slap him. He hasn't done anything, and he's very upset and terrified.'

Agnes looked as if she couldn't believe her ears. 'The boy was trick-acting in the back of the church during Mass.'

'He wasn't really, Agnes. He was only doing what his parents were letting him do.'

'Exactly.' Agnes's mouth was pinched, her sharp nose quivered, and her delicate skin became patched with red. 'And that's why he must be punished. He needs to know his parents are wrong in the way they behave, unless you mean to let him follow them down the path to damnation?'

'Ah, Agnes, surely you don't think...' Grace could hear her voice failing. It always made her doubt herself when Agnes accused her of not caring for her pupils' souls. She tried to inject more strength into her voice. 'He's only a small lad, and he meant no harm –'

Without waiting for her to finish, Agnes stepped past her and whipped open the door to the juniors' room, barking, 'Mikey O'Shea! Come here at once.'

As the poor boy slowly emerged from the room, Grace longed to snatch him in her arms and run away with him. But she couldn't run, not with her leg – it would look ridiculous. Hating herself, she walked stiffly back into the juniors' room as poor Mikey was marched by Agnes, his head drooping, into the seniors'.

She shut the door and picked up 'Tóraíocht Dhiarmada agus Gráinne' again, hoping if she read aloud in a strong enough voice, she would spare her pupils the horrible sound of Mikey's punishment. But it was no good; there was only a thin partition wall between the two rooms. The slap of the leather was loud and clear, and Mikey's wails made the children go pale and quiet.

Grace found herself unable to speak as the leather sounded again like a crack of lightning in the still air.

No. Just no.

Without saying a word to the children in front of her, she walked out of her classroom and into Agnes's room without knocking. The scene that greeted her steeled her resolve. The older children were watching, sitting bolt upright, terrified to move in case they were next. Agnes stood at the top of the room with her arm raised high, the leather gripped in her fist, gathering all her strength to slap poor, tear-stained Mikey for the third time.

The arrival of Grace made her stop, mid-wallop. 'What are you doing here?' she demanded, lowering the leather.

Grace swallowed the terror she felt and clenched her fists to stop them trembling. 'I've come to take Mikey back to my room,' she managed to say, quietly but firmly, as she crossed to where the boy and her sister stood.

A series of emotions in quick succession appeared on her sister's thin, pale face. Confusion, indecision, followed by cold fury as she raised the strap high again…

Before she could bring it down, Grace pulled Mikey away. 'Come with me, Mikey. It's time to go.'

The little boy turned to her as his saviour and grabbed her outstretched hand like a drowning man on a rope. Together they walked out of Agnes's classroom.

Once back in her own room, she tried to hush her excited chattering class, but they were too thrilled by what had just happened to quieten, so she dismissed them with twenty minutes left on the clock. News of what she'd done with Mikey would be the topic at every dinner table for miles around this evening.

A few minutes later, after tidying up her own room, she also left. Normally she stayed behind to clean the senior room as well, but Agnes would have to do that today. Another mad act of defiance. She crossed the schoolyard with her head held high, not looking back towards the windows to see if her sister was watching, her heart beating furiously.

She felt strangely exhilarated. Whatever the consequences of her public defiance of her sister were to be, and she dreaded to think, she would face them. Because Agnes was wrong.

CHAPTER 3

By the time she let herself back into the house, she wasn't feeling quite so brave because she'd begun to panic about the children. There was a real chance Agnes would dismiss her from her post, and the prospect of leaving the little ones to be taught by her sister filled her with anxiety and guilt, even if by saving Mikey she'd done the only thing she could do in that moment.

As for herself, she'd survive, even if Agnes turfed her out on the street without a penny. She hated the idea, though, because this was the only home she'd ever known; it was full of her precious childhood memories, even if it was a very different place from when her parents were alive.

Eddie and Kathleen Fitzgerald had been very busy people, and the household they'd kept was warm and bright but also slightly chaotic. Since they drowned, Agnes had kept it much tidier, but also dark and cold. She never lit the fire before November because 'turf makes a mess and coal is too dear', and she liked to keep the cotton curtains drawn 'to stop the sunlight fading the upholstery'.

The many trinkets – Mammy loved finding odd-shaped stones that she gathered on the windowsills – had been thrown out, and everything else – the books, their mother's artworks, their father's fishing rods and knitted jumpers – had all been consigned to the storage room upstairs.

At least the piano was still in the sitting room, though hidden by a dust cover, and the gramophone, pushed into the corner and also covered with a cloth. Mammy had bought the gramophone the summer before she died. Her favourite recording had been *London Calling!*, a musical revue written by Noël Coward of sketches and skits and funny songs, and it made her laugh every time. Mammy had been such a light-hearted person; in Grace's memory, she seemed to always be laughing. And Daddy would be smiling too, delighted by her.

Hesitating in the hallway, torn between staying downstairs to face her sister or hiding away in her bedroom, Grace's heart missed a beat as she heard the creak of the gate at the end of the path. But instead of the front door flying open with a furious crash, there was a soft, nervous knock. It was just Patrick coming to get his precious football back. Of course. She'd left the school with it still in her bag.

'Miss Fitz, you were wonderful,' he whispered as she gave him his ball. 'But the mistress is awful mad. She didn't say nothing, but her face is red as Janie O'Shea's hair and her eyes have gone all strange looking.' And having imparted this breathless information, he scuttled away with the ball clutched to his chest, glancing nervously around him in case the dreaded mistress suddenly appeared.

Grace glanced towards the gate in the wall before closing the door, her stomach churning with anxiety. It wouldn't take Agnes long to lock up the school. Maybe giving her some time to calm down would be a good idea.

She headed for the stairs and climbed them as quickly as she could. She had to lead with her left and pull the right leg up after her.

She stood on the landing to get her breath, her hand on the banister. There were four bedrooms off the landing. The first was the largest, her parents' room, which Agnes now used as her own; like the sitting room, it was now a lot tidier but less welcoming somehow.

Grace tried to keep her own room, which she'd had since she was a baby, more in her mother's style. The rag doll Mammy had made for her when she was five, which she'd brought with her to hospital, was called Nellie after Dame Nellie Melba, Kathleen Fitzgerald's favourite singer. It rested against the pillow of her single childhood bed, which was still big enough for her because she was so small. The red wool rug on the dark wood floorboards had come from her *mamó's* house, Daddy's mother. Some of her mother's paintings were on the walls, and Grace had crocheted a bedspread in all different colours, mostly taken from woollen jumpers she'd outgrown. She knew Agnes thought she lived in a pigsty, but Grace found it a bright, cheery oasis in their cold, too-tidy house.

Now, instead of going into her own room, she went into Maurice's, which was opposite hers and was kept the way Agnes liked it, empty except for the bed, which was always made up and turned down, even though the absent priest had not been home to sleep in it since before their parents died. The window of this room looked down at the schoolhouse next door, and she could see Agnes still in her classroom, going through the filing cabinet that stood by her desk. She hadn't cleaned the blackboard yet, so whatever her sister was doing, it looked like Grace still had a few minutes to spare.

The last bedroom off the landing had belonged to Agnes but was now the spare room, and it was full of things Grace remembered from her childhood.

Boxes of old schoolbooks, Mammy and Daddy's clothes and personal effects – the room was full to the ceiling. Nobody but Grace ever went in there. It was where she retreated when she wanted to feel close to her parents.

She went in there now and did what she often did for comfort – she held Daddy's old *báinín* sweater to her cheek. It had been knitted by Mammy with wool that had the lanolin still in it, to keep out the rain and the spray, and the scent of it brought back the image of him, tall and strong, striding through the schoolyard on a soft misty day, his pipe held in his teeth, a permanent smile on his face. He was the master, but the children knew they had no more to fear from Master Fitz than they did from Santa Claus. He never slapped a child, ever.

He handled poor behaviour by giving the child a few extra jobs, or if it was a repeat offence, telling the errant young criminal how disappointed he was, how he was sure they were better than that, how he hated to see them let themselves and their family down in such a way. And sure enough, it worked; they couldn't bear to disappoint Master Fitz.

Mammy was loved by the children too, and she also would never hit a child. She believed that teaching them art and music was just as important, maybe even more important, than arithmetic and writing. Mammy's easel was here in the spare room too, leaning against an old dresser, and her paintbrushes were on the shelf. Grace wished again that Agnes would let her teach the children to paint, the way Mammy had done.

Also on the dresser was an old Boland's biscuit tin, with a picture of a little girl with a parasol on the front. It held a bundle of letters that had been written by her parents to each other when her father was in teacher training college in Dublin and her mother was at home in Knocknashee. This was what Grace had come for.

She picked it up and carried it into her own room, shutting her door behind her. On impulse she pushed a chair under the handle to block the door from being opened too suddenly, then sat at her dressing table and brought out her parents' letters from the box. They were worn on the creases from her reading them, but even though she knew them by heart, it always made her happy to read them again as they were so full of humour and love.

There were her daddy's funny observations of life in Dublin. It was before the Great War, and he described the dresses of the ladies he saw as he walked to and from the college. Her mother replied that while she had asked him about the fashions, he was not to be looking at the ladies too closely. She spoke of how lonely her life here was without him.

Daddy wrote of how hard he found the mathematics part of the course and how he feared for any child learning mathematics from him because he had no numeric skills at all.

In another letter, Charlie McKenna was mentioned with warmth;

he and his late wife had been great friends of her parents. Agnes didn't allow Grace to talk to Charlie, even when he brought the post. It was a pity – he might have good stories of their parents in the old days. But Agnes disapproved of him because he took to the drink after his wife died and his children were taken into care. It wasn't until Nancy O'Flaherty from the post office rescued him with the offer of a job that he'd begun to piece his life back together.

It sounded like Charlie had been a different person when her parents were friends with him, a warm, funny, loyal, trustworthy man. He had no land or boat, so he had worked as a farm labourer for some of the more wealthy families who could afford to pay a man.

She opened another letter. Her Mamó Nóinín, her mother's mother, died the year Daddy was in Dublin. *Nóinín* was the Irish word for a daisy, and every time Grace saw one, she thought of her *mamó*, wishing she'd met her. In this one and a few that followed, Mammy poured out all her loneliness and loss. She wrote of seeing a robin on her windowsill every morning in the months after, and how it gave her comfort in her grief. Mammy was a big believer in signs and always told Grace that a robin was the soul of a loved one passed on, of that she was certain. And then she spoke again of how much she missed Daddy and longed to have his arms around her.

Resting her chin on her hand, Grace wondered if she would ever have someone to write to in such a passionate, loving way. Sometimes she wished she was the kind of girl men looked at, the ones with the trim figures and pretty faces, the ones with hair curled with rags at night and washed in rainwater for shine, the ones with two good legs. Like Tilly, who was so beautiful and drew men's eyes, even when she was dressed in a shirt and tie. But she wasn't beautiful like Tilly. And no man would ever want her. Who'd want a person like her staggering up the aisle to meet him? Nobody, that's who.

She had no one to write to, no one to whom she could pour out the pain and worry in her heart. She wished her mother were still alive, as she was the kind of person one could confide in, however hopeless one felt…

St Jude. The patron saint of hopeless cases. That was who she'd write to. If any saint was the one for her, it would be St Jude, because Grace was nothing if not a hopeless case.

She took out her notepad, a fancy one she'd bought when she was fifteen on a rare trip to Cork City arranged by the nurses to give the children a break from the hospital. Sister Ailbhe, a very kind nurse, had asked Dr Warrington, and he'd not only allowed it, he'd accompanied them, much to the children's delight, and gave them each a shilling to spend. The ten children well enough for the outing were taken down the main street, St Patrick's Street, on the electric tram, and allowed to visit the Munster Arcade. Dr Warrington told them how, as the biggest department store in Cork, it had been destroyed by the British the night they burnt the city to the ground in 1920 as a punishment for the rebellious actions of the IRA; but the Corkonians were not called the Rebel County for nothing and had built it back up again. Dr Warrington was an Englishman, so it was funny to hear him speak in this way, but he had come to love his adopted home and everything about it, and he was as proud of that city as any Corkman you'd meet.

Grace had spent her shilling on some fancy notepaper and a pen that could be filled with any colour ink you wanted. She'd selected a bottle of purple ink, called Lilac Dream, and had imagined using it for writing love letters when she was older, but that was never going to happen now. She'd written to Tilly from the hospital, but that was all.

Maybe she should write to Tilly now...

But Agnes had forbidden her to talk to her old friend ever again, and although Grace hadn't expressly agreed not to do so, she'd been defiant enough for one day.

No, she would stick to her plan of writing to St Jude.

She filled the barrel of her fountain pen with the lilac ink and began, in her small, neat, cursive hand.

Dear St Jude,

I am writing this to you because I have not a single soul in my life in whom I can confide. I feel a bit silly, but I have to get this out of me somehow, and given your portfolio, I thought we might be a good match.

My name is Grace Fitzgerald, and I live in Knocknashee, Co Kerry,

Ireland. I am seventeen years old and an assistant teacher in a school run by my sister, who, God forgive me, I am very angry with right now for beating a little boy for messing at Mass, and I made matters so much worse for myself by walking in and taking him out, mid-punishment.

I wish my parents were alive. They were the teachers before Agnes and I, and they never slapped anyone. I suppose I should be happy for them being in heaven with you and all the other saints, but I miss them.

By the way, I do realise I'm very lucky that, thanks to my sister, I have a roof over my head and food, when so many go poor and hungry. It's not that I'm ungrateful, and she has some wonderful qualities, and she only is hard on the children because she thinks it's for their good in the end, but still. It was a very hard day today. She thinks I'm too soft. Maybe I am.

I had polio and was in hospital for four years, and though I have a limp and my back often hurts, I know I was spared far worse.

Dr Warrington says it's important to rise above the polio. He says some people let their illness define who they are, that they allow the world to see them through the lens of a disease, that they even like the attention it brings, but mixed in with the attention is pity, and that's not something that does any good. Dr Warrington encourages all his young patients to stand up and be counted. We had polio, that's a fact and can't be changed, but he drilled it into us, 'You have polio, you are not *Polio with a capital P. You're a Person with a capital P, with something to contribute to the world. Don't let the world see you as a Polio Victim and not a Person. Don't let it win.'*

He's very funny, Dr Warrington. He says each child in the polio ward is allowed two minutes of an organ recital every morning. That's what he called our complaining about all our aches and pains. He used to encourage us to be cross, or sad, or frustrated, or downright grumpy – he said it was good to let it all out. He even let us say one bad word about the polio once a month – that was a very funny day – and then no more. He said complaining was a bad habit we shouldn't cultivate.

He's right, and I will try harder to do as he says. I know I'm letting him down whenever I feel sorry for myself about the fact no one will ever marry me and I'll never have children. It must be ten times worse for Agnes than it is for me, because she knew what love was and she was expecting to get married until Cyril's mother persuaded him to leave her because I had polio and she was afraid of the disease. And so my sister's heart is permanently broken, which I think is what makes her so sad and unhappy.

I know I complain too much, and I know I am so blessed by the beautiful mountains and sea around me that God made for our enjoyment, and being able to read books and escape that way from what sometimes feels like the smallness of my world. If I'd worked harder at my exams, maybe I could have gone away to teacher training college...

As she wrote this line, a tear dropped onto the page, smudging the ink not yet dry. It didn't matter, though; nobody but St Jude would ever read this, so she might as well get it all out.

But Knocknashee is my world now, and I'm sure it's for the best. I just wish I knew better how to get along with my sister. Why can't I love her like I know I should? Or love her at all?

She's going to be absolutely livid with me for what I did today, and I'm scared stiff of her, that's the truth.

Here she stopped and read back over the lines, and a pang of guilt and shame washed over her. What sort of a person could not love their sister?

Please help me, St Jude. Please intervene so Agnes doesn't sack me, leaving the little ones at her mercy, and could you also make sure she doesn't throw me out on the side of the road, because I have absolutely nowhere else to go.

THE FRONT DOOR SLAMMED. Sharp footsteps crossed the hall and mounted the stairs. Her heart beating rapidly, Grace tore the sheet from the pad, quickly folded it and put it in the pocket of her skirt.

The doorknob rattled, but the door wouldn't open because of the chair wedged under the handle. Grace stayed frozen at the desk. What should she do? How stupid to push the chair under the knob; of course it was just going to make things worse...

'Grace, open this door immediately,' snapped Agnes. The knob rattled again. Her sister tried to force the door, but the legs of the ring-backed chair were wedged against a floorboard that stood slightly proud of the others, so it didn't budge. 'Grace, I will count to five, and if you do not open up, then I will… I will…'

You will what, Grace wondered. And then, as if writing the letter to St Jude had already taken a weight off her shoulders, she stifled a daft giggle at the prospect of Agnes shouldering the door and eventually bursting in covered in dust and splinters of wood like you saw cowboys doing at the cinema. A big, very bad part of her wanted to wait, to see if it might happen.

But the kinder and more sensible part of her knew that to upset her sister even further would be wrong and would also make Grace's situation worse. She stood and crossed the sunny bedroom. Quietly she removed the chair.

Before she could open the door, Agnes made another attempt to force it and burst into the room with an almost comical expression of surprise, stumbling forwards and tripping over the rug with a squawk of fury, landing on her hands and knees.

Grace would have saved her if she could, but she couldn't move that fast. And then an even worse thing happened. The giggle she had suppressed at the idea of Agnes bursting through the door like a cowboy rose up in her again, and the next minute she couldn't help herself – she laughed and laughed, her hands pressed to her mouth. It was the funniest thing…

'How dare you mock me, Grace Fitzgerald!' gasped Agnes as she clambered to her feet. 'How dare you! How dare you… Stop laughing at once!'

But Grace couldn't. 'I'm sorry, I'm so sorry,' she spluttered. 'So…' It was no good. She had to get out of there. Every time she even looked at Agnes's outraged pink face, it set her off again. With as much dignity as she could muster, she headed for the stairs. She wished she could make a speedy exit, but she had to ease down them one step at a time, clinging to the banister, which made the whole thing even more comical, and in the end, she was laughing as much at herself as at Agnes.

'Where are you going?' screeched Agnes from the top of the stairs, enraged. 'What are you doing? For goodness' sake, you're not a child – stop behaving like one! Don't you dare go out in the street like that...'

Still breathless with merriment, Grace took her coat from the hall-stand, placed her felt hat on her head and let herself out the front door. She had no idea what she was going to do next, but she felt it was better she stay away from Agnes for a while.

CHAPTER 4

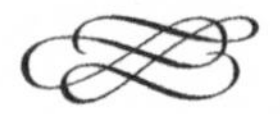

A number of her pupils were out playing on the patch of grass in the small town square as she passed. When they saw her, they waved excitedly and some of them even cheered and clapped until she frowned a little and put her finger to her lips. Such goings-on wouldn't do them any good with Agnes if Grace was sacked and they were left to her sister's mercies.

They chorused their greetings as she limped past. '*Dia dhuit,* Miss Fitz! *Dé bhúr mbeatha,* Miss Fitz!' Agnes was referred to as 'the mistress', but the children all called Grace 'Miss Fitz' and she liked it. It showed they weren't scared of her.

Seven-year-old Leonard O'Flynn, Patrick's brother, was up in a tree with a rolled-up newspaper up to his eye. 'I'm Bartolomeu Dias and I can see India! We've done it, lads, we got around the Cape of Good Hope,' he yelled, punching the air in victory, and Grace smiled up at him. It was wonderful what memories even the little ones had for stories that captured their lively imaginations.

'Be careful up there, won't you, Leonard? I don't want to hear you fell out of the tree,' she called.

The cheeky boy grinned. 'Sure I'm like a monkey, miss. I can get up and down not a bother.'

She laughed. 'I'm sure you can, but still, be careful.'

Clearly they'd all recovered from their fright of earlier. Even Mikey was out playing and sucking a lollipop, though the poor little fella wasn't climbing any trees; his hand would still be too sore for that. She was glad to see he was being fussed over by his cousin Janie, who was fourteen years old and a pillar of sense and kindness.

As she passed them, both the O'Sheas gave her a little wave and smile, and Grace waved and smiled back but didn't stop to speak to them. To discuss what had happened would only add fuel to the fire.

Áine Walsh stood at the base of the tree, surrounded by small children, wearing a red curtain. 'I'm the pope and I've decided that all the new land must be divided between Spain and Portugal, so I'm going to draw a line.' She and some other children had made a map with pebbles on the grass, and she traced a line with a big stick. The Treaty of Tordesillas was being ironed out.

There were a few people waiting at the bus stop outside the wall of O'Connor's undertakers and pub. Seán 'The Last Man to Let You Down' O'Connor stood on his doorstep, chatting to everyone in the queue. He was unusually jovial for an undertaker, Grace thought, always joking and laughing, but he'd been so kind when Mammy's and later Daddy's bodies were washed ashore. He'd seen life in Knocknashee in all its forms and knew that death is a great leveller; it doesn't matter who you are or what you have, it's coming for everyone in the end.

Beyond the undertaker's was Peggy Donnelly's mint-green drapery, which sold everything from a needle to an anchor. The window still displayed the pastel cardigans and nice skirts, so she must have taken no notice of Agnes's objections. Her husband, Matthew, had dropped dead a few years ago, lifting bags in from the back, then and there in the shop. They never had children, so poor Peggy was left very lonesome. She'd eaten her troubles away and was now a woman of considerable girth.

Beside Peggy's was Bríd Butler's sweetshop, and even from here, Grace could smell the delicious aroma of her home-made toffee, ready for the children with a ha'penny after Mass tomorrow. Bríd had a cold box too, and if families were feeling *fláthúlach,* they'd buy a pint of vanilla ice cream frozen in a block to have after their Sunday dinner as a treat. They'd cut it in slices and put it between two wafers. Grace remembered Daddy bringing home ice cream when she was small, but Agnes would never allow such an extravagance now because of them having to survive on a single wage. Bríd was a stocky but timid woman who looked permanently startled.

Then there was Pádraig Ó Sé's cobblers, where the shoes of the parish were reheeled and resoled for years after their natural life. Pádraig was as ugly a man as she'd ever seen, with a bulbous nose and wild hair that looked like it was stuck on rather than growing out of his head, and he had a terrible temperament to match. A person's shoes would want to be in a woeful condition altogether to run the gauntlet of Pádraig Ó Sé's tongue. The children loved repeating stories of his rudeness. Apparently he'd told the curate, Father O'Riordan, that his new soutane was too tight for him, that he must be eating too much of the housekeeper's sweet cake, and he told Peggy Donnelly that the reason her heels were wearing so fast on her good shoes was because she had a 'quare walk' on account of her being so fat. Grace would never forget the day he'd told Agnes that she was the living spit of Winston Churchill with the sour puss. Agnes did always look cranky, but Pádraig was the only one who ever mentioned it. His blunt rudeness was legendary, and he didn't defend himself, merely said he was being truthful. After the Peggy Donnelly episode, which had the children in stitches, Grace had had to do a whole lesson on the difference between honesty and rudeness, trying to drill into them that the world didn't necessarily need the benefit of their opinions on every little thing and maybe if one couldn't think of something nice to say, saying nothing was a good answer sometimes.

Beyond Pádraig's was O'Donoghue's grocers. Biddy O'Donoghue, the woman of the house, was a desperate gossip, and her ample bosom spent the day resting on the counter as she traded the comings and goings of everyone. But for all that, she was kind. She was the one who gave Grace bread and jam or a few apples to make up lunches for the little ones who came to school without one. She always looked well put together – her hair was always set neatly, and she wore a series of pastel-coloured shop coats – but everyone knew her husband, Tom, was too handsome for her. Their first son, James, had arrived seven months after the wedding, so that explained the disparity. Not that anyone would dare say anything about it, because if Biddy O'Donoghue took a set against you, you were goosed. She'd pass stories that were true or true-ish, and if she couldn't pick something up, she'd make it up. Tom went to the wholesaler's in Cork once a month, though he could have got all he needed in Tralee, and he stayed away overnight. It was noted that Tom O'Donoghue might have an eye for the ladies, but it was never remarked upon.

The church came next, set back through wrought-iron gates. With its large main steeple and two smaller ones, it seemed incongruously large for as small a parish as Knocknashee was, but it was probably representative of the level of influence the Church of Rome had on the lives of those who lived beneath its spires. The departed clergy of the parish were laid neatly to rest in the manicured green grass of the grounds. The graveyard where her parents were buried, along with everyone else, Reilig Naomh Ide, was a wilder place, just outside the town, with Celtic crosses and headstones seemingly randomly placed. Some of the gravestones were from the 1500s, and there were people buried there since well before then, it was said, so it was never really planned, not like the churchyard where the clergy were.

Across the street from the church was the entrance to the large, well-appointed parochial house. Canon Rafferty lived there with his housekeeper, Kit Gallagher – she of the sweet cakes – and the chubby curate, Father O'Riordan.

Canon Rafferty was a tall, thin man with a long nose and sparse white hair. He was silent almost to the point of being invisible but with a cutting tongue when he decided to use it. He was a huge admirer of Agnes – they could often be seen talking after Sunday Mass. That was how Mikey's punishment was decided on; it was probably the canon's idea. Grace shivered at the thought. She liked going to Mass, but it was very hard to like the canon.

She did like the curate, though, a small tubby fellow with spectacles so thick, they made his eyes look like saucers. The children were the same; they were afraid of Canon Rafferty, but they loved it when Father O'Riordan visited the school. He asked them about their football, he told them he played hurling himself when he was at school, and he praised their stories and then said their prayers with them.

Behind the parochial house rose the hill for which Knocknashee was named, with the Mass Rock at the top. It was a site of magic and fairies and the banshee long before St Patrick brought Christianity to Ireland in 406 AD, and to this day, people were wary of it. The Church had tried – and failed – to rid people of their pagan superstitions for centuries. Yet during the Penal Laws time in the 1600s, when the English forbade the Irish to practice their religion, priests said Mass in remote areas, often under cover of darkness, and the top of Knocknashee was the place they chose. The rock they used as an altar was still there, and as a child, Grace had often run up there, then down by the old ring fort, then past Tilly's farm, then along the strand back to the village.

Nowadays she couldn't climb the hill, but she could still walk as far as the strand, if she didn't mind the pain.

When he brought her home from Cork, Dr Warrington had left a wheelchair for Agnes to push her long distances, but Agnes had put it away in the spare room immediately, after treating her little sister to a lecture on the bracing effects of sea air and how being pushed around when capable of walking was only for the lazy. 'The devil makes work for idle hands' was one of her favourite sayings. Grace couldn't walk as far as the sea in the beginning; she could only just about make it from the house to the school, and she had to stop and rest frequently. These days she could manage to walk in one go through the village to the strand, though it was hard. So maybe it had done her good, the way Agnes made no allowance for the polio; maybe it had toughened her up.

* * *

As she approached Trá na n-Aingeal, the angel's beach, she saw the tide was well out. That was good because it meant she could walk on the hard sand at the shore; the softer sand up the beach was impossible for her with her calliper.

The water was clear, and she suspected it was cold enough to stop one's heart, but she wondered what it would be like to paddle. She'd better not, she thought. Getting her steel on and off was an undignified process, not one to be shared with the parish.

She walked slowly and deliberately, careful to maintain her balance. She was expert at realising how far she could walk, as she'd have to do the same journey on the return, and she knew that today she could get as far as Our Lady. There was a small cave with a platform above it, halfway down the cliff from the high road above, and on that platform was a statue of the Blessed Virgin.

It had been there for as long as anyone remembered, and every feast day of Our Lady, the people made a pilgrimage to the Mass Rock on the top of Knocknashee and stopped at the little grotto on the way back and sang the hymn 'Hail, Queen of Heaven, the Ocean Star'. It was an appeal to the virgin to protect the people of the parish from the ocean, a plea to watch over them.

She always loved that hymn, and she sang it softly to herself now as she walked. 'Hail, queen of heaven, the ocean star, guide all the wanderers here below. Thrown on life's surge, we claim thy care; save us from peril and from woe. Mother of Christ, star of the sea, pray for the wanderer, pray for me.'

Maybe the Blessed Virgin would hear her prayer and intercede on her behalf. But to do what? She didn't even know what she wanted to happen.

Maybe a handsome sailor would turn up one day, whisk Agnes off her feet and tell her that he would die if she didn't return to Valparaiso with him on the next tide. But handsome sailors from Valparaiso didn't usually pitch up on the Dingle Peninsula. The only sailors they knew were locals, with ruddy faces and calloused hands and who smelled of fish.

Almost everyone around here earned their living by farming or fishing or a mixture of both. The ocean was the lifeblood of this place, but it could be cruel, and there were few families untouched by a maritime tragedy in some way. She should probably be angry at the sea for taking her parents, but she wasn't. It gave and it took; that was the way of it. The Fitzgeralds were just two more added to a long list of people from the peninsula lost by drowning.

The afternoon was warm, and the ocean was calm and glittering. As she gazed out across the smooth surface of the water, it was hard to picture it churned up and angry, as it had been that day when the squall overturned her parents' boat. When Daddy's body was finally given up, a week after Mammy's, the fisherman who found him, Oliver Daly, told her he recognised it by the pattern on Daddy's jumper, the same pattern as the one she had held to her cheek in the spare room. Mammy always knit the same cable stitch.

She rested for a while on a flat rock at the entrance to a cave. When the tide was in, the cave filled with seawater, but for now the water was way out. Lugworms made their little spirals on the hard sand, a few razorbills wheeled around, and seals basked on the rocks over to her right, but other than birds, seals and worms, she was alone.

A bit of the way to the cave, a ray of sun twinkled on a heap of something shiny. She got up to investigate, hauling herself up onto her bad leg. But it was just a few empty poitín naggins, half buried in wet sand, left by some of the older boys and girls, no doubt, coming down here drinking and courting, away from the prying eyes of the town. Yet two more things Grace would never do – illicit drinking or canoodling with a boy. She was too old for such blackguarding now, even if she didn't live under Agnes's eagle eye, but sometimes she thought that if only she'd had some kind of youth, even a tiny bit of wildness, maybe settling down to the life of a spinster wouldn't seem so very hard.

She stooped awkwardly to pick up one of the bottles. The label had been washed off. She unscrewed the top and sniffed; though the naggin was empty, it still carried the pungent smell of alcohol. She rubbed the glass clean of wet sand and found 'Paddy Old Irish

Whiskey' in raised letters on the glass. She set it back down, and to clean her hand, she brushed it hard on her skirt...and heard the crinkle of paper in her pocket.

Her letter to St Jude.

She took it out and looked at it. What was she going to do with this? How did one post a letter to a saint?

With a sudden thought, she picked up the bottle again, rolled the letter into a tube and fed it into the neck of the bottle. She screwed the cap on tightly, and without allowing herself time to change her mind, she walked the long way across the sand to the edge of the tide and flung the bottle out as far as she could into the smooth, flat ocean. Perhaps her parents would read it in their watery graves and send her a sign of their love.

'Mammy, Daddy, do something, please...help me somehow.' As she watched the bottle sink beneath the waves, she felt a tear slide down her face. She didn't normally cry, but today she couldn't seem to stop. She felt so sad and alone.

A pair of brown eyes peeped out of the water. There were lots of seals here, and at low tide, they liked to loll about on the rocks, so it wasn't a surprise, but the soft kindness in the animal's gaze caused the tears to flow in earnest. The seal ducked down and popped up again several times, as if trying to cheer her up with its antics. People believed the *roan*, the seals, embodied the dead. And to harm one would bring great misfortune. Maybe this was a sign?

The seal ducked a few more times before swimming off. The tiny ankle-biter waves lapped gently on the rippled dark sand. She had better go back, she thought; the tide was turning.

As she trudged home, she saw a slim, tall figure running at speed towards her across the sand, and for a scared moment thought that Agnes had come to find her... But no, it was Tilly.

Even though she wasn't supposed to be talking to her old friend, Grace beamed in delight. 'I like your hair,' she said as Tilly came to a halt in front of her.

'It's good, isn't it?' Tilly grinned, revealing a crooked front tooth, and put her hand to her short dark-brown crop. 'No more pins or rubbish. Ma nearly had a stroke, of course, but she'll get over it.'

'You're giving more than your mother strokes with the shirt and tie,' Grace laughed, running her eyes over Tilly's outfit. It must have been the one that caused such a stir in the town yesterday. A man's shirt, a navy-blue tie, a yellow cardigan, a brown skirt and flat lace-up boots.

'I know. You should have seen them when I got off the bus.' Tilly fell in beside her, matching her usually lightning pace to Grace's slow, heavy stroll. 'You'd swear I was in my birthday suit.'

Grace chuckled. 'I wish I'd been there to see their faces. Where were you off to when you saw me?'

'Looking for you, of course. Everyone in Knocknashee thinks you're as brave as a lion.'

Grace stared at her. 'What do you mean?'

'I was in Biddy O'Donoghue's – she was out of our eggs, so I brought her in a few boxes – and by good luck, she was full of gossip about how you'd stuck up for Mikey and sent the children home early. Janie O'Shea had been in telling her, and she gave Mikey a lollipop to take his mind off his sore hand, and then she said you'd come through the town without stopping, when usually you're on some errand, so she was sure you and Agnes had fallen out. Did ye fall out? You should.'

'Oh, well, I...' Grace felt torn. It would be lovely to confide in her best friend, but she'd just written to a saint asking his help to be a better person, and talking about Agnes behind her back and creating a division in the town didn't feel like the right thing to do. So instead she asked, 'Why were you looking for me, Tilly?'

Tilly beamed and pulled two slips of cardboard from her cardigan pocket. 'Tickets! There's a show coming to Dingle, a cabaret troupe. They've not been here for five years, and apparently they were wonderful before, acrobats and magicians and everything, and it's a bit of a dance night after as well on the Saturday. It's called Cullen's Celtic Cabaret.'

'Oh, you're so lucky!' Grace took one of the tickets and looked at it longingly. She'd never been to any sort of show. She'd be happy with anything at all, but Cullen's Celtic Cabaret was famous. 'How on earth did you get these?'

'That auld eejit next door who's ever making eyes at me over the ditch – well, making eyes at my fields, more like – he gave me the tickets and said did I fancy a trip to Dingle, so I said yes!'

'Seriously? You're going with Tomás Kinneally?' Grace was surprised. Tilly was always so scathing about the poor man with the farm next to hers, dismissing his declarations of love as being only a ploy to get his hands on her dead father's land.

'Ah, would you have a hair of sense! I am not indeed doing anything of the kind, I want to go with you. Maybe he was hoping I'd say let's go together, and I could look down on his shiny bald head all evening and watch him totting up my cheque from the auctioneer in his mind, plotting for when my lambs sell this summer. No, but I had the perfect companion in mind, so I thanked Tomás Kinneally for his kindness in thinking of me, gave him a big basket of eggs so as not to be beholden and showed him the door.'

'Oh, Tilly...' Grace was half laughing, even though she felt sorry for poor Tomás getting 'the harsh negation', as her father used to say. But it was silly of him to try. He did have a bald head and he was much too old, and despite the short haircut and the manly clothes, Tilly O'Hare was gorgeous. She had grey eyes that mesmerised people, and high cheekbones and a rich, full mouth. She turned heads wherever she went; she could wear a meal sack and look amazing. The men fell over themselves to get her attention, and it wasn't at all just to do with her land.

'Well, if you won't go with Tomás Kinneally, there's any number of suitors you could take instead of me? Paudie Lehane couldn't take his eyes off you at Mass, and he has a big farm and doesn't need yours.'

Tilly rolled her unusual eyes. 'I could take Paudie, of course I could, but I won't, because I want to take you.'

'I wish I could go with you, I really do...'

'What do you mean, wish?' Tilly pretended to be confused, though she knew well Grace's problem.

'Look, it says here on the ticket, it won't be over until ten at night, and...' She tried to hand the ticket back, but Tilly pushed it away.

'So? I know it's too late for the bus back, but we can stay in a boarding house and come back in the morning.'

'I can't, Tilly, you know I can't. Agnes wouldn't like it.'

Tilly snorted and rolled her eyes again. 'Ah, for God's sake, Grace, will you ever cop on? You're seventeen, for the love of God. How long more are you going to be dictated to by that old *cailleach*?'

'Please don't call her a *cailleach,* Tilly, she *is* my sister... And anyway, I haven't a brasser to pay you for the ticket or the bus or the overnight stay. So no, I'd love to, but I can't.'

Tilly exhaled impatiently. She was not a person to allow anyone or anything to get in her way. Her father died two years ago and her only brother, Alfie was away in Spain, and anyway he had no interest in a small scrabby bit of a farm on the side of a windy hill. Her sister, Marion was up in Dublin with the married man who couldn't show his face down here for fear of the scandal. So that left Tilly – who had only just turned sixteen at the time – and she said she'd farm the land herself. People scoffed and told her mother that she wasn't able, that she'd be better off to let the land to the local men, who'd farm it for her and give her a few bob for rent.

'A few bob is right, Ma,' Tilly had told her mother. 'Very few bob, I'd bet, and we starving to death here, the two of us. No, Daddy made a living for us on all of that land, and so will I.'

So, defying everyone, Tilly started farming. It was hard for her, as it had been for her father; the land wasn't much use for anything but mountain sheep. Tilly was smart, though. She bought a young ram for next to nothing, a docile fellow who didn't look like he'd be up to much because, like Grace, he had a gammy leg. But Tilly was wise enough to know appearances were deceptive, and that ram – she called him Clark Gable, after the film star who was such a ladies' man – made sure every ewe of Tilly's had a lamb the first spring, and now the farmers were used to her face at the fair day.

With the extra money that came in from selling the lambs, Tilly got beehives, with bees that flourished on the yellow gorse that was nearly always in bloom, and twenty chickens and even a cow, which she grazed on a piece of land she'd reclaimed from a wet corner of the farm by digging a ditch to divert the stream. She extracted the honey from the hives and sold it in Dingle and in Tralee, and the eggs to O'Donoghue's grocery in the town, and she encouraged her mother to make more of her brown cake to sell, as well as apple and rhubarb tarts from the gnarly apple trees, and stalky rhubarb that grew around their cottage.

At first everyone said the O'Hares were mad to be selling cakes and pastries on top of everything else – sure didn't everyone make their own brown cake and apple tarts – but they were wrong. There were women in the town now who'd much rather pay a few shillings and have the benefit of Mrs O'Hare's light hand with pastry and soda bread.

So successful was Tilly's enterprise, and her mother's as well, that there was money to spare at the O'Hares' these days.

Now Tilly stood before her, blocking her way. 'That's it, enough *ologáning* now,' she said, her face stern and her jaw thrust out in disapproval.

'Look at me, Grace. You are going to get on the three o'clock bus to Dingle with me on Saturday, and no more about it. I've the money to pay for it. We sold all the baking and honey yesterday, and a woman who owns a boarding house is one of our best customers – she wants jam and honey and as much soda bread as Ma can churn out, so I'm flush. And I asked her if she'd have a room for us for the night, and she has, so it's all arranged.'

Still avoiding her friend's eyes, Grace stared down at her shoes – the black flat one and the other awful, ugly built-up shoe. The truth was, it wasn't even just about Agnes, or her lack of money. What right did the likes of her have to get dressed up to go out for a fancy night in Dingle – and Tilly had said there'd be dancing involved? 'Don't think I'm not grateful, Tilly, but you don't want to be spending your money on me –'

'I can and I will.' Tilly's grey eyes blazed now. 'You put up with that auld *cailleach* – yes, I will call her *cailleach* because that's what she is –

day in, day out, listen to her carping and farting fire about all and sundry and not letting you spend your own wages, and you need a day out.'

'But you said there's dancing at the end, so you'd be better going on your own even. You'd talk to the wall, so you'll get a partner easy for the dance at the end of the show. You hardly need Hopalong Cassidy here, slowing you down…'

Tilly's eyes softened. 'Don't call yourself that,' she said nudging Grace with a smile.

Grace fought back another sudden urge to cry – what was the matter with her today? 'It's what I am and what I'll always be, Tilly. You might meet the boy of your dreams there and want to stand up with him. You don't want the likes of me spoiling your fun.'

Tilly's eyes grew fierce again. 'Stop this, Grace. I wish you could see yourself properly – like really see yourself as everyone else sees you. You're really pretty. Other girls with mousy hair and boring old blue eyes would kill for your colouring. And you think the lads don't notice you, or all they see is the limp, but you're wrong. So what if you have a bandy leg – who cares?'

'Ah, Tilly, give over –'

'I will not give over! That auld crow of a sister of yours has you convinced high up and low down that you're a burden and not a full person, but she's the one lacking, Grace. She might have two good legs, but she's missing a shred of humanity, and you have that in spades.'

Grace laughed, trying to make light of it. 'And that's what men are after, is it? Shreds of humanity?'

'No,' Tilly replied, all traces of humour gone. 'Well, I don't know exactly, but I know that you're…well, you're beautiful, Grace.'

'I am in my eye, but thanks for trying to cheer me up.'

'You are actually,' Tilly said, her eyes downcast kicking a pebble. 'But you won't see it.' Then she turned and skipped alongside, pleading, 'Please, Grace, please come. And I'm going to keep on and on asking until the answer is yes.'

With a sigh, Grace looked again at the ticket she still had in her hand. She knew Tilly was just saying that stuff about her looks and lads noticing her to cheer her up, but hearing it did make her happier, even if it wasn't true. And she would so love to see the show. There was no obligation to dance herself – she could sit and watch Tilly – and it would be lovely to have some fun for once.

Besides, if Tilly said she was going to keep on about it until Grace gave in, then that was exactly what she'd do. So maybe she should just give in now and say yes? At the thought of it, a surge of excitement rushed through her body, her bandy-legged body.

'Coming or not?' asked Tilly. 'And I'm going to keep –'

'Right. Fine. I am. Yes.' She put the ticket in her pocket where the letter had been and exhaled. 'Agnes will probably murder me stone dead when she finds out, but sure I'll die happy. We'll go.'

CHAPTER 5

Grace did her best to listen to the instructions her sister gave before Agnes left, but all she could think about was how strange and what amazingly good luck it was that Agnes had chosen this very weekend to be away on a pilgrimage for four whole nights. Maybe St Jude had heard her pleas.

Agnes was highly devout and believed in the need for sacrifice and suffering to ensure salvation, for herself and anyone she tried to help. She was always going on pilgrimages and retreats, though she didn't usually take time off school – but apparently this was an emergency. She didn't explain why.

Poor Agnes. She'd been so upset and shaken when Grace finally came home from the beach. She'd said Grace had laughed in such a strange way, it seemed like the devil had got into her, especially with her twisted leg and her mad red hair and how she had cackled all the way down the stairs.

Grace couldn't fathom why, but Agnes never brought up the subject of Mikey. She had been bracing herself for the tirade, or whatever punishment was coming, for saving the little boy, but Agnes said absolutely nothing. The only thing that happened was that Mikey brought a lovely apple tart to school the following day as a present from his mother, and Grace had shared it with the whole class at small break.

Tilly said when they met on the beach yesterday to discuss their trip that it was because Agnes was a bully, and when you stood up to a bully, they were never as brave as they made themselves out to be. But Grace wasn't sure; maybe it was the 'devilish' laughter that had done it.

Either way, Grace had apologised profusely, and Agnes had gone some way to forgiving her, because it was Christian to forgive. But even so, for Grace's sake, Agnes felt she had to make this trip to Lough Derg, an island in County Donegal where, legend had it, St Patrick was given a glimpse of purgatory by the Lord in order to provide him with proof of the wonders of heaven and the terrors of hell. This knowledge was to help him as he converted the pagans of Ireland to Christianity in the fifth century. And apparently it was vital for Agnes too, right this minute.

'Now, Grace, it is critical that the house is swept every day, and I know I usually do it because it takes you a lot of time with your leg, but honestly, if I can do the pilgrimage to St Patrick's Purgatory, for three days, in my bare feet, fasting and staying awake overnight in prayer, I think a little light sweeping –'

'I'll do it, Agnes,' said Grace, feeling very guilty about sneaking off to see the cabaret with Tilly while Agnes was going on such a hard pilgrimage.

'And tomorrow and Monday you'll have to have both classes, and the presses in school will need tidying, and the inkwells should all be removed and washed and dried thoroughly. And Canon Rafferty is away himself as well, so Father O'Riordan might call, so ensure everyone knows their catechism off by heart.'

'Of course, Agnes.' Grace felt a surge of relief that it was Father O'Riordan and not Canon Rafferty, who, like Agnes, was a great believer in the strap.

'And when you're relaxing in the evenings with nothing to do, feel free to get on with the basket of darning I've left by the fire.'

'I will, Agnes.'

Satisfied, Agnes turned to examine her reflection in the oval mirror over the hallstand and adjust her hat. She looked very dressed up for a person going to an island in the wilds of Donegal, in her pale-blue dress and coat and cream and navy hat, but she always said that looking your best when you went to Mass was a way of showing respect to God, and so Grace thought it must be the same for a pilgrimage.

'I saw Peggy Clifford at Mass,' Agnes said, with a hint of unkind pleasure in her voice. 'She's gone very old looking, and that coat she had on looked like something you'd use to line the dog's basket, and her with all her money.' Peggy Clifford was the mother of Cyril, the man Agnes should have married.

Reminded again of how her illness had ruined Agnes's life, Grace made an apologetic sound, then, as their father's clock struck the hour in the kitchen, added, 'You'd better go, Agnes.' She felt suddenly fearful that Agnes might miss the bus and call the whole thing off.

'Oh, the canon is going as far as Tralee anyway, so he's offered me a lift,' said Agnes as she patted her hair in satisfaction. At that moment there was the sound of an engine coming down the street, and a smile spread over Agnes's face – a real smile, which made her look suddenly pretty. 'And there he is, right on time,' she said as she stooped to pick up her little travelling case. There were only two cars in the village, Dr Ryan's and the canon's, and the doctor was gone away for the week, so she didn't need to check.

'Well, have a nice drive. And Agnes, you do look nice.'

Agnes inclined her head but didn't acknowledge the compliment. 'And it really is such a pity you can't come with me, Grace, but rest assured, I will pray for you all the time. You be sure to get the jobs done and be a good girl, and think about the Lord's example and how to be a better person.'

And with this parting advice, Agnes swept out of the house and away down the path.

* * *

THAT AFTERNOON GRACE went down to the cove again and walked the beach at low tide, but of the bottle there was still no sign.

The morning after she'd thrown it into the sea, she had woken up certain the stupid thing would wash ashore and someone would read the letter inside and show it to Agnes. Since then she'd been down at every low tide, searching for it.

Today, trundling slowly up and down the beach, her leg paining her, she decided to accept it was gone and would not reappear. And finally allowed herself to exhale. It had probably sunk to the seabed and was becoming encrusted with barnacles and periwinkles while she was up here going out of her mind with worry.

She would forget about it and never do something as stupid as that again.

* * *

ON SATURDAY the bus was at three, and Grace knew it would take her seven minutes to walk the two hundred yards to the bus stop. She planned to time it perfectly so she didn't have to loiter around the bus stop for too long, risking being noticed by Biddy O'Donoghue, whose shop was in sight of the bus stop and who might ask Agnes all innocently where Grace was off to at that time on a Saturday afternoon.

Grace didn't know what Tilly was going to wear to the show, maybe a dress for once, or maybe trousers and a shirt and tie, which would cause a stir, but either way Grace was wearing her best cornflower-blue dress and wine cardigan; she thought she looked nice in them – well, as nice as she could look anyway. The shoes were and always would be clumpy and black, one of them built up with her steel attached.

She often gazed with envy at the elegant high heels she sometimes saw women wear on their way to the dance in the village hall, or the dainty sandals on summer days, knowing she would never own anything pretty like those. But every time she went down that rabbit hole, she did as Dr Warrington suggested and counted her blessings. 'Focus on what you have, not what you haven't,' he would say. 'You have one good leg, two good arms, a working heart and lungs and a fine brain. You'll do great things, Grace Fitzgerald, mark my words.'

That hadn't materialised with her exams. The memory of her failure still stung; she'd worked so hard. But maybe there was time yet.

As she waited for the minutes to pass, she pinned on her wine felt hat, one she'd bought for cheap at a jumble sale and decorated herself with embroidery – she had a good hand for that sort of thing – and donned her overcoat. Her overnight bag she had stored in the press under the stairs, under the winter coats and behind the wellington boots, in case Agnes came home early because of bad weather – which often happened on the islands – and spotted it in the hall and forbade her to go. It was an ancient brown leather case that she'd found in the spare room; probably it had belonged to Mammy. Maybe it would look a bit odd, her walking through the town with it, but she was a teacher and had to carry all sorts of things, so hopefully nobody would think it meant she was staying away overnight.

At quarter to three, she could stand the wait no longer. The tick of her father's clock in the kitchen drilled into her brain, and she felt she might scream if she didn't begin her adventure right now. Somehow she managed to hold off five more minutes, until ten to three...and then decided if she walked even more slowly than usual, she'd be fine.

The busy town bustled, ideal, because it made her less noticeable. The once monthly mart was set up, with men driving cattle and calves, sheep and lambs and even some goats for auction. The overpowering cacophony and smell assaulted her senses as they picked their way across the dung-covered the street. Grace had to pick her way around a woman who extracted a loudly protesting hen from a cage and held it aloft by its feet, wings flapping and the poor bird squawking, as Mrs Lenihan, a local farmer's wife, examined it. Grace had heard from Con Lenihan how the fox had got into his mother's chicken coop and had a frenzy of killing, and so she would have to replace her small flock.

The bus wasn't outside the undertaker's yet when she got there at one minute to three. Tilly wasn't there either, and Grace felt a sickening sense of panic. But then from around the corner that led to the creamery, Tilly appeared, hitching a lift on the back of a donkey and cart bearing empty churns.

'Thanks, Neilus!' she called as she jumped down. The old farmer simply waved. Neilus Collins and his four geriatric brothers had a farm out towards Slea Head, none of them married, and they lived and worked together in total disharmony. Dr Ryan was forever going out there to patch one or another of them up after yet another scrap.

'So you made it,' said Grace, with a quick, nervous glance towards Biddy O'Donoghue's grocer's shop.

'You made it too.' Tilly beamed as she came to stand right beside her. 'I was afraid I'd land up and I'd be all on my tod because you chickened out. Oh, and don't be anxious about that gossip Biddy O'Donoghue telling on you. As soon as we come back from Dingle, I'll make sure she knows it will cost her more than it's worth to blab on us, 'cos she won't get another egg out of me if she does, and they're the best to be had – our hens are fine and healthy.'

'I wasn't anxious...' protested Grace. She was, but she was ashamed to be caught worrying about what people – especially Agnes – might think of her talking to Tilly.

Tilly laughed. 'You were, but I don't mind.' She was dressed eccentrically as always, though thankfully not in trousers, just another shirt and tie, and to dress it up, she'd got rid of the cardigan and was wearing a waistcoat from a man's three-piece suit. She had no stockings under her skirt, only a thick pair of socks and brown lace-up boots, and her hair was slicked back with hair oil. There were murmurs in the bus queue, but Tilly stuck her thumbs in the buttonholes of her waistcoat and looked around with a grin, enjoying the shock and scandal she caused. No wonder Agnes disapproved of Tilly O'Hare; there wasn't a respectable bone in the girl's body.

'Time to stand up to the *cailleach,* Grace,' added Tilly with a smile, delighting in the scandal she caused, as if she'd just read Grace's mind, while poor Grace glanced around in an agony of fright in case anyone in the queue had heard them. *Bobby the bus driver had better get here soon,* she thought, and just then, the bus came down the street.

'Come on, let's get you a seat!' Tilly had an old haversack that had seen a great many better days slung over her shoulder, and she picked up Grace's bag too so Grace could use both hands to get up the steps into the bus.

Normally if Grace had to do a message for Agnes, she would wait until last to get on the bus, not wanting people to have to wait for her, but this time Tilly urged her on first, because the bus was almost full and there would be standing room only if they didn't move fast. She felt cumbersome and awkward, climbing the steps with people waiting behind her, and she was worried she might not find a suitable seat; she needed an aisle seat on the left-hand side so she could stretch her right leg out.

Luckily there was one double seat still empty on the left, so Grace stood until Tilly took the inside and then sat down. She knew her leg was in the way for people trying to get further back, and she apologised to each person as they passed, but to be fair, everyone was kind.

'Wisha don't be worrying yourself, Miss Fitz. Sure amn't I like a spring goat.' Oliver Daly chuckled as he stepped over her. Oliver was the fisherman who'd found her father's body, and he was eighty if he was a day. His white hair stuck out at every imaginable angle, and blue veins threaded his cheeks – a lifetime on the rough ocean catching fish did that to men. The bulbous red nose he'd done to himself through the consumption of whiskey. He was to be heard singing at all hours on his way home, and to the people of Knocknashee, Oliver Daly's light opera was as familiar as the squawk of the gulls or the kittiwakes.

His daughter Assumpta was with him, and she carried a baby, her grandchild presumably, as her daughter was in the hospital in Tralee. That's where they were headed, Grace assumed. People were saying it was consumption, but Grace hoped not. Noirín was only young and had a child to rear.

The bus took off, and as they left Knocknashee behind, Grace felt like all her fears and worries faded away and her heart lifted.

As they trundled along the small winding road, she gazed out of the window and drank in the beauty of where she lived. The mountains, just flushing purple with the rhododendron that would take over the entire range by May, tumbled down to the crashing azure ocean on their right. Ancient forts and cottages dotted the landscape in white stone, and mountain sheep grazed happily, oblivious to the people passing. Men looked up from the bogs where they were cutting turf with the *sleán*, the spade with a blade attached, specifically designed for that purpose, using their moment of inquisitiveness as a respite from the back-breaking work.

After half an hour, the bus made several stops on the way, they descended slowly towards Dingle, passing farmyards full of hens, the puffs of blueish smoke from turf fires dissipating in the clear sky. Out on the bay, brightly painted fishing boats bobbed and gulls wheeled overhead, cawing and screeching; the trawlers would be coming in soon on the afternoon tide, and the seabirds would have their fill of fish guts.

Another bumpy ten minutes later, the bus stopped on the quayside in Dingle. Tilly threw her haversack on her back and jumped down, with Grace's overnight bag swinging in her other hand. Grace waited for everyone else to get off, then followed her out. She took a deep breath of the briny air, the not-unpleasant smell of seaweed and freshly landed fish competing for supremacy in her nostrils.

'We did it, Gracie girl, we got out of Knocknashee.' Tilly laughed as they stood admiring the bustling scene of the big town. 'Dingle today, maybe New York next week?'

Before they went anywhere else, Tilly insisted on buying them fish and chips in a corner café just off the pier. Grace hadn't realised how hungry she was until she tasted the crisp batter and soft flaky cod inside and the delicious salty chips. She ate every morsel, and then, despite Grace protesting that she'd already spent enough, Tilly got them an ice cream each from a little huckster shop on the quay, which also sold sandwiches and lemonade to the holidaymakers. As she licked the sweet, lovely coldness, Grace was in heaven. It had been so long since she'd had any kind of treat. Dr Warrington knew she was partial to a Fry's Chocolate Cream and to Hadji Bey Turkish delight, and often brought her one at the hospital after a trip into town. But in the house she shared with Agnes, there was never enough money to buy sweets, or an ice cream from Bríd's – or God forbid, a whole block to share – or a cream slice from the Wooden Spoon bakery in the village, or anything like that.

Grace understood Agnes's logic, but maybe her older sister would be happier with life if she could be persuaded to allow Grace to squander a little bit of that money occasionally on a treat for the two of them.

'Mm...this ice cream is so nice. I can't remember the last time I had one.' Grace sighed and licked more of the cold cream.

'You really should make her let you spend your own savings on something nice, Grace. It's your money, and it's not up to her what you do with it,' said Tilly as they sat on a bench overlooking the sea, and it was like she'd read Grace's mind for a second time that day.

'Yes, I might suggest it to her. We could have a cake for tea or something.'

'I didn't mean for *her*.' Tilly gave the customary snort that seemed to come out of her every time Agnes was under discussion.

'Ah, Tilly, don't be like that. I feel bad enough, here licking ice cream with you while Agnes is doing St Patrick's Purgatory for three days, in her bare feet, and praying and fasting all night.' Grace sighed, fighting the guilt.

But Tilly's only response was an even louder snort.

CHAPTER 6

The tent was set up in the field just outside of Dingle. By the time Grace and Tilly arrived in the big, long cart drawn by two horses, which shuttled to and fro giving lifts to the field from the town, the crowds were already gathering at the entrance.

Cullen's Celtic Cabaret had last been here five years ago and had been an enormous success, so everyone who could get a ticket was going. The town had been all agog as the performers wandered round earlier today. The lady who sold them the ice cream told them about a woman with a long black-lace dress, down to her ankles but skin-tight, and a red enamel comb in her hair. She was the famous Aida, and she had come in to buy ice cream for a pair of twin boys who called her mama and spoke in Spanish. The lady in the shop said she didn't look like a woman who had ever given birth, but the two boys were the spit of her, with dark skin and eyes but with white-blond hair. Their father was Peter Cullen, it would seem, the man who owned the show, but he was married to another woman and she'd left him for someone, his brother or something? Grace hadn't really followed her – she was all nods and winks and nudges – but it all sounded very racy, whatever it was.

Grace could hardly believe she was going to see the show. The performers were household names in Ireland now, and they'd toured all over Europe and even America, yet here they were in this little town.

They had been putting on a show every night since Monday, and some of the people on the cart had gone to more than one performance. This one was the grand finale, where everyone was going to perform, and people could stay behind to dance afterwards with the actors. The men were talking excitedly about Aida and Maggie, and the women were on about Enzo the trapeze artist, who was married to a very posh English lady, Lady Florence something – they had three wild-looking children who performed with their father, swinging from the rafters.

As the crowd filtered into the tent, they were greeted by Peter Cullen himself, and when Grace hobbled past him, he gently took her arm and showed her to a comfortable aisle seat with a cushion, where she could stretch out her leg but still have a good view. He was very good-looking and wore the most amazing suit, black satin with gold buttons, and Grace blushed to the roots of her hair at being on the receiving end of his special attention.

The tent continued to fill up until there was standing room only, and finally Peter Cullen introduced the opening act with a flourish, accompanied by a roll of chords on the piano, played by a very big, aristocratic-looking man whose hands were surprisingly nimble for their size.

The hilarious act had the crowd in stitches, two women, clearly, but one of the women was dressed as a man, with a top hat and cane, and the other all dressed up as a French lady. They performed several comic songs together beautifully. The one dressed as a man desperately tried to court the French woman, and they did it so realistically, it could have been a man and a woman.

The acrobatic act made her and everyone else gasp as Enzo swung through the air, catching his four-year-old son as he dangled in the opposite direction. There was a kind of trampoline where two little girls bounced up so high, spinning and tumbling as if they were monkeys. The finale was on the trampoline, Enzo on the bottom, his daughter on his shoulders, his other daughter on hers and the little boy on top. How they managed it was a mystery, but they seemed to do it as if it was nothing at all.

She and Tilly sat mesmerised then as Nick Shaw, the big pianist, and his wife, Maggie, who had hair the same colour as Grace but looked about a million times more glamorous, sang duet after duet, her soaring alto blending perfectly with his rumbling baritone. Maggie Shaw was dressed in an emerald-green velvet dress that accentuated rather than disguised her obvious pregnancy, which Grace thought was lovely. She knew there were women in Knocknashee who would have been scandalised; to their minds being pregnant was a necessary part of life but it should be concealed as much as possible. It was nice to know everyone didn't think that way. If she ever had a baby, thought Grace, which of course she never would, she would like to carry her bump with pride, not shame.

The couple finished their set with what Peter Cullen announced to be 'the signature song of the most glamorous lord and lady in Ireland', and when Nick sang to Maggie, with his big soft eyes full of love, 'If you were the only girl in the world and I were the only boy,' everyone sang along, and the volume of melody Grace was sure could be heard back in Knocknashee.

A tall gangly Scotsman came on next and told hilarious story after hilarious story that had the entire tent wiping their eyes with mirth.

At the interval there was a raffle, and Tilly insisted on treating them to a cup of tea and a bun at a stall at the back of the hall. People were crushed in, and it was a struggle to be served.

'It's marvellous, isn't it?' Tilly asked, her eyes shining.

'It really is. I can't believe I'm here,' Grace replied, then bit into a delicious cake with lemon crème filling. She was having to stand, but she was so happy, her leg hardly hurt her at all. 'What's been your favourite so far?'

Tilly sipped her tea and thought. 'I loved Millie and Celine. I thought they were wonderful.'

'Me too. Like you'd know Millie was a woman, but still she is very convincing. It looks almost real, the relationship between them.' Grace giggled, and Tilly nodded.

'How about you? What's your favourite?'

'Oh, it was wonderful to see how much Nick and Maggie love each other. The way he looked at her, and she at him. And I'm really excited to see Magus the Magician next – one of the children in school said his brother saw this show when they were here last and that he's just amazing. But Two-Soups is so funny, I could listen to him all day.'

'He really is. That story about getting leave from the war and it taking so long to get to Scotland that he had to choose between his sweetheart and his mother for a kiss on the platform before getting back on the train, I thought I'd wet my pants,' Tilly whispered, and she and Grace both laughed. 'But I'm really looking forward to seeing Aida too. She's dancing with Peter Cullen himself at the end.' Tilly ran her finger down the colour programme she'd bought.

'They're together, did you know that?' A girl standing beside them, her hair in ringlets, gossiped. 'Even though he's married to someone else.'

'Really? Well, I suppose that's their business,' said Tilly, with a cool smile. Tilly was used to this sort of gossip – her own sister, Marion, was married to a man who had been divorced in England, and Irish people wouldn't recognise an English divorce since in the Catholic faith, marriage was for life. There was nothing half as scandalous about Marion and her man as people liked to make out. The first wife had dementia, and she was in a hospital in London and knew nobody. Though Marion's husband had divorced her, he still paid all her bills and made sure she was well cared for, but he needed a mother for his six children.

'Yes, they are. And you won't believe this,' the girl added, 'but my uncle is a doorman in Dublin, so he knows them all. Peter Cullen left his wife for Aida, and his wife left him for his brother, Eamonn, and now she runs a theatre in Dublin and Peter acts there sometimes – it's very strange they still get on. I can understand Mr Cullen going off with the Spaniard – no man could resist her if she set her claws in him – but the brother is not nearly as good-looking as Peter, so maybe he was the consolation prize…'

'Well, I think they're wonderful, and I'm sure they're good people. And from what I've seen so far, they look like they all get along just fine, so I wouldn't listen to all you hear, either.' Grace coloured after giving her little speech, but it wasn't right to speak about people that way. The girl looked sour at being admonished, and Grace felt very uncomfortable. She tried to get away but failed because of her calliper, which made it awkward to escape the crush. As she and Tilly looked around for some sort of way out, a willowy girl with very dramatic make-up and dark hair cut in a very modern style, wearing a gold sequinned ankle-length dress and carrying a violin, joined them.

'The rules don't apply to us, that's what makes us so interesting.' She grinned, clearly having overheard what was being said. 'Aisling Cullen, nice to meet you,' she added to the ringleted girl, with a gleam of satisfaction in her eyes. 'Peter Cullen is my father.'

The girl clearly wished the ground would open and swallow her. She blushed crimson and stuttered, 'I'm s-sorry, Miss Cullen, I was just…'

'Gossiping, I know,' Aisling said, cool as a breeze, with a sideways wink at Tilly, who was grinning. 'I hope you enjoy the rest of the show.' She turned then to face Grace, with a lovely, warm smile. 'My father sent me over to help you back to your seat, Miss…um…'

'Miss Fitzgerald,' Grace was embarrassed at being singled out. 'Thank you so much. But please, call me Grace.'

'Thanks for sticking up for us, Grace,' Aisling whispered as she let Grace lean on her arm as they walked. 'You know how stories get legs, and they love to dig up a bit of dirt on us.'

Grace had never spoken to anyone as mesmerising as Aisling Cullen. She was like something from a film, not a real person you'd know. 'You're welcome,' was all she could manage.

Aisling got her settled very comfortably, and the rest of the show was as wonderful as the first half.

The magician held the audience enthralled, and the hilarious ventriloquist with a dummy who thought Two-Soups was his uncle had everyone in gales of laughter – and the funniest thing, they did look very alike. Then a line of chorus girls came on and danced their hearts out. Aisling performed next, and she played the violin in such a sweet and plaintive way, it had everyone moved almost to tears. And finally came Aida Gonzalez and Peter Cullen, and you could have heard a pin drop as they danced the tango. Precise and technically perfect, yet at the same time so passionate and wild.

After the finale, some of the chairs got taken away and the audience was invited to dance with the chorus girls and other members of the cast, both male and female, or each other if they preferred. A couple of young men came up to Grace and Tilly; they worked for the cabaret as roustabouts, putting up and striking the tent as the cabaret moved from place to place, but they also got called on to dance with the ladies. Grace declined of course. And so did Tilly, which was all very well and nice of her at first, but then she kept on saying no to any man who came up to her, even though Grace made it clear she didn't mind one bit.

It was exasperating.

She could understand why Tilly might not be interested in what Knocknashee had left to offer in the way of men. So many of the good young ones were gone abroad, leaving only those with very little get up and go. The ongoing economic war with England led by Mr de Valera, with his instructions to 'burn everything British but their coal', was possibly hurting Ireland more than the old enemy. Under the terms of the 1921 treaty, signed by Michael Collins amid much furore, Ireland was supposed to keep paying back debts for land purchases that were accrued during the last century, and Mr de Valera refused to pay. He said that land was never British to begin with, that the Crown were colonisers, that the Irish didn't owe them a shilling and they could go and jump in a lake if they thought the Irish were going to pay them rent for their own land.

Most people agreed with him, as did Grace, but the trade war was taking a heavy toll. The British had landed a heavy tax on all products coming from Ireland, and Ireland retaliated in kind and did the same with British goods entering the country. The upshot was that Irish produce was being rejected by the British housewives as too expensive, and in Ireland a lot of things couldn't be got at all and what was available was very dear. And so many young men were leaving in search of work. Where she and Tilly lived was picture-postcard beautiful, but you couldn't eat scenery. Work was scarce, and if a lad hadn't a farm or a business of his own, the only option was the emigrant boat; between America and England, half the parish of Knocknashee was gone.

In Dingle, though, several of the young men who came up to Tilly looked less downtrodden and more prosperous than the men in Knocknashee, maybe because the land around here was more fertile. And of course there were the busy harbour and tourists and general bustle; the local businesses could make a profit instead of just scratching a living, as there were more people around to buy their wares.

So Grace kept nudging Tilly to say yes...but over and over, Tilly refused. The last to be rejected and go off in a huff was now dancing with the gorgeous French woman, Celine, while Celine's partner in the first act, Millie, stood looking around her with a cool smile. She was still dressed as a man and had been making up the numbers by dancing with the ladies, who were more numerous on the dance floor.

Just then Peter Cullen came over and offered Grace his hand. 'Will you do me the honour?' he asked, and she didn't know where to put herself. Even though he was older than her, he was still gorgeous, and it was so kind of him to offer.

'No, thank you, no.' She blushed furiously again, indicating her poor crippled leg.

Instead of walking away, he went down on his hunkers and took her hands. 'Look at me, Grace,' he said, his eyes searching her face. 'Is it all right if I call you Grace? My daughter said that was your name.'

'Yes, of course, Mr Cullen...'

'Peter.' To her astonishment he sounded nothing like the cultured MC from the stage; his accent now was much more ordinary, more Dublin. 'So, Grace, listen to me. As you heard from our gossipy friend

– don't worry, Aisling told me how you were trying to get away from her, how you stuck up for us – Aida and I are together.'

'She's very beautiful,' she said, with a catch in her throat.

'You're right. The first time I saw her, I thought she was the most beautiful woman I had ever seen. But that's not why I fell in love with her, Grace.' He was still holding her hands, his dark-blue eyes intense. 'I fell in love with her after she was tortured by the English in Dublin Castle and left crippled, her feet broken, her hair torn out and face scarred and unable to walk. I loved her then for who she really was, behind the beauty. I loved her for her courage, her strength, her determination.'

'I'm so sorry she suffered that way,' she whispered. 'And I'm so glad she got better and learnt to dance again.'

'She did get better. Because one day, despite her pain, despite her suffering – and often her feet still hurt, a great deal – she stood up and danced. Because she'd realised that the dancing was not in her feet. It was in here...it *is* in here.' He pointed to his heart. 'If you have a heart, you can dance, that's what Aida taught me, and that's why I love her. So I ask you again – Grace, would you like to dance?'

This time she felt unable to refuse. She accepted his hand, and he helped her stand. Nick smiled at Peter and changed the tempo to a slow waltz, and Peter supported her carefully as they danced a gentle circle on the floor. For the first time since she had polio, Grace didn't feel stupid or ugly or clumsy. She wasn't a cripple, she wasn't a polio victim; she was just an innocent girl dancing in a haze of happiness.

When the song ended and Peter saw her back to her seat, and offered to bring a glass of lemonade, which she declined, she realised Tilly had also stood up to dance. The funny thing was, it still wasn't with a man – it was with Millie. Nick on piano was playing a quickstep now, and the two women were spinning around and laughing together. Grace clapped as she watched them. She was going to remember this forever as the most perfect night of her life, and she owed it all to her oldest, most loyal friend, so she was delighted to see Tilly having her own fun.

CHAPTER 7

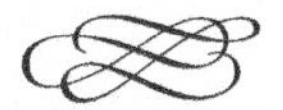

The following day, tired but so very happy, Grace got back on the bus. The night hadn't ended with the dance. The woman who owned the boarding house was at the cabaret, and when everyone left the tent after the performance and went to the hotel for a drink, their landlady did too, and so Grace and Tilly took full advantage of the opportunity. They would never have dared put their heads around the door of Creedon's Bar in Knocknashee – it was for men – but they could risk it here. The bar was full of women as well as men, girls as well as boys, and soon a session of music started up, fiddles, uilleann pipes and an accordion, and a man from Killarney started a sing-song. Grace sat inside a table, so her leg was hidden, and a man down from Kildare on a fishing holiday offered to buy her a shandy. She declined, but it was nice to be asked. It was almost two in the morning when they finally got into bed.

The only bus back before this evening was at ten in the morning, so they'd got up at eight for their breakfast – served by a yawning landlady – then wandered down the quay for a last look at all the bustle and fun.

Even at nine on a Sunday morning, the place was buzzing with tourists and traders, and everywhere were families in their Sunday best. Over at the pier, a man had set up by one of the benches, and Grace and Tilly stopped to watch as a family took a seat and the young man took their picture with a camera, then handed them some sort of docket.

'Want a snap yourselves, ladies?' he asked them with a cheeky wink when he saw them watching. His accent was not local, and he was dressed in a lemon-coloured shirt with short sleeves, no tie and flannel trousers. A cigarette dangled from the side of his mouth. Agnes would be appalled at her associating with such a person.

'How much is it?' asked Tilly, who had no such qualms.

'For you darlin', two shillings,' he said, resetting his camera. 'Come on, have a seat. I'll take your snap, and your chap will be delighted with it in his wallet.'

He winked as he beckoned her over to the bench. Tilly laughed and sat, and he quickly took her picture.

'And another for my friend here,' said Tilly, waving Grace over.

'Oh no, Tilly, that's too much…'

'One and six, since she's such a beauty.' He grinned at Grace, dropping the butt of his cigarette and quenching it with his heel.

Grace blushed to the roots of her hair; he clearly was making fun of her. She started walking away.

'Grace, wait, come back! I can't be the only one who has my photo taken! And one of us together, for free?' Tilly added to the man.

'I'll do her by herself, then one of you together, for two shillings,' he offered. 'So four altogether.'

'Done. Grace, get over here!' Tilly opened her purse and gave him four shillings, and he pocketed it.

'I… Well…all right…' There was no way out now; the money was paid.

After taking a photo of the two of them together, their arms around each other, the man waved Tilly away and concentrated on Grace. If he noticed her leg, he never commented. He focussed on her face, then he moved her chin slightly to the right. 'There, the breeze is blowing your hair back. You look like a Celtic goddess now, wait till you see.'

He took the picture, examined the camera and gave her a docket. 'Come back tomorrow, after four. I'll be here with your snap.'

Tilly had moved on, gone to chat with the ice cream man, and a young couple were waiting. She blurted out in a hurry, 'Oh, I'm sorry, we can't come tomorrow, we live too far and…'

He looked at her for a second and sighed. 'I don't normally do this, but what's your address? I'll post the photos to ya 'cause you're so lovely. And your friend's not bad either.'

She laughed. 'I am not, and she's the beautiful one, as you well know, but thank you. It's Grace Fitzgerald, Knocknashee, County Kerry.'

He didn't laugh as he wrote it on the back of his notebook. Then he looked up and gazed directly at her. 'You are, actually, but the fact that you don't know it is part of your charm. Now, next…' He turned to the young couple and had them on the bench in seconds.

After all that they nearly missed the ten o'clock bus, which would have been a disaster, as Grace had to make the eleven o'clock Mass.

Tilly said she'd probably go directly to the farm to milk the cow and not go to Mass at all today, an idea so shocking to most people in Knocknashee that they couldn't even countenance it, but Tilly didn't march to anyone's drum but her own. Her mother didn't care either; she was a *bean feasa*, a wise woman of old. They said her family had the *bean sidhe*, and so she was more interested in the old pagan ways, not that she'd say it out loud – the canon would have her locked up probably – but it was the truth.

Besides, she was just so grateful to have her one capable daughter to help her, as the other two O'Hares were, according to their mother, neither use nor ornament. Mrs O'Hare thought Alfie's high political notions on communism were a load of old codswallop, and she thought Marion was an awful eejit altogether to get herself landed with a man with a living wife and six children.

Grace had to be at Mass, though; she was a teacher – well, teaching assistant – and she couldn't afford not to be seen. It was bad enough she was going to the later one. She and Agnes always went to the nine o'clock on Sunday mornings; the one at eleven, Agnes said, was full of young fellas scutting and caffling and fellas half cut from spending the night in Creedon's drinking more porter than they could afford. It would be better that Grace went at eleven than not at all of course, but she knew she was doing yet another thing Agnes would disapprove of if she found her out.

She was beginning to think she should make a clean breast of it when Agnes came home tomorrow. She'd had the best night she would ever have in all her life, and she wouldn't have changed it for the world. Why should she lie? She'd done nothing wrong.

The weather had changed overnight and become windy and cold again. Where the sea had sparkled azure yesterday, today it was gunmetal grey with whitetops crashing on the rocky shoreline. The gulls sounded more threatening today too, and there was rain on the wind. Yesterday the landscape had looked like a painting, the clouds shadowing the glens between the mountains, the sea glorious. But today it was different; it held a sense of foreboding, of something bad about to happen. She shook herself. *Such nonsense.* It was just the weather in west Kerry, where you could easily have all four seasons in one day; only a mad person would start thinking the weather reflected what was going to happen.

The bus pulled away from the quayside, and they settled into their seats. Before long Tilly nodded off and rested her head on Grace's shoulder, caring not a bit that to sleep in public was very unseemly for a lady. Grace was lost in a reverie, imagining what it would be like to be beautiful like Aida Gonzalez and have a handsome man like Peter Cullen in love with her. To drive a man so wild with desire and passion that he would scandalise the world to be near her. She'd never seen anything so romantic around Knocknashee.

Normally what happened was people courted for a while, a ring was produced, the banns read and the marriage solemnised up at the church. A year later the woman had a baby, and then another, and on it went. She assumed the baby-making process was nice – it didn't sound that nice, but people would hardly keep doing it if it wasn't, would they? She knew it was bad to think this way, but it was hard not to try to imagine couples she knew engaging in the marriage act. It seemed all so incongruous and undignified, but the place was swarming with children, so they must all be doing it. She glanced to the seat opposite and saw Mrs Lehane watching her.

She blushed deep crimson, as if Mrs Lehane, the mother of handsome Paudie Lehane, Tilly's latest suitor, could see into her mind and the indecent thoughts she entertained. Mercifully they were nearly home, so she nudged her friend as they approached Knocknashee.

'We're back,' she murmured.

The bus pulled up at the stop, and she and Tilly made their way to the door. The bus went all the way out to Dún Chaoin, so it was still half full. When they alighted, a strong gust almost knocked her sideways as she came down off the bottom step.

Tilly and a few others followed, and it wasn't until Murty Kelleher, the local blacksmith who'd been on the bus, handed her the overnight bag did Grace see her, in her navy hat and the pale-blue coat she always wore to Mass, advancing with the light of fury in her eyes.

'Agnes,' she gasped, feeling sick and nearly falling again in her panic. 'I didn't –'

'Grace, go directly home. I want a word with Miss O'Hare.' Agnes's voice, so imperious, cut like a hot knife through butter.

'Agnes, please don't...' She was horribly aware that the crowd getting off the bus and the gathered few getting on were all ears.

'What do you want?' Tilly asked, her square jaw at the defiant angle Grace knew only too well.

'I'll tell you what I want.' Agnes rounded on Tilly as Grace stood rooted to the spot. Around them nobody moved; this was going to be something to see. 'I want you to stay away from my sister.' She had the attention of at least twenty people now, because despite the inclement conditions, this was gossip gold.

'Agnes... Agnes,' whispered Grace, 'please come away. This is my fault. Let's talk about this at home...'

'If you wanted to talk at home, you should have stayed at home.'

Her sister's voice cracked like a whip, and her eyes glittered with unspent rage. 'What do you imagine I thought when I came back yesterday evening because the weather was too bad to risk a boat in a storm and I found the house empty? I went looking for you around the town, and Biddy O'Donoghue told me you were off to Dingle with this...this...'

'This *what*?' snarled Tilly.

Agnes barked a short, harsh, unhappy laugh. 'Oh, you know well what you are, Tilly O'Hare. My poor sister spent years in hospital, she's a cripple and been sheltered from the world, and she hasn't the sense to know you and yours are heading straight for the pit of hell. But don't think you have me fooled. Your whole family are unnatural, you dressing like a man and running wild, and your sister shacked up with a married man, and your brother a communist, bad enough...'

Grace's face burnt. Being called a cripple and easily led in front of the whole town, it was mortifying. But Tilly wasn't mortified; she was incandescent with fury.

'You shut your mouth, you old *cailleach*!' she roared. 'My sister is a legally married woman and a saint to be minding six children who aren't hers, and our Alfie has indeed gone to Russia, because he's a true Irish patriot and a big follower of James Connolly and Jim Larkin and believes the poor people of Russia had more in common with the poor people of Ireland than with the high and mighty of our own country who care nothing for the poor and weak, only showing off to the neighbours about how holy they are when in reality they haven't a Christian bone in their bodies. If Jesus Christ were to come back this very minute, they'd be the very ones he'd be casting down to hell.'

Agnes blanched but stood her ground, rapidly making a sign of the cross. 'Tilly O'Hare, I'll not listen to another word that comes out of your dirty mouth, but I will protect my sister from you.' And then she seized Grace by the arm and barked, 'Home. Now,' as if Grace were a dog.

Grace did as she was told, staggering along beside Agnes, her overnight bag in her hand. She knew she looked like a dreadful coward, but she knew anything that came out of her mouth now would make things a thousand times worse, and she'd done enough already. She shouldn't have gone with Tilly to the cabaret, bringing Agnes down on top of her friend; it was always going to happen.

At the house Agnes ordered her up to her room, and she sat up there all day, in such a state of misery, she didn't even care that she was hungry. Dreadful feelings churned around inside her. As she'd confessed to St Jude in her letter, she did want to love her sister – they were family – but now even the wish to love Agnes was gone, replaced by a horrible hot burning in her stomach.

She hated her sister right now. Hot, oozing, burning, acid hate.

And what must Tilly think of Grace, standing there saying nothing while Agnes abused her in public – Tilly, who had just treated Grace to the best night of her life. And Grace had turned her back and walked away. She'd chosen Agnes over Tilly, that's what it must look like. How could her old friend ever forgive her for being so spineless? She had to apologise; she had to explain how she'd been so afraid of making it worse. But how? She couldn't make it as far as the farm on the hill, and Tilly would certainly never come to her. Maybe they'd meet around the town, but she wouldn't blame Tilly for walking straight past her on the street, and Grace wouldn't be able to run after her however much she wanted to.

Maybe she could write to her. Then even if Tilly threw the letter in the fire, at least she'd know how sorry Grace was. The paper and lilac ink were still on her desk. But even that was fraught with difficulty. Most people posted their letters in the postbox outside the post office, but Charlie McKenna collected the Fitzgeralds' post, both from the house and the school. And if Agnes saw the envelope with Tilly's address, it would fire the whole thing up again.

* * *

GRACE SLIPPED into the post office, and to her relief, there was nobody else there. Nancy O'Flaherty, the postmistress, was a lovely person, a really kind-hearted woman, but she was also very chatty, so buying a stamp could take a half an hour some days if she was in a mind for talking. Grace had left fourteen-year-old Janie O'Shea in charge of the lunchtime playground for five minutes, and everyone had promised faithfully to be good, but she didn't want to be gone any longer than necessary.

She certainly couldn't afford to have Agnes notice her absence.

'Morning, Mrs O'Flaherty. Can I get a ha'penny stamp please?' she asked. It was a great piece of luck that she had a ha'penny. She'd found it in an old purse of her mother's, in the spare room, and had put it aside, thinking maybe she would buy a piece of toffee from Bríd Butler one day when she was desperate enough to need it. To take one of the household stamps would have required an explanation. Agnes never failed to notice even the slightest alteration in the house.

Nancy was a widow and she always reminded Grace of her rag doll, Nellie. She had a broad, kind face with pink cheeks, and she had a squint in one eye. Her salt-and-pepper hair was pulled back in a bun, and she dressed in a brown skirt and cream blouse every single day, but today she had brightened her look with one of the new cardigans from Peggy Donnelly's, an orange one.

'You can of course, Grace.' She smiled as she opened the book of stamps. 'Did Charlie tell you his big news?' she asked as she handed over the stamp and Grace gave her a ha'penny.

'No, I didn't see him this morning?' Not that she would have spoken to Charlie at length if she had, due to Agnes' disapproval.

After his wife, Maggie, died, he turned to the drink, so baby Siobhán and six-year-old Declan had to be put in the orphanage as an act of kindness by the canon. Agnes didn't think Nancy should have rescued Charlie; she thought it was setting a bad example to the other men in the town to reward such a waste of a father with a good, steady job at the post office.

'Oh, he won't mind me telling you. He's walking on air. I'd say his rounds are going to take twice as long today because he's telling everyone.'

'What happened?' Grace wondered what good news he'd received. Despite Agnes not liking her to talk to Charlie McKenna, she often saw him slip a child a bullseye from the packet he kept in his postbag. According to her parents' letters, Charlie was one of the kindest people you could meet, and so she'd always had an interest in him.

'He got a letter from his son, Declan. After twelve years of searching and trying to find his boy, he got a letter and Declan is coming home.' Nancy beamed. 'He's eighteen now.'

Grace felt a tear sting her eye; this was miraculous news. She hadn't realised Charlie had kept trying to find his children. Her parents' letters had been written when Charlie's wife, Maggie, was still alive and neither of the children born yet. All she knew of Charlie's story was what Agnes had told her.

'Oh, that's wonderful.' The emotion choked her. 'I'm so happy for him. Maybe he will find his baby girl now. Will Declan know where she is?'

A look of sorrow passed over Nancy's normally cheerful face. 'That little *cailín* is gone, I'm afraid.'

'Did she die?' Grace was horrified.

'Oh no, nothing like that…but I doubt very much he'll ever see her again.'

'Please, Mrs O'Flaherty, tell me.' She should be going back to the schoolyard, but she had heard such conflicting reports of Charlie from her parents' letters and then from Agnes, she couldn't help wanting to know the story, if it didn't take too long.

Nancy rested her arms on the counter. 'I'm surprised you didn't know, but I suppose you were only little and then you were away. Siobhán was probably adopted, *a stór*. Charlie was only a farm labourer at the time, and the canon didn't think he'd be able to raise his children on such a low wage with no woman to help him, so they stepped in. And there's people who will pay big money for a baby they can pass off as their own.'

'And you think someone might have paid for her?' Grace could hardly believe what she was hearing. She knew children were adopted, but money changing hands? 'Who did they pay?'

'Ara, look, 'twas probably the canon arranged it – he has connections everywhere. And well… Look, 'twill serve nobody dragging all that back up again, and Charlie got nowhere with the canon before, that's why he turned to the drink, the poor man.'

Grace blinked. 'Charlie McKenna didn't take to the bottle until *after* his children were taken?'

Nancy O'Flaherty's face told her all she needed to know.

'I thought that it was before...'

The kindly woman patted her hand as she took Tilly's letter for posting now that Grace had stuck the stamp to it. 'Don't go worrying. Charlie has his house here now, and his job, and the place is nice, and it's a home for Declan to come to.'

'It was so good of you to help him get the postman's job, Mrs O'Flaherty,' said Grace, her heart full.

Nancy dropped her voice to barely a whisper. ''Twas your father came and asked me about it. He said he'd vouch for Charlie, write him a reference for the application and all the rest of it – it was breaking poor Eddie's heart to see his friend brought so low. Charlie was proud, still is, and wouldn't accept charity. God knows your father and mother, God be good to them both, tried their very best with him, but losing his babies so soon after poor Maggie just broke him, it really did. He lost his house because he didn't pay the rent. He was on the side of the road, but Eddie and myself worked out how to get him in the job, and your mother, Kathleen, put him through the exam for it, and it came with the cottage as well, so that was a blessing. And sure he's been all right since, but he never gave up hope of finding his children.'

* * *

BY THE TIME she got back to the playground, it had been more like ten minutes than five, but Janie O'Shea had kept everyone in order. The child would make an excellent teacher one day, thought Grace as she looked around. Mercifully there was no sign of Agnes.

Standing in the doorway, watching the children play, Grace went over and over in her mind the conflicting stories she'd heard about Charlie. She was very sure Agnes had said the canon had only stepped in because Charlie was drinking a bottle of whiskey a day. Yet according to Nancy, that was only after the children were taken.

It was hard to know what to believe. She thought of raising it with Agnes, to try and get the story straight, but then she decided not to; she wanted to think the best of Charlie, her parents' friend, and Agnes was so inclined to see the badness in everyone, maybe it was best not to ask.

CHAPTER 8

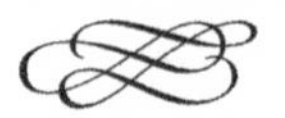

It was the first day of the Easter holidays. Agnes entered the kitchen, carrying the post, and sat down with the two envelopes in front of her plate, both brown with harps on the front, the way government correspondence always came.

Grace couldn't help feeling disappointed. Two weeks had gone by since she'd posted her letter to Tilly, and she kept hoping for one back. And then there was the matter of the letter with the photographs, which still hadn't arrived.

'Are you expecting something in the post, Grace?' Agnes's gaze was steely.

'No, I... No. Nothing.' Grace concentrated on taking the top off her boiled egg. She missed Tilly so much, but as the time passed after Agnes's awful attack, she had to assume Tilly's silence was deliberate. If her old friend wanted to contact her without Agnes finding out, she could have given a note to one of the children, so it was true that she wasn't really expecting anything in the post. And the photographer was obviously a fraud; she could have guessed that from how he kept going on about her being beautiful. Four whole shillings down the drain, on top of everything else Tilly had spent on her.

'Please don't keep secrets from me, Grace.' Agnes glared across the table, her blue eyes boring into Grace from behind the horn-rimmed spectacles. Even from here, Grace could smell the Yardley lily of the valley talcum powder that Agnes liked; she must have used a lot this morning. 'Not telling me the truth is the same as lying. And you promised you'd never lie to me again after that terrible, terrible occasion with the cabaret...'

'I don't have any secrets,' said Grace, and without meaning to, she stuck out her chin, Tilly-style. Maybe Agnes would call that a lie, because she hadn't said about writing to Tilly, but she didn't intend to draw her sister down on her old friend ever again. They had to be kept apart.

After another long, hard, suspicious stare, Agnes opened both envelopes and extracted two cheques from the education department, one made out to her as headmistress and the other to Grace as an assistant teacher, and folded them.

'I'll lodge these this morning in the post office.' She tucked them into her pocket and pulled the toast rack and butter towards her.

The cheques reminded Grace of something she'd been thinking about since Dingle. Up to now she'd been too upset to suggest it, and Agnes too upset to listen, but the sisters were stuck together for life – they both had to accept that. And things couldn't just carry on forever like this, dull and unhappy. The only place Agnes ever went was on hard pilgrimages. Surely she would be a happier woman if only she could allow herself a treat.

'I know you're saving it up for my future, Agnes, and I appreciate it,' said Grace, still with her chin slightly raised. 'But maybe we could use a little bit to do something fun, something nice, like a trip somewhere, a day out maybe?'

Agnes looked at her as if she had two heads. 'Are you seriously suggesting we spend the money on frivolities, when your care and future are all I worry about?' Two bright-pink dots appeared on her pale cheeks, as if the very idea was something akin to heresy. 'Grace, you really are a child. Of course we can't do that. Going off spending your hard-earned money on rubbish and days out? Nonsense. No, this money has to be saved, because you'll need every shilling for your care when I'm gone. You're infirm enough now, and that will only get worse. Imagine when you're old and alone. At least if you have some money, you can pay someone to mind you.'

Grace's courage evaporated. She didn't like to think about the future. Would her leg get worse? It was hard to know. Agnes could be difficult, more than difficult, but at least with a sister, she wasn't alone in the world. Maurice clearly had no intention of ever coming home, and her best friend, Tilly, was lost to her. So the idea of Agnes dying and her having to fend entirely for herself was a frightening one.

* * *

THE FOLLOWING morning Grace woke early, still on the school time, and she decided to go out. The ancient graveyard of Knocknashee was a little way up the hill, a higgledy-piggledy affair that had been used for hundreds of years, and it was too late to try to put manners on it now. Her parents were there, and though she found even that gentle climb hard with her leg, Grace went up once a month, just to say a prayer and have a quiet chat with them in her head.

It was a warm enough day to go without her coat, so she felt quite free as she walked slowly up the hill out of the village to the cemetery. Wild garlic grew in abundance in a field to her right, and the air was scented with its oniony aroma; she remembered her mother adding it to stews and the delicious scent filling the house.

The breeze was stiff but not biting, and she welcomed it. The sea was calm today, and the red, blue and white buoys bobbed on the water, waiting for the fishermen to return and tie up after the day's work. The seabirds circled overhead. She'd seen a puffin only yesterday. They were mainly on the islands, but if you looked carefully, you could find an odd stray. They were such comical little birds, it lifted her heart to see them. Razorbills, guillemots and fulmars were all starting to breed now too, so it felt like the beginning of something, not the end.

Some older children who had finished school for Easter were on the lookout for gannets, the big seabirds that nested in pairs in the rocks of Little Skellig. And as she crossed the field to take a smooth, well-trodden shortcut to the graveyard, she spotted a *maidrín rua*, the vixen leading her cubs out of the den. The fox's brush was long and luxurious, and she stopped to observe Grace with her yellow eyes for a moment before loping on calmly, her babies in her wake.

Grace entered the graveyard through the rickety gate, hanging by one hinge. Clumps of pale-yellow primroses dotted the entire cemetery, blooming in profusion. Daffodils and crocuses bobbed in the salty breeze. Her parents were in the top corner, and she silently greeted the final resting places of neighbours and friends of her family as she picked her way across.

She always passed Maggie McKenna's grave on the way in. Maggie was buried with Charlie's mother and father, long gone now, and it always struck Grace as so sad that the three of them were there and their children desperately needing them. Why did God send children to people, only to take the parents away when they were needed? One of her many questions.

Most families had a plain stone, or maybe a little Celtic cross. She remembered Mary O'Hare telling them when they were children that the ring in the Celtic cross was to represent the sun and the moon, and that when the early Christians came, they didn't dismiss the old pagan ways, they just incorporated them. But when she told Agnes that, Agnes snapped that paganism was not a word she wanted to hear. But people here did believe in the old ways every bit as much as the new.

Agnes had decided on a black marble headstone with gold lettering for their parents, which to Grace seemed a bit too austere and showy. But slowly even this stone was settling into the grass and wild flowers.

She perched on a flat rock beside the grave. Like all the land on the peninsula, the graveyard had to be fought back from the limestone beneath, which cropped up through the green grass everywhere in white slabs.

She read the inscription that she knew by heart, the one Agnes had chosen.

In memory of
Edward John Fitzgerald 1880–1932
And his wife,
Kathleen Mary Fitzgerald (née Moriarty) 1883–1932

It was a bit impersonal. A little prayer or a quotation or something to soften it might help to indicate the kind, loving parents they were, that they were much admired teachers and loved by so many. Maybe it was something she could use a bit of her savings for in the years to come when she'd be left to look after herself.

'Hello, Mammy and Daddy, it's Grace,' she said to the grave, then stopped to think what to say next. She didn't want to complain, or let them know their daughters weren't getting on, but there were things she just had to get off her chest.

'Mammy and Daddy, I wrote a letter to St Jude three weeks ago, and I threw it in the sea, and I wonder did you read it too? I don't know, I just feel a bit...well, a bit lost and alone honestly. Agnes is good to me, and God knows she had to give up so much because of me...'

She blushed and lowered her voice, though she was entirely alone in the cemetery. 'I think I'm not really living, you know? I don't mean to complain – it could be much worse – but I keep feeling angry with Agnes. And I turned my back on my best friend, Tilly, and I'm worried she'll never talk to me again. I wish I could see Dr Warrington. He was the one who told us all to go out and live our lives, but I don't think I'm really doing that. I wish I could have a dose of his positivity, but I don't like to bother him.'

She paused then, watching the vixen lead her cubs back into the den, then looked back at the grave. 'You always told me, Mammy, that the dead never really leave us, so I hope you can hear me now, because I think you and Daddy are all I have. At least I know that, wherever you are, you love me and I love you.'

There was a chill in the air now, and her bad leg felt cold, like clay. She heaved herself up and winced at the pain, then kissed her fingers and pressed them to the stone. 'So it's *slán* for now. Rest easy, and don't mind me moaning about everything – I'll be fine.'

She listened for a moment, maybe for an answer, but only heard the breeze in the heather and the yap of the cubs, and then, to her surprise, the creak of the graveyard gate being opened. She turned to see the chubby little curate, Father O'Riordan.

'Oh, hello, Father.' She smiled as they made their way slowly towards each other across the uneven ground.

'Hello, Grace. All alone, I see?' He smiled, his eyes as saucer-like as ever behind his thick spectacles.

'Just visiting my parents, Father.'

'Ah yes.' The huge eyes twinkled. 'I've heard what a wonderful couple they were, so good to the children and such good teachers. I must say, from what I see, I think you take after them. I think it's lovely, the way you teach the boys and girls. They all hang on every word you say.'

It was nice to know he approved. She'd had the children doing a project on the South Pole explorations, because a local Kerryman, Tom Crean from Annascaul, only twenty-five miles away, had been part of Robert Falcon Scott's effort to reach the South Pole, only to find Amundsen got there before them. And later on Ernest Shackleton's trans-Antarctic expedition that resulted in their ship being crushed by pack ice and having to navigate to South Georgia, a journey of over a thousand miles, in a small boat to get help for the stranded crew. There were drawings of sleds and dogs and penguins and ice shelves all over the classroom, and the children had really enjoyed it. Tom Crean still ran the pub in the village of Annascaul, the South Pole Inn, with his wife and daughters.

'Thank you, Father. I do enjoy the work,' she said with a smile, he was so much easier to talk to than the Canon.

'I wish more teachers were like you. Your sister must be glad to have you.'

'I'm not sure she is,' Grace said, with a small smile. 'She thinks I can't keep order at all.'

'The children seem very well behaved to me,' Father O'Riordan said, with a wider smile back at her.

'Ah, but the thing is, I can't slap anyone.'

'There's far too much slapping goes on, in my opinion.' He stopped smiling and shot a slightly nervous glance around him.

Grace remained silent, not sure what to say. The curate obviously had the same differences of opinion with the canon as she did with her sister, and like her and Agnes, the two of them were forced to share a house. She felt a wave of sympathy for him.

'I might pop in to see the children after Easter if that would suit you?' He still didn't sound at all sure of himself.

She liked him for asking. The canon never announced when he was visiting the school; he just turned up and expected everyone to drop everything while he tested the children on their catechism and half scared them to death in the process.

'Of course, Father. As soon as they're back after the holidays, you'd be very welcome any time. I'll have their religion copies ready for you to inspect.'

'Oh no, I'm sure that's all fine.' He brushed her offer away. 'I was just very interested in what you were teaching the last day, about the explorers, and I thought I might come in and tell them a bit about my granduncle who was in India with the British Army. He's dead now, but he had some great stories, and I thought the children might like to hear…' His voice tapered off, and he actually blushed; he seemed easily embarrassed, shy even.

'Oh, they'd love that, Father,' she said, he was a bit unsure of himself so she wanted to encourage him.

'Would they?' his round face was anxious.

'They really would, and especially if it was a relation of yours. They love hearing stories about faraway places and people who did interesting things.'

He seemed to take heart from that. 'Did you ever hear of Jean-Baptiste de La Salle, Grace?'

She shook her head. 'I don't think I did – is he a saint?' Admitting she didn't know of a saint was something she wouldn't dare have done with the canon, but Father O'Riordan seemed so nice, she didn't mind being honest.

'He is. He was a teacher in Reims in France in the seventeenth century, but he was very unusual for the time. He believed that you could not use fear and punishment as a teaching method, and that the emotion necessary for teaching was love. He allowed all the children into his schools, rich and poor, and he insisted his teachers taught with kindness and compassion. He was a remarkable man for the time.'

'For any time,' she said, and they both knew what she meant. St Jean- Baptiste de La Salle would most certainly not approve of Agnes's teaching methods.

'I would have loved to have been a teacher myself, but...' He sighed; clearly what he wanted was not important.

'Maybe you could come in another time and tell the children about him as well, if you were free?' she suggested.

'Well, I don't know if the canon would really approve...' he began, and she felt his pain.

'If it was part of catechism... I could do a series of lessons about saints?'

He smiled then and exhaled, his myopic eyes bright. 'I'd love that, Grace, if I wasn't getting in your way.'

'Not at all, Father. I'd love it, and I'm sure the children would too.'

As she left the graveyard, she realised she felt much happier than when she'd arrived. It was a bit like after she'd thrown the bottle into the sea, wanting to feel special, loved. Tilly had turned up right away then, with those wonderful tickets, and this time it was Father O'Riordan offering to come and tell the children stories. Neither of them had been quite what she'd envisaged as the answer to her prayers, but still, it did feel like someone was giving her a helping hand.

She felt a sudden hope that things would be right between her and Tilly, and even looked out for her as she was trudging through the town. Somehow things seemed brighter and happier, with the jubilant voices of the children ringing in the springtime air. It was only the second day of the Easter holidays, and they were like spring calves let out to the pasture for the first time, leaping and bucking, hardly able to believe their freedom.

Almost every shop was open. Peggy was doing her window with a selection of Easter bonnets that nobody ever bought. She used the same ones every year. They were flamboyant, and the women of Knocknashee would feel too self-conscious in a hat with flowers on it or bedecked with ribbons, however they might secretly wish they had the courage to wear it.

Only Bríd's sweetshop was still shuttered. She closed every Lent and went to visit her sister and her family in Limerick. Bríd's mother lived with the sister, and she was infirm and cranky as anything, so Bríd went to give her sister a break. There was no point her having the shop open, because all children and most adults gave up sweet things for Lent. Many men gave up drinking porter and women gave up tea, all to show solidarity with Our Lord, who had to suffer in the desert for forty days and nights. It was almost the end of Lent now, which meant Bríd could open her shop again.

It would be Spy Wednesday next week, a Black Fast day where no meat, milk, eggs or sugar could be consumed. Last year Grace was so hungry, she fainted onto the bulk of Ned Harrington, one of the fishermen, in the church at morning Mass, much to her embarrassment. He was lovely about it and helped her back up and led her outside for some air. He slipped her a clove-rock sweet, which was strictly forbidden, but he assured her it was strictly medicinal.

The Easter services would begin in earnest on Thursday with the Holy Thursday Mass, where the canon would wash the feet of twelve of the congregation to symbolise the Last Supper. The twelve were selected based on their underlying level of personal hygiene. There had been a moment a few years ago when poor old Dinny Murphy was one of those selected and the general consensus was that was the first time he'd taken his socks off in a year. The canon nearly keeled over with the smell, and so since then, the disciples were carefully vetted, chosen ahead of time and given plenty of notice to wash their own feet before coming to the church for fear of offending the delicate nostrils of the canon.

Then the altar would be draped in black cloth for the Good Friday Stations of the Cross, and the canon would visit each of the Stations, recalling in prayer and sorrow the sufferings of Jesus on his way to

Calvary. When Grace came back after her years in the hospital, she couldn't bend her leg. The ceremony involved more standing, kneeling and sitting than she remembered, and she felt very conscious of being looked at. Agnes had turned pink with embarrassment, though she said nothing.

Still, something about Good Friday appealed to her. There was not a sound to be heard between midday and three – no radio, no talking – as every individual contemplated the agony of Jesus as he carried that heavy cross up the hill of Calvary. Then slowly and without a word, the people of Knocknashee would walk towards the church for the Stations at three. Only the birds ignored the silence, and their cawing cut through the stillness in an atmospheric way.

Then Holy Saturday, where no Mass was said and the faithful were called upon to remember in prayer the passion of Jesus. A select few, again chosen by the canon, would maintain a vigil in the church overnight until the joyous Easter Sunday, when the church was in highest celebration that Jesus had risen.

Children deprived of a treat for the forty days of Lent leading up to the Easter Sunday might get a bar of chocolate or a few sweets from Bríd if they had benevolent parents, and everyone would have a lovely roast dinner, lamb usually. Mammy used to make the Easter Sunday dinner, and Grace's mouth watered at the memory. She and Agnes never had a full roast – it was too much for just the two of them – so they would have a chop each and some boiled potatoes and carrots.

It wasn't as nice a meal or as happy a life as when her parents had been alive, but maybe that was just part of growing up. It was her life, and she would just have to find a way of living it. Her pupils were such a source of joy; she lived in her parents' house and their things were there, if packed away in the spare room; she had a body that mostly worked; she had a good education; and she was on good terms with mostly everyone.

If she could just fix things with Tilly.

And find a way of living with Agnes.

CHAPTER 9

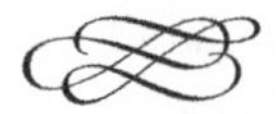

SAVANNAH, GEORGIA

September 1938

RICHARD LEWIS TAPPED the horn of his brand-new Buick; he was impatient to begin the two-hour trip to join his parents at their summer house on St Simons Island on the Georgia coast. It was going to be wonderful to get out of the city heat. The oppressive Georgia summers were something one never quite acclimatised to.

The summer house was on the East Beach on the island, and the breeze and the salty, cold Atlantic were all he'd been able to think about for weeks. His brother, Nathan, and his family had already gone ahead; his sister, Sarah, had decided to go with them instead of waiting for Richard. Everyone of their set was heading as fast as they could to the coast, to Tybee or the Golden Isles, anywhere to escape the furnace.

The soft roof of the car was rolled back, and the sweet scent of tea olive filled his nostrils. In the distance he could hear the clanging of the Gino's ice cream truck, calling children with their coins in exchange for the delicious gelato, made from a recipe that was seventeen generations old, according to Gino anyway.

He beeped the horn again.

'Coming! Goodness! So demanding!' Miranda Logan, looking like something from one of his mother's glossy magazines, finally arrived down the steps of the wraparound porch of her beautiful house off Forsyth Park, which was almost as big as his own family's house on Jones Street. He watched as she sashayed through the well-tended garden. Two overheated servants staggered along behind her, weighted down by leather bags and hat boxes. She'd bought a new dress yesterday – she'd told him she was planning to – though she had hundreds as far as he could see; this one was a cream linen, which fitted her perfect figure like a glove. Her blond hair was expensively coiffed and styled – two dollars at the Guarantee Wave Salon on Bull and West 36th – pinned back from her pretty face with its expertly applied make-up, and on her feet, she wore strappy sandals that he could not imagine were even remotely comfortable. Miranda was the daughter of a Southern belle, and she took grooming extremely seriously; he'd never once seen her with so much as a hair astray.

He got out to help. 'Gee, Miranda – do you really need all this? It's only for a week!'

'Darling Richard, it's the bare minimum...'

The servants were already piling the hat boxes into the back seat, and Richard opened the trunk and helped put more bags in, grumbling mildly all the time.

Miranda Logan was beautiful and smart, and there was no point refusing her anything she considered to be her due. Her father, Theobald Logan, was an antiques dealer, with a speciality in jewellery, and the family was very well-to-do. Mother adored Miranda and considered her a very suitable match for Richard – she had the looks, the poise, the air of entitlement that came with old money. It was assumed by everyone – including himself – that he would propose to her sooner or later.

And Richard, of course, was very fond of her.

The only problem was, while everyone expected him to follow his father into banking, he wanted to be a poet. A writer. Or an artist. Or something. A sculptor maybe. He felt like he had so much pent-up creativity inside of him. He was forever doodling, or composing songs in his head, or imagining plays performed on stage. But someone like Miranda Logan would not settle for the life of a starving artist in an attic, that was for sure.

'A what?' She had pealed with laughter three nights ago as they walked home from the Bijou movie theatre, so delightfully air-conditioned that nobody really cared what movie was on.

'Maybe a novelist,' he'd said, idly kicking a stone along the brick-work sidewalk, his light cotton jacket slung over his shoulder.

She laughed again. 'Oh yes, and I'll dance the can-can, will I, Richard? It's a cute idea, but you know your mama and she is never going to accept that. There's a seat on the board of the bank coming your way if you play ball, and your cute tush is gonna fill it, like it or not.'

'I hate banking.' Another kick of the stone.

She sighed, like he was being a child and not a young man of twenty. 'You've been there a month, Richard.'

'And I hate it already. I want to stop. Numbers, numbers, numbers. The darn marble halls. The droning voices of the accountants and clerks. Ugh. I hate it all. Why did Nathan have to be a doctor?'

His brilliant older brother should have entered their father's bank and been groomed to join the board and eventually take over from their father as chairman, but he'd had his heart set on medicine. Father hadn't been pleased, but Nathan had prevailed, and four years ago had graduated summa cum laude from Harvard Medical School and was gainfully employed in an intern surgical programme at the famous Henry Ford hospital in Detroit built by its namesake. Father wasn't very happy about the Detroit thing either, often accusing his older son of being 'a real Yankee now', but Nathan had at least partially redeemed himself by marrying a very rich heiress whose family owned an insurance business; they had two charming little daughters.

And after all, as Father had said, at least there was Richard.

'Why not Sarah?' Richard had asked, to much amusement around the dinner table. Sarah did have a head for numbers; however, by virtue of her sex, she was not required to do much but look pretty, which she was, and marry well. At the moment their mother, worried her daughter was getting too old at twenty-five, was pushing her at a real bore with a nasal tone and lots of money in the bank, who was on his way to being a partner in his father's luxury yacht business. Sarah had other ideas, but she was a lot better at handling their parents than he was. She agreed with Mother on every little thing, and even dated the guy – what was his name? Algernon? Gideon? Something like that – but behind Mother's back, she was as wild as a March hare with a passion for unsuitable men; the last he'd heard, it was some photographer fellow.

So it was Richard who got saddled with the bank. He had no relevant qualifications. He hadn't paid much attention at school; there was so much else to do in life apart from study – parties, for instance, and girls, and cars. But fortunately – or unfortunately, for him – being the son of the chairman of Lewis Holdings meant he could walk in as the chairman's son without having to jump through the normal hoops.

He'd been in the Savannah branch almost a month now, and he was exhausted, another reason he was so looking forward to this vacation, swimming and boating and plenty of champagne, he hoped, and falling asleep to the sound of the waves.

Miranda pecked his cheek after getting into the car, and as they pulled away from the curb, she glanced at him and said approvingly, 'You're looking very handsome, Richard. Nice outfit.'

He'd selected a pale-blue button-down short-sleeved shirt and some tailored shorts that stopped above the knee to wear on the trip.

'Thanks. Mother will have conniptions, I imagine.'

'Nothing like the fit she'll throw if you mention being a poet. I'd suggest getting over your bohemian stage, darling.'

Richard sighed. Miranda was right. It would be carnage if he confessed he wanted to be some sort of artist. Yet he felt much too young to settle down, and anyway, why live the life your parents did? There was a big world out there, and while Savannah was beautiful and he loved it, the stuffy drawing rooms of the Savannahian upper class were not for him.

'Talking of artistic nonsense,' Miranda said, fanning herself with a folded glossy magazine, her elbow resting on the rolled-down window, 'Sarah's not being as discreet as she should be right now, Richard. You should have a word.'

'Oh, yes? What did you hear?' He doubted there was any point him having any kind of a word with his sister, though. She was far too proud to listen to her younger brother, even if he was going to be chair of the board one day.

'That her latest fling is unsuitable to the point of being disreputable.'

This was worrying. Miranda's sister Fenella was friendly with Sarah, and normally both she and Miranda found his sister's antics hilarious, even though they would never do such things themselves. Had Sarah crossed the line in some terrible way?

'I did hear she was knocking around with a photographer?' he probed keeping his eyes on the road ahead.

'Yes, some freelance newspaper guy, which is unsuitable enough because they live on a shoestring, those types,' said Miranda, before adding, unkindly he thought, 'Hardly better than poets.'

Stung, he gripped the steering wheel, 'I actually think it's honourable to make a career out of something you love.'

'Sure, if you want to be as poor as a church mouse all your life and marry someone with no standards. But joking aside, Richard, you need to know this. This time it's much, much worse.'

'He's married?' Richard's heart sank. His parents would definitely disinherit Sarah if she brought such a horror upon them. The family cast out Uncle Harold when he took up with a married woman, and he'd been Richard's godfather and a great favourite. Richard sometimes spent a weekend boating in Tybee, where Harold now lived quietly with the lovely Marianne, but if he happened to run into his uncle, he never mentioned it to his parents.

'No, not married...'

'Oh, thank God.'

'Far, far worse.'

He racked his brains for what could possibly be worse. 'Catholic?' Mother was a WASP to her core, and so was Father, and they were very conscious of their position in society. A big part of the 'Uncle Harold scandal' was that the woman involved was a Catholic, hence the lack of divorce. Not that divorce was considered reputable either.

'Sorry. Worse than that.'

'Oh, come on...'

'He's a socialist.'

'*A socialist?*' He turned to her and the car swerved slightly, almost into the path of an oncoming truck. The driver blew his horn. 'You're not serious.' He could hardly imagine the shades of purple his father's face would attain if he caught wind of such a thing. Roosevelt and the New Deal were a forbidden topic of conversation around the Lewis family table.

'I am. And Richard, I'm truly sorry, but it's even worse than that.'

If Miranda hadn't sounded so serious, even a little upset, he would have suspected her of enjoying this. 'Come on, spill the beans,' he said, steeling himself.

'He's Jewish.'

Richard groaned. 'Oh God.'

'Exactly. So as I said, you need to talk to her.'

He shook his head. 'No. Not me. She'd never listen to me, Miranda. Maybe Nathan...'

'I really wouldn't tell Nathan.'

'Why not? It could work. I know she's headstrong, but she's always wanted him to be proud of her, and he wouldn't betray her.'

'He wouldn't, but if he told that wife of his...'

'Darn. You're right.' Rebecca's family was every bit as bad about this sort of thing as his own, and Rebecca was the same. 'Maybe we should just leave it.'

'That's your answer to everything, isn't it, Richard?' said Miranda, sighing and raising a perfectly plucked eyebrow. It was a complaint of hers, that he tended to drift into things rather than apply himself properly.

'No, but I'm right about this. She'll get tired of him, like all the rest of them, and maybe a lot quicker if we don't do anything about it.'

She laid her hand on his arm as he was changing gear. 'The thing is, Richard, she's told Fenella it's getting serious. They're…'

He glanced at her with a furrowed brow. '*What?* No…'

All nice Southern girls were expected to be virgins when they married, and all Southern gentlemen knew that to expect a girl to go to bed before she had a ring on her finger was futile, but Miranda had hinted before that Sarah might have flouted that rule too.

'This could ruin her life. You've a duty to protect her, Richard.'

Turning his eyes back to the road ahead, he nodded as he drove on. He had to admit, he agreed with Miranda now.

If he ever did go off and find some creative expression, become a poet, or an artist, or musician, or whatever he might turn out to be good at, then of course he would have friends who were photographers, even ones who called themselves socialists, maybe even Jewish, because the Jews were everywhere in the arts and many of them were geniuses. He had no reason to dislike the Jews – he didn't know any well, as they didn't mix in the same worlds – but his family would not think that way.

And this was his sister's future they were talking about. Impossible to know where to start, but he would do his best to talk to her.

They were far out of the city now. Peach orchards as far as the eye could see across the flat landscape.

He half listened as Miranda chatted on beside him; she was full of stories about people in their set. Jamie Fulcrom had been accepted to Stanford. His parents were thrilled and so was Jamie, because he heard Californian girls were more free and easy with their favours than the Southern girls, who were all on a tight rein from their mothers.

The Ridley sisters had both got engaged the same weekend, Eloise to Jack Brandon, the son of the gynaecologist Professor John Brandon, and Lucille to some guy from Chattanooga, Tennessee, who owned a distillery there. The joint engagement party was on their parents' yacht next month and would be *the* event of the fall.

That, and the wedding of Rhett Tomkinson and Olivia Stanway. Miranda had hated Olivia Stanway since she took some guy Miranda liked to the prom when they were in high school, so Richard knew better than to ever say anything nice about her. Not that he particularly wanted to – Olivia was OK but not that interesting.

Miranda moved on to talking about her father and how he was looking forward to retiring. He had his millions made long ago, so he and her mother were only waiting to see her wed and then they were going to Europe for a while. They had a place in St Tropez.

This was Miranda's strongest hint yet that she was waiting for Richard to get down on one knee, but he said nothing in reply. Privately he thought it crazy that all his friends were getting married so young, before they'd been anywhere or done anything interesting – their highest ambition was to be carbon copies of their parents. Noting his silence, Miranda shot him a narrow-eyed look. He cast around for a way to change the subject.

They were crossing the causeway to get to St Simons.

'Did you know the guy who built this causeway, Fernando Torras, was so innovative? They tried several times before to find a way to link the islands but always failed, but Torras, who studied engineering at Georgia Tech, by the way' – Richard looked at Miranda; she only regarded the Ivy League schools as worthy of praise – 'managed to do it in 1924. It only took a year or so to build and cost $418,000.'

'Really?' She couldn't have been less interested.

He ploughed on regardless. 'Yeah, after he graduated, he went to South America, in the jungles, and he built roads and railway lines and bridges.'

'Urgh, sounds sticky.' She fanned herself.

'It might have been, but imagine the adventure, Miranda. Imagine doing something you are passionate about and feeling fulfilled, getting into bed tired every night after spending your energy on something that matters to you. Wouldn't that be something?'

He wished she could understand, could see beyond the ivory tower of their privileged but so small life. But she was like a hothouse plant, beautiful and perfect but raised to bloom in a specific environment and nowhere else. He was so fond of her – she was such fun when she wanted to be, and she was so gorgeous – but he was beginning to think she was not the person he wanted to share his life with.

But telling her or his parents he didn't want to get married or settle down just yet, or maybe never...well, it would be as bad as telling them he'd rather be a poet or artist or something, anything but a banker.

He pulled the car up in the broad driveway of the Lewis summer house.

The two-storey home, though it was called a cottage, was as big as their house in Savannah, painted turquoise and white, with a wide porch, a high-pitched roof and a front yard that gave way to a boardwalk, then sand and an idyllic beach.

Esme, the coloured housekeeper, stood at the foot of the steps, talking to Jimmy, the coloured man employed to take care of the grounds. Esme was dressed in the uniform all help wore: a blue dress, white apron, white stockings and flat black shoes. Her beam at the sight of him made him feel welcome, and he remembered how he would run into her arms as a little boy, her softness so comforting. His mother thought he was too familiar with Esme, but he didn't care. Esme was the kindest woman he'd ever met; he loved her no matter what anyone said. And now he jumped out and ran up and hugged her, just as he did back then.

'Mr Richard, you're early. We wasn't expectin' you till suppertime. Your mama said you ain't comin' till six. Boy, I do believe you've grown some! I thought you was done growin', but you're like a dang tree.' She chuckled and her whole body shook. .

'Hello, Esme. It's so good to be back – the city is so hot. You remember Miranda?'

By the look on Miranda's face, she was a little taken aback by this exchange. Esme's demeanour returned to a more neutral expression; she nodded respectfully and said, 'Good afternoon, Miss Logan. Welcome back to St Simons.'

'Thank you, Esme,' Miranda said, not rude but not warm either. Miranda, like all of her class, didn't really see the help; they were omnipresent like the furniture. She made an imperious little gesture to Jimmy, who promptly sloped off to the car and began unpacking the bags.

'Richard! How wonderful you got here so early.' Caroline Lewis appeared on the terrace above them, holding a glass of something cold. She was in a pale-blue dress, and like Miranda she was made up and coiffed perfectly. 'Miranda, you look wonderful.'

'So do you, Mrs Lewis.' Miranda smiled as she tripped gracefully up the steps to the terrace.

'But Richard, what have you come as, dear?' His mother looked him up and down as he followed Miranda. 'Did I say it was fancy dress?' She raised a perfectly arched eyebrow.

'It's just a shirt and shorts, Mother,' he said, and kissed her on the cheek. 'It's what people wear nowadays.'

'People? What people? Not any people I know.' She turned to Miranda. 'Miranda dear, let's get him inside before the neighbours think we've got a new pool boy.' The tinkly laugh held no mirth. 'Richard, I'm just going to call your father. Make Miranda something nice to drink. Nathan and Rebecca are out shopping with the girls, but they'll be back shortly, I'd imagine.'

She left them, passing through the double-width front door into the large octagonal reception area and continuing up the stairs.

Off to the right of the octagon was another set of doors leading to a long glass conservatory filled with greenery. Sarah and the beau their parents intended for her – Algernon Smythe, Miranda had reminded him – were playing backgammon and drinking cocktails. They got up to greet the new arrivals as they entered.

'Hello, brother, nice knees,' Sarah teased, and Algernon shook his hand limply – it was like grasping a wet fish. Unlike Richard, he was formally dressed in white trousers, a white shirt and a navy-blue blazer with gold buttons, a gold cravat at his throat, and his prematurely thinning hair was brushed back off his high forehead. No doubt Caroline Lewis considered Algernon perfectly dressed, but in Richard's opinion, he looked like a fool.

'Good afternoon, Richard, Miranda,' he boomed, and turning to Miranda, he said, 'I see your brother bought the forty-three-footer. I saw it for sale at the Isle of Hope Marina when I was down there with Dougie Pilkington – he was selling his…' Algernon had one topic of conversation: sailing. If you wanted to talk mainsails and booms, masts and jibs, he was your man, but anything else, forget it.

As Algernon launched into some yachting anecdote that could go on for an hour but in which Miranda seemed immediately fascinated, Richard used the opportunity to draw his sister aside, over to the table with the drinks.

'What's going on with the revolutionary? Are you trying to give our parents a heart attack?' he murmured as he fixed a martini for Miranda and a gin sling for himself.

Sarah winked at him as she topped up her own glass, adding ice and slices of lemon from cut-glass bowls. 'Aren't you the nosy boy.'

He did his best to look stern and authoritative. 'And what about Algernon? He's bound to find out if you keep it up.'

He was met with a peal of laughter. 'Oh, he only cares about boats. The only way he'd notice anything about me is if I had a mast coming out of my head.' She jerked her shoulder in Algernon's direction, and sure enough, he was still explaining to Miranda about different models of yacht.

'Seriously, though, Sarah, this is not going to fly. Best put an end to it.'

'Because you said so?' She clinked her glass off his. 'Relax, little brother, you'll like him. He's…' She paused, then said in a low voice, 'Interesting.'

'But Miranda said he's a socialist and a –'

'A what, Richard? What is his shocking secret?' Sarah's eyes danced wickedly.

'You know what I mean,' he whispered. 'He's Jewish. Ma and Pa will never, ever allow it.'

'Then I will never, ever ask them.' She winked, taking a long slug of her drink.

She was so reckless with her reputation; it made him despair. 'You're playing with fire, Sarah. Why would you want your name linked to a man like that?'

Instead of laughing this time, her eyes glittered, and she spat back, 'Maybe you could take a leaf out of his book, doing what he wants, not caring about what his mommy and daddy say. You could learn from him, Richard, instead of condemning him out of hand. Going on about being a poet or an artist – oh yes, Miranda told me! She thinks you're hilarious…but I doubt you could survive without the fancy clothes and the new car. But just because you can't, you shouldn't judge those who can.'

With a toss of her pretty dark curls, she moved back to Algernon and Miranda and stood listening with a rapt expression while Algernon explained to them both how the yacht Miranda's brother had just purchased had a maple deck, which was superior to a pine one for some incredibly long and boring reason.

Even though his father hadn't come downstairs to greet him yet, Richard decided to escape to the kitchen. As he wandered through the huge house to the back, he thought about what his sister had said to him. The walls of this house were hung with beautiful paintings, expensive vases stood on mahogany side tables, and velvet curtains hung at the windows. Every sumptuous inch of it spoke of his family's wealth. Could he walk away from all of it? It was all he'd ever known. Could he live more simply? Truthfully he didn't know if he even had the courage to try.

In the kitchen Esme was preparing the salads to accompany the barbeque they would have later. He offered to help her, but she shooed him away.

'Why don't you take Doodle for a walk, Mr Richard? He's been cooped up all morning, and he needs a long run. And it looks like you do as well, young man.'

'I do, Esme.' He grinned, bending over to kiss her plump cheek. She was a big woman and looked forbidding, but she wasn't at all. Not when you got to know her. Esme was soft-hearted, and Richard knew that while she loved Nathan and Sarah, he was her favourite, always was.

'Come on, Doodle.' He coaxed the old chocolate Labrador out of his basket. The dog who'd been in the Lewis family for years and years, and now lived permanently at the beach house, was nowhere near as decrepit as he made out – he was actually just really lazy – but to see him creep creakily out of the basket, you'd imagine he was on his last legs.

'Doodle, Mr Richard is going to take you to the beach,' Esme said with a smile, and immediately the dog perked up. He disliked his daily trot along the boardwalk on his leash, but a trip to the beach where he could gallop and cavort to his heart's content, that was an entirely different prospect. 'I sure wish I could take you there myself…' she added with a sigh.

'Are your knees no better, Esme?' Richard asked as he attached the leash to Doodle's collar.

'The doc says I ain't to be walkin' on no sand. It's fine on the sidewalk, not so much pain, but on sand…' She made a wincing face and raised her hands in despair. 'Poor Doodle misses his beach walks. He'll be so happy now you are here.' She patted Richard's cheek affectionately. 'Don't y'all forget to come home now, Mr Richard – don't you be doin' no daydreamin' in the sun. Dinner is at six, and your parents will expect you to be here.'

CHAPTER 10

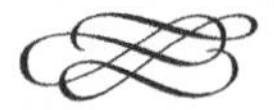

The tide was out, and the sky was blue. Families were spread around on picnic rugs and striped deckchairs, and the children had buckets and spades with them. He lifted his face to the sun, enjoying the cool, salty breeze on his skin. The city had not had a breath of air in weeks, but here it was strong enough to ripple his thick blond shock of hair. When he reached the edge of the ocean, he took off his shoes and socks, carrying them in one hand, as Doodle bounded ahead, splashing and bouncing in the water, unrecognisable from the reluctant creature that had to be coaxed out of his basket.

He followed the dog through the edge of the surf for a while, then stopped to look at the newly constructed Coast Guard station. After the economic crash of 1929, which had decimated the country, President Roosevelt had set up various projects to try to boost the economy, and this was one of those, built to assist swimmers in difficulty or boats that ran aground on the many salty marshes of the coastline and to log all ships and airplanes in the area. It sounded like a fun life. More fun than the bank, he was sure. Two boys he knew from school, Chip Sanderson and Albie Winters, had joined up rather than follow their fathers into their respective family businesses, and they were having a wonderful time by all accounts.

Maybe if he got some sort of paying job in the arts, it would make it more palatable to his parents? Not as a poet, but writing lyrics for musicals, something like that. Look at Cole Porter – he defied his wealthy family. They wanted him to practice law, but instead he became a songwriter, and now look at him.

On he walked, swinging his shoes in his hand, trying to come up with a good song in his mind.

Walking on the golden sand, dreaming of you...

But dreaming of who? Somehow Miranda didn't seem like a girl you'd write songs about. And what rhymed with Miranda? Not a lot, which made it awkward.

A little girl with reddish-blond hair of around six or seven and a smaller but even redder-haired boy were busy making a sandcastle, and he stopped to admire it. He then felt a pang of hunger and checked his watch. It was getting close to dinner time, and his mouth watered at the thought of the burgers and shrimp they would have. Mother would never dream of serving hamburgers at home, but here at the beach, it was somehow acceptable. Esme would make her special grits, and he'd load up his plate. He and Doodle better be getting back. But when he looked around, Doodle was nowhere to be seen; he'd been so lost in thought, he'd forgotten to keep an eye out.

'Doodle! Doodle!!' he shouted, scanning the dunes.

'He's up by the picnic tables,' called the little girl, looking up from her castle-making.

He smiled at her in surprise. 'You know Doodle?'

She nodded. 'He lives in the house next door to our new summer house. I know him – he comes to our back door looking for scraps. He's up there by the picnic tables. He's probably trying to eat the end of the picnics.' She had a slow Southern drawl. She beamed, showing her missing two front teeth.

'So you *do* know him.' He chuckled. 'That dog has no off button when it comes to food. I'm Richard, by the way. What's your name?'

'Amelia, and this is my brother, Robbie.'

'Nice to meet you, Amelia, and Robbie. That's a neat sandcastle you got there.'

'Thanks.' The little boy was sticking a series of small white pebbles on the top.

'You'd better get Doodle,' said Amelia. 'He stole a man's hot dog last week, and he was madder than a wet hen.'

These kids were from what his mother would call 'new money'. No child of their class spoke in that Southern accent. It was trained out of them by elocution teachers.

'You got it!' Richard laughed and strode on up the beach. Typical Doodle to be scrounging for scraps. He was bordering on chubby, but he could still give picnickers a pathetic look that said he hadn't eaten for weeks. Last summer Esme had whispered to Richard that Doodle had helped himself to a whole cooked chicken from an unsuspecting family's picnic basket.

And sure enough, there he was, on the far side of the tables at the top of the beach. Sadly for Doodle, the tables had emptied out, so all potential marks for a treat were gone, but he was burrowing frantically nearby, presumably for some tossed-away hot dog or hamburger or other morsel.

Richard checked his watch, and it was past five thirty. He thought he'd better go home via the road to save time. 'Come on, buddy! Let's go!'

Doodle just kept on digging.

While Richard waited for him to unearth whatever it was, he sat down at a table to replace his shoes and socks. The dunes changed shape here all the time depending on the storms, and now there was a huge pile of debris dumped all around the area in the form of sticks and dried seaweed, which would be sharp on his feet when he crossed over it to the road. After he'd tied his laces, he took Doodle's leash from his pocket and went to clip it onto his collar.

'Come on, buddy, time for dinner.' His watch told him it was twenty to six now. Father didn't tolerate tardiness to the table, and he needed time to freshen up as well. But Doodle showed no sign of giving up, even when Richard pulled on the leash. 'What are you after, buddy?'

He stooped to look. There seemed to be a small flat bottle trapped between two pieces of driftwood that for some reason the dog was determined to get at. Gently pushing the dog's nose aside, Richard used his fingers to dislodge the bottle.

'Is this what you're after?'

He straightened up with the find in his hand, while the Labrador sat panting and grinning, looking up at him with his eyes crossed. The bottle was made of thick glass, opaque now from the abrasion of the sand and water, with a cork stopper, and in raised letters in the glass he could just make out the words 'Paddy Whiskey'. There was something inside, he thought, a bit of trash someone had shoved in there before throwing the bottle away. He tested the cork, but it was swollen with the saltwater and stuck fast.

The dog was still watching him hopefully, his sandy tongue lolling.

Richard wagged his finger at him. 'Sorry, buddy, can't give you this. The glass might break in your mouth. People shouldn't leave things like this on the beach.'

He stuck the bottle in his pocket to dispose of at home and set off across the seaweed and up the road, with Doodle limping along grumpily behind.

* * *

HE CAME in through the kitchen, giving the little whiskey bottle to Esme to throw away with some other empties, then went to wash his hands upstairs in the bathroom. He came down to the terrace, where the chairs and tables had been set outside under an awning. Jimmy was helping out by turning the shrimp on the barbecue.

It was ten past six, and his father frowned as he checked his chunky gold watch before shaking Richard's hand by way of a greeting. 'There you are, Richard. I was beginning to think something had happened to you. Your mother was very worried. And Miranda as well, weren't you, Miranda?'

'Absolutely frantic with fear,' Miranda said sweetly, reminding Richard of how much he liked her when she was being light-hearted.

'You see?' declared his father triumphantly. He never could tell when a woman had been deliberately funny; in his world women didn't make jokes.

'I'm so sorry, Father. I just lost track of time. The breeze was so refreshing after the stickiness of the city. Hello, Nathan, hello, Rebecca.' He greeted his brother and his wife and looked around for his little nieces. 'Where are the girls?'

'I wanted them to stay up to see you, but Rebecca sent them off to bed with the nanny.' Nathan smiled as he stood up to give Richard a hug.

'Which is where they should be at this time,' said Rebecca, calmly peeling a shrimp without getting a speck on her blue silk dress. She was a great believer in children being seen but not heard, and often not even seen.

'I'm sorry I missed them. Thank you, Esme.'

The housekeeper had appeared with a plate of salad and grits for him, and he moved to the barbecue to add shrimp and a burger, then brought the whole lot over to the table. Miranda had perched between Rebecca and his mother, so he took the remaining chair next to Sarah. On Sarah's other side, Algernon was still managing to drone on about yachts.

'I'll bring the girls swimming tomorrow if you like, Nathan,' he said across the table to his brother.

'Aren't they a little young for that?' asked Rebecca, looking anxious.

'Oh, don't worry, Rebecca,' said Sarah, speaking across Algernon, who was mid-sentence about a squall off Bermuda; she'd clearly stopped listening to him some time ago. 'They'll be safe with Richard. Swimming is the one thing he genuinely excels at.'

'Thank you, Sarah.' Richard shot his sister a look as he forked up a mouthful of grits; she grinned back at him. She was right, though; he'd been captain of the school swim team, and it was the only thing for which he'd ever won awards.

'Don't tease your brother, Sarah. The boy will go far at the bank,' pontificated their father from the other end of the table, using his napkin to flick shrimp from his bushy moustache. 'If he only pulls his socks up and keeps his head down and his shoulder to the wheel.'

'Goodness. All at the same time?' Sarah's eyes glittered with amusement. 'He'll give himself a hernia.'

'I was speaking metaphorically, Sarah,' Arthur Lewis explained, his tone patronising.

'Oh, of course, silly me...'

'Sarah? Sarah?' Algernon tried to regain her attention. 'I've been meaning to tell you, Dougie Pilkington is planning to take his new yacht on a small cruise around the islands next Thursday, with cocktails and a few friends. It will be splendid fun. You'll love Dougie, he just adores –'

'Yachts. Yes, Algy, I know,' snapped Sarah, without even looking at him. 'Can we please talk about something else for a change?'

'Sarah.' Their mother glowered from her end of the table.

'But Sarah, you'll love it.' Algernon was confused and hurt.

'How do you know I'll love it, Algy?'

'Well, I...'

'Have you ever asked me? Have you ever asked what I think about anything at all?'

'Sarah,' repeated their mother, glaring at her daughter now, while Rebecca and Miranda both shifted uncomfortably in their seats. Women in their set weren't supposed to make any sort of a scene.

'What is it, Mother?' There was a dangerous glint in his sister's eye now, the same as when he'd warned her to step away from her Jewish socialist friend.

'Sarah,' said Nathan with a slight shake of his head.

'Yes, Nathan?'

Richard said nothing but nudged her with his elbow. Bad mistake. She turned on him, eyes flashing.

'What are you elbowing me for, Richard? Do *you* want to say something?'

'Sarah, please...'

'Please what? Please behave myself? Do exactly as I'm told? Like you do?' She turned and addressed the whole table, her voice getting louder with every word. 'Mother, Father, everyone, did you know Richard wants to be a poet? He doesn't want to work in the bank at all – he wants to sit in an attic and scribble by candlelight. But he doesn't dare tell you because he's such a coward.'

'Oh, Sarah, you know that's not true,' protested Miranda, with a forced laugh. 'Whoever heard such nonsense.'

'Yes, don't talk nonsense, Sarah,' boomed their father. 'Boy's never written a word in his life, have you, Richard?'

Nathan looked at him. 'Richard?'

Algernon stared at his hamburger, struck dumb for once.

'Tell them, Richard. No time like the present…no point in dragging it out.'

Mother's knife and fork clattered onto her plate. 'Sarah, you've said quite enough for one day.' Her voice had an edge of steel. 'Richard, tell your father right now that your sister is being ridiculous –'

'But I'm not being ridiculous, Mother.' Sarah cut across their mother mid-speech, something very few people ever dared to do. 'You want to be an artist, don't you, Richard?'

He opened his mouth to deny it, but closed it again, his cheeks flushed and burning. It was terrible of Sarah to do this to him. Everyone's eyes were on him; he couldn't stay here to be mocked and sneered at. He wiped his hands on his napkin and threw it on the table, got up without saying anything and went into the house and upstairs to his room.

His suitcase was on the bed, where Jimmy had left it. In a fit of miserable rebellion, he opened it and took out his notebook, fountain pen and an inkwell. Sitting at the desk by the window, he laid the things out in front of him, then filled the pen and wrote, *Walking on the golden sand, dreaming of you…*

After a few minutes, he stood up and thrust his hands in his pockets, staring out to sea, tears in his eyes.

Then sat down again and reread, with blurred vision, what he'd written.

Walking on the golden sand, dreaming of you…

Again, tears pricked his eyes, and he scrubbed at them fiercely with his wrist. What was he thinking of? He'd never be able to do this... It was just a stupid dream. He got up to stare at the ocean again, then went over to the bed and threw himself down in despair.

* * *

He drifted out of a shallow dream. He'd been walking on the beach with some unknown woman whose face he couldn't see.

The tap on the door came again. 'Mr Richard?' To his relief, it was Esme, and he got off the bed to open the door.

'What can I do for you, Esme?'

'I just thought you might like to see this, Mr Richard.' She held out the whiskey bottle he'd left with her. 'That little bottle you gave me earlier, well, the cork dried out in the heat of the kitchen, and I couldn't resist a peep inside, and well, see for yourself...'

'What is it?' He took the bottle, tipped it and drew out a single spool of paper, slightly bent at one end.

'I had a small look, but reading ain't my strong point, Mr Richard, so I put it back to show you how it fit. But looks to me like it's a kinda letter, and I thought since you found the bottle... Well, the good Lord sure works in mysterious ways, Mr Richard, and I thought maybe this was meant for you.'

He smiled. 'It was Doodle who found it really, Esme. But thank you for thinking of me.' He had the bottle in one hand and with the other tried to unroll the spool; it kept springing together again, but he could see the paper was covered in small, neat purple handwriting.

'Is it anything, Mr Richard? Or just trash? Do you want it, or will I take it away again?' Her voice sounded uncertain now, unsure that she'd done the right thing.

'No, leave it with me.' His curiosity was piqued.

'Very well, Mr Richard. Good night.'

'Good night, Esme.' As the door closed behind her, Richard brought the find over to the window to avail of the last of the fading light. He weighted one edge of the paper with the bottle and flattened out the letter with his hand.

Dear St Jude, he read.

St Jude? He wasn't big on the saints, but even he'd heard of this one. Something to do with hope and impossible causes. He wondered who was writing to such a saint for help. And why did they throw the letter away, stuck into a bottle? What an odd thing to do.

Dear St Jude,

I am writing this to you because I have not a single soul in my life in whom I can confide. I feel a bit silly, but I have to get this out of me somehow, and given your portfolio, I thought we might be a good match.

So that's why the writer had thrown this away. Clearly it was never intended to be read; it was just a way of getting things out of their system. *What a good idea.* He might do it himself, maybe it would make a writer of him.

My name is Grace Fitzgerald...

He wondered if she lived locally.

...and I live in Knocknashee, Co Kerry, Ireland.

He stopped and reread the address in amazement.

Knocknashee, County Kerry, Ireland?

Surely not.

But there it was in black and white... Or lilac and white. Could this bottle have come all the way from there? He tried to recall the map of the world on the wall of his eighth-grade classroom and Mrs Gold, his teacher, having them learn off by heart various world capitals. They would chant, Paris, France; Rome, Italy; Budapest, Hungary; London, England. What was Ireland? Durban? Something like that? And where was Ireland exactly? He'd have to check the atlas at home.

He carried on reading.

I do realise I'm very lucky that, thanks to my sister, I have a roof over my head and food, when so many go poor and hungry. It's not that I'm ungrateful...

I had polio and was in hospital for four years, and though I have a limp and my back often hurts, I know I was spared far worse.

It was like taking a private peek into someone else's soul. A heartfelt letter written by a seventeen-year-old girl who seemed much more grown up than his twenty-year-old self; articulate and well educated, he could see that, and brave, and grateful for the small things she had, and struggling to be a better person, the best she could be. Though all along, her frustration and despair radiated off the page.

Please help me, St Jude. Please intervene so Agnes doesn't sack me, leaving the little ones at her mercy, and could you also make sure she doesn't throw me out on the side of the road, because I have absolutely nowhere else to go.

The letter finished abruptly there, and he got the impression the writer had been interrupted. He hoped she didn't get into trouble with that sister, who sounded very hard to live with. But then this girl had managed to put the note in a bottle and throw it out to sea, so she must have found a way to hide it from her. How long did it take for the ocean to deliver her message, to be dug up by Doodle on the beach? There was no date. It might have been written years ago. He wondered how old Grace Fitzgerald was now, or if she was even still alive.

And did she ever escape her impossibly small world? It was very sad about the polio, and she clearly had no money of her own, so it seemed unlikely. He hoped she hadn't become bitter. She was clearly so brave and naturally good-hearted. Even at this distance in space and time, she made him feel rather ashamed of himself. He was Richard Lewis, fit and young and healthy, and he hadn't one tenth this young girl's courage or goodness.

CHAPTER 11

KNOCKNASHEE, DINGLE

ctober 1938

GRACE CAME out of the school, a basket of exercise books over her arm. It was a blustery October day, the heat of the summer long done, and there was a wind that could cut you in half. The fishing boats that bobbed all summer on their moorings were now being pitched around by the grey Atlantic.

She wished Agnes would allow her to light a fire in her bedroom tonight; the chimney was swept and ready. Her leg was always cold, but now that the weather had turned, the whole lot of her was chilled to the bone. Agnes, though, said it was a waste of money for them to light the fires upstairs before November, so she would have to mark these essays downstairs in the dark kitchen.

Agnes said that the canon thought there would be a war, and if there was, everything would be scarce, including coal, so they shouldn't waste anything. They never did anyway, and even if there was a war – and she thought it was unlikely; Germany would surely not start another one so soon after the last – Mr de Valera would keep Ireland out of it.

She was dying to read her pupils' versions of what they'd learnt today, from the sentence or two written by the four-year-olds – PIRITES AR BAD – to excited stories written by the eight-year-olds. She'd prefer to read them in private, to chuckle at their funny perceptions and to give a star if a child did particularly well, but with Agnes double-checking her marking, with enthusiastic and vicious use of the red pen, that was impossible. She'd just have to whisper to each child how good they were.

The history part of the schoolday was their favourite and incentivised them to learn their prayers, letters and sums as fast as possible, to get to the good bit, as they called it.

Today the lesson had been mostly about pirates. Doreen O'Boyle had proudly brought in a book her father had about the pirate raid in West Cork, the next county over, where Barbary pirates entered the town of Baltimore in 1631 and took almost two hundred people captive and brought them to Algeria as slaves. There wouldn't be much going spare in the O'Boyle household – the book had been an ill-judged gift from a visitor years ago, as Finbarr O'Boyle could hardly read or write – but the beam on little Doreen's face, to be able to contribute something to the conversation, was priceless. Grace had passed the book around the classroom, and they recoiled at the pencil drawings of terrifying Ottoman Turks. Doreen was walking on air.

Grace told them more about pirates then, and they were all agog about Blackbeard, Edward Teach, who had smoke coming out of his ears due to burning bits of candles or fuse he placed there to make him even more ferocious. They lapped up stories of the port town of Port Royal on the island of Jamaica, where the rule of the buccaneer was law. She told them why the Jolly Roger had a skull and crossbones, because the men who sailed beneath that flag knew they were destined for the hangman's rope anyway and therefore had nothing to fear.

She was at great pains to explain that was long ago, that there were no pirates nowadays, but she was a little worried they'd all be awake tonight listening out for the creak of oars and the soft march of pirate boots.

Agnes had asked her to pick up half a pound of butter from O'Donoghue's, and that took a few minutes because Biddy kept talking about how she would happily pay that girl Tilly O'Hare an extra farthing for a dozen eggs if the foolish, headstrong girl would only stop bringing them to the grocer's in Dingle instead. Clearly Tilly had made good her threat to boycott Biddy for gossiping to Agnes, and the grocer's wife thought Grace had a way of influencing the situation...which of course she didn't.

As she walked past the post office, thinking sadly of how much she missed her old friend, a voice whispered, 'Gracie,' and she stopped and turned.

Charlie McKenna, a small, slight man with a receding hairline, was standing at the door of his postman's cottage, a thatched two-up, two-down to the right of the post office.

'Hello, Mr McKenna.' Grace was always sure to address him respectfully, to make up for her sister's rudeness; Agnes tended to treat Charlie as if she were a duchess and he a potboy.

'Ah, will you stop. Call me Charlie for God's sake, Gracie.' His words were gruff, but there was kindness there. 'When your father was alive, you called me Charlie as soon as you could talk. Come in, quick now, before anyone sees.' He looked up and down the street, which was almost empty because of the piercing wind. The bus was just gone, and there were only a few children around.

She stepped inside uncertainly as he held the door open for her. She didn't really remember this man from her childhood, and apart from the 'good morning' and 'thank you for the letters' each morning, she'd not had a conversation with him since she came out of hospital, and she'd never set foot in his house. But she liked the way he'd called her Gracie. It was what her father had called her; it brought him closer somehow.

He led the way down a passageway to the back kitchen, which was sparse but clean, and gestured that she should take one of the súgán chairs beside the range; it creaked slightly as she rested on the hemp seat. The room was spotless, the floor swept and the table clear of debris. The blackened kettle hung on the hook over the fire. There was no woman's touch in the McKenna house, no nice tea towel or picture on the wall. Everything was practical and functional.

'I have something for you, Gracie.' He went to his postal sack hanging on a nail on the wall.

As he rummaged in the deep bag, Declan opened the back door and seemed a little nonplussed to find her there. Visitors to the McKenna house were rare, she imagined. Like her own house.

'Hello, Declan.' She smiled warmly at him. He'd been back a few months now, but apart from a hello from her on the street, met with a nod of acknowledgement from him, they'd not spoken since his return. When she was five, he must have been in the same classroom in school – he was only a year ahead of her in age – but when he was six, he'd been spirited away to the orphanage in Letterfrack, and she had no memory of him.

'Grace,' his voice gentle and gravelly. 'How are you?'

'Very well, thank you.' She smiled again. 'And you?'

'I'm all right.' He looked surprised that she asked, then quickly crossed the kitchen and disappeared into the hall.

She gazed after him, thinking how like his mother Declan must look, because apart from being rail thin, he was nothing like his father. He was a lot taller for one, and his face had a defined jaw and deep-set indigo-blue eyes under beautifully arched dark eyebrows. His dark-brown hair was silky, and he wore it longer than most men; it hung over his eyes almost, and you got the distinct impression he was hiding behind it.

Charlie found what he was looking for and came towards her, a thick letter in his outstretched hand. 'Here you are. I thought you might want to get this in private.'

'Oh, thank you, Charlie!' She took the letter with a cry of delight, feeling the heat rush into her face. This had to be from Tilly! Because who else would write to her? Charlie would have heard about the row in the street and be worried Grace would get in trouble with her sister if this came to the house. It was so kind of him to be discreet…though a bit embarrassing that everyone in town clearly knew her business.

Yet when she looked at the envelope, it wasn't from Tilly at all.

There was her name, Miss Grace Fitzgerald, and her address, Knocknashee, County Kerry, Ireland, but the handwriting was unfamiliar, and some of the letters were formed differently to the way an Irish person would write them. There were three stamps stuck to the top righthand corner, pink in colour, all showing the head of an old man, with '2 CENTS' printed on each one. The envelope was covered in round black ink-smudged stamps, and another rectangular stamp in blue ink said 'Air Mail'.

She studied it in disappointment. 'Goodness…I don't recognise these stamps. And what does it mean, air mail?'

'It means it's come by plane from America, instead of by ship,' said Charlie.

'From *America*?' She looked up at him in astonishment. 'Sure I don't know anyone in America!'

'Well, someone in America knows you.' He smiled at her.

'But who?'

'Well, Gracie, there's a way to find out easy enough.'

Grace stared at him, her brain in an absolute whirl. 'How?'

'Take it home and open it?' he suggested a mischievous smile playing around his lips.

'Oh, yes. Yes. Of course.' Laughing and feeling silly as well as still very confused, she got to her feet, her basket in one hand, the letter in the other. 'I'll do that right now.'

'And why don't you pop it into one of those books you have in your bag, Gracie, to keep it safe until you do?' he suggested as he walked her to the door.

That made her uncomfortable, as if he thought she was having a secret correspondence behind Agnes's back with someone other than Tilly. It was kind of him to want to protect her, but still…

'I know nothing about who this is, Charlie,' she assured him. 'And I'm sure I'll show it to Agnes anyway.'

'Whatever you like, Gracie, but if you want to write back to whoever it is, you just drop your letter in to me at the house here. Just to make sure it doesn't go missing. By accident, of course.'

'By...accident?' She stared at him, confused.

In the dim hallway, he met her eyes. 'All I'm saying is, your sister has a terrible habit of losing things, Gracie. So you'd have to be careful.'

'Careful about...' Her voice tailed off. Was Charlie McKenna really implying Agnes would take a letter, written by Grace and sealed, from the stand in the hall, and 'lose' it before it was posted? Agnes, who insisted on honesty above all else? It was a dreadful accusation. She thought she really should say something firm to Charlie. But then she remembered the mysterious disappearance of the leather football that belonged to the Murphy boys.

She left the little house with the American letter still openly in her hand, to show she had no fear of her sister, and limped up the street, empty even of children now.

The smell of turf fires was on the evening air. Milking was almost over. The men were already in from the sea and off the land. The children would be helping at home or doing homework on kitchen tables as mothers served up potatoes and fish, maybe a few carrots or a turnip. It being a Monday, there would be no sweet after dinner; that was reserved for Sundays or maybe a Friday if a family was feeling *flúirseach*.

When she was nearly at the schoolhouse, but still out of sight of its windows, Grace came to a halt and thought for a moment. Then she rested the basket on the windowsill of an empty cottage – the Lynns were away in Tralee at a funeral – and tucked the letter into one of her hardback history books before she walked on home.

* * *

AT BEDTIME she brought the book upstairs to her freezing bedroom, got into her nightie, said her prayers by candlelight, then waited a while until she was sure Agnes had gone to bed and to sleep. By the time she took out the letter and tried to open it, her hands were so numb with cold, she was all fingers and thumbs and tore the envelope a little in the wrong direction.

There was a thin wooden bookmark on the bookcase, painted with a red poppy, that her mother had made for her; she fetched it and used it to slit the envelope the rest of the way and extracted several sheets of paper covered in handwriting, the same neat cursive as was on the envelope.

Dear Miss Fitzgerald, she read.

My name is Richard Lewis, and while walking my dog, I found your bottle on the beach here on St. Simons Island, Georgia.

A pounding began in her ears and her mouth felt dry. Her letter? The one from the bottle? The one she was sure had sunk to the bottom of the sea had floated across the ocean to America? She exhaled with the sheer wonder of it.

The bottle turned out to contain your letter. I realize it wasn't sent to me but to St. Jude, so I hope you will not regard it as impertinent for me to reply on the saint's behalf, but I wanted to thank you for your help.

For her help? What could he possibly mean by that? Her wonder deepened...

I don't know when you put the bottle in the ocean—I assume you did that in Ireland—but I found it on September 2nd of 1938 on the Georgia coast. It's fall here now, but we're in the South, so it doesn't get as cold as the north. Does Ireland get snow in the winter?

I must confess to needing an atlas to see where exactly Ireland is. I had an idea, but I was not good at paying attention in school, I'm afraid.

I have a picture in my head now of where you are, based on the bit you said, and it sounds beautiful, like a kind of paradise. I imagine a kind of tropical place with trees with big leaves and lots of wilderness. Am I wrong? If I'm honest, you could write all I know about Ireland on the back of a stamp.

Do you know much about Georgia? As a teacher, you probably do, but I'll tell you a bit about it anyway just in case.

Georgia is just above Florida and below the Carolinas on the East Coast of the United States. The state was founded in the 1700s—I should know the exact date, but I was probably gazing out the window on the days we learned this—by a guy called Oglethorpe. Lots of things here are named after him. Georgia's famous for peaches. We grow a lot of crops here, and we fish—we love shrimp, so lots of shrimping boats.

We've got baseball, though we are not in the top leagues in that, so we follow the Detroit Tigers. We're only willing to overlook our opinions on Yankees generally in this one case. If you are a big baseball fan, and we are, you have to look to the north for the Major League teams—New York, Boston, Chicago, Philadelphia. There are some on the West Coast too—San Francisco and Los Angeles—and some in the Midwest—Ohio, Missouri—but not so much down here.

Grace was mystified. What was baseball?

Well, I guess baseball isn't that interesting to an Irish girl, but once I get on that topic, I get carried away. There are lots of dances and movie theaters and things like that too, and the city of Savannah is particularly beautiful. It's my hometown, so you might think I would say that, but everyone says it. People come from all over to visit. The city is made up around lots of gardens, with fountains and trees for shade. In summer it's hotter than blue blazes, but the magnolia smells so sweet and the buildings are real pretty too.

To give you an idea, I've enclosed a photograph of my house in Savannah and also our summer cottage on St. Simons, which my grandmother left to our family and where we all go when the heat is too much.

With a thrill of excitement, Grace looked into the envelope again, and sure enough there were two photos, one of three young people, the boys tall and blond and the girl willowy, with dark hair cropped into a short bob.

Tilly would love to see that. Grace smiled.

The three of them were standing outside a huge, beautiful city house with a fruit tree in the garden – were those apples or peaches? She'd never seen a peach, so she had no idea. On the back he'd written *134 Jones Street, Savannah,* and she marvelled at the idea of any street having 134 buildings on it. Knocknashee had one main street and a bit of a square, and it petered out on both sides after around two hundred yards. No house or business needed a number; everyone knew everyone anyway.

The second photo was of the same three people, plus another girl, standing on the terrace of a gorgeous two-storey house with a beach in the background, and on the back was written *Our summer cottage, East Beach, St Simons*. She laughed out loud at the idea of calling such a mansion a cottage. Astonishing that one family could own two such enormous houses – and one just for the summer!

That's me on the left in both photos, by the way, in the shorts.

She studied his face eagerly and felt her heart melt a little. So handsome!

The others are my sister, Sarah, and my brother, Nathan, and at East Beach, the girl in the green dress is Miranda. She's my girl, or she was at the time of the photo, and Mother would like to see us get engaged; her family is well connected. I don't know, though. I like her a lot, but I think she might be getting tired of me at the moment, for the same reason my parents aren't speaking to me. Don't worry, I'll survive!

Miranda looked like something out of a magazine. Poor Richard. Even though he was being brave about it, he must be heartbroken if Miranda was changing her mind about marrying him. And what on earth had he done to deserve his parents not talking to him?

Grace, before I say any more about myself, I sure am sorry to hear about your own mother and father. That's a hard thing to face, losing them so young, and I'm not comparing my troubles to something so horrifying and final. I'm certain your parents are looking down on you from heaven, just as you imagine.

I'm also sorry to hear you had polio. That's hard as well. Are you aware our president, Mr. Roosevelt, has polio too? We have a place called Warm Springs in Georgia—it has an 88-degree natural spring, and Mr. Roosevelt goes for treatment there. He's made it into a place for other polio sufferers as well—or should I say People with a capital P who happen to have polio with a small p (I really like your Dr. Warrington). Of course I can't advise you, I'm not a doctor, but my brother, Nathan, is. He works at a hospital in Detroit, and he has a colleague who is trying to get an Australian nurse named Sister Kenny over to America. She is another one who believes in treating polio with hot water and massage. I asked Nathan to ask his colleague about you, and he said maybe you should go to England, because that is where Sister Kenny is visiting now.

Amazed, Grace had to smother a laugh at the idea she could just pop over to England for a polio cure. What a world of possibilities this wealthy young man had at his feet... He obviously had no way of imagining the smallness and poverty of her life.

Anyway, talking about Nathan kind of brings me around to myself. I hope you don't mind, but I feel it only fair that I tell you something about my life, since I feel I know so much about yours from your letter. Also, your example is such a good one, committing your feelings to the page. I have ambitions to be a writer, and I hope this will help me.

Of course, you may not care in the slightest about the angst of a young American man, but I shall write it, and if you deem it beneath your interest, feel free to dispose of it in the nearest fire.

The thing is, if Nathan had followed my father into the bank and been groomed as chair of the board, then I would have probably been allowed to live my life the way I choose, which is to be an artist or a poet or something like that—maybe a songwriter, I don't yet know. I'm only twenty, and I'm trying to find out what I want before I settle down with the bank and marry Miranda—if she'll still have me—and everything that means. Do I sound spoiled and ridiculous? I probably do.

Grace considered the question. On the one hand, it did seem strange that such a privileged boy, in the fullness of his health and with such a beautiful girlfriend, should be unhappy. But at the same time, she understood the pain of being forced into the wrong box and feeling your life is too small. Maybe families and their stifling expectations were the same everywhere; maybe money didn't make you free.

Anyway, as I was saying, Nathan decided to be a doctor instead and a Yankee to boot (living so far north in Detroit), which as far as my parents are concerned is not a good thing.

I don't know if you know about the Civil War we had here, but it divided the country into north and south. We are very much in the south. It's to do with slavery and being ruled from the north, among other things. Southerners dislike almost everything about Yankees. We think they're uppity, and they think we're dumb. Don't quote me, but that's the gist of it. The main difference is the South is segregated, meaning colored and white people live separately, go to different schools, live in different neighborhoods, that sort of thing. It's not a good story, truthfully—the colored people are much poorer and are often treated badly—but it's how it is.

Have you ever had anything like that in Ireland?

Thinking of the way the English treated the Irish for hundreds of years, Grace wondered where to begin...

Anyway, back to the point. Because of Nathan not doing what he was supposed to do, my parents decided I should work at the bank instead. So I did. And I hated it. But I said nothing.

And then when we were on vacation at the beach house in early September, my sister, Sarah, told my whole family I wanted to be a poet—she did it just to annoy me—and everyone thought it was hilarious. I stormed off to my room like a child. And that was when I read your letter, from the bottle. So Grace, this is where I have you to thank.

The candle guttered at that point, and for a panicky moment, she thought it was going out. She lit a second candle from it just in time, spilling wax on the desk as she did so.

Because it blew me away, how brave you are, and I realized how weak I was, hiding in my room. So I went back downstairs and told my parents that I needed to spread my wings.

All hell broke loose, but I stood firm (ish), and then they decided I was just "going through a phase" and gave me a few months off from the bank, with my promise to go back if, and when as they see it, I fail. And so here I am, still on the island, banned from my home in Savannah, trying to figure it all out. I don't know if I will, but I'm trying. For instance, I'm working on a song at the moment, though I haven't gotten very far.

Miranda is being very nice about my "breakdown" and has been to visit a few times, but I can feel her patience wearing thin. She really needs someone more like Algernon, Sarah's intended—if Sarah behaves herself. But anyway, we'll see.

So that's my story, Grace. I wish I could be more help about your own sister; sisters can certainly be a pain in the you-know-what. But I hope the two of you are getting along better.

Yours sincerely,

Richard Lewis.

PS I honestly have no idea how old you are now. You may have thrown the bottle in the ocean years ago and are now an older lady with everything worked out. If so, I'm sure you would think it's very dull to correspond with an ignorant young man. But if you are still alive and would like to correspond, write to Richard Lewis, 51 Clematis Drive, East Beach, St. Simons Island, GA. It will reach me if I'm still here, and Esme the maid will forward it on if I've already gone home to Savannah with my tail between my legs.

L.

By now the hands on the little clock by Grace's bed were folded at one o'clock, but there was no way she could sleep. This was the most exciting thing to ever happen to her. She could hardly believe that the sheet of paper in her hand had once been in America. And a letter to her, not from a woman or a child or an old man, but a boy her own age who understood her, who gave her an insight into his life in return. It was incredible.

And he'd asked her to write back!

No better time, she decided, than in the dead of night, when Agnes was fast asleep. She opened the lilac inkpot and filled the cartridge.

Dear Mr Lewis,

What a lovely surprise to receive your letter. Thank you for writing to me. I had no idea who the letter could have been from, and I have never received a letter from someone abroad before, let alone all the way over in America. It's the middle of the night here, but I've just finished reading it, and I'm too excited to sleep and couldn't wait to write back...

She paused. Did that sound gauche? Unhinged? But this relationship had started on raw honesty, a state most people never get to even after years, so to pretend she was more worldly than she was would be pointless; she might as well be honest. And to be fair, if he didn't think she was unhinged after the last letter, she was probably safe enough now.

In answer to your question about whether I'm still alive, I threw the bottle in the sea in April of 1938 and my birthday was in June, so I'm now eighteen years old.

I am sorry that your first introduction to me was through such a tirade of misery. I won't say I didn't mean it, because I did, but it isn't generally how I introduce myself!

Thank you for telling me about Georgia. It will be the next place I teach my pupils about.

Your description of your home city sounds wonderful. Shrimp boats and baseball and dances – it all sounds like something you'd see at the pictures, not real life.

Perhaps I should tell you a bit more about Ireland, which isn't the tropical place you're imagining, I'm afraid; it's often fairly wet and cold. It's beautiful, though, and a very ancient place. We have castles and forts and lots of pre-Christian settlements everywhere.

I live on a peninsula on the southwest coast. It's called the Dingle Peninsula and is like a long narrow finger pointing into the Atlantic. And while it is very beautiful – green fields, high mountains, cliffs and crashing ocean on both sides – it is difficult to make a living here. Most people farm and fish, and that keeps them going. I am a schoolteacher – well, not a fully qualified one or anything, more of a teaching assistant. But I have my own class, and I teach children between the ages of four and eight. I really love it.

The peninsula is a Gaeltacht area, meaning the people speak Irish here as our first language, though some people speak English as well. My sister, the headmistress, thinks we should teach mainly through English, but I allow the children to converse in their native tongue when she's not within earshot. They prefer Irish. It's more expressive than English. We have a lot more words to describe things, so it's easier to say what you mean exactly in Irish.

She hoped that didn't sound rude, him being an English speaker, but it was true. Only today Bill Lucey, one of her students, was trying to explain something in English and had struggled. Maybe she would tell Richard this, to explain what she meant.

For example, take the English word 'clever'. In Irish we have lots of words for different types of cleverness. One of my students was trying to find an English word for the Irish word glic. *It means clever in the way a fox might be – a bit sly, or even devious, but instinctive rather than learnt, and for a particular purpose. I hope that makes sense. Maybe I'm being too much like a schoolteacher, always trying to educate people. That would be fierce annoying altogether, so write back and tell me if I am. But I do love being a teacher and wouldn't want to be anything else, even if I do one day get to travel the world, which is a dream of mine.*

She inhaled. Perhaps she was being too open about herself. But he'd been very open too, describing all his problems with his family wanting him to go into the bank when he wanted to do something creative instead. Banks were just about numbers, she supposed. She didn't know much about them, only post offices, but she supposed the principle was the same. You put money in and took it out again.

I think you're right to tell your family you don't want to be a banker if you want to be an artist. If you don't love what you're doing, you'll only make a mess of it. My sister is a teacher out of duty, but it doesn't suit her, and that's bad for everyone.

This girl I know, Tilly, she doesn't want to marry, and I'm sure if she did, she would be a terrible wife. I don't know why she plans to be a spinster – it's not something I would do out of choice – but people are all different, I suppose.

She feared Tilly would never speak to her again after the dreadful scene in the square and the long silence afterwards, with Tilly not answering her letter. But writing about her old friend comforted her, she realised; it seemed to bring her into the room somehow.

Tilly is very funny and loves to cause scandal. She cut her hair short like a boy's, which might be a fine thing to do over there in America, judging by the picture of your sister, who is beautiful – I'd love to show the picture to Tilly – but I assure you, it is most certainly not all right here in Knocknashee. She dresses like a man too, which causes sceitimíní *left, right and sideways. She says it's more comfortable for farming, and she's probably right, but it drives some people half daft.*

Tilly is very funny and bright and brave. Far braver than I am. In fact, I'm not a bit brave. But around Tilly I am a little bit bolder than when I'm on my own.

We watched a wedding in the village last year where the bride's surname was Cooney, and she married a man called Martin Crowley. There's an old piséog *here that says if a bride 'changes name but not the letter, it's a change for the worse and not for the better.' Tilly and I laughed so much, poor Bríd*

Cooney had no idea what had us giggling, but Tilly said even if they were an A and a Z, she wouldn't swap places with the bride for a gold clock.

Stop, she thought. A wealthy, wordly boy like Richard Lewis wouldn't be interested in the silly antics of two girls in a little Irish village.

She considered crossing out what she'd written, but that would look strange. She supposed she could rewrite the whole letter, but that seemed ridiculous. So she left it in. He'd probably already decided she was a bit tapped in the head after reading the first one anyway.

Ignore me, Mr Lewis! I'm daft as the crows.

I'm sure Miranda is lovely and will support you in whatever you do once she gets used to the idea, and I know your parents will forgive you, whatever you do. That's what parents are for – they have to love you, however annoying you are.

Thank you for your suggestion that I should go to England to see Sister Kenny. If I had the money, I might do it, even though it's very far and I wouldn't be sure how to get there, but my sister puts all my savings into the post office for my future and so we only have the one wage to live on. I didn't know your president had polio – it's never talked about here. I will say it to Dr Warrington if I ever see him again, and he's sure to tell me that proves everything he says about the sky being the limit for me. He was always very encouraging, even though I've let him down by not going very far at all.

Thank you for writing back to me and being so honest and so kind. It's made me very happy.

Yours sincerely,

Grace Fitzgerald.

PS I don't have a photo of myself to send back to you, I'm afraid. Yours was very nice. Your houses are lovely.

It was true, because the photographer hadn't sent the photos to Knocknashee. She was glad of that now, because at least she didn't have to tell Richard Lewis a lie.

CHAPTER 12

She spent the day happily teaching the children all about the Southern states. And why Georgia, Virginia and the Carolinas were named as they were.

In her excitement she'd barely had two hours' sleep, and she had risen long before Agnes, which gave her time to find a particular book in the spare room, a book that had belonged to her father and that she was sure – and she was right – had a chapter about James Oglethorpe, the founder of the colony of Georgia and the extraordinary set of circumstances and run of good luck on his part that enabled him to set up and build Savannah.

To the Irish children, who inhabited a rich and wild landscape where the only planning in evidence was that of the divine, the idea of a new city, with twenty-four green squares surrounded by handsome houses and civic buildings, was fascinating. They listened, captivated, as she made the dull chapter come to life by telling it in her own words. They were even willing to overlook Oglethorpe's English nationality in their admiration of him.

Usually her pupils were fascinated by stories of the Catholic conquistadors but very against the rampaging of the English Protestants. These were the children of the Irish Rebellion. Their fathers and uncles had fought the British to liberate Ireland in the last generation, so they cheered for the Spaniards and Portuguese in any conflict over land between them and the English, and adored any story in which England was in strife. The pilgrims on Plymouth Rock, the Sioux, the Apache, the Choctaw – they loved all that. Sometimes she wondered if it was quite seemly that she taught in such an animated way, as it led to her pupils taking such fervent sides.

It would all change when they moved up, though, she told herself, so if she could teach them with a bit of joy, then it was worth it.

And today she was full of joy herself, and very conscious of the letter to Georgia, in America, that she had in her basket of books. Agnes, she knew, was paying a visit to the canon after school to discuss some important Church business or other, and she was going to seize the opportunity to bring the letter to Charlie's house. She'd forgotten altogether that she was going to need a stamp, and had no idea what type was needed to get this letter to America, but she planned to do a bit of cleaning or baking for Charlie if he would see his way to finding her one.

Thank goodness for Charlie. He'd been so right to be discreet. If Agnes had seen Richard Lewis's letter, Grace would have had to explain everything – the throwing of the bottle into the sea and the obvious fact that she'd been writing about Agnes in a less than complimentary way.

It would have been worse than being caught out going to Dingle with Tilly O'Hare.

* * *

CHARLIE WAS HAVING a bowl of home-made soup when she tapped on his front door, and he immediately invited her in to join him.

'Thanks, I'd love it.' She sat at the end of his kitchen table, her bad leg outstretched. There was an ache there all the time now, but she tried to ignore it as best she could. It wasn't too painful during the day, or when she was too busy to think about it, but at night when she got into bed, the ache there almost made her weep sometimes.

He ladled out a steaming bowlful of rich vegetable soup and handed her a spoon. 'Is the leg sore today?' he asked, kindly. Nobody ever mentioned her leg, so it was a bit of a jolt. She just nodded, and to her horror, her eyes filled with tears.

He took the spoon from her hand and put his arms around her. ''Tis all right, *alanna*. I saw you making a face on you coming in. You poor *craythur*. It must be wicked sore to say you're in tears over it?'

She could only nod. It wasn't any worse today than usual, but to have someone be kind to her about it, or even mention it at all, had touched something in her. Her face rested against the soft cotton of his Posts and Telegraphs–issue shirt; his uniform jacket hung on the back of the chair. He smelled of pipe tobacco and fresh air, and it reminded her of her father.

When she stopped crying, he gave her his handkerchief. 'It's clean.' He smiled. 'Why don't you write to your Dr Warrington? You never know, he might be able to do something for you.' His voice was kind as he handed her the spoon again.

'Agnes says not to be bothering him, that he has enough to be doing.'

He sighed and rubbed his stubbly chin. 'But I've heard tell from Dr Ryan he's a decent man and a great doctor, and he'd want to see you as well as you can be, so why not tell him it's hurting you?'

'Mm…' She took a spoon of the delicious soup. She had in fact sent Dr Warrington and his wife a long thank-you card when she'd got home from the hospital, but she'd never heard back. It did bother her a little, but they were so busy. They had children on their hands who were dying, and so many patients, and they'd probably not even had time to read yet another thank-you card.

Too tactful to press her further, Charlie emptied his bowl, then stood and took it to the sink and washed it, dried it and placed it back on the dresser. 'Cuppa tea?' he asked, and she just nodded.

Silently he made tea, taking two clean cups from the hooks, while she finished her soup. He placed the teapot on the scrubbed pine table, along with a jug of milk from the windowsill, then sat back down and looked at her, his intelligent hazel eyes weighing up whether to tell her something. Then he exhaled slowly and spoke. 'If you ever want to write to the doctor, or anyone, Grace, make sure you give the letter to me – will you do that?'

Grace felt uncomfortable. Charlie was doing it again, suggesting she was better not leaving her letters among the post to be collected at home. But why? There was hardly anything shameful about a letter she might send to Dr Warrington. Agnes knew he was a very respectable person. It wasn't like being caught writing to Tilly, or blabbing about everything to a boy in America...

Which reminded her, she had the letter to Richard in her basket.

Blushing, she took it out and placed it on the table. 'I've written back to America, Charlie. But I don't have a stamp for it, and I was wondering, could I do a bit of housekeeping for you in return for one?'

He smiled. 'There's no need to do anything for me, Gracie. I owe your parents so much, I'd just be paying it back. I'll see it gets there.' He held out his hand, but she placed her palm over the envelope on the table.

'No, Charlie. I can't give it to you unless you promise me I can work off the cost of the stamp.'

Seeing she was in earnest, he relented. 'If it makes you feel better, Gracie, I'll find something for you.'

'Do you promise me?'

'I promise.'

She handed him the letter then, and he went to put it in his sack without even looking at the envelope, as if he thought she'd prefer the address to be a secret.

'It's not what it seems, Charlie,' she said, blushing again. 'I really didn't know who that letter was from when you gave it to me. What happened is –'

'You don't have to tell me, Gracie, if you don't want to. It's your own business.'

'No, it's all right. I know I can trust you.'

He smiled slightly as he added some milk to his tea. 'You've no business being *béal scaoilte* as a postman. Right enough, I'm no Biddy O'Donoghue. So if you want to talk, your secret is safe with me.'

'I...well...' Grace began but hesitated, 'Agnes can be a little bit... difficult, I suppose. And she was very rude to Tilly – you probably heard – and I was so vexed with her, so furious really, that I wrote a letter, pouring it all out. I'd nobody else to tell, you see. She drove Tilly away, and Tilly was my only friend. And I...' She felt foolish saying it; it was such a fanciful thing to do, like something out of a novel or a picture in the cinema, putting notes in bottles.

Charlie sipped his tea and let her speak with no interruption.

'Well, I put the letter in a bottle and threw it into the sea at Trá na n-Aingeal, and it seems this person found it, in Georgia, in America, and he wrote back.'

'And it got all the way over there?' The postman beamed and ran his hand over his thinning hair. 'Well, doesn't that bate all?'

'And would it be right to write back to this person, do you think?' Grace asked.

'Well, does he seem all right, not some kind of an *amadán*?'

'I think he does...'

'Well, sure even if he is, there's thousands of miles of ocean between ye, so he can't do much to harm you with a pen and paper anyway. And you can leave your letters here if you want to. In case you don't want them found. Nobody will look at them. I'll find a box for you, with a lid, and you can put them in it and leave them in the bottom of the dresser there – you'll be the only one to open it.'

It was a kind offer, and maybe a sensible one. 'Thank you very much, Charlie, maybe that would be a good idea.' She felt a rush of warmth towards him. 'You and Daddy were very good friends, weren't you?'

'Sure we were. Your father was my best man, did you know that? And I was his. And your mother and Maggie were great pals. They were together the night Eddie and I met them. He said he'd take the one on the left and I could have the one on the right. As luck would have it, we got them the right way round, and Eddie married Kathleen and I married Maggie.'

Grace smiled. She loved hearing stories about her parents.

'But then Maggie died, and the canon decided I wasn't fit to care for Declan and the little girl – I called her Siobhán. Your father tried to stop it happening, but sure the canon is the chair of the school board. He has all the power in the town – a schoolteacher was nothing to him. He overrode your father, and the little ones were taken away.'

He sighed again; telling this story was hard for him. Her heart ached for him.

'I've no idea where they were sent, the canon wouldn't tell me. And all your father could do for me was try to pull me out of the gutter when I sunk into it. He persuaded Nancy O'Flaherty to give me a job on condition I cleaned myself up, and Kathleen put me through the examination for the Posts and Telegraphs herself. And I'll always be so grateful to both your parents, because at least I was ready to be a father when Declan finally came home, to mind him and help him to move forwards with his life.'

'Has he got any plans at the moment?'

He shrugged. 'Nancy is saying she needs to take on another person. The round is getting too big, and with the telegraphs and the banking and all the rest.'

Grace was delighted. 'Oh, that would be perfect. It will bring him out of himself having to speak to people, even if only a little bit.'

He poured them both another cup of tea, still looking doubtful. 'He wants it, and he's bright enough for anything. Sure he's a genius with all the gadgets. He fixed the auld wireless. 'Twas banjaxed entirely and I was for dumping the bloody thing, but he took it apart and soldered it, and now it works grand, so it does. But what lets him down is his handwriting is so bad and shaky, and I'm worried he'll fail the exam because of it. He was left-handed, you see, and the Christian brothers in Letterfrack beat him for it and forced him to write with his right…' He shuddered. 'The poor boy doesn't say much, but what he did say about what they did to him…'

Grace reached across the table to touch Charlie's hand, which was also shaking. His jaw was set, and his voice held all the pain and grief of a parent whose child is suffering.

'Could I help him, Charlie? Maybe that's what I could do for you, in return for the stamp. I teach letters to little children every day. I'm sure it would be nothing to teach someone as clever as Declan to shape his letters more clearly.'

He looked at her then, and hope and relief came into his face. 'You're so like Kathleen, Gracie, you know that? She was so kind too. And such a good teacher. If you could get my boy through his exams, it would be worth a lot more to me than one American stamp. But wouldn't it get you in trouble with your sister?'

'It's none of Agnes's business, Charlie.' Her heart thumped as she said the words; she could hardly believe they'd come out of her mouth. Richard Lewis had called her brave, but she wasn't at all, writing all her complaints secretly and throwing them into the sea.

Maybe, just maybe, she was beginning to be the girl the boy in America imagined her to be. If he could stand up to his family, then so could she.

CHAPTER 13

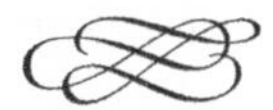

Grace was using her free Saturday to take a lot of boxes out of the spare room so she could poke into the back of it. She was searching for a map; she was nearly sure one used to hang on the wall of the seniors' room before Agnes replaced it with the terrifying Shroud of Turin, bearing the image of the crucified Christ.

A colourful map of North America on a roll of good cloth, showing all the states and going down as far as Mexico...

She'd been at it for two hours already. There was so much stored away in here, and it was taking her so long with her leg. She knew she really should give up soon and use the time for polishing windows. As Agnes had pointed out before she left for her latest pilgrimage, the salt air had encrusted the glass. And she had also promised to weed the front flowerbed, even though it was very hard to do with all the bending involved.

Of course, Agnes had the harder task this weekend. She was doing the path of St Finbarr pilgrimage in Cork, all twenty-two miles from Drimoleague to Gougane Barra. 'I'm offering it up for the sins of the parish,' she'd told Grace. 'That my sacrifice may be seen by the Lord, and He will show mercy on those of this parish who have fallen into the way of sin.'

'You're really wonderful to do that, Agnes,' Grace had said, though a bad part of her – the part that had said 'It's none of Agnes's business, Charlie' – thought maybe Agnes should think of her own sins for once, instead of those of other people. And how did it even work? Did God look down and say, 'Well, look, there's Agnes Fitzgerald doing a very long walk, so I'll let so-and-so off with stealing?' It didn't make any sense at all.

'Well, somebody has to, and it sure as eggs won't be you.' Agnes had sighed theatrically as she adjusted her best navy-and-cream hat and left the house in time for the Friday evening bus.

And there it was. To Grace's delight she caught a glimpse of a red and green and yellow corner of cloth stuffed right at the back, under a box of her mother's clothes. But when she pulled it out, the mice had made shreds of it; somewhere under the floorboards, she thought there must be a very comfortable mouse nursery, woven in all sorts of primary colours.

With a sigh, Grace spent another hour putting everything back as it was and hiding the shredded map. Agnes had once threatened to burn everything if Grace kept leaving the carefully stacked boxes untidy, and if she knew there were mice in here, she might carry out her threat. It would break Grace's heart if she no longer had her parents' things to look at.

When she was finally done, she clumped downstairs, fetched the hoe from outside the back door and pulled on her shabby brown coat. She would weed the front garden before she started on the windows.

It was cold outside, but at least it was dry, and the soil was easy enough to turn.

'Hello, Grace, though I feel I should call you Miss Fitz?'

Grace looked up from her work to find Father O'Riordan beaming at her myopically through his ridiculously thick glasses.

'Why hello, Father. And Miss Fitz is a fine name – it's what the children call me and I love it. But Grace is fine too. What has you out on such a cold day?'

'Well, I'd like you to call me Father Iggy.'

Grace smiled. She'd never known the curate's first name.

'It's short for Ignatius. I'm named after my grandfather. I was always called Iggy growing up – my friends call me it still.' He blushed crimson.

'Father Iggy it is.'

'Visiting the sick, Miss Fitz. Poor old Tommy Meaghar is not the best, I'm afraid.'

'I'm so sorry to hear that.' She felt a lump in her throat. Tommy Meaghar was still a young man, with two small children in her class, but he'd had the TB for a year and it was getting worse.

The tubby little curate also looked sad. 'Yes, it's a great worry. I pray daily to God for his recovery, or at least to ease his suffering.' He sighed deeply as he peered over the fence at her work. 'And how about yourself, Miss Fitz? Would you not leave the weeding until a warmer day?'

'I want to get this done while Agnes is away on the pilgrimage, Father. She's doing twenty-two miles from Drimoleague to Gougane Barra, for the sake of the souls of Knocknashee.'

'Drimoleague to Gougane Barra? Well, well. Is that so.' For some reason his easy-to-read face seemed more puzzled than impressed; maybe he had the same thoughts about doing pilgrimages for other peoples' souls as she did. But then he perked up and said, 'Little Betty Meaghar and Tomásín tell me you're teaching them about a place named after an old king that's full of peaches.'

She brightened. 'Georgia! Yes, I am. And I've wasted my whole morning searching for a map of America. I thought I'd found it but…' She pulled herself up short. She didn't want it to get out about the mice. If Father O'Riordan thought it amusing and told the canon, and the canon told her sister during one of those intimate two-person huddles they had after Mass, who knew what Agnes might do? 'But it wasn't what I thought it was, Father. I wonder how much one would be to buy?' Not that she had the money.

'The school should buy one, and one of the whole world, I think, not just America,' he said with enthusiasm. 'With all the countries you teach them about, it would be a great help and well worth the money. Write off to the bookshop in Cork to send you one. They do splendid ones. Have you their catalogue?'

'We do, Father.' She'd found it in the school filing cabinet one day when she was fetching a new attendance book and had been quite excited by it. She'd made suggestions to Agnes about what they might get – an atlas, an encyclopaedia maybe – but Agnes was as penny-pinching on the school's behalf as she was on their own; she didn't even want to splash out on powder paint from Mr Delaney, their travelling supplier. So Grace didn't imagine she'd have any success at suggesting they buy a huge expensive map from the bookshop.

Trying to hide a fit of irritation with her sister, she jabbed the hoe into the ground, turning over a clod of earth. Father Iggy didn't move on but stood watching her with a sympathetic expression; he seemed to know just what she was thinking.

'I'll tell you what,' he said suddenly. 'The canon is off on his travels this weekend as well – he has business in Bantry apparently and can't be contacted – and while he's away, I'm in charge of the school board. So if you pop into the school and find me that chequebook and the catalogue, Miss Fitz, I'll write you a cheque and you can send off for the map.'

A few days ago, the old Grace would have been quite scared at such a suggestion. But now she thought, *Why not?* and leant the hoe against the fence. 'Thank you, Father, that would be wonderful. Just give me a moment, to see if...'

Agnes usually kept the bunch of her school keys in her coat, but she'd put a different coat on, her pale-blue Sunday one, for the pilgrimage. Sure enough, in her black schoolmistress's coat, hung behind the door, were the heavy bunch of keys.

She popped her head out into the garden again. 'Will I make you a cuppa, Father, while I go and find the chequebook?'

He smiled as he came up the path. 'I won't stop, but I'll stand in out of the cold if you don't mind.'

'Of course, Father, come in.'

She made way for him, and while he waited by the hallstand, she walked as fast as she could through the gate in the wall and to the seniors' classroom. The filing cabinet was locked, but the third key fitted it, and she flicked through it, removing the catalogue and the chequebook, which was with a bank in Tralee.

She took out the wrong chequebook first; there were two of them in the file. The first one she looked at had the stubs written out to hotels and restaurants – an ice cream shop in Ballyferriter for only a small amount but a lot more to a wine bar in Cork, which was puzzling, especially as the handwriting looked so like Agnes's. But of course the wine wouldn't be for Agnes. Apart from the ridiculous expense, Agnes was a Pioneer who had taken the pledge not to drink alcohol when she made her confirmation. The name on the account was 'Knocknashee National School Board of Management', so she thought this must be part of Canon Rafferty's work as chairman; the Church did like to wine and dine its patrons. Agnes had acted as his secretary, no doubt, filling out the cheques when she received the receipts.

Putting the wrong one back, she took out the right chequebook, in the name of Knocknashee National School, and brought it with the catalogue over to the house.

Back in the hall, Father O'Riordan quickly chose the biggest map in the catalogue – it would cover nearly a whole wall, realised Grace in horrified amusement – and, resting the chequebook on the hall-stand, wrote one for the correct amount, made a note of what it was for on the stub and signed on the line with a flourish. 'There you go, Miss Fitz,' he said, handing her back the chequebook and catalogue with a mighty wink of one of his magnified eyes. 'And you tell that nice postman, Charlie McKenna, to warn you when it's being delivered, and I'll come to the school right away and make sure you get in no trouble for it.'

'Oh, but Father…' She wanted to say he might get in terrible trouble with the canon himself, and to be careful, but that seemed a bit daft to say to a grown man and a priest.

He knew what she meant, though. 'Ara, I'll be fine. The world won't end, though it might shake a bit.'

His round face was flushed with merriment, and Grace nearly started giggling herself; they were like a pair of bold schoolchildren. She suppressed an urge to say 'While the cats are away, the mice will play...' because it felt a bit close to the bone, calling Agnes and the canon cats.

'I'll be gone then, Miss Fitz,' he said, still pink-cheeked with amusement, settling his hat. 'I've another call to make to Peggy Donnelly. She has arthritis of the knee and wants a blessing, though I think maybe it's loneliness which is her problem. At least I can help with that better than with the arthritis.' And he waved his way out of the door and off down the street.

As soon as he was gone, Grace felt her bravery evaporate a little. But the thing was done now, the stub written on with 'World map for Junior Room, five pounds', and the curate had picked out the map and signed the cheque. She couldn't countermand a man of the cloth; surely even Agnes could see that.

Back in the school, she returned the catalogue and the chequebook to the filing cabinet and hoped she had left everything in order. Agnes was a very, very tidy woman, and if she thought Grace had left a mess, she might be even angrier than about the curate writing a cheque for five pounds. Everything in the cabinet was carefully labelled with tabs that stuck up, reading things like 'pilgrimage expenses' and 'school receipts' and...'Grace'...

Why was there a file in here marked 'Grace'? Again, before Richard Lewis's letter, she would have been inclined to let it well alone. She wasn't one to snoop, and she already felt bad enough for going into Agnes's pocket for the keys. But this file did have her name on it, after all...

She pulled it out, sat at the teacher's desk and took out the documents one by one. There was her birth certificate. Grace Kathleen Fitzgerald. She loved that her middle name was the same as her mother's. Bills from her hospital stay. Poor Agnes, she'd cost her so much. A post office savings book. She wondered how much was in there; it would be a year's wages now. But when she opened it, it was blank. It must be a new one, or a spare.

And next was a letter that had been opened and kept in here, addressed to her in a familiar strong, sloping hand. The same hand in which Tilly had written to her at the hospital every month for four long years.

But this envelope was addressed to 'The Schoolhouse, Knocknashee'. Puzzled, Grace checked the date of the postmark. April of that year. Only a few days after she'd posted her apology to Tilly in the post office.

Her heart turning over, she took the letter from the envelope. It was very, very long.

Dear Grace,

Of course I'm still your very best friend, though I wouldn't blame you if you kept away from me for a while! I understand why you had to go off with the cailleach *– it would only have made everything worse if you'd stood up to her. Let's meet on the beach next Wednesday...*

Grace's hands were shaking. Despite it being freezing in the school, she felt hot and sick. Tilly's letter had arrived for her, yet it never reached her. What must Tilly have thought when she didn't turn up at the beach? This was horrible...

Was this what Charlie had been hinting at when he said to give any letter she wanted to send into his own hands, and kept the American letter to give to her in private? Had he found something out about Agnes interfering in her post?

Putting Tilly's letter aside to read in a moment, she dove into the cardboard file again.

A stiff envelope. And inside, three photographs: One of Tilly. One of her and Tilly together. And one of her by herself, sitting on a bench with the sea behind her, her leg out of sight and her face turned sideways, in profile, her hair blowing a little in the wind. The photographer from Dingle had sent the pictures after all.

Her mind in a whirl of disbelief, she dipped her hand in again.

Another, much thinner letter, and this postmark was dated a year ago in August...

Her heart in her mouth, she opened the envelope and began to read.

My dear Grace,

How proud you must be with your leaving cert results. In the top five percent! Well done indeed!

Though Lizzie says she's not surprised. You are the cleverest child she's ever taught. So I was discussing you with Lizzie last night, and she came up with a wonderful idea.

How about you attend teacher training college here, in Cork?

As for your accommodation, Lizzie and I would be very happy for you to come live with us during term time. We have the space, and it would be a pleasure.

In return, perhaps you would like to spend a few hours a week with the children in the hospital, most of whom, as you were, are here for a considerable period of time. They would benefit hugely from meeting someone as invigorating as you, and as you are a 'Person who has had polio' (I hope you've remembered to mind your P's!), you would serve as an inspiration for what can be achieved if they put their minds to it.

The advantage for you would be that you would have daily access to the hospital, and I am confident we can extend your range of mobility.

I know you have your own beloved parents, God rest their souls, but I hope you won't mind me saying that to us, you are like the daughter we would so love to have had.

Please consider it carefully, Grace.

Kind regards,

Hugh (Let's dispense with the Dr Warrington title now that you're a grown woman!)

Alone in the freezing schoolroom, Grace put her head down on the desk and wept. Hot, furious, angry, despairing tears.

How could she? How could Agnes keep all this from her?

She'd not failed her leaving cert after all – here was Dr Warrington telling her she'd done very well. And suggesting she go to teacher training college in Cork. And offering for her to live with him and his wife, who would be like parents to her. Oh, it was too much, too much to bear.

'Come out, ya *cailleach*! Get out here, you black-hearted witch!'

With a start, Grace raised her head, tears still running down her face.

'Come out, ya *cailleach*, before I come in and get you myself!'

The roaring was coming from outside in the schoolyard, or at any rate no further away than next door. Grace wiped her eyes on her sleeve, wondering what to do. It sounded like someone was after Agnes, but Agnes wasn't there, so maybe they'd go away again.

'I'm giving you ten seconds...'

Grace stuffed everything back into the file and returned it to the filing cabinet – though at the last moment, before locking it, she took out the three letters and shoved them into the pocket of her shabby brown coat. She could return them later if she decided not to confront her sister.

She hobbled across the schoolyard to the gate in the wall to find Madge O'Sullivan standing in the front garden of the schoolhouse, wielding the hoe that Grace had left leaning against the fence, swinging it dangerously close to the curtained bay window of the sitting room.

'Come out and face me!' Madge was bright red in the face with rage.

Grace was fairly sure she knew what this was about.

The O'Sullivans were sheep farmers on the western part of the peninsula, and the last three of the seven children in the family were still in school. The youngest, Eily, was in Grace's room, but the boys, Paddy and Ger, were in with Agnes. Grace had heard from Eily on Friday that Agnes had taken the strap to Paddy but that he'd smirked when she slapped him, so she went for the stick and in her fury hit the boy so hard he'd run howling out of the school.

'Ten, nine, eight...' roared the furious mother. Madge O'Sullivan was not a person you'd trifle with. Rumour had it that she actually bit someone who tried to steal money from her at the mart when she was selling lambs. He reached into her pocket, and by all accounts, she grabbed his hand and actually bit down hard to get him to let go of the money. 'SEVEN, SIX, FIVE...'

'Hello, Mrs O'Sullivan, can I help you?' Grace tried to sound professional as she stepped through the gate, but she was quaking inside.

Madge spun to face her, brandishing the hoe, but when she saw who it was, her big face softened. 'No indeed then, you can't, Miss Fitz. 'Tis your sister I'm after,' she said, lowering her voice a few decibels.

'I'm so sorry, she's not here today. She's actually on a pilgrimage. She's gone to walk St Finbarr's pilgrimage in Cork, from Drimoleague to Gougane Barra –'

Madge reared up again. 'She is, is she? And so her going off on the bus yesterday evening all done up like a dog's dinner in her fancy hat and shoes was to go walking twenty-two rocky miles in the wind and the wet, was it?'

'I promise you, Mrs O'Sullivan, she's doing the pilgrim path today. She told me –'

'And the canon is gone with her, I suppose?' Madge interrupted with a snort of derision. 'In his fine, fancy car? Meeting her in Dingle on the way?'

Grace had no idea what Madge meant. 'I don't think so. She said she was going alone to pray.'

'Ara, did you come down in the last shower?' demanded the thick-set farmer's wife.

'I don't know what you mean, Mrs O'Sullivan?'

Madge stopped and eyeballed Grace for a long moment, then snarled, 'You might not, though you must be blind as a bat. But you tell her from me that I know what she's up to, and more than that, she broke my boy's finger with her stick – the doctor is above with him now. So you tell your sister she'll want to be sleeping with one eye open, because you do not hurt one of mine and get away with it.' She drew a step closer, leaning in, and hissed into Grace's face, spraying spittle as she spoke, 'You tell her that from me, Miss Fitz.'

And she threw the hoe down with a mighty clatter and left.

* * *

IN THE KITCHEN Grace made herself a cup of tea and a piece of toast with shaking hands, and even though it wasn't November yet, she decided to light a proper fire that was capable of warming her.

After that, she sat at the kitchen table with the three letters before her, trying to make sense of what she'd just found out – not from Mrs O'Sullivan but from the file in the filing cabinet.

It was impossible to believe Agnes would deliberately set out to destroy Grace's life; there had to be a way she believed she was doing the right thing.

Sitting there in the kitchen, Grace desperately tried to debate the matter in a way that didn't make her feel like she was all alone in the world...or worse than alone, sharing her house with an enemy.

Try to see this from Agnes's point of view, she told herself.

Tilly's letter she could almost understand. Tilly was a 'bad influence', and so Agnes would have thought she was protecting her. And maybe that was the same reason Agnes had hidden the photos from the trip to Dingle, so Grace wouldn't be reminded, or even pin up the one of her and Tilly in her room.

But what was she protecting Grace from by hiding her leaving cert results, and Dr Warrington's offer?

Maybe she feared Grace wouldn't be able to manage away from home? But Grace could have lived with the doctor and his wife – it sounded like they really meant the offer.

Maybe the explanation was more to do with Agnes than with Grace. Maybe Agnes had hated being by herself in this house for four long years. Maybe she had done this to ensure Grace would never leave her again. Maybe *everything* that Agnes had done came from a place of fear and loneliness.

If only Cyril Clifford, or his mother anyway, hadn't been so afraid of the polio, and Agnes hadn't been left to manage everything alone.

She read the doctor's letter again, so kind, so warm – what must he think about her never replying to him? Was there any point in her writing back now? It would be so humiliating to have to explain about Agnes, and maybe he and his wife had put Grace out of their minds and found another girl to be like a daughter to them. She would have to think very carefully how to reply.

Suppose he repeated his offer for her to go to college in Cork. Did she want to leave Knocknashee? She thought of the children she taught here, how they bounced in the door every day, delighted to be learning. It would be wonderful to be properly trained, but could she leave them to Agnes? Could she abandon her lonely, miserable sister, whose only joy in life was going off on pilgrimages?

Thinking of her pupils, she fetched some ordinary writing paper and ink from the dresser and wrote to the shop in Cork for the map, enclosing the cheque. She didn't feel one bit guilty about doing that now. She even used one of the household stamps, which all had to be so carefully accounted for.

Then, after making herself a second cup of tea, she settled down to read Tilly's letter. At least when she wrote back to Tilly, she wouldn't have to be ashamed about Agnes, because Tilly knew all about her already.

Dear Grace,

Of course I'm still your very best friend, though I wouldn't blame you if you kept away from me for a while! I understand why you had to go off with the cailleach *– it would only have made everything worse if you'd stood up to her. Let's meet on the beach next Wednesday.*

But now I'm going to tell you all about the day I've had.

First thing was, Ma decided I should marry. I think she has a hankering for grandchildren of her own. It doesn't look like Alfie will ever get her any – he's more likely to be killed now he's gone to Spain.

Grace had heard about this from a scandalised Agnes. Alfie had joined the Fifth International Brigade in April to fight Franco, who had the pope on his side. Irishmen like Alfie were denounced from altars the length and breadth of the country, whereas on the other side, the bishop blessed the Blueshirts – General Eoin O'Duffy's Irish Brigade – who were off to fight for the Spanish dictator, believing they were defending their Catholic faith.

You'd think she'd be satisfied with Marion's six, but apparently they're not good enough because they're not her blood relations, and besides, Marion can never come home with them because of the canon – I'll tell you about him in a minute.

So now over breakfast she started going on about Paudie Lehane. 'He's a nice lad,' she says, 'handsome, and he's a decent worker, and he has a fine farm of land and so you can't say he's after our bit of a bothán *here now like you usually do.'*

'Well, Mammy,' I says, 'that's all very well, but I don't love him.'

She only snorted at that, as if love had anything to do with it.

And then as if that wasn't bad enough, Canon Rafferty turned up out of the blue, which was a first. He wouldn't normally lower himself to call on the likes of us – he prefers the homes of the strong farmers, where he can get a glass of brandy and a slice of cake – but it was obvious your sister sent him, after that row in the street.

He began by 'seeking clarification' on the subject of Marion.

I half expected Ma to run him like she did to your sister that one fine day in school, when she called her a cailleach *in front of everyone. But she got all mumbly and stammering.*

I suppose, to be fair, standing up to Agnes Fitzgerald is one thing but standing up to a priest of the Church, well, that's a line even my ma isn't willing to cross.

She did try to explain about how Marion's husband – you should have seen his face at the word 'husband', making it clear he didn't think she was properly married – had six children who needed a mother. And you know what he said?

'Those children should not have been left in that man's care if he's incapable. There are places for such misfortunes, and that is where they should have been put, instead of dragging a God-fearing woman into the ways of mortal sin.'

I so wanted to show him the door, but Ma would never forgive me for giving cheek to the priest. He would bring such trouble down on our head from the pulpit that no one would dare buy our honey and eggs again, not even in Dingle, and we need that business to keep food on the table.

'And your sssson, where issss he?' he asked.

Grace smiled at the row of s's that Tilly had written. The canon spoke so quietly, he was hard to hear, and he had a slight lisp. Tilly used to do impressions of him when they were children, making the old cleric sound like the snake Kaa from *The Jungle Book*, and she would have the whole class in fits of giggles. Now that Grace thought about it, that's why Agnes had leathered Tilly until she bled that day, which led to the infamous intervention of Mrs O'Hare.

'He's in Spain, Father,' said Ma, looking as scared as I've ever seen her, Grace.

'Ah, I see. And if the rumours are to be believed, Mrssss O'Hare, and you musssst correct me if I'm wrong, he'ssss over there fighting for communissssm and barbarissssm and the undermining of the Holy Catholic Church.'

It was like watching her on the rack.

Then, Grace, you won't believe this, but the old cadaver demanded to know why I wasn't married!

'And now, to top it all, we have young Matilda here, refussssing any decent propossssal?'

Poor Ma, she tried to stick up for me.

'She's young, Canon. She has plenty of time for that.'

But his brow furrowed as if he'd never heard such an outlandish sentiment in his life.

'My good woman, a dessssire to marry is not the issue. A young healthy woman should be married and should produce children – it is what she is here to do – and worsssship the Lord and obey her husband. Farming 'tissss no work for a woman…'

Oh, Grace, it was so creepy. He turned then and looked me up and down with such disgust. Of course, I was wearing Daddy's old trousers tied up with a bit of baler twine and a hand-knit báinín. *I'd been out with the sheep – was I supposed to be wearing high heels? 'A woman shall not wear a man'ssss garment, nor shall a man put on a woman'ssss cloak, for whoever does these thingssss is an abomination to the Lord, your God. Deuteronomy,' he says, and then without another word, he silently glides out of the house as if he moves around on castors and not like a mortal man.*

I waited until the car was well down our boreen before speaking. 'Mam, don't be worrying about that auld priest,' I said. 'We aren't doing a thing wrong here, only minding our own business.'

But she just sat and stared into the fire.

Grace knew that fire well, from when she was a child and could run up the steep hill to the O'Hare farm. It was kept going in the hearth day and night, winter and summer, with turf from their own bog. They cooked their meals on it, dried their clothes beside it and used it to give comfort on the long dark nights. She had happy memories of eating bread-and-butter pudding, her favourite thing – the layers of buttered bread, demerara sugar, currants and custard, all baked into a delicious pie – in the heat of that fire.

She went back to the letter.

'There's nothing I can do about Marion,' Ma said at last. 'She's made her bed and must lie on it. And there's nothing I can do about Alfie. He is as daft as the crows, always was. Even as a garsún *there, he'd half-cracked notions about the world. I only pray every night that he won't be in the way of some bullet. But as for you, Tilly...' And there she stopped.*

And Grace, I was so scared. I thought she was going to say something again about Paudie Lehane and take the priest's side, because I was the only one left at home she could do something about.

But then a miracle happened – wait till I tell you.

Instead of going on again about Paudie, she said, 'I'm very proud of you, Tilly. I always was and I always will be. And your daddy, Lord have mercy on him, would be too, the way you took this place on and provide for us. You're the best daughter a woman could want.'

I nearly couldn't answer, I had such a lump in my throat, but I knew this was a once-in-a-lifetime conversation, and I had to know. So I coughed a bit and said, 'You do know I won't be marrying anyone, ever. You realise that, don't you, Ma?'

And she said, 'I do, alanna *I do.'*

And Grace, I think that will be the last word we will ever have on the subject of me and marriage, and it's all thanks to that old bag of bones Canon Rafferty sticking his long drippy nose into our business! So what do you think?

You can tell me when you see me!

Don't forget, next Wednesday!

Your best friend as ever,

Tilly

CHAPTER 14

ST SIMONS ISLAND, GEORGIA

November 1938

RICHARD LAY STRETCHED out on the very long cushioned wicker sofa in the conservatory of the East Beach house, among the palms and tropical flowers, a tartan blanket thrown over his legs; he was rereading with amused interest the letter that had arrived that morning.

He'd been surprised to find Grace Fitzgerald was still only a girl, eighteen since her birthday in June. Which meant the bottle had taken just a few months to cross that vast expanse of ocean. Incredible.

And his geography had been way off. Since sending his letter, he'd looked it up in the atlas in the library, and Ireland was quite northerly, it seemed. And they spoke two languages there, Irish as well as English. He wondered if it was hard to speak both. It was difficult enough to be good at English, as he'd discovered, now that he was trying to be a writer.

He hadn't yet managed to produce anything worth reading, but he'd been strangely comforted to find this unknown girl from a country he had only just found on the map supported him in his vague ambitions.

I think you're right to tell your family you don't want to be a banker if you want to be an artist. If you don't love what you're doing, you'll only make a mess of it. My sister is a teacher out of duty, but it doesn't suit her, and that's bad for everyone.

This girl I know, Tilly, she doesn't want to marry, and I'm sure if she did, she would be a terrible wife.

That had made him smile, as did the nonsense about surnames and initials and unlucky brides. Perhaps he should mention to Miranda that her surname, Logan, began with an L, like Lewis, so they were surely doomed as a couple!

There was another part of the letter, though, that forced him to think hard about financial planning, not something he usually cared to do.

Thank you for your suggestion that I should go to England to see Sister Kenny. If I had the money, I might do it, even though it's very far and I wouldn't be sure how to get there, but my sister puts all my savings into the post office for my future and so we only have the one wage to live on.

Although Richard disliked banking, he was still his father's son, so he couldn't help knowing a thing or two. And he knew the highly dislikeable Agnes shouldn't be hoarding her sister's wages in a country post office.

If a sum of money like that was going to be put beyond reach for years, it should be in a high-interest account in a proper bank. Better, though, would be to spend some of it on things that were necessary to Grace right now. Like a trip to England to see this Sister Kenny, to help her leg. There was a difference between being sensible with money and being miserly. That's why banks lent money to businesses instead of locking it up in a vault. Money had to be used to make the world go round – that's what Father said.

He leant his head back against the cushions, the letter resting on his chest. The sun striking through the glass roof was pleasant on his face; it still had plenty of heat in it. Closing his eyes, he yawned so widely, his jaw cracked. In a moment he'd get up and start working on a short story or something…

Gosh, he was exhausted today. He'd stayed up for hours last night, playing the piano, working on his song.

He'd had piano lessons when he was a kid, but Mrs Klein was cross and said he lacked application, so the lessons were soon deemed a waste of time and money. Yet he'd kept on playing, by ear. He hadn't the patience for the dots, but he could hear a tune once or twice and be able to do a reasonable version. Last night he'd been trying his hand at setting music to the lyrics he'd been working on. Even though it had started coming to him in September, he'd still not got much further.

Walking on the golden sand,
thinking of you.
My girl across the sea,
yellow hair and eyes of blue,
when will you come to me...

He'd added a handful of nice chords to it, though, and a bit of a melody, and was hopeful he'd soon think of a second verse.

That morning Esme had said as she served him breakfast, 'I heard lovely music wafting through the walls to my room, and I thought how lucky I am to be sung to sleep in my old age.'

'You're not so old, Esme, and I think you're gorgeous,' he'd teased, and the old housekeeper had laughed as she handed him this letter, which had two green stamps and his name and address written in lilac ink. What a surprise it had been to find she'd written back.

Now, with his eyes still closed, he drifted in his mind, imagining himself in the little village of Knocknashee…

Someone laughed, a soft tinkle, and he was walking the beach again with a woman whose face he couldn't see…

'So I will support you, will I?' said an amused voice, and he opened his eyes with a start to find Miranda sitting on the wicker chair near the foot of the sofa, a jug of Esme's home-made lemonade on the little wrought-iron table beside her.

'How long have you been there?' He sat up, rubbing his eyes.

'Well, "hello darling, lovely to see you" to you too, Richard.' She was dressed in an elegant aquamarine dress with a fabric belt, and her blond hair was as perfectly styled as ever. The summer had left her very lightly tanned, despite her best efforts to hide from the sun under hats and parasols, and it showed off the blueness of her eyes. She was beautiful, it was true. Guys gave her a second glance every time she walked down the street. 'I'm glad to see you working away at your art, following the advice of...an eighteen-year-old Irish girl called Grace?' She held up the letter, wrinkling her nose in amusement. 'How long has this little affair been going on, Richard darling?'

He forced a smile, though he felt a stab of annoyance at her reading his private correspondence – she must have picked it up off his chest. 'Oh yeah, that. I have to tell you about that.'

'Yes, Richard, you really do.' She poured him a glass of lemonade, tart and cold, and handed it to him, then spread out Grace's letter on her knee and read in a mocking childish voice, '"I'm sure Miranda will support you in whatever you do once she gets used to the idea..." What idea, Richard? And what on earth does she think I'll "get used to"?'

'Me being a writer, I imagine,' he said. Being dismissive of his dreams was one thing but her mocking Grace gave him a wave of dislike for her he'd never felt before.

She laughed, with a cool glint in her eyes. 'Well, that's unlikely, even if you actually were one. And this...' She jabbed at the paper with her painted fingernail. '"Thank you for your suggestion that I should go to England to see Sister Kenny..." Who on earth is Sister Kenny?'

'Someone who has a different way of treating polio, Miranda. Grace Fitzgerald had polio as a child.'

'Polio? Goodness.' She looked taken aback, almost scared, but then a bit relieved. She glanced at the postscript again. 'Well, I can see why she didn't want to send you her photo. Is she very badly crippled, the poor thing?'

The words were sympathetic, but he suspected she wanted him to answer that Grace was very badly crippled indeed. 'Maybe. I suppose she is.' He felt oddly guilty for saying it, though, as if he was wishing it on the unknown girl.

'You don't know?'

'In her first letter, she said her leg and back hurt very much, and she said she'd never be married because of it.'

She smiled, then frowned again. 'But Richard, *how* did she come to be writing to you in the first place? I really don't understand any of this.'

He sighed and pushed one hand through his shock of blond hair. 'I know it seems strange, and it is, but if you give me a chance, I'll explain. The thing is, the first letter wasn't addressed to me at all…'

When he'd finished his story, she sat shaking her head in disbelief. 'What possessed you to write back to a stranger? A poverty-stricken Irish peasant with a gimpy leg who's probably in love with you already…'

'Miranda, don't talk nonsense. She lives thousands of miles away.'

'And she's probably a Catholic as well! Can you imagine if she turned up here, looking for you?' She pealed with laughter at the thought. 'Your poor parents… A Catholic! You'd certainly get disinherited then.'

He took a mouthful of his lemonade and wondered if it was too early to add a dash of gin. 'How are they?'

She wagged her finger. 'Very upset with you, Richard. You need to get over your bohemian stage sooner rather than later. Or should I call it your "sleeping on a sofa" stage…'

'I wasn't sleeping, I was resting,' he sighed, tired of her haranguing.

'You were sleeping, Richard.'

'OK, maybe I was, but only because I was up working on a new song all night. Esme will tell you about it – she enjoyed it…'

'Goodness, Richard, I'm not going to go asking the help for her opinion of your songwriting!' She looked shocked at the very idea, but then her face softened and she patted his hand. 'Why don't you come home to Savannah, darling, just for a weekend? Try to mend a few bridges.'

He noticed that she didn't ask him to play her his song, which in one way was a relief, as there was so little to it, but in another way depressing. She really didn't have any belief in him at all.

He got off the sofa, went to the drinks table at the far end of the conservatory and added a finger of gin to his glass. 'I don't think Mother and Father care for me much right now, Miranda. Would you like a drop?' He waved the bottle at her.

'Too early for me, Richard. I'm not a bohemian like you. Well, if you won't listen to me, why don't you listen to your little Irish friend? "I know your parents will forgive you, whatever you do. That's what parents are for – they have to love you, however annoying you are."' Again she adopted that mocking childish voice, and he shot her a sour look, which made her laugh even more. 'You're not seriously carrying a torch for your little Irish peasant with the gimpy leg, are you, Richard?'

'Don't be ridiculous,' he snapped.

Realising she had made him cross, she stood and came over to him and wound her slender arms around his neck. 'Ah, don't get grumpy with me, darling. I'm only teasing.' She kissed him, her lips lingering on his, then ran her finger down his cheek, regarding him with her beautiful deep-blue eyes, set off so nicely by the trace of golden tan. 'Aren't you glad I came to visit you?'

'Of course I'm glad,' he said, not really meaning it. 'I just wish you would take me seriously sometimes.'

She dropped her eyes, then raised them again, and this time there was no laughter in them. 'I do have something serious to tell you, as it happens, Richard. Something a lot more important than writing songs to entertain the help and sending letters to an Irish peasant. While you're idling around here, being all bohemian, your sister is at the point of throwing away her whole life.'

He winced. 'The socialist photographer?'

'The socialist photographer *Jew*, Richard. His name is Jacob Nunez.

Fenella and I have tried to talk her round, but I think it's time to offer him some money to go away.'

Richard took another mouthful of his drink. *Damn.* He had a few thousand dollars' inheritance from his grandmother, but he'd been planning to fund himself for a whole year while he found his feet in the art scene. 'Would that work, do you think?'

She laughed at him. 'Money always works, silly boy. And don't worry, he's poor as a church mouse. Of course, he's a Jew, so he might try to drive a hard bargain. But once you've explained that your parents will disinherit your sister if they find out, a few hundred should do it. I can help, if you need more money.'

'Where would I even find him?' he wished this problem would just go away.

'I'll tell Sarah you want to meet him, and she'll probably bring him to see you. Now that you've gone all bohemian, she'll think you won't mind. Then you sit up chatting with him, have a few beers. Explain the situation to him, put your money on the table.'

'If he refuses and tells Sarah…'

'He won't. But if he does, you were testing to see if he really loved her. And were shocked by the speed with which he pocketed your money.'

She was so devious, he had to admire her. Unlike Sarah, a wild child who needed rescuing from herself, Miranda knew exactly how the game of life was played.

'But before I do this for you and your sister, will you do something for me? Go to see your mother and father?' She looked up at him with her beautiful blue eyes and kissed him again, with more passion than she normally did. 'For me, Richard?' she murmured against his lips.

He sighed. 'OK, OK.' He wasn't crazy about the idea, but maybe Grace Fitzgerald was right about parents always loving their children, even if they found them annoying. He was lucky they were alive, he supposed.

'And one more thing, darling…'

He groaned. When she was in this seductive mood, he could never refuse her. 'What is it?'

'I really wouldn't write that little Irish girl back again.'

This time he stepped away from her, ostensibly to refresh his glass. 'Why on earth not?' he asked, with his back to her.

'Fix me one of those. I'm sure its five o'clock somewhere. Why? Because she's an innocent uneducated child, Richard. She's poor, she's a cripple, and you are gorgeous and rich and exotic. She's seen your photo, hasn't she?'

Richard shrugged, vaguely embarrassed that she knew he'd sent a photo to the Irish girl; he guessed it was an odd thing for him to do. 'It was only to show her what Savannah was like, and this place. It wasn't a picture "of me", if you see what I mean. Nathan and Sarah were in it too. And you. I told her who you were, you know.'

'Yes, Richard, I gathered as much from her reply.' She studied him with one arched eyebrow as he handed her glass to her. 'The materialistic girlfriend who is refusing to support you in your crazy dreams.'

He squirmed slightly. 'I didn't say that...'

'Oh, I think you did. And so she's setting herself up as the opposite – the one advising you to follow your dreams. Richard, wake up, it's so obvious. Even at the distance of a thousand miles, that poor girl is dreaming about you every night. You are her fairy prince. The only person in the world who cares about her. So don't lead her on, Richard, by sending her pictures of fine houses and writing to her about miracle cures that she can't afford. Just remember she's a young, very innocent girl, and if you break her heart, she may not recover.'

'I don't plan on breaking anyone's heart, Miranda.' He was stung that she would accuse him of such a thing.

She gazed at him, her huge blue eyes full of reproach. 'Don't you, Richard? How about *my* heart?'

'Miranda, I would never...'

There were tears in her eyes now. 'You know I can't marry you if you don't snap out of this songwriting nonsense? I love you so much, but I can't live in poverty with you. I just can't. My parents would never allow it.'

She looked so upset, he felt obliged to reassure her. 'I promise you, Miranda, I will never make you live in poverty.'

'I knew it!' All smiles, she kissed him again, full on the mouth, until he couldn't help but kiss her back. She really was beautiful.

'Be nice to your mother, Richard,' she murmured, her lips to his. 'Please. You need her to make your peace with your father. Tell her you're sorry for upsetting her. Don't cut yourself off from them. For my sake, Richard. Please.'

'I don't know, Miranda…' But he could feel himself weakening.

'Oh, Richard, please. And while I'm here, why don't you play me your song?'

She was buttering him up now, but he didn't mind. Maybe she would realise he did have potential. Genius even!

Sitting at the piano in the living room, he played her the one verse of his song, and then again, because it did sound very short just playing it the once. She stood in the curve of the grand piano, sipping her gin and lemonade, her face unreadable. When he'd finished, she said, 'Yellow hair and eyes of blue? I hope that's me, Richard. Though yellow isn't the colour of hair any woman would want.'

'Of course it's about you, Miranda.' He didn't like to mention the woman in his dreams, who was walking with him on the sand but whose face he couldn't see.

'Though I'm hardly from across the sea.' She glanced out of the window towards the Atlantic.

'You are, of course – I'm here on the island and you're in Savannah.'

'Mm.' She looked at him sideways with a wry smile. 'I wonder if you were thinking of me at all.'

'Yes, I was, but the point is, do you like it?'

She glanced towards the ocean again. 'Oh sure, what there is of it. It kind of reminds me of that other thing, that one by Nat King Cole… very popular, going around at the moment…' She hummed a few bars, then began to sing in her pleasant alto voice 'Goodnight, Irene, Goodnight'. His heart sunk a little, because the melody he'd written was a bit similar; he hadn't realised. To cover his disappointment, he launched into 'Goodnight, Irene, Goodnight' on the piano and sang along with her. They ended up laughing and enjoying themselves, and he felt a sudden surge of relief and happiness.

This was fine. Miranda was fun. They were having a nice time.

CHAPTER 15

SAVANNAH, GEORGIA

He'd only been away for a couple of months, but it felt like years. He parked his Buick a street away from the handsome DeSoto hotel and bought a copy of the *Savannah Evening Press* from a boy on the street. He'd have a cold beer in the Sapphire Room and read the paper first, to relax and calm his nerves.

Though it was November, it was much warmer than out on the island, and he was glad he was wearing only a light-grey linen suit and an open-necked shirt. The other men in the street were wearing heavy coats over their suits, and the ladies were in furs; they were used to the heat and thought sixty-five degrees was freezing.

Mind you, even in the summer, the men of his class would wear neckties and buttoned-up collars. The city was handsome, but it demanded a certain decorum of its inhabitants, and it got it. Sometimes he imagined Savannah as an old lady from the last century, dressed in lace and pearls and looking down her pince-nez disapprovingly if a gentleman undid his top button or a lady thought she might remove her hat.

As he crossed the road, two coloured nannies pushed prams down the sunny side of the street, wearing navy coats over their uniforms. They stopped talking and stood aside to let him pass, and when he thanked them, they looked surprised. There wasn't much social contact between white folks and Black folks ever in Savannah; he'd almost forgotten that after chatting to Esme every day.

Not that he knew anyone Black apart from Esme and Jimmy the groundsman, who never said much. Coloured people didn't go to the same restaurants or clubs or schools or anything; they even had their own churches, and white people like himself didn't know what went on in them. As a child he'd been amazed to see a group of Black folks being dipped in the Frederica River; his older brother, Nathan, always the smart one who knew everything, had explained to him they were being baptised.

He bounced up the steps of the hotel, and in the Sapphire Room bought himself a cold beer and settled down to read the newspaper. Out on the island, he'd been avoiding the news for the last few weeks, and as soon as he started reading, he realised he'd been right to do so.

It looked like Hitler was getting madder than ever. It seemed the Jews weren't allowed to do anything now, practise medicine or law, be teachers or civil servants – not even own a private garden. It all sounded a bit unbelievable, and he hoped, like most people he knew in Savannah, that the papers were making it sound a lot worse than it was.

Nobody wanted to be dragged into another world war.

After the Great War, there was a growing sense of 'let Europe deal with their own issues – why should the US have to step in?' The banking collapse of 1929 had led to a shortage of cash, and people still remembered being paid by companies like the Sea Island Company in 'scrip', a type of currency that could be used at local stores. Even now, America was still reeling from the Great Depression, and the last thing people wanted was to get involved with Europe's problems again. America had to come first for once.

There had been some marches and protests about the treatment of Jews by Nazis, and trade unions were asking people to boycott

German-produced goods; thousands of people signed a petition, expressing outrage. Two years ago there had even been talk of not sending a USA team to the Berlin Olympics. But it was complicated, and overall, people couldn't get that worked up about the whole thing.

It wasn't as if there wasn't segregation and discrimination against people here too, so it would be a bit hypocritical to get worked up about Hitler anyway. The National Association for the Advancement of Colored People didn't even want Black athletes to represent the USA in the first place at the Olympics, saying it was wrong to compete for a country that treated them so badly, but they were convinced in the end, and the mighty Jesse Owens won four gold medals.

There had been a lot of talk in the press at the time about Hitler snubbing Owens because he was Black, but since Owens was never invited to the White House afterwards, and had to take the freight elevator to the parade in his honour in New York – he wasn't allowed through the front doors of the Waldorf Astoria hotel – Owens would be right to think he didn't need to go abroad to witness discrimination.

Richard turned to the sports pages. There was nothing of interest there either. Baseball season finished up last month so there was nothing happening. It was a pain, but up north the weather was too cold and snowy for baseball now. The New York Giants would probably win the NFL but he didn't care too much about football. He folded the newspaper and finished his beer. Time to see if Grace Fitzgerald was right and his parents still loved him, however annoying he was.

He left the hotel, got his car and drove slowly along River Street. A cargo ship made its slow progress up to the port of Savannah, the pilots either side. It was a striking scene. He'd love to write a piece about this city, the history, the colour, the ghosts and the huge ships going up the narrow river. He loved Savannah – to know it was to love it. It was a city like no other in the country, probably the world, and he would love to show it to Grace. Maybe if he wrote a piece, he could get it published in a newspaper if it was good enough.

Though when he imagined putting pen to paper, it wasn't as a newspaper article, it was as a letter. And the letter was to Grace.

Which reminded him, she'd never answered his question about discrimination in Ireland. And now he'd never know what she thought about that, or anything else for that matter, because he'd listened to Miranda and hadn't written back.

Now if he could just get Grace Fitzgerald out of his mind...

He still wasn't sure if he was doing the right thing. In Miranda's world, girls were always looking for the right kind of boy – handsome, rich, able to move them into places in society that they wanted to go. A rich fairy prince of some sorts. He wasn't sure Grace was cut from the same cloth, though. She seemed like an open, sensible girl who just spoke from the heart. It was refreshing. She'd called him kind and honest. And not writing back to her seemed neither of those things. When Miranda talked about it, it kind of made sense. Grace's world and his were so different. He was wealthy; she clearly wasn't. She was Catholic; he definitely wasn't. She had no place in his life. The trouble was, now that he thought about it, he wasn't sure he had much place in his life either.

He pulled up at the kerb outside his childhood home and realised how much he'd missed being here. Even in November the flowers tumbled from baskets around the door as well as trailed down from the balcony above. The porch was spotless, and the brass shone on the front door. The double-swing seat was still there, upholstered in peacock-blue fabric; as a child he'd been allowed to sleep on it when the house was too warm.

Would he be welcome? He stood at the front door, wondering if he should knock, and then decided that would be ridiculous – it was his home.

He opened the door – it was never locked – and entered the dark wood-floored hallway. It was large and square, the stairs to the left, the telephone on the antique table opposite the door, a large oval mirror over it. The mahogany door to the right of the table was into Father's study, out of bounds to everyone.

To his right behind the study were the pair of double glass doors that led to the living room. He opened them to find a tiny Black woman dusting the bookcases, their maid, Delores, who had been with them forever. She looked old, but it was hard to tell her age. Her hair was grey around the temples and at her roots, and her face was deeply wrinkled.

'Hello, Delores, are my parents in?'

She stopped what she was doing. 'Mr Lewis is at the bank, but Mrs Lewis is in the library, Mr Richard,' she said, indicating with a nod towards the back of the house. She barely opened her lips when she spoke. Then she stood there, head down, until he passed.

He walked through the immaculate living room with the two double sofas facing each other, the large glass coffee table in between, the magazines on the shelf below arranged as if by a set square. The painting over the mantel was a portrait of a beautiful lady from the last century dressed to the nines, which Mother liked to pass off as a long-dead relative of hers, though Nathan had once told him she'd picked it up at an auction.

The dining room led off the living room and was just as neat and tidy. Everything was as he remembered it. The thick cream rug under the large teak dining table, the linen-covered dining chairs, complete with carved arms. More mirrors, not a smudge daring to be seen. A candelabra, brass and gleaming, stood on the sideboard, two antique serving platters on display beside it. The clock ticked loudly on the mantel.

Behind that was the kitchen, where Delores prepared their meals, except when they were entertaining – then a white freelance chef was employed. Monsieur de la Croix was his name, and he was much sought after, though Nathan had told Richard he was as French as Mickey Mouse.

He tapped on the door of the library and went in. His mother was reading a magazine on a chaise longue, sipping an iced tea, but when he opened the door, she sat up with a cool but not unwelcoming smile. 'Hello, Richard.' She put her magazine down, some interiors thing.

She was in a blue polka-dot dress and navy-blue sandals, and her dark hair was pinned perfectly. Her coral lipstick matched her painted fingernails, he noticed as she proffered her powdered cheek for a kiss, which he dutifully delivered. He couldn't remember ever seeing his mother in anything approximating dishevelled.

'Hello, Mother.' He withdrew and stood awkwardly in the centre of the silk rug.

'Sit down, Richard.' She pointed to a nearby armchair, and he did, crossing his legs at the ankle and trying to look relaxed. 'Now, what brings you to Savannah?'

'I came to see you,' he answered. Biting back, *I would have thought that was obvious.*

'Why, might I ask?'

He paused. He knew she was expecting an apology, and he had promised Miranda. He didn't want to give up on his dreams just yet, but at the same time, he did owe it to her not to cut himself off from his parents altogether, not to close doors.

'To say I'm sorry if you and Father were upset by my saying I didn't like the bank.'

'If we were upset?' Her voice rose in slight incredulity.

'Well...yes...'

She sighed deeply. 'Oh, Richard. Your father and I were much more than upset. Your actions were that of a spoiled child, throwing away a perfectly good future, a career, your marriage to a beautiful, clever woman. But I suppose I must forgive, because Miranda tells me she has forgiven you and that you're ready to come home. I will have to talk to Father, of course, and persuade him to give you back your job...'

He stiffened; he felt a stifling sense of panic. What was this? He'd never told Miranda he was ready to come home. 'What did she say to you, Mother?'

'Oh...' She flapped her hand with a pout. 'I can't remember the exact words. I'm sure she spoke very nicely about you.'

'About me how, Mother?'

She sighed. 'Very well, if you really must know, she told me that you are wasting your days doing nothing and we should rescue you before you go to the dogs completely.'

He flushed, hot with annoyance. For Miranda's sake he'd been willing to reconcile, but she had clearly plotted this ambush, exaggerating his failures and assuming he would crumble as soon as he was in his mother's presence. How could she have so little faith in him? Was he that weak and spineless?

'I'm not wasting my days, Mother.'

She cast a glance then, one of sheer disdain. 'Drinking gin in the morning and fraternising with the help?'

He stared at her in shock. 'That's just not true...'

'Sleeping in the sunroom after being up all night playing music to Esme? Richard, this is not the way you were raised, and you know that. Now I suggest you bring in your case – I assume you've brought your case with you – go up to your room and unpack, and I will speak to Father as soon as he comes home. And if you behave like a dutiful son, I may even suggest he offer you an increase on your already very generous remittance. You will need more money if you're going to be married.'

This had Miranda's fingerprints all over it. 'Money always works' was one of her favourite expressions. He jumped to his feet, his cheeks burning. 'I'm sorry to have given you the wrong impression, Mother. I do want to be a good son, but you and Father did agree I could have a few months to explore my artistic side –'

'You've had a few months, Richard. And what have you done with them?'

'Only two months, Mother, and I'm currently writing a song.'

'Ah yes, I heard about your song.' A contemptuous little smile played around her lips.

It was like she'd stuck a knife in his heart. He didn't know what Miranda had told her, but it clearly hadn't been along the lines of her second son being a genius who would soon be making as much money as Nat King Cole.

'I'm working on it, Mother,' he protested. 'It's nowhere near finished, and I'll probably change it completely, but I'm enjoying it. I'm happy – can't you at least be happy for me that I'm happy, Mother?'

She looked at him then, down her long, elegant nose, in cold astonishment. 'Happy that you are throwing your life away doing something so pointless and foolish as to be an embarrassment to your family? Happy that you have taken the privilege your father and I have worked so hard to give you and thrown it back in our faces? Why on earth would I be happy about that, Richard? That I have a son who is a complete and utter waste of my time and his father's money?'

'Very well, if that's how you feel, I'll be going. There is nothing more to say.' He stood his ground, waiting for her response.

His mother shrugged and returned to her magazine.

He stared at her. Where was the inevitable fight, the shouting, the drama, the hysteria?

He tried again. 'So, goodbye, Mother.'

No answer.

Still he stood there, hoping for something, some sign he meant more to her as a son, as an individual, than a mere clone she had created to follow in his father's footsteps, work at the bank, marry the girl they'd chosen for him, become the dutiful mirror of their lives.

She flipped a page and sipped her iced tea. She didn't ask him to stay or try to fight with him. It was as if she had cut him out of her heart, and it didn't seem to bother her at all. It was far worse than if she'd screamed at him or slapped him or burst into tears.

Shaken, his heart pounding, he retraced his steps through the place he'd called home for twenty years. Was it possible this would be the last time he'd set foot in this house? Had his mother really that little love for him?

He remembered Grace's words from the letter. *I know your parents will forgive you, whatever you do. That's what parents are for – they have to love you, however annoying you are.*

What a different world she lived in from this hard, cold place. Miranda had told him not to write back to Grace because she might come to see him as the only person in the world who cared about her.

It was the other way around. He was beginning to think Grace Fitzgerald might be the only person in the world who cared about him.

Damn it, he *would* write back. But first he had to finish that song or she would think he was a useless spoiled rich boy. And somehow he didn't want that.

CHAPTER 16

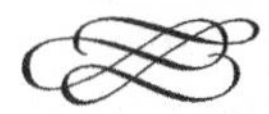

KNOCKNASHEE, DINGLE

ebruary 1939

THE MAP HAD ARRIVED in January and took up most of one wall. The children were saucer-eyed with amazement at being able to see where they lived in relation to everywhere else in the world, and how small Ireland was, and England too.

Agnes had been furious of course, but the curate knew from Charlie when the map was coming and was straight round to the school to admire it and to tell Agnes at length how he'd insisted Grace bring him the school chequebook. Agnes, though seething, was unable to argue with a man of the cloth.

That Sunday there had been a particularly fervent discussion between herself and the canon in the churchyard, and Grace had been afraid the map would get taken down and burnt or something and the curate get in terrible trouble, but Agnes merely made a snide remark over their meagre Sunday dinner (two chicken legs and a scoop of unbuttered mash) about it being no use crying over spilt milk and the money was gone now. The money was from the school fund, not their own, the money the government allowed for the running of the school, so why she was behaving as if Grace and Father Iggy had dipped into her purse was another mystery.

Grace prayed her sister wouldn't notice she'd removed the Dingle photographs from the filing cabinet. She'd returned Dr Warrington's and Tilly's letters and the photographer's cardboard envelope, now empty, but Agnes had such an eagle eye for a hair out of place. Nothing came of it, though she did catch Agnes looking at her oddly from time to time, and when Grace went to get a new attendance sheet, the handles of the cabinet were padlocked together as well as the drawers locked with the ordinary key.

It was odd, in a way, that Agnes didn't say more, or demand to know if she'd gone rooting. If anything her older sister seemed nervous and almost slightly cowed by what Grace had done.

The best thing was, she was now in regular correspondence with Tilly, thanks to Charlie McKenna. Tilly thought Grace should confront Agnes about stealing her letters, but Grace still wasn't sure, even though she didn't feel as powerless these days. She felt more like she was waiting for the right time. She still hadn't written back to Dr Warrington.

In the meantime she'd received another letter from Richard Lewis, which she was now reading in Charlie McKenna's kitchen.

It was St Brigid's Day weekend, so the children had a long weekend off school, and Agnes was spending it in bed with a cold she'd picked up on her last pilgrimage. She had sent Grace out for a list of messages, and Charlie had beckoned to her as she passed his house, holding up the now familiar envelope with the pink American stamps.

'Gracie! He's written again!' He sounded almost as gleeful to say it as she felt to hear it.

He left her alone in his kitchen to open it, and she sat by the range slowly reading it through, savouring every word, trying to picture

Richard sitting writing it, his thick blond shock of hair falling forward as he bent over the pen and paper.

Dear Miss Fitzgerald,

Here I am in America still trying my best to write a song and impressing no one, not Miranda and certainly not my parents, who I suspect don't feel about me in quite the same way your parents felt about you. They must have loved you a great deal, and still do, from where they are in heaven of course.

She had no idea why someone as sophisticated and handsome and rich as Richard Lewis of Georgia would want to be in touch with someone like her, who had never been anywhere or done anything, yet the opening couple of sentences made her feel sorry for him. Maybe his parents were more like her sister than Eddie and Kathleen Fitzgerald, just not very good at showing their love.

I won't bore you with that, though, because something interesting did happen to me. I wasn't planning to write back until I had my song finished, in case you come to think I'm a waster and a hobo like the rest of my family think, but now I find I can make some money out of writing after all, just not the way I imagined.

Grace smiled at the idea this young man could value her opinion of him. She was sure he was just being nice.

OK, here is the story. My sister came to visit in January, a couple of weeks ago, and she brought a Very Unsuitable Man with her for me to meet. Unsuitable how? you may ask. Well, for one thing, he is a newspaper photographer, a highly disreputable profession.

She nearly laughed at that. She thought she knew what he meant. That photographer in Dingle had been disreputable. Though her opinion of him had gone right up now that she realised he'd sent the photographs after all. Tilly had been delighted to get her picture, and Grace had also sent her the one of them together so Tilly could pin it up on her wall, as she wasn't able to do it at home. The two of them were waiting for Agnes to go on another pilgrimage before they dared meet up in real life – somewhere far from prying eyes. Grace didn't want to draw the priest down on Tilly and her mother again; Tilly said she didn't care about herself but she did for her mother.

For another thing, he's a socialist, which means he supports Roosevelt's

New Deal and everything and says nice things about Russia and the Republicans in Spain. And that does not go down well in my world. I hope you're not too shocked, Miss Fitzgerald.

She wasn't shocked at all. She was well used to it from hearing Tilly defend her brother, the one who was now off fighting Franco, to the despair of his mother. Alfie had written to Tilly recently. He was frustrated. The government still held huge territory, and the Basque country largely supported the Republicans, but the exhausted armies of resistance were no match for Franco's might. Thousands of refugees were fleeing to the Republicans for protection and shelter. It seemed the war had been fought to a bloody stalemate, and it was looking increasingly unlikely by the week that they would ever succeed in defeating the fascist dictator.

The last thing is, he's a Jew.

Now, that was a surprise. She didn't know how she felt about that, because she knew nothing about them. The only thing she'd ever heard about Jews was that they'd killed Christ. And there'd been a few items in the paper recently about Hitler wanting to get rid of the German Jews – though exactly how he intended to do it, she wasn't sure.

He's not one of these new immigrants from Germany and France, though. So many Jewish people are getting out of Germany and Austria now, and all of Europe, I think, trying to find somewhere safe, but his family has been in America longer than mine, though I wouldn't dare tell that to my parents. Two hundred years his family has been here, while Mother and Father think we're the crème de la crème because we've been here since the 1800s.

It was amazing how new the New World was when Grace thought about it. Not like Ireland. She had no idea how far her own family went back. Fitzgerald was a Norman name, so at least eight hundred years.

I never knew this, but Savannah has nearly the oldest Jewish congregation in the United States, according to Nunez—that's the Very Unsuitable Man, Jacob Nunez—and Mickve Israel, the synagogue here, holds the oldest Torah in America. I've learned so much from Jacob, the history of our city, things that were under my nose my whole life but that I never took any notice of. I think I told you about James Oglethorpe, the founder of the state of Georgia?

Grace smiled at that. He certainly had, and that's why she'd taught the children all about Oglethorpe out of that old history book of her father's. And if it wasn't for wanting to know more about Georgia, she'd never have got talking to Father Iggy about wanting a map. And then she'd never have gone to the filing cabinet, never have found her stolen letters. This stranger from beyond the sea had already made such a big difference to her life, without him knowing. She would have to tell him.

Well, at the beginning, Catholics weren't allowed to settle in Georgia because the Catholic Spanish were right next door in Florida, which belonged to Spain at the time. I don't know if you know anything about the different colonizers of America?

She did, and so did all her pupils in the school. She'd better not tell him they were mad keen supporters of the Spanish conquistadors over the English.

And the Jews were forbidden too, but when a group of Portuguese Jews fleeing persecution landed in London and heard of the opportunities in the New World, they decided to take a chance. When they got to Georgia, Oglethorpe had lost many of his original group of settlers to disease and sixty others were very sick, and the doctor he'd brought was sick as well. But the Jews had a doctor among them, Samuel Nunez, and he healed many of the sick and charged nothing, so Oglethorpe let him stay along with all the other Jews. And this Jacob is a descendant of that first Nunez. What do you think of that? It just goes to show, you can't judge people by their religion.

Grace wondered if this Richard Lewis had guessed she was a Catholic, and if he was trying to say something polite about that without actually saying it.

The thing is, people do judge, all the time, and so did I until I met Jacob. Miss Fitzgerald, I'm highly ashamed to say the reason Sarah brought this Nunez fellow to the island was because Miranda suggested it. Sarah was unaware, but Miranda's plan was that I could get Jacob alone and offer him money to stay away from my sister.

Grace's heart sank miserably. What a horrible plan. Like Cyril

Clifford's mother insisting on him breaking up with Agnes because of the polio.

But when I came to it, I couldn't go along with it...

Her heart lifted again. She knew he wasn't that sort of person.

...and the reason is to do with you.

She blinked in surprise and reread that sentence. How could it be to do with her?

Sarah insisted on knowing what I'd been doing with my time, and I played that bit of song I'd written about hearing from a girl across the sea. Nunez asked me where the idea came from, and I ended up telling him about the bottle and how I found your letter.

Grace felt a prickle of alarm. She hoped he hadn't shown it to them.

I didn't show them the first letter because it wasn't addressed to me, but it reminded me of what you'd said about your sister being sad and bitter all the time because Cyril's mother persuaded him to leave her, and it came to me that I didn't want to do that to my own sister, in case she never recovered. I don't know much about love and romance, but my sister lights up around Jacob Nunez in a way I've never seen anyone do before. Algernon Smythe, the guy my parents picked out for her, is just so boring. He only talks about yachts, literally no other topic of conversation, so he and Jacob are as different as night and day.

Grace shook her head, marvelling that she'd made a difference to his life, in the way he had made a difference to hers.

And then Nunez said how my finding the bottle would make a good story for the paper, and he could take a photograph of it where it was found, and did you have a photo of your own to send? Well, I said I'd already asked you and you didn't have one, and maybe you wouldn't want your picture being in the paper anyway...

She felt a slight twinge of sadness. He probably thought she hadn't sent him a photo because she was ugly and twisted. Well, he was right in a way – even if she had one, she wouldn't have sent it.

Nunez wanted to do something together, and we ended up agreeing to collaborate on a piece about the local Coast Guard station, which is near where I found your bottle.

The station was set up as part of the New Deal, of which Nunez is a big fan, and it happened I know a couple of the guys who work there at the station. We interviewed them about what they do – well, I interviewed them, and Nunez took pictures. I thought I knew about boats. My sister's intended, the dreadful Algernon, has told me a great deal more about yachts than I ever wanted to know. But never have I learned so much about seafaring, boat maintenance and the potential hazards at sea! This area of the United States is made up of islands and marshes and saltwater inlets and can be dangerous if you don't know where you're going apparently.

They also log all passing planes and ships, and they're on alert now to look out for enemy attacks.

It seems crazy to think anyone would attack America, but Nunez says there's going to be a war in Europe, and whether the right side will win will depend on whether the Americans get into it. And sure enough we found there was a rumor going around the Coast Guard that Roosevelt was going to swap the Coast Guard over to the Navy, just in case. We spoke to this colored fellow as well—he was the janitor at the Coast Guard station—and he told us he would love to join the service, as he can swim like a fish, but he wouldn't be permitted because of the segregation laws, so he had to be happy mopping floors and polishing brass. Nunez thought it was a good example of how the US services would be stronger and better able to fight without segregation.

Anyway, Nunez suggested I lead the story on the war angle, and I did, and The Capital *paid money for it! So what do you think of that?*

I don't know if I want a war, though Nunez says what's happening in Germany is very bad, worse than the papers report.

How about you, Miss Fitzgerald? What do you think about it all? Is Ireland planning to get into a war if it happens, or stay out?

Now to a subject I actually know something about, which is money. I hate banking, but I come from a banking family, so if you don't mind, I'll be blunt.

Your sister is no doubt doing what she thinks is best for you, but your money needs to be under your own control, and you need to use it in a different way. There's no point in not being able to travel to England to see Sister Kenny while she's there, when by improving your health, you will improve your life prospects. Being afraid to spend money on the right things,

things that make you happy and healthy, is not a good way to live. At the same time, it is a good idea to save a portion of your salary, but it needs to be in a high-interest savings account in a bank, not a post office.

Can you arrange to have your salary paid to the post office directly? Contact your employers and ask them to do that for you? It happens here, so I assume it could happen there too. You can transfer a portion every month to your high-interest account in your nearest bank and keep the rest as spending money.

It was something she had never considered. Both she and Agnes were paid by a cheque sent every month in the post from the Department of Education. Agnes took both, and Grace never saw them again. But was it possible to have her wages paid directly to her own post office account? If it was, would she dare to do it? Agnes would have a fit.

That's a lot for you to think about, and I hope I haven't offended you in any way, but if you need any more advice on money, just ask.

Yours sincerely,

Richard Lewis.

PS Did you ask your Dr. Warrington what he thinks about Sister Kenny yet?

PPS I hope you don't mind, but I showed my sister, Sarah, your second letter. And she wants to know, has Tilly ever read a book called The Well of Loneliness*? No idea what she means by that.*

THINKING DEEPLY about what he'd said, she folded the letter and replaced it in the envelope. The clock on the wall said half an hour had passed. She should do those messages; Agnes was waiting for a hot lemon and sugar drink. And she had to bring Agnes's good shoes to the cobbler's as well – one of the heels was broken. No doubt Pádraig Ó Sé would have something rude to say about Grace or the shoes or Agnes. He was indiscriminate in his insulting, at least that; everyone got the same tongue-lashing.

She rose, and the deep pain in her leg that seemed to have got worse these days made her wince. She placed the letter in the tin box

Charlie had left for her in the bottom of the dresser. It was emblazoned with OXO, a brand of stock cubes. Safer here than at home, away from Agnes's suspicious eyes.

As she straightened, holding onto the dresser to support herself, the door from the hall opened and Declan appeared.

'Hello, Gracie.' He smiled. He was much more relaxed around her these days, since she'd started working with him on getting him through the exam that he needed for the job in the Posts and Telegraphs. 'Do we have a lesson today?'

'Not today, Declan, but I'll come on Monday evening.' She hoped and prayed she would be able to improve his penmanship sufficiently to make his writing legible at least so he could pass the exam when he sat it in Tralee in a few months' time.

As she hobbled out of the house, Declan opening the front door for her, she noticed she didn't glance nervously up and down the street as she would have done before. And not just because she knew Agnes was in bed. She really had got bolder since the episode with the map; she hadn't even bothered to hide she was teaching Declan.

Agnes had made a big fuss about it when she found out, and said it was beneath Grace to teach a rough boy who had been in Letterfrack. 'You have no business getting involved with that person...'

'It's my private matter, Agnes,' Grace said, and she had stood and limped out of the room. For a moment she thought her sister might follow her and spin her around by the shoulder – she wasn't above the use of physical force – but she didn't. It was the most insolence she'd ever shown to Agnes, and she had quaked inside at doing it, but once she'd said her piece, she felt a surge of something like liberation. Between that and buying the map, she was getting braver.

She liked teaching Declan McKenna. There was something about him that made her heart go out to him as well, a fragility that wasn't common in men from these parts. The constant battering by the sea toughened people, physically but emotionally as well. Life was hard, making ends meet a constant source of strain, so there wasn't much room for softness. But Declan was not robust like the men of the sea, or those who farmed the hard stony ground.

As his father had told her, the young man was very bright, fluent in Irish and quick at mathematics, but his handwriting was almost illegible due to his being left-handed and the Christian brothers forcing him to use his right. The end result was his writing looked like a spider was dipped in ink and ran across the page.

She'd suggested he just write with the left if it was more comfortable, but he couldn't do that either; it had been beaten out of him. So she painstakingly helped him relearn how to form his letters using one of the children's handwriting exercise books with red lines to show where capitals stopped and blue for the smaller letters.

Declan followed her instructions, trying to force his unruly hand to do his bidding. He was still scared of getting anything wrong, even when being taught by a little thing like her, always hiding behind his hair, wearing it long, with his eyelashes lowered over his worried eyes. When they were working, she could only see his mouth and chin, and the light smattering of freckles that crossed the pale skin on the bridge of his nose.

One thing he did say, whispering it to her one day, was that he'd like to be a teacher like her. 'Not like the ones in Letterfrack...' He shuddered when he said the name and just shook his head when she asked him what they were like. His hand had started to shake too much to carry on with the lesson.

Grace told him to relax, go for a walk, get some air while she had a cuppa with his father, and that they could try again in a bit.

'The poor lad is broken, that's the only word for it. Broken entirely,' Charlie had said, after Declan closed the back door behind him.

Grace shook her head. 'He's bad today but he's getting better, I think. When he passes the exam in Tralee, he can start getting his life back.'

'The bit of it they didn't destroy,' said Charlie, a darkness crossing his normally happy features..

'He will recover, I'm sure of it. You're such a good father to him. And maybe he will be a teacher one day – he says that's his dream. And isn't it a sign he's getting stronger that he's thinking of his future?'

'Whatever he achieves, it will be down to you, Gracie. You're the only person he's able and willing to learn anything from. He's so afraid of authority. When he sees the canon in the street, he puts his head down like a terrified little boy.'

'Well, I hope he's not afraid of me, Charlie.'

'No more than I was afraid of your mother.' The postman smiled, and they'd sat and drank their tea. And after ten minutes or so, Declan had returned much calmer, and he and Grace were able to go back to the lesson again.

CHAPTER 17

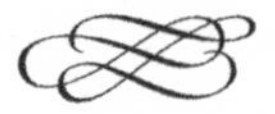

After she'd bought the lemon and sugar from Biddy O'Donoghue, Grace went on down to Pádraig Ó Sé's, the cobbler, and left Agnes's shoes – the pale-blue ones she wore to Mass and to the pilgrimages and which were surely too fragile for climbing over rocks; it wasn't surprising one of the heels was broken.

Pádraig Ó Sé, as wild-looking and bad-tempered as ever, looked at the shoes in disgust. 'Broke her heel climbing over rocks? Stuff and nonsense, there's not a scuff on them. The soles are perfect. No surprise there, Miss Fitz. Your sister's a *cailleach* – maybe she flies on her broomstick, her feet never touching the ground. Broke the heel knocking off a treetop, for sure!' He cackled, delighted at his own joke.

Grace fled as fast as her leg would allow her before Pádraig Ó Sé could get any worse. Walking back past Bríd Butler's sweetshop, two people, a couple in their twenties who must have been having a few days' holiday, came out of the shop licking ice cream sandwiched between two wafers, and she remembered the ice cream she'd had in Dingle and how lovely it was. It was only February, but there was a clear blue sky of spring sunshine, no breeze and a hint of warmth in the air, daffodils poking up in people's front gardens. She had a few coins in her purse of her own, payment for teaching Declan, and her mouth was watering.

Agnes would be very annoyed with her for wasting money. But Richard Lewis had said money was no good if it was never spent on something that would make you happy or healthy, and right now she felt a treat would make her happy.

On a whim, and knowing eating in the street was a bit disreputable, she pushed open the door of the shop. The bell tinkled overhead.

'Ah, Miss Fitz, 'tis yourself. What can I do for you?' Bríd smiled.

Grace realised she hadn't been inside the shop since her parents died. She'd never had the money for sweets, only that ha'penny she'd found in her mother's pocket and saved for a toffee, and then spent instead on a stamp for her letter to Tilly. That seemed so long ago now.

The shop smelled of sugar, and there were glass jars on the counter and on the shelves, each one containing different brightly coloured sweets. Cinder toffee, jelly babies, bullseyes, clove rocks, apple drops, barley sugars, acid drops, lemon sherbets, iced caramels, pear drops, liquorice, chocolate bars, toffee apples. She remembered Dr Warrington taking them to Cudmores in Cork, where there was a similar display. He would watch patiently as the children asked for one of those and one of those, the whole expedition taking hours.

'I was… I'd like an ice cream please, Mrs Butler,' she said, colouring slightly.

'Of course, Miss Fitz.' Bríd opened the cold box, extracted a block of ice cream, cut a thick slice and placed it between two wafers.

'What do I owe you?' Grace asked as she accepted it.

'Well, I'll tell you what now, you can have that one on the house.'

'Oh, thank you… I really shouldn't, I suppose, but I saw that couple leaving, and it's been so long since I had one.' Grace licked the side of the slice, and the creamy sweetness was like nectar.

'You enjoy that now, Miss Fitz, and sure have it in here if you don't want to go outside. I'm glad of the company.'

She pulled out a stool from behind the counter, and Grace sank onto it, glad to take the weight off her leg. 'You're very kind, Mrs Butler.' She was savouring the treat.

'Ah, 'tis nothing. I'm happy to give it to you,' Bríd said, resting her ample bottom against the counter. 'How is the...your sister?'

Grace had a feeling Bríd had been about to call Agnes 'the *cailleach*' like Pádraig Ó Sé had done and was grateful Bríd had stopped herself. She agreed, but at the same time, she didn't want to be openly disloyal. 'Agnes is above sick in the bed, and I feel a bit guilty getting a treat for myself, but she isn't one for sweet things – she probably wouldn't approve at all.'

Bríd snorted, a bit like Tilly always did when Agnes's name was mentioned. 'Your sister is fond of an ice cream herself, let me tell you. Sure don't herself and the canon have one every time they go back to Ballyferriter. Mrs Duggan who has the shop back there says she and the canon are her best customers, so don't you feel one bit bad, Miss Fitz. You're as entitled as anyone else to have an ice cream if you feel like it, and don't mind what anyone has to say about it.'

Grace was taken aback. When had Agnes been in Ballyferriter with the canon? And more than once? And eating ice cream? She couldn't imagine Canon Rafferty doing anything as normal as eating an ice cream, but surely neither Mrs Butler nor Mrs Duggan had any reason to lie.

* * *

BACK AT THE SCHOOLHOUSE, she made the hot lemon and sugar drink for Agnes. Most people would have put a whiskey in it, but Agnes was a Pioneer, so she just added a couple of cloves and took it upstairs.

Agnes was lying in the bed in the darkened room that had once been such a bright and cheerful place when it was their parents' room, decorated in their mother's style with lilac-sprigged wallpaper and a lilac bedspread and cushions, instead of the brown 'hard-wearing' colours it was painted and upholstered in now. Kathleen Fitzgerald had loved lilac; that's why Grace had chosen lilac as the colour of her ink.

She set the steaming glass down on the bedside table and stood looking at Agnes for a moment. Her older sister did look very like their mother, who had been very pretty, but somehow Agnes's grim expression spoiled her nice features. Now she looked up from the Bible she was reading, her pale-blue eyes wary. 'Do you wish to say something to me, Grace?' she asked, with that odd, angry nervousness she seemed to feel around Grace these days.

Grace did want to say something. She wanted to ask about the ice cream with the canon. About the letters. But Agnes was sick in bed, and besides, if she challenged her, it would lead to a terrible row. And what if they fell out forever and she had no family left in the world? 'I was just wondering if you wanted something nice for dinner, Agnes. Maybe a dessert.' She added, daringly, 'Ice cream?'

'What an idea.' As always, when Grace suggested spending money, two crimson spots appeared on her sister's pale cheeks. 'Every spare penny in this house is for your future, Grace. Please stop acting like a child and be grateful you have a wage at all. Where are you going now with that face on you? The potatoes need peeling for the dinner. And the front garden needs weeding.'

'I'll do that, Agnes.'

* * *

SHE DID TAKE the hoe from beside the back door, but she did only a small bit, because Agnes talking about her savings again got her thinking about Richard Lewis's letter. After a while she left the hoe leaning against the fence and walked slowly down to the post office.

Nancy O'Flaherty was sending a telegram for the young couple who had bought the ice cream earlier, and Grace waited until they'd paid and left.

'Now, Miss Fitz, what can I do for you?' asked the kindly post-mistress. As usual her salt-and-pepper hair was pulled back in a bun, and she wore a brown skirt and cream blouse. Last time Grace was in here, she'd been wearing one of the cardigans from Peggy Donnelly's, an orange one, but today it was a pale purple.

Maybe it was the sight of her mother's favourite colour that gave Grace the courage to act, but almost without thinking about it, she blurted, 'Mrs O'Flaherty, if I was to write to the Department of Education and have my wages paid here instead of by cheque, would that be possible?'

Nancy smiled broadly, as if she approved of the question. 'It would, but you'd need an account.'

She was surprised. 'I have a savings account?'

Nancy looked at her slightly oddly. 'Mm, no, you'll need to open a new account for your wages to be paid directly in.'

'Oh, I see. And how would I do that?' Her heart was beating fast with the excitement of it.

'You'd open one here with me,' answered Nancy, as if it was the simplest thing in the world.

'It's as easy as that?'

'More or less. You fill in a form, I open an account in your name, and then you can deposit or withdraw money as you have it using your post office book.'

'And the Department would pay my wages into that account for me to use?'

Nancy nodded firmly. 'They would. You'd need to write and instruct them to pay you like that rather than by cheque.'

'So would I need Agnes to…as the school principal…or the canon, as chair of the board of management… Would they need to agree?' Despite her newfound courage, she felt quite sick at the thought of asking them.

'Not a bit of it.' For some reason Nancy's normally sunny face looked quite cross and pink at the idea. 'It's nothing to do with her or him, *a stór*. Your wages for your work are your business, nobody else's. So will we open that account?'

'Now?' This was going so fast.

'No time like the present.' The postmistress ducked down behind the counter and re-emerged with a large white form, which she spread out on the counter. She began filling in the white spaces without even asking Grace the questions because she knew all the answers already.

Name: Grace Kathleen Fitzgerald.

Date of birth: 20th June 1920.

Home address: The Schoolhouse, Knocknashee, Dingle, Co Kerry

Previous accounts...

This time she stopped and looked at Grace inquiringly, but Grace just shrugged. 'I'm sorry, I don't know it. I've never used it to take anything out. It's just where Agnes has been putting my wages since I started work as assistant teacher in the school.'

Nancy looked a bit taken aback, and her cheeks flushed. 'I'm sorry?'

'And I wanted to talk to you about that, Mrs O'Flaherty. But first, is there anything else?'

'No, um, oh... No...that's all.' The normally unflappable Nancy seemed a bit confused. 'Right, sign that here so...' She pushed the form towards Grace, and Grace took the pen from her hand and wrote her signature. *Grace Fitzgerald.*

Nancy took the form back and started writing in a large ledger, pressing rather hard with her pen, her mouth tight, filling in the details. Then to Grace's surprise, she reached under the counter again and this time took out a new little book with a green cover, a gold harp emblazoned on the front and 'Posts and Telegraphs Savings Account' printed on it in black. She wrote Grace's name and account number inside and handed it to her.

'So you can have your wages paid here, and nobody but you has access to the information – it's private. You don't need to share it with anyone, and I'm legally obliged to keep it confidential.'

Grace took the book and gazed at it. Was it really as simple as this? 'Thank you for all your help, Mrs O'Flaherty,' she said, her voice wavering, turning to leave.

'Wait there, Grace.' Nancy pulled out a sheet of notepaper, set it before her with a pen and announced in a very businesslike fashion, her cheeks redder than ever, 'Now, you write your letter asking the department to pay your wages into this new account. Give them the number and the name of it – that's your name – and the address of this post office. They will sort it out before you're next paid.'

'That soon?' With a slightly shaking hand, Grace picked up the pen and wrote the short letter as Nancy watched over her, reading out the account number. Nancy then took the letter from her and folded it into an envelope, wrote the address of the Department of Education on the front, licked a stamp, stuck it on and popped it into the box behind the counter. 'Now, Miss Fitz, that will go out with the next mail.'

Grace took out her purse, but Nancy waved her ha'penny away, just as Bríd had waved away her attempt to pay for the ice cream. It was as if the whole village was conspiring to help her defy her sister. It was heart-warming but a bit nerve-wracking as well.

'Thank you so much, Mrs O'Flaherty,' she said, ready to leave again.

'Did you not want to talk to me about your other savings account, Miss Fitz?' said Nancy.

'Oh, well, yes, I suppose I might.' She turned clumsily back. Her leg was getting very painful with all the walking she'd done today, and like Bríd, Nancy came out with a stool and set it down for her to sit on, to take the weight off. 'Thank you, Mrs O'Flaherty.'

'A pleasure, Miss Fitz. Now...' Nancy went to the door, and to Grace's surprise, turned the sign to 'Closed' before she came back again and stood behind the counter with her arms folded. 'Just what is it you want to know about your other savings account, Miss Fitz? Ask me anything.'

'I don't know, really. I just... Let me think.' She tried to remember back to the letter now sitting in the OXO tin in the bottom of Charlie's dresser. 'You see, a friend of mine, he knows something about banking...'

She glanced at Nancy, expecting her to be very surprised that Grace had a friend like that. But Nancy just stood looking at her, waiting, expressionless, with that odd flush on her cheeks.

'Well, this friend, he said if I was going to be saving all my wages – he said not to save all of them, but he said if I was saving a portion, I should put it in a high-interest savings account, one that can't be touched by anyone for a while. So I was wondering, is it possible for you to do that, Mrs O'Flaherty? He said I should go to a bank, but maybe you have such a thing here, in the post office?'

'We don't, Grace. You'd have to go to the bank in Tralee. And if you want to save some of your wages, I can send them there for you surely.'

Grace got a heady rush of joy – money of her own! She remembered Richard's advice to visit Sister Kenny in England.

'And what of the savings I have already? I was wondering how much that was? I might put a small part of them into my current account now, if you wouldn't mind, Mrs O'Flaherty, but the rest I think I should put into the bank. What do you think, if I took out a third now and moved the other two thirds to Tralee when I set up a savings account there?'

The postmistress looked at her for a long moment, her mouth pressed tight shut, like she desperately wanted to say something but was holding herself back. Then she took a deep breath and burst out in a rush, 'I'm so sorry to tell you this, Miss Fitz, but your post office savings account has never had a lodgement made to it and is now defunct. I swear to you, I did not know until this moment that you thought it was an active account, but I can assure you, it's not.'

'I'm sorry? What?' Her mind grappled to understand what had just been said. 'But Agnes always puts –'

'Have you ever signed for another account in your name, Grace?'

'No, just the one here. I don't understand. Agnes said…' She felt weak, sick. Agnes took her cheques to lodge for her every two weeks, yet her account was…empty?

Nancy's face was a picture of alarmed concern. 'If you're telling me something has been done you didn't agree to, Miss Fitz, which you didn't know about, which would be a terrible thing to happen, if something's been stolen from you against your will, then Sergeant Keane will have to be involved…'

'*Sergeant Keane?*' She clung to the sides of the stool. There was a terrible roaring in her ears now, like the boom and suck of the waves when a winter storm was blowing, though it was a mild spring day.

'Grace, do you want me to call someone?' The postmistress's voice sounded very far away, drowned by the thunder of the waves. 'Will I call Dr Ryan? You look very faint.'

'No, I'll be fine.' She leant her head forward, breathing, pressing her hands to her temples. The roaring of the ocean was in her own head. 'I'm fine.' She rose unsteadily to her feet.

'You're white as a sheet, Miss Fitz. Will I call Charlie?'

'I'm fine, Mrs O'Flaherty. I...I just need some time.' Almost blindly she went to the door and fumbled to open it until Nancy came to unlock it for her. The postmistress asked Grace again if she needed anyone to help her, and then insisted on walking her the short way to the schoolhouse. She stood there anxiously as Grace stumbled her way inside.

* * *

THE HOUSE WAS DEATHLY QUIET. Grace mounted the stairs as softly as she could. What had been their parents' bedroom door was closed, and when she listened, she could hear Agnes breathing. Asleep. How could her sister sleep?

It seemed to her that so many people had been trying to tell her the truth, or what they knew of it. Charlie by insisting all her letters go through him. Madge O'Sullivan by asking her did she come down in the last shower and telling her that the canon had been seen picking Agnes up in his fancy car from Dingle. Only that day Pádraig Ó Sé had rubbished the idea that Agnes was really going on pilgrimages. And then Bríd Butler telling her about Agnes being seen to eat in Ballyferriter with the canon. Even the curate sending her to the school filing cabinet.

A memory struck her like a thunderbolt. The other chequebook in the file, with Agnes's writing on the stubs. There had been one made out to an ice cream shop in Ballyferriter. And then all those hotels, those dinners...

Was it possible? Were Agnes and the canon spending her money? Jaunting around, having a great time, putting her wages in the wrong account and spending the money on themselves?

She refused to believe it. She mustn't believe it.

She had to talk to someone, find out if she was going mad.

She ran through the possibilities in her head. She couldn't go to the guards. If this went to court, the Fitzgerald name would become a byword for shame and disgrace. Her poor parents. A daughter, accused by their other daughter of being a thief. Whether it turned out to be true or not, it would be impossibly shameful. They would both have to leave Knocknashee, the school. She and Agnes were tied to each other and this town.

Charlie McKenna. But supposing he went to have it out with Agnes on Grace's behalf? She and the canon would destroy him. The same with Tilly – she mustn't hear a word of it. The curate? Canon Rafferty probably had more absolute power over the curate than anyone else; he would probably fire him off to deepest Africa, and Knocknashee needed Father Iggy – he was the good face of the Church.

No, there was no one she could talk to. She sat on the edge of her bed in a state of shock and stared across the room at the window, listening to the noises from the street. Her town. The place she'd lived and intended to live all her life. The dray horse pulling churns up the street was making a racket, and a breeze had got up, causing the sign outside O'Donoghue's grocery to creak in the distance, a familiar sound. She could hear the chatter of men, Packie Keohane and his cousin John, who were the gravediggers, walking past. A grandfather of one of the children in Agnes's room would be buried later today.

Sitting on the windowsill behind the desk was the bottle of lilac ink.

Richard Lewis.

He was thousands of miles away. He knew no one she knew. And he was discreet. He'd shown her second letter to his sister, but not the first, because it hadn't been addressed to him but to St Jude. And he'd refused to put the story of the bottle in the paper without her say-so, even though that man Nunez had said it was a good story.

And unlike her, Richard Lewis knew about money, and the world.

She got up, went to the desk, sat down and filled her pen.

Dear Mr Lewis, she wrote in her neat hand.

I hope you don't mind me asking you not to show this to anyone, but I need to know if I am going quite mad to think what I do about recent events.

It all began with you writing to me about Georgia...

She went on and on for six pages, until she felt he must be sick of hearing about her mad thoughts and finished the letter apologetically.

So that's my story, Mr Lewis, and I'm sorry for going on and on about my own troubles – I hope I haven't bored you.

I'm sorry to hear you are still in difficulties with your parents. I hope that's resolved by the time you get this.

I'd say they must be very proud of you for having a story published and of course if it helps your career to write about the bottle on the beach, then do it – you've been so much help to me, I'd like to help you. It's not like I'm ever going to meet anyone in America. But please, Mr Lewis, please don't mention anything I've told you about Agnes. I would die of shame if it was printed in a paper over there and somebody from Knocknashee ever got wind of it.

She sat there then with the pen in her hand, wondering about his new request for a photo, which he'd couched very carefully. *Maybe you wouldn't want your picture being in the paper...* And it was true.

But then she heard Tilly's voice in her mind, from when they met on the beach before taking the bus to Dingle. *That auld crow of a sister of yours has you convinced high up and low down that you're a burden and not a full person, but she's the one lacking, Grace. She might have two good legs, but she's missing a shred of humanity, and you have that in spades.*

Tilly was right. She was a human being. Why should she be afraid of having her picture in the paper? If it would help Richard Lewis to tell the story of the bottle – not with all the awful stuff about Agnes, but just as a story about a message crossing the ocean – then why not send him a photo?

As Dr Warrington had reminded her in his letter, the one to which she had still not replied, she was a person, entitled to a future and a life as much as anyone else.

She could just reach under her mattress for the photo of herself posing in Dingle with her hair in the wind… But then she heard Agnes's bedroom door open and Agnes cross the landing. She threw the writing pad into the drawer as Agnes opened the door, standing there, rake-thin, in her long brown dressing gown.

'Are the potatoes done, Grace?' she snapped, with a suspicious glance towards the drawer, which was still slightly open.

'No, Agnes. I forgot,' said Grace, eyes cast down.

'You haven't?' Her sister seemed astonished at Grace's total lack of shame. 'Did you even weed the flowerbed?'

'I started but didn't finish it yet.'

'So instead of doing as you were asked, you sit here gazing out the window like a simpleton?'

At that Grace raised her head and looked directly at her sister. 'I'll do it all now, Agnes.' She sat there, waiting for her sister to leave the room.

Agnes didn't move either; she was clearly very curious about what Grace had been up to, and no doubt would search her drawers in a heartbeat as soon as her back was turned. 'Well, what's keeping you?' she asked, her sharp nose quivering.

'I need to adjust my steel. It's hurting me.'

The ruse worked in that it got rid of her sister. Agnes had more than once snapped at her to 'stop fiddling with that wretched thing'; she said it turned her stomach to see it.

'Oh, very well. See you don't take all day and all night.' Agnes spun on her heel and went back into her own room.

For a long moment, Grace just sat there, staring at the closed door. She never felt more useless or more ugly than when Agnes openly shuddered at the sight of her twisted leg, encased in its calliper. It made her wonder what was going to happen to her. If she and Agnes fell out over the money, where then would she live? Who would have her? Who would want her?

She took the letter back out of the drawer and added another paragraph, answering his question about Ireland and a possible war, saying the same things were in the papers here but that Ireland would remain neutral. She hoped it wouldn't come to that. Surely the men in power would sort it out – they couldn't think it was a good idea to go to war again, not after the carnage of the last one. Then she signed it. She was no longer inclined to send the photo from Dingle, but she was glad to have got things off her chest anyway. She clumped downstairs and out the door with the letter hidden under her cardigan.

She was off to post her letter to America.

The potatoes could wait.

CHAPTER 18

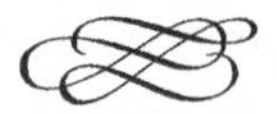

ST SIMONS ISLAND

March 1939

THERE WAS a letter waiting for him on the hall table when he got back from his long day swimming and lazing and seeing his friends, Chip Sanderson and Albie Winters, who'd had a day's leave from the Coast Guard.

He'd been spending quite a bit of time with the guys since he'd interviewed them for the newspaper, and it felt nice to be part of that community, men of the water. Nothing like the bank, where the men had soft white hands and wore their collars buttoned up. Or sitting over the piano, desperately trying to come up with an original tune.

That evening there had been a dance in aid of the Coast Guard, at the King and Prince Resort overlooking the beach, and the music had been fun and the girls had been pretty, though none of them as pretty as Miranda Logan, who had been ignoring him for weeks now.

He missed her. In January he'd sent her a picture postcard of the East Beach, saying 'Wish you were here.' A few days later, he'd received a postcard of Savannah saying 'Wish you were here.' And nothing since.

And now here was a letter, addressed to him…

But with green stamps, and the address written in lilac ink. Not Miranda after all, but at least Grace Fitzgerald was still writing to him, and he was surprised how much it lifted his heart to see it, to know she was thinking of him, even if she was on the far side of the ocean.

He picked up the letter, weighing it in his hand. It seemed thicker than the last one. He was very tired and had drunk a lot of beer; maybe he should save it for the morning, read it in luxury over breakfast with coffee and a glass of orange juice? That would be the sensible thing, but instead he decided to open it and scan a few lines, check everything was OK with her, see if she'd taken his advice.

He carried it with him into the living room overlooking the beach. There was an oil lamp burning, turned down low, the curtains open and a window ajar, and in the warm spring night, beyond the beach, the moon was setting, laying a silver road across the ocean. Esme had left a tray of lemonade and biscuits out for him on the table by the sofa, and he poured a lemonade and threw himself down on the cushions, slitting the envelope open with the little penknife he carried on his key ring.

There was a lot of it, three pages written on both sides, and as he started to read, he snapped wide awake.

Dear Mr Lewis,

I hope you don't mind me asking you not to show this to anyone, but I need to know if I am going quite mad to think what I do about recent events.

It all began with you writing to me about Georgia...

His eyes widened as he read on. He wasn't at all surprised the poor girl felt like she was going mad. The tale she had to tell was like a detective story from a magazine; he had to keep going back over sentences as he went along. The map, the curate, the two chequebooks, the receipt for ice cream, the stolen letters, the people in the village dropping dark hints, the postmistress locking the door before telling her about the empty savings account.

I'm so grateful to you, Mr Lewis. If it wasn't for you, I'd never have wanted to get a map, and then I'd never have talked to Father Iggy, and discovered the secret of the filing cabinet. And I'm so grateful for your advice about money. If it hadn't been for that, I'd never have spoken to Nancy O'Flaherty...

How extraordinary to have had such an impact on someone else's life. A pretty devastating impact, but he was pleased to see Grace refused to be defeated.

So I'm going to use my first wage check to travel to Cork to see Dr Warrington. I am fully resolved to write to him now, asking if I can visit at Easter. I will tell him the letter went astray. I am too ashamed to tell him the truth. The only person I dare tell is you, because you are so far away beyond the ocean. And I trust you not to put it in the paper!

I'M sorry you're still having difficulties with your parents. I know better than most that families can be complicated. Feel free to write whatever and whenever you like. I promise to afford you the same confidentiality you do me. Maybe things are better with them now? I hope so.

I'D SAY they must be very proud of you for having a story published,

He smiled briefly at that. He had sent a copy of *The Capital* article to his parents' house, and to Miranda's as well, but his parents said nothing and Miranda reported back that nobody was impressed by him scribbling a few lines for a Yankee rag, and a Jewish-owned one to boot. And quoting a coloured man in the story! Nor had it escaped Miranda's notice who the photographer was. She'd asked Sarah a lot of hard questions about that.

You ask what I think about the war. I don't think Ireland will be joining any war where we have to fight on the side of the English, but we don't like Germany either. We're not all like Tilly's brother, mad keen to fight everyone we disagree with; we've had enough of that after the last eight centuries and want a bit of peace. So best to stay out of it, which I hear is what America is going to do.

He wasn't surprised that's what she'd heard, though he suspected that might change. Chip had been full of war talk at the dance; his brother had applied for the Navy and was currently being trained at the base in Norfolk, Virginia.

'So what about it?' Chip had asked everyone at their table, raising his voice over the music. 'There's a war coming, everyone says so, and we get in early, we get moved up. We're the ones with experience. Coast Guard has gotta stand for something, right? We serve the war with the brass, not down below hauling rope.'

'You really think we should apply?' Albie had asked. 'Will the Coast Guard let us go?'

'They'd let us transfer if we wanted to, and the Navy will be glad to have us. They took our Doug, and he ain't no genius, let me tell ya that, so you and me, we'll be shoo-ins. Officer class, I'm telling you.'

Chip was no academic, no more than his brother Dougie, which was why he preferred physical outdoor work, but he had that sense of entitlement that came with a privileged background. Chip's father was a wealthy trader, but unlike Richard, Chip was one of nine sons, and he joked that nobody had even noticed when he left Savannah to join the Coast Guard.

'And we get more girls? That's a guarantee?' Albie was also one of several boys and had escaped the family net.

'Solid-gold certainty, my friend.' Chip clapped him on the back. 'Is that a yes?'

'Why not?' Albie agreed, and took a drink of his beer. 'If the war comes, we'll get drafted anyhow. Might as well be in on top.'

Nobody had asked if Richard would be interested. But after everything Nunez had said to him, he was beginning to think that he should play his part somehow. Nunez had been talking about going to Europe, being there when it kicked off to document what was happening.

'The world is on the brink of something, Richard,' he'd said. 'I don't know what exactly, but I don't like it. Fascists are gaining ground, President Roosevelt talking about quarantining aggressive nations, Lindbergh and his wife went to Germany to inspect their planes. English royalty meeting Hitler. Germany, Italy arming to the teeth and cosying up to each other, the Nazis growing in power all the time, wiping out any opposition to them. And it's no shock the Jews are on the front line – they always are. When things go wrong, it is always blame the Jews. Whether it's for killing Jesus, or poisoning the wells during the black death, or becoming moneylenders when we were forced out of every other trade – the list goes on and on. There's trouble in Palestine, and that lunatic Stalin won't be happy till he's slaughtered everyone. The Japanese won't hear any reason on the subject of China...and we're trying to help the Chinese. The bombing of Shanghai last year killed thousands. There are so many stories to tell, Richard. I think I should be there.'

He went back to reading, but the letter had come to an end, quite abruptly.

So that's all from me for now.

Yours sincerely,

Grace Fitzgerald.

* * *

He couldn't sleep for thinking of her extraordinary story. He kept rereading her letter. He'd set this whole horror in motion, this dreadful discovery, and he couldn't help but wonder if he'd done the right thing.

It must have been heartbreaking for Grace to discover that her sister didn't care about her at all. It reminded him of his last encounter with his mother, when he'd realised his only worth to her was if he did her bidding, was the son she wanted him to be, a replica of his father married to a replica of his mother.

It was worse for Grace, though. He couldn't be thrown out of this summer house because it was partly his, thanks to his grandmother, and he had his inheritance from that same grandmother to draw on and plenty of wealthy friends to tap, but Grace's loss had practical implications as well as emotional ones.

I was feeling so hopeful, he read again, and he thought the ink was a little smudged at that point, as if a tear had fallen. *Right there in the post office, I decided to take your advice to see Sister Kenny in London. And then Nancy O'Flaherty told me my account was empty and that lovely dream came crashing down.*

This was his fault as well, for meddling with this girl's life. It's what Miranda had accused him of. *Don't lead her on, Richard, by sending her pictures of fine houses and writing to her about miracle cures that she can't afford.*

He turned on his side, putting the letter on his nightstand, and slowly, slowly drifted to sleep and dreamt he was walking on the beach with a woman whose face he could not see.

CHAPTER 19

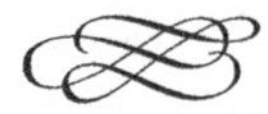

KNOCKNASHEE, DINGLE

aster 1939

GRACE WAS LIVING on her nerves, constantly sick and faint.

The Department of Education had written back to say they would pay her next wages straight into her new account. She'd crept into the post office to let Nancy O'Flaherty know, and the kindly woman had patted her hand.

'You don't need to tell me your business, and don't look so worried, Miss Fitz. It's been done now, so 'tis just a matter of *haulting your whist* till the payday comes. I won't be saying anything and mind you don't say a blessed bit either. Let your sister work it out for herself and see if she has the brass neck to say anything. You keep your own counsel.'

The rest of March dragged by, and the beginning of April.

The wages were due the Wednesday before Easter. And Grace's

cheque simply wouldn't arrive. She'd decided what to do when that happened. When Agnes got confused about where it was, she would drop a casual remark about having opened a different account and leave it at that. She wasn't going to accuse Agnes of stealing or embezzling or anything. She was just going to let Agnes work it out for herself that she knew what had happened and hope Agnes would do as Grace planned to do – never mention it again. They were sisters, they were stuck together in this house, in the school. Agnes was all she had in the world, and Grace was all Agnes had as well.

Anyway, if Agnes did get angry, she had a place to escape to while her sister simmered down. She had written to Dr Warrington to explain how she was very sorry, that she hadn't received his letter until recently, that it had gone astray. She was overwhelmed when he responded quickly and with great enthusiasm, asking her to come to Cork over the Easter school holidays. Mrs Warrington would collect her from the station and take her to their house, where she could stay for the whole week.

Her wages would be in by then, Nancy O'Flaherty had assured her, so she could take the bus to Killarney and the train from there to Cork.

It was just a question of waiting it out now. Finally, on the Wednesday before Easter, Charlie knocked on the front door. Agnes went to open it – it was one of the few jobs she didn't make Grace do for her – and came back holding a brown envelope with a harp on it. It took her a moment, standing there, to realise she was holding only one envelope and not two. She opened it and double-checked the contents with a puzzled expression, then, without a glance at Grace, who was sitting there sweating, she hurried to call Charlie back from the front door.

'There's a letter missing!' Grace could hear her imperious tone.

'No, Miss Fitzgerald,' she heard Charlie call back, cool as a breeze. 'That's all the post addressed to your house for today.' And his wheels squeaked and his bell tinkled as he hopped up on his bike and rode away.

Agnes came back in and sat down to breakfast, looking mightily vexed. She buttered her toast with a frown, muttering about the post office and how unreliable it was. Grace couldn't answer. She sat there unable to eat; she felt like she had a potato stuck in her throat. Now was the time to mention about her new account, but the courage had drained out of her. She would wait until she was sure her own wages were safe in the post office, she decided.

When Charlie arrived the next morning, Agnes went out to meet him on the step, while Grace remained in the kitchen, quaking. Her wages had gone in; Nancy had told her yesterday afternoon. Now she would have to say something.

'Where is Grace's cheque?' she heard Agnes demand. 'What have you done with it?'

'I don't know what you're talking about, Agnes,' the postman called back cheerfully as his wheels creaked away. Grace was beginning to wonder if Nancy O'Flaherty had dropped Charlie a hint, despite her having to keep everything confidential about people's money.

'It's Miss Fitzgerald to you!' Agnes barked after him, then stormed back into the kitchen, white with rage apart from the two pink spots high in her cheeks. 'The insolence of him. I've half a mind to report him...'

Now. She had to say it. *Now.*

She opened her mouth. 'I'm going away for a few days, Agnes. I've been meaning to tell you.' It was not quite where she'd meant to start, but oh well, it had to be said anyway.

Agnes stared at her in amazement. 'Going away? Where? How? It better not be to that Tilly girl's house – I've warned you...'

'It's not Tilly. I'm going to see Dr Warrington, in Cork. I'm getting the bus to Dingle at nine thirty and the train from there to Cork. I'll be there by evening.'

Agnes cast her a withering, almost amused look. 'Don't fantasise, Grace. Even if you had the money for such a jaunt, the consultant has better things to do with his time than see the likes of you. You would only be imposing on him, turning up out of the blue. You were just another patient, Grace. Don't be so foolish as to imagine you were ever something special to him. He was just doing the job he's well paid to do, but typical of you to read more into it.'

'I'm not imposing on him, Agnes.' She wished she could keep the shake out of her voice. 'He wrote to me, inviting me to stay, and his wife is going to pick me up from the station.'

'Wrote to you? When did he write to you?' Agnes went white, then pink. 'You're making this up, Grace. You didn't receive any letter... You haven't had a letter from anyone!'

'I did, Agnes. It came in the post, addressed to me. I suppose I made it to the door faster than you for once.'

'But... I... You... What do you mean?' Agnes's mouth opened and shut like a fish hooked out of the water and landed on the pier. She couldn't say what she wanted to say, which was how dare Grace get her hands on her own letters, so instead she burst out with, 'And where are you getting the money for this foolish trip?'

Now, Grace. Just say it.

She took a deep breath and said so rapidly it was almost one word, 'I asked the Department of Education to pay my wages into my new account.'

'You did what?' This time Agnes went purple, then white again, and when she spoke, she actually sprayed Grace with spittle, just as Madge O'Sullivan had done the day she'd threatened to put the schoolhouse windows through with the hoe because Agnes had broken her son's finger. 'You have no right...' Every sinew of Agnes' body was tense, as if she was about to pounce.

'I have every right.' Grace was terrified, but she tried to keep her voice as calm as if they were discussing the early arrival of the swallows. 'I'm entitled to have a post office account the same as anyone else. I've taken advice –'

'Taken...advice?' Agnes could hardly talk, she was so livid.

'Yes, from a banker.' Richard wasn't exactly a banker, but she was throwing caution to the wind here. 'And he says they are my wages, to do with as I see fit. So we'll say no more about any of this, Agnes, will we? What's been happening this past year, no one will know about but us. And perhaps the canon, though I hope not. Now I'd better go and get my bus.'

Agnes just stared, her jaw clenched, breathing through her nose. Grace had caught her off-guard; she had no defence. Grace didn't look back as she stomped away down the hall. She bent awkwardly to get her packed bag out from under the stairs, then took her coat and hat from the hook in the hall.

'Goodbye, Agnes,' she called over her shoulder as she opened the front door, then paused for a moment to see if there was any kind of reply, and when none came, she had a sudden bad feeling and went back to look through the kitchen door. Suppose this time Agnes really had had a heart attack or something and was lying there...

What she saw was more horrible than she could have imagined in her worst fears. As she came in the door, her sister stood where she'd left her, stock still.

'*Go n-ullamhuighe an diabhal tinne dhuit*,' she spat at Grace, with a venomous hiss. The old Irish curse: May the devil have a fire ready for you.

Grace's blood ran cold. It was as if a mask had been stripped from her sanctimonious, Mass-going sister, the holy Agnes of the retreats and pilgrimages, always exhorting Grace to think of her soul and the souls of those in her care. Her heart pounding, she stumbled away as fast as she could, and as she fled down the garden path, she could hear from the sitting room windows Agnes shrieking that terrifying curse again, as if she really had turned into a *cailleach*.

'*Go n-ullamhuighe an diabhal tinne dhuit*!'

A woman carrying a baby wrapped in her shawl glanced across the cobbled street in horror and crossed herself, and Grace's face burnt with the shame and pity of it as she hobbled away.

CHAPTER 20

Lizzie Warrington, the doctor's wife, collected her from the train station in Cork, and the welcome she gave to Grace was so heart-warming, it made the hours on the bus and then the train worth it. 'It's so wonderful to see you, Grace.'

'It's so wonderful to see you as well, Mrs Warrington.' Grace smiled as they embraced. The doctor's wife was plain, square and tending to plump, with a round face and a rather large nose, but she had a heart of gold. As well as teaching the children in her husband's care, she mothered them, reading bedtime stories, remembering birthdays with a present and a home-baked cake, always wiping away tears with a kiss and a biscuit.

'Call me Lizzie, please,' begged the older woman. 'Let us be Lizzie and Hugh to you, Grace. We've missed you so much.'

'I've missed you too, Lizzie, more than I can say.' Her heart felt so full, she almost cried.

'You have a special place in our hearts, Grace. Oh, you look prettier than ever! But how is your leg?' She cast a worried glance at Grace as they walked towards the tram. 'Is it hurting you very much? You must ask Hugh to look at it. We have some new callipers in, and I've heard about this new treatment...'

'It's fine, not hurting at all,' said Grace, though it wasn't true, her leg ached. This evening she didn't want to be a patient, she just wanted to be Grace.

'Well, tomorrow then,' said Lizzie, understanding her meaning straight away. The tram was already there when they got to the stop, and she insisted on carrying Grace's bag on for her, then sat next to her on the window side, beaming at her, while Grace thrust her stiff right leg out into the aisle.

'I can't believe you're really here, Grace. I'm so glad our letter to you turned up in the end – it must have gone the wrong way around the world to get to you. We almost thought you didn't want to see us, but we said to each other that we understood, that it must have been such a difficult time for you here at the hospital. We thought maybe you just wanted to forget and put it all behind you.'

Tears pricked Grace's eyes at the thought of the Warringtons trying to find the best possible reason for her neglect. 'Please don't ever say that. You and Hugh were like parents to me. I never was going to forget you – didn't I tell you that in the thank-you card I sent you?'

'You sent a card?' Lizzie looked surprised. 'Oh, I wish I'd seen that. Did you send it to the hospital ward? They usually pin them up on the noticeboard?'

'No, I sent it to you, Lizzie, and Hugh, at your home address. It was a card with bluebells on it and inside was a letter...' She stopped as an awful thought struck her, making her stomach lurch. Had Agnes been interfering with her post from the very beginning? Grace had been too ashamed to explain to the Warringtons why their letter had taken so long to get to her; she'd just said it had gone astray. And now it looked as if they hadn't got her card either.

'Dear me, it must have gone missing as well,' Lizzie said, with a puzzled air. 'What a coincidence.'

The tram stopped then at the end of the Warringtons' street – a humble little red-brick cul-de-sac where Hugh and Lizzie Warrington lived in a two-storey terraced house. Agnes had said Hugh was 'well paid' to do his job, but now that Grace was old enough to notice things like the size of people's houses, she found herself wondering if the pair of them ploughed some of their salaries back into the hospital, because this was nothing like the huge Victorian house that Dr Ryan owned in Knocknashee.

When Dr Warrington greeted her at the door, he was in the same suit as he'd always worn. His shoes were scuffed and had been reheeled and resoled many times. He was completely grey now – he'd still been quite dark-haired the last time she'd seen him – but his twinkly blue eyes were the same, and he was as tall and broad and handsome as ever. Grace knew that whenever a new nurse started at the hospital, she would giggle about Hugh Warrington being so much better looking than his wife, but you didn't have to know the couple long to realise they were devoted to each other, and then people forgot about the discrepancy.

'Hello, Dr Warrington!'

'Hugh,' he corrected her as he enveloped her in a bear hug.

'I mean, hello, Hugh.' She beamed, hugging him back. It was so good to see him, and he did feel like a father to her. She'd been lucky, she realised, to have had her daddy, a kind and happy man, and then Dr Warrington in her life – or Hugh, as she had to call him now, though she suspected in her head he would always be Dr Warrington.

After they'd had a cup of tea and Grace had told them all about her long journey down on the bus and then the train, Lizzie showed her to her room. It was downstairs and very small, squeezed in to the right of the front door with a bathroom behind it; it only had room for a narrow single bed, a chest of drawers and a desk.

'There's a bigger room upstairs,' explained Lizzie, 'But we thought it might be easier for you to be on the ground floor, not having to climb stairs every day.'

'It's perfect, and thank you so much for thinking of me.' The tiny room was so warm and cosy, with a feather mattress, linen sheets, a thick woollen blanket and a patchwork quilt on the bed and a simple blue vase full of daffodils on the chest of drawers. It struck her how much better it would have been for her if there had been a downstairs bathroom at home, instead of having to climb up and down the stairs every day, with the constant wear on her hip that entailed.

After Lizzie had left her, she got changed into her favourite dress, the cornflower-blue one, and added the wine-coloured cardigan, and when she entered the kitchen, the Warringtons sat her down, refusing all help. Working together, they served up a lovely, simple dinner of roast ham and buttered cabbage and floury potatoes.

'Did you know, Hugh, Grace sent us a thank-you card here to the house after she left us?' said Lizzie, after finishing her dinner. 'It must have gone missing, just like the one we sent to her.'

'Oh?' He looked astonished as he folded his knife and fork. 'That's right strange?' The broad vowels of the north of England had never left his accent.

'It didn't go missing,' said Grace, the words out of her mouth before she was even aware of what she was going to say. 'It was...' Avoiding their eyes, which were full of concern, she looked down at her plate and blushed with shame, thinking how much her parents would hate to hear her say this. 'It was stolen. By my sister, Agnes.' There, it was out, and then the awful memory of the last time she'd seen her sister came flooding back. The happiness of seeing the Warringtons had pushed the memory away, but now it filled her mind – the bitter snarl, the wild hair, the staring eyes, the pointing finger... that terrible curse...

She burst into tears and buried her face in her hands.

Moments later she felt their arms around her, which made her cry even more, but eventually she calmed down and blew her nose. Hugh made her a cup of tea while Lizzie sat by her, holding her hand, and eventually they coaxed the whole miserable story out of her.

When she'd finished, Hugh marched round the kitchen, running his fingers through his grey shock of hair. 'I have held my tongue on the subject of your sister these many years now, because I knew she was all you had in terms of family and I'd assumed there was some good in her despite her never coming to see you. Though that summer when I drove you home, when I was leaving, I told her how well we expected you to do in your exams, and she passed some snide remark about you failing…'

'Did she?' Grace was miserable..

'Yes, and I should have known then something was very wrong, but she passed it off as in jest and I gave her the benefit of the doubt. Though I did say to her, "Only a very foolish person would underestimate Grace, Miss Fitzgerald, a very foolish person indeed." I can't believe she was so cruel and dishonest to tell you you'd failed.'

'I think maybe she was afraid of losing my company,' said Grace, who even now found it hard to believe her sister could hate her that much.

'Afraid of losing you as an assistant teacher in the school, more like,' said Lizzie, with a rare flash of anger. 'And an easy source of money to go wining and dining that Canon Rafferty. I hope he didn't realise it was your money she was spending on him, the silly, deluded woman. What was she buying for him?'

'All sorts of treats. She's never drunk a drop in her life, but there were stubs written out to wine bars and everything. Though it was the ice cream that made me realise…'

'The ice cream?' asked Lizzie, bewildered, and Grace explained about Bríd Butler, and the frequent sightings of the pair in Ballyferriter, and how Agnes had made out a cheque even for such a small amount.

'Imagine that – he wouldn't even pay for his own ice cream,' said Lizzie, shaking her head. 'Well, she wouldn't be the first spinster to get starry-eyed over a priest.'

'Some of them are so arrogant, they think it's their due never to put their hand in their pocket,' agreed Hugh. 'It makes them feel important to be worshipped, particularly by the women.'

Lizzie squeezed Grace's hand, sympathetic and encouraging. 'It's horrible that Agnes spent your money on a silly crush. But you are free of her now, Grace, which is a blessing. You must do your teacher's training here in Cork, and stay with us, as we said in the letter. You missed starting last September, but there might still be places for this year.'

'I don't think there'll be any of my money left to pay my fees.' She wasn't going to ask anyway. There didn't seem much point, not after seeing all those extravagant payments marked in the chequebook. It was still her plan to carry on like nothing had ever happened.

'There's another way of managing your fees, though, darling. Hugh and I were discussing you last night while we were waiting for you to arrive –'

'Please don't offer to pay them for me,' interrupted Grace, alarmed. 'I can't take your money. I know you spend it all on the children. I wouldn't take any of it away from them...'

'Stop, Grace, stop!' Lizzie was smiling. 'That was Hugh's idea, but I told him you'd refuse. No, I have a better one. You can pay your way through college by helping me teach the children in the hospital, a proper teaching position, not just a few hours a week. We'll even make a proper schoolroom, and the Department of Education will pay for it, I am quite certain, because we have so many more children now, more than I can cope with alone.'

'Oh...' She was overwhelmed by this sudden offer. 'I don't know... It sounds wonderful...'

'Please say yes, Grace. It would be so lovely to have you.'

'And I would love to come, it's just...'

'Just what, Grace?' The doctor's wife looked anxious. 'I'm sure we can sort out any difficulties, and you can stay here, as we said...'

'And that's so kind of you, but how can I leave my children in Knocknashee? You don't know how bad it is, Lizzie. The children are scared witless of Agnes. She slaps them all the time and makes no allowances for anything. If I wasn't there to give them some bit of joy in learning... I'm not saying I'm marvellous or anything, but they like my class and they get four years of me before they have to go in to Agnes. I don't think I can bear to leave them... I don't think I should.'

'You have your life to live as well, Grace,' murmured Lizzie, her eyes full of admiration as well as disappointment. She took both Grace's hands in hers. Hugh stopped pacing and stood by Grace's chair, patting her shoulder.

'There's no need to make up your mind about it right now,' he was gruff, as if he had a lump in his throat. 'We will apply to the Department of Education for the post anyway, and it will be there for you if you want it. But will you come to the hospital with us tomorrow, to speak to the children?'

'Oh, I will. I'd love to,' Grace was excited at the prospect.

'And while we're there, I will have a look at your leg.'

'Hugh, Grace doesn't want to talk about polio this evening,' intervened Lizzie gently, and he nodded, understanding.

'Of course, of course. Now, Grace, tell me all about these children of yours.' He pulled up a chair, and both the Warringtons listened avidly as Grace told them all about her many charges: Mikey O'Shea with his cheeky smile, and his cousin Janie who was so sensible, and Patrick who loved his football so much, and Leonard O'Flynn pretending to be Bartolomeu Dias with a rolled-up newspaper for a telescope, and Aisling Walsh wearing a red curtain to act as the pope sorting out the Treaty of Tordesillas...

Lizzie laughed. 'You must be a wonderful teacher.'

'I learnt it from the best, Lizzie.' Grace smiled. 'I think you were better than any teacher training college, you know.'

That night as she lay in her bed, so comfortable with the feather mattress, she thought about how much she would love to live here with the Warringtons, and how, despite what she'd said to Lizzie, she would love to be properly trained. She did her best with her natural talents – when telling the children anything, she modulated her voice and facial expressions for emphasis, and she was never complacent about being able to hold their interest – but she was sure there were methods that could make things even better for them. She also thought about how much she dreaded going home to Agnes.

There was something she dreaded even more, though. If she never went back, if she wasn't there to protect the little children from the worst of her sister's wrath... It didn't bear thinking about. Her life was in Knocknashee.

CHAPTER 21

Sister Ahern, the matron and one of her favourite people, brought her on a tour to show her all the improvements to the wards and the communal areas.

'This is Grace, do you remember Grace?' The matron kept saying to every nurse they met, and everyone who had been there when she left, nearly two years ago now, recognised her at once and seemed thrilled to see her.

'Of course we remember Grace. She was so bright and happy all the time!' It was like being enveloped in a warm glow to have people care about her, be happy to see her. The hospital was a big clinical institution, and it smelled the same as ever, disinfectant and overcooked vegetables, but it felt like home too, more like home than Knocknashee. Four years was a long time in a child's life, and she'd never been treated with anything but kindness here.

In a room full of children's books, a new student nurse was reading a story to a group of children. They all, like her, had polio.

'I'm sorry to interrupt, Nurse Eileen,' Sister Ahern said as she opened the door. 'But here is someone I would like you all to meet.' She beckoned Grace in. 'This is Miss Fitzgerald, and she was a patient here for four years, when she was a girl, just like you are now. And she got better and became a teacher. Isn't that marvellous?'

All heads turned to look at her, and Grace remembered how sad this place could be as well as happy. The little faces were pale and tired, eyes like holes burnt in a blanket. She found she desperately wanted to give them hope. The endless medicine, exercises, pain, was hard enough for an adult to endure, but she remembered as child it was close to impossible for her to imagine any other life.

'I thought I'd never be able to go home,' she said, sitting down on one of the chairs, her bad leg outstretched. 'I didn't see anyone from my family for four years, and I tried to imagine what it would be like when I got out, but I couldn't. And then one day, Dr Warrington said to me, "I think we'll let you go home in about two weeks, and I'll drive you myself."'

She had their rapt attention now, just as she was able to captivate the children in the junior class.

'Well, I was shocked, and honestly a bit frightened. I'd been here for so long, and I didn't know what kind of life I would have away from here. I had friends here, and the doctor and the nurses were so kind, and they felt like my family.'

She didn't mention her parents were dead. It wouldn't help.

'But Dr Warrington told me something when I said I was a bit nervous about going home. He said that I was as brave as a lion' – she made a growl, and they tittered – 'and that I had been through a lot, but that all of that would stand to me because it had made me so much tougher and more courageous than other people, even adults. And the same is true for all of you.'

'And did you have friends when you went back to school?' a pale little girl of about eight, with her fair hair tied back in a ribbon, asked. She was in a wheelchair.

Grace nodded. 'I did. My best friend, Tilly, and I wrote every week when I was here, so I knew all the news, and I went back to school' – not strictly true as she was too old for school by the time she was released, but this little girl needed to be reassured – 'and it was as if I never left. And I got used to walking with my steel, and it hardly hurts at all now. It was very sore at the start, but I am quite nifty now, and I'm able to do whatever I want to do.' Again, this wasn't strictly true, but it was what they needed to hear.

'Can you climb trees?' asked a boy with freckles and spiky brown hair. Both his legs were in callipers.

She laughed. 'I can't, or at least I haven't tried, but I can go to the beach and I can climb stairs. And I know if I was a boy and your age, not climbing a tree might be a big problem, but I did learn that if you want to do something badly enough, you'll find a way. I just don't really want to climb trees.'

'Have you got a boyfriend?' a girl around thirteen asked. She was so thin, her wrists were like twigs. The veins on her temples were visible, and her collarbone stood out sharply from her neck.

'I don't...' But then she stopped herself, because it was clear the girl felt as Agnes had made Grace feel, that she would never be loved by a man, or have a family or anything. 'I don't here in Ireland, but I have a friend who is a boy in America, and we write to each other and exchange photos. He's very handsome and rich and kind.' It was the first time she'd even mentioned Richard to anyone except to Charlie, and he had never asked her anything about him since that first time, just gave her the letters.

'Will you go to see him?' The girl's eyes shone with the possibility of it all; clearly she thought maybe she could have her own fairy prince one day.

'I might, or he might come here.' Grace didn't believe a word of this, of course. She'd seen the photo of Miranda, with her shiny hair and perfect smile, the kind you saw in magazines, and she knew she was a nobody from Knocknashee with a banjaxed leg. But she didn't want to stop this child from dreaming. 'I hope to do a lot of gallivanting.' She laughed. 'And if I change my mind and don't go, it won't be because of the polio.'

'There she is, my star patient.' Everyone turned as Hugh Warrington came in with a big smile on his handsome face. 'Is she telling you how bold she was when she was here?' he asked the children, going down on his hunkers to be their height, as Grace remembered him doing with her and her friends.

The children shook their heads, grinning, used to his play-acting.

'Oh, she was a right divil altogether. She used to escape at night and slide down the drainpipes and go looking for stray dogs and cats around the city, and other times she would put worms in the nurses' tea, and once, and this was the worst...'

He paused, his finger in the air, and they gazed at him with the same adoration she remembered herself and her fellow patients feeling for him. 'I was having a very important meeting with the board of governors, a very serious one about money and grown-up things.' He made a serious face, and they laughed again. 'And they were just about to start the meeting when she sailed through the air outside on a rope swing she'd made, just like Tarzan in the films, and the chairman of the board, a very scary man with a huuuuge moustache, said, "Oh, dear me, Dr Warrington, it looks like you're running a zoo, not a hospital."'

'And did you really?' the children asked Grace, eyes wide as saucers.

'Don't you be listening to his daft stories,' Grace said with a chuckle. 'He's always talking nonsense.'

'Oh, she was wild, all right,' said Dr Warrington with a conspiratorial wink. 'But she's a very respectable teacher now, so it must be our secret, all right? No telling tales on her, or she might lose her job.'

'We won't!' they chorused breathlessly.

'Now, I'm afraid I have to take her away with me.' He stood up, helped her from the chair and led her outside, his arm around her shoulder, as behind them the student nurse went back to the story.

'Let's have a look at you,' he said, once they were alone in his consulting room. He placed his big hands on her shoulders and held her back from him, looking her over. Then, without any warning, he dropped to his knees and examined her leg.

'Right, let's get you up here so I can take a proper look.' He brought her across his office and helped her up on the examining table, where he untied the lace that held the leather cuff around her thigh and undid the buckles that held the knee brace in place. Further down another leather strap went around her shin, holding the steel bars. Once all the straps were loosened, he pulled the steels from the built-up heel of her shoe.

As always when her steel was removed, there was a feeling of release but also a throbbing ache. She did her best to hide her wince, but he caught her expression.

'You're in pain.' A statement not a question.

'Just a small bit, not too bad.' She still felt shame at anyone, even him, seeing her leg. It was much thinner than her good leg, and the knee was misshapen, with chafe marks everywhere. Her foot pointed towards the floor, the muscles unable to tighten enough to pull it up without the brace, and her toes were swollen with chilblains due to her poor circulation.

He ran his hands over her calf, feeling for muscle. 'Is it cold?' he asked.

She nodded; that leg was always cold.

He finished his examination and helped her into a sitting position on the table, then he pulled a chair up and sat near her. 'We have some new steels that are much lighter than this one, and the leather cuff around the thigh and knee are padded with wool, so it won't chafe you any more, and the blood should flow better. We'll get you fitted for one this afternoon. Is there anything else you think I could do to help?'

Because she'd just been talking about Richard Lewis, the suggestion in his first letter came instantly to mind. 'Someone I know...' She blushed, then carried on. 'Well, his brother is a doctor in America, and he said the president there, Roosevelt, he had polio when he was a child...'

Hugh beamed at her as she knew he would. 'You see, Grace, the sky's the limit! You wouldn't know that man had it, would you, by his photograph in the papers? He keeps it very quiet on the world stage. What else did your friend say?'

'Well, the president goes to this place called Warm Springs for the hot water baths, and he suggested I ask you what you think of an

Australian nurse called Sister Kenny – she's come up with a new way of treating polio. Have you heard of her at all?'

'I have, of course.' He nodded, and a twinkle came into his eye. 'And I'm glad you asked that.'

'My friend's brother says a colleague of his is trying to get her over to Detroit. He didn't say much else about her, though.'

'She's Australian, as you say, but of Irish parents. She has published a paper suggesting we treat our patients without plaster of Paris or callipers or even surgery. Instead she says we should warm up and soften the affected limb with hot compresses and hot baths, and then manually work the muscles, looking to awaken unaffected neural pathways.'

Seeing her look of confusion, he explained, 'Polio cuts off the muscle from the brain, and modern science thinks keeping the muscle immobilised is the best way to keep it from wasting away. But Nurse Kenny says that by her treatment, she can encourage the muscle to go back to working by itself, by finding another pathway through the nerves to a different part of the brain. Like finding a different way around if you come to a broken bridge on the road.'

'And have people been cured?' She was sure they were not but had to ask. She'd long ago come to terms with the fact that this was her lot in life; it would never improve and most likely deteriorate as she aged.

'Not cured completely, but she claims she can create a greater range of function and a better quality of life overall,' said Hugh.

'How wonderful for those children! And are you going to try out her method here at the hospital?' Grace felt a sudden surge of hope. Not just for herself but for all the others affected.

He shook his head. 'I'm afraid her treatment is in direct contravention to the accepted wisdom. All the academic journals reject her ideas, so that means no funding. And it's expensive and time-consuming. It requires hot compresses and hot baths more than once a day, and manual manipulation of the limb by nurses afterwards, and we have neither the resources nor the staff to do that as well as follow the accepted treatment. I did suggest to the board of the hospital that we run a very small trial here in Cork, with one or two children perhaps, but they think Sister Kenny is a foolish woman and refuse to approve the idea.'

'I'm sorry,' Grace said, feeling a wave of compassion and love for this kind man, who only wanted to do his best.

'Would you like to try it?'

'I'm sorry?' She stared at him, confused. 'What did you say?'

The twinkle was back in his eyes. 'I have something to confess to you, Grace. My wife thinks Sister Kenny is only being dismissed as a crank because she is a mere nurse, and a woman to boot, so when she came to London recently, Lizzie went to see her and came back with lots of illustrated information about the treatment. She's only been dying to get her hands on someone to experiment on, but as nothing can be done on hospital grounds, or to anyone who is an actual patient of ours...which you no longer are...'

* * *

THE BATHROOM IN THE WARRINGTONS' house was downstairs next to her own room, and the huge claw-footed bath was wonderful, the water hotter than she'd ever had and deeper too.

At home the bathroom was tiny, and they only had a small hip bath that would be no good for this, and the water had to be carried upstairs, cooling on the way. Agnes used it occasionally, demanding that Grace climb the stairs with a fresh kettle every five minutes. But somehow Agnes never had the time or energy to return the favour, so Grace used to clean herself thoroughly every morning with cold water standing at the sink and only wash her hair once a week, shivering as she did so.

Now she luxuriated in the hot water, the heat slowly and gradually permeating her bad leg, and for the first time since she could remember, there was no pain. Lizzie told her to top it up as she wished – she could just about turn the tap with her foot on her good leg if she slid halfway down – and she'd added more hot water twice already.

After half an hour, there was a knock on the door, and Lizzie called in that it was time to do the exercises now. And so she very reluctantly got out of the bath; it was difficult but there were handholds on both sides to help, and she managed it. She put on her underwear and dressing gown and was just tying the belt around her waist when Lizzie appeared.

'Was that a nice bath?' she asked as she entered.

'The nicest ever.' She was too embarrassed to admit she hadn't had a bath since she went back to Knocknashee.

'Right then, let's see what we can do here.' Lizzie smiled. 'I've tried this out on Hugh. I'm sure I don't know what I'm doing, but I took lots of notes from the demonstration and I'll do my best. Tell me if I hurt you, and I'll stop straight away.'

She led Grace to her bedroom, sat her up against the pillows of the settle bed and placed a heavy woollen blanket over her legs to keep them warm. 'Now what Sister Kenny showed us is, we don't just work on the affected limb, we work the whole body, because we are trying to create new memories in the brain. So first just rotate your head to your shoulder, then over to the other side.'

Grace, sitting upright, did as she asked.

'Now the arms. So as you move your head, open your arms out from your torso, and as your head comes back to centre, return your hands to your lap. That's excellent.' She smiled as Grace followed her instructions. 'This must never hurt or strain – it should be easy. If it hurts, then stop.'

Grace nodded.

Together they exercised every part of her body, arching and rounding her back, distending and pulling in her abdomen, rotating her shoulders. Her upper body was strong – it did most of the work for her in her daily life – but she was concerned about how well she would do with her lower half.

She need not have worried. Lizzie took her through raising her knee and bending it slightly – did she imagine it, or was her knee more flexible than it had been? Lizzie rotated both her feet. 'How does that feel?' she asked, and Grace saw a beauty to the doctor's wife. It wasn't apparent at first, but there was something so gentle about her. Grace could see why her husband loved her.

'I think I'm definitely moving a bit better after the long soak, and I wouldn't even have tried to do some of those movements myself,' Grace was honest.

'Perhaps when you go back home, you could have a bath once a day and try this yourself? If you had someone to help you do the exercises?' She asked.

Grace smiled but said nothing. The chance of her being allowed a hot bath every day, even if the hip bath was big enough, was slim to nothing, and as for getting someone to help her, she didn't see how. On the few occasions her sister had seen her leg, she'd wrinkled her nose as if it were a bag of rancid fish.

Lizzie, often able to tell what people were thinking said, 'But never mind that. Even warm compresses on your leg, hot water bottles even, before an exercise session can help. Any movement, according to Nurse Kenny, is better than none, but do make sure to warm the muscles first. Now I'll leave you to dress, and I'll make the dinner. Hugh says he'll be home by six thirty, but the reality is it will be closer to seven thirty – you know how he is. So take your time.'

Alone in the room, Grace dressed, and she definitely felt better. The light steel Sister Ahern had measured her for was not as tight, and she didn't feel the ever-present ache. If only one session had achieved this, perhaps she could make herself more mobile over time if she really tried?

And then if she ever did get to meet Richard Lewis in person… She shook her head, smiling to herself. Impossible dream.

As she left her room for the kitchen, she felt quite mobile and cast a prayer of thanks for Nurse Kenny and hoped she was robust enough to take on the medical establishment for better outcomes for all polio patients. There was no cure, so a treatment that made things more comfortable for the many people all over the world affected by this disease was the best hope any person could have.

CHAPTER 22

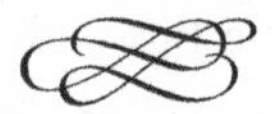

After the best and only holiday of her life, she got off the bus outside the undertaker's. Seán O'Connor stood on the doorstep of his pub, greeting everyone as they alighted. When he saw Grace, he smiled even wider than he usually did and came forward to help her with her bag.

'Good to have you back, Miss Fitz. There was a rumour flying round you'd packed up and gone for good, and my grandchildren are in the horrors thinking they'll be taught by the caill...I mean, your sister, when school starts back tomorrow.'

'Of course I'm back. I've only been on a little holiday,' said Grace, though she blushed and felt a bit guilty because she had asked herself many times during the last two weeks whether she could bear to leave the Warringtons.

She'd had such a wonderful time in Cork. It was so big and busy compared to Knocknashee, and she'd gone on adventures every chance she got. She'd loved the ladies' reading room in the City Library and was amazed to find they got a newspaper called the *Savannah Morning News* once a week. She'd spent a very happy hour reading about developments to Salzburger Park, and about a court case involving a man from Brunswick who had some kind of altercation with a woman on Abercorn Street. There were stories about places she'd never see and people she'd never meet, but it was amazing to be able to read about Richard's world in such detail. It helped her to picture it, the streets he walked on, the buildings he saw every day. She hoped he was home now and had made it up with his parents, as she planned to make it up with Agnes. Life was too short to fall out with family, however badly they'd behaved.

Lizzie and Hugh had been so kind. They hadn't let her do a bit of cooking or shopping to pull her weight. Lizzie had given her Sister Kenny's therapy twice a day, and her leg felt so much softer and less cold. One of the days, she even felt she could pull her foot up a bit, and another day she moved her toes, which no longer had chilblains.

She'd taken advantage of her newfound mobility – the lighter calliper really helped as well – to visit all the cathedrals in Cork, even a Protestant one by mistake, which she thought might be some kind of sin, but she didn't ask and nobody seemed to care. People were so busy there with their own lives, they didn't seem to bother too much with other people's doings. It was very refreshing.

One night Lizzie brought her to the city hall to hear the army band play. It was to raise funds for a good cause, one of the many the Warringtons were involved with. As well they went to three plays; there were so many theatres in the city with things on all the time. Two were funny ones put on by local groups, but the third was Shakespeare's *Hamlet* staged by a Dublin theatre company normally based in the beautiful Saoirse Theatre in Dublin but that was on tour for the summer. To Grace's amazement Peter Cullen played the forlorn prince of Denmark; she wouldn't have recognised him but for his name on the bill, he was so compelling and believable. She went to the stage door afterwards to congratulate him. She felt a bit forward doing it, but then she was glad she had, because he remembered her from the dance night in Dingle and seemed delighted to see her. He signed the playbill for her and told her how well she was looking.

He introduced her to May Cullen, his wife and owner of the theatre company, who was charming and pretty and teased Peter mercilessly.

'You look so much better, Grace. Be sure to keep dancing,' he said to her. Lizzie overheard and asked what Peter had meant by it, and that night the doctor's wife put a record on the gramophone, 'Goodnight, Irene, Goodnight' by someone called Nat King Cole, and Hugh moved the kitchen table aside and danced Grace slowly around the floor. It was such fun.

All the way back on the train and bus, she'd been asking herself if she was doing the right thing to come home, but now after that greeting from Seán O'Connor, she knew she belonged here in Knocknashee. She walked slowly through the town, greeted by so many friendly faces – it was market day and sunny, and everyone was out; the place was bustling – and children kept rushing up to her shouting, 'Miss Fitz! You're back! We thought you'd left us!' So it seemed it wasn't just the undertaker's grandchildren who'd had the strange notion she'd left them without a word.

'Why on earth did ye think I'd run away?' she asked as Mikey O'Shea and Aisling Walsh insisted on carrying her bag between them, one handle each.

'It was the burning, miss!' confided Aisling. 'Mammy said the *cailleach*' – in her excitement she'd forgotten not to use that word aloud – 'was burning clothes and things, a big bonfire in the garden the day you went, so we thought you weren't coming back at all.'

'Well, here I am, so there was no need to worry. Sure maybe she was having a clear-out.' She smiled reassuringly, and they relaxed. 'Now I'm thinking, if it's a good summer, we can take advantage of the fine weather and maybe plant our own little garden again and grow some more vegetables and flowers?'

Last summer she'd delighted in seeing the sense of achievement on the children's faces as they took home their own carrots or potatoes for dinner. It was worth all the hard work of digging and planting and treating the greenfly with soapy water and harvesting. With a lighter calliper and her exercise, she hoped it would be easier on her back this year.

'Oh yes, Miss Fitz, please!' Her two little helpers were distracted from their fears and wild stories about bonfires.

She took her bag back from them at the corner by the post office – she didn't want them to witness a scene if Agnes was still angry with her – and limped on alone. As she turned into the front garden of the only home she'd ever known, she noticed a burnt patch of ground and a lumpy heap of dampened ashes beside the gate into the schoolyard next door, with something metal poking up among them, and black scorch marks on the white wall. So it was true; Agnes had been burning things. It was strange. There was only a small yard behind, but for her sister, normally so private, to do something like that on full display of everyone was odd.

With a slightly hollow feeling in her stomach, she tapped on the front door, then opened it and stood for a moment, listening. No sound. Nothing in the hallway had changed...except when she turned to hang up her coat, there was a man's black jacket on the hook she normally used. Keeping her coat on because there was no other hook, she peeped into the dark sitting room to see if there was a visitor. No one there, but a trace of a fire in the fireplace, something she'd never seen in here before. Agnes usually kept it closed up until the summer made it warm enough for her to sit in, enjoying some 'peace and quiet', as if Grace was playing the trombone in the kitchen every morning.

Everything seemed much the same in the kitchen as well, though there was a new mug on the dresser. Her own mug, the one with the violets, which she'd brought home from the hospital with her – Sister Ahern had given it to her as a leaving present – was nowhere to be seen. She hoped Agnes hadn't broken it in a rage and then bought her this rather horrible plain brown one as a replacement. Before their last encounter, she would never have even considered that Agnes might break one of her treasured belongings on purpose, but when she thought back to that moment, with Agnes screaming that awful curse, it seemed only too possible.

And it wouldn't be unlike her sister to think the brown mug was nicer than the one with the violets, which she'd always considered frivolous.

Leaving her bag in the hall, she climbed the stairs, noting with pleasure that even after the long journey, she was a little bit more limber thanks to all the hot baths, and went directly to her bedroom. All her clothes and books were still there. She felt a rush of relief and realised that Aisling Walsh's childish gossip about the bonfire had troubled her more than she'd thought. Though she couldn't see Nellie, the rag doll her mother had made for her. She checked under the blankets. Not there.

No, even if Agnes had been cruel enough to burn poor Nellie – and that was a lot harder to believe than a broken cup, so Nellie must be somewhere – one little rag doll was hardly going to make that big bonfire. Agnes had been talking a lot about replacing the mattress on her bed. Maybe that was it, and she'd burnt the old one? The steel springs might explain the metal poking up from the ashes.

The door to Agnes's room was ajar, and it didn't look like the mattress had been changed. It was hard to tell, though. Maurice's room was a shrine to him as always, dust motes dancing in the air in the almost empty room.

A strange thought popped into her mind. Had Agnes burnt Grace's hospital wheelchair? She'd always hated that chair and talked often of getting rid of it.

She opened the door into the spare room where Agnes had shoved the chair out of sight, the room with all her parents' belongings.

It was empty.

Not technically empty. There was a new single bed and a desk and a chest of drawers with a mirror on top. But it was empty of what should be here – the boxes of her parents' things, the shelves of their clothing, her father's beloved jumper that Kathleen had knitted for him, the easel, the artbooks, the Boland's biscuit tin that contained their letters. All of it, gone.

As Grace stood frozen, there were footsteps on the stairs behind her, and through the throbbing in her head came voices, a man's and a woman's, and then a little laugh, the one her sister usually used with the canon when she was being at her nicest.

'Goodness, Grace, fancy seeing you here,' Agnes trilled. 'What a surprise. I wondered whose bag that was cluttering up my hall. I had no idea you were coming home today.'

Grace turned, pivoting on her good left leg to face her. 'Where are Mammy and Daddy's things, Agnes?'

A dour-faced, black-haired man stood beside Agnes, staring dolefully, but Grace was in too much shock to even acknowledge him.

'In a moment, goodness…' Again the fake laugh. 'Francis, this is my sister, Grace, who has been filling in as assistant teacher while I was short of help. Grace, this is Francis Sheehan. He's a fully trained teacher. We're so lucky to have him with us.'

The dour man muttered, 'Nice to meet you, Miss Fitzgerald,' before turning sideways to sidle past Grace into the room that had been emptied of her parents' things.

'Where are Mammy and Daddy's belongings, Agnes?' Grace repeated, fighting to stay calm.

'Goodness me, take that look off your face – and you could at least say hello to Francis, who is lodging here.' Agnes was still trilling and smiling, though Grace could sense the fury bubbling beneath.

'Where are they, Agnes?'

Agnes sighed, making it clear Grace was testing her patience. 'That rubbish? I burnt it. It was taking up space and of no use to anyone. I gave the clothes to the convent in Dingle for distribution to the poor and burnt everything else. Why do you ask?' She raised an eyebrow, as if Grace had been enquiring about a bundle of old newspapers or something else insignificant.

'I don't believe you…' She could hardly get the words out; acid bile rose in her gullet. 'You couldn't have…' Maybe her sister was joking, just to be cruel.

Francis had closed the spare room door behind him now, and this time Agnes didn't trill her answer but spoke in a low, dry and toneless voice. 'I've no idea what was there, but everything, yes.'

'Mammy and Daddy's letters? You didn't burn those?'

Agnes fixed her with a look, her pale-blue eyes entirely emotionless. 'Letters? Oh, those old papers…'

'How could you?' She was hoarse with tears now. 'You know that was all I had of them…'

'All you had?' Agnes's brow furrowed in mock confusion. 'Nothing in that room was yours, Grace, in the same way that nothing in this house is yours. It's entirely my business who I rent my rooms to, and it was necessary to make space for Francis. There was nowhere else to put things – we have to keep Maurice's room ready for him at all times.'

'You could have at least put their letters in *my* room!'

'*Your* room?' Agnes's tone was as cold as ice. She took a step closer. '*Yours*? You don't own that room, Grace. This is my house. That is just the room you sleep in, and you only get to stay in it for free out of my generosity.'

'For free?' The accusing question came bursting out of her; she hardly recognised her own voice. 'For *free*, Agnes?'

Agnes shrank back and half closed her eyes, then opened them again, as hard as before. 'Yes, Grace, for free, and I suggest you go to that room now, until you've calmed down. Because I have things to do and I've no time for this childishness.' She turned then and went down the stairs very quickly, clearly not expecting Grace to be able to catch up with her.

But Grace did. Between her leg being so much better and the rage she felt, she was able to move faster than she'd ever done before.

'*Free?*' she spat as they reached the bottom of the stairs, and Agnes spun round with a gasp and recoiled in fright, shocked to find Grace standing right behind her. '*Free*, Agnes, when you've been spending every penny of my wages on jaunting around the countryside with Canon Rafferty? Does your precious priest know you've been stealing from me?'

Her sister gasped in outrage and threw a sharp glance up the stairs towards Francis's closed door.

'Stealing from you?' she hissed back, white now but for those two red high spots on her thin cheeks. '*Stealing*? How dare you, when I've done so much for you. I paid your hospital bills. I gave you a place to live, fed you and bought you clothes. I had no obligation to care for you. I could have sent you to the orphanage when our parents died, but instead I saddled myself with you, you ungrateful wretch. You're the reason I'm not married to Cyril. You're a scrounger and a drain, and yet you *dare* to complain that I bought a few things to make my life easier, and maybe gave a little to the canon for charity for the poor children. You're selfish and spoiled to want to deprive them of it –'

'And did the poor children enjoy the hotels and the wine?' Grace hissed back. She hadn't wanted to say it, but the sight of that empty room... Well, she couldn't keep silent any longer simply to keep the peace.

Agnes recoiled again, her ramrod-straight back pressed to the hall-stand, next to which hung her pale-blue coat and the man's black jacket.

'I *knew* it,' she choked out. 'You've been snooping around in *my* filing cabinet, reading *my* school files. How dare you spy on me, Grace! You're lucky I couldn't believe it of you. If I'd known, I would have written to the Department of Education and had you dismissed for gross misconduct. As it is I merely informed the canon, as chair of the school board, that you had decided to resign due to ill health, and now we have a proper teacher at last. We're so grateful for Francis – he came from Northern Ireland.'

Grace stared, shaking, rendered entirely speechless. So that's why Agnes had pretended to be surprised she was home, even though the summer term started tomorrow. Francis Sheehan wasn't just a new lodger; he was her replacement at the school.

Agnes tried and failed to hide her smirk, so delighted at causing even more pain to Grace that she couldn't disguise it. 'Oh yes, Grace. So maybe you'll remember from now on which side your bread is buttered. Maybe now that you have no job, you'll be a little more grateful to me for giving you a roof over your head and food on the table, all for nothing. And don't worry – you can pay me back by lighting the school fires in the morning and cleaning and cooking for myself and Francis, because we will be busy teaching the children in the way they should be taught instead of you filling their heads with nonsense and showing them maps of places they will never get to see, encouraging them to dream dreams that will never come true, as if the lives they live here in Knocknashee are not enough for them…'

Grace picked up her bag from the hallway and walked out of the front door.

Before stepping out into the road, she turned aside to look at the pile of ashes, all that remained of her parents' belongings. The half-buried metal on top of the heap was the Boland's biscuit tin that had contained their letters, the girl in the parasol barely visible. A drift of paler-grey ashes spilled out of it as she stroked it with her hand, and there among them were two little blue buttons that once were eyes. Nellie, the rag doll.

Agnes stood watching from the door as Grace limped to the gate. 'Where do you think you are going?' she barked.

'I don't know, Agnes. Anywhere but here.'

Agnes chuckled then and rolled her eyes like Grace was just being silly. 'Yes, yes, Grace, always the dramatic. Until you realise there's no money for you to go anywhere, and no one to take you in. Then we'll see who'll be in need of a sister.'

Grace paused to look back at her, hand on the gate. 'As far as I'm concerned, I don't have a sister.'

Agnes sniggered. 'I'll see you before nightfall, Grace.' And she stepped back inside and closed the door.

Standing out in the middle of the cobbled street, Grace felt curiously numb, no tears, no despair.

What should she do now?

She still had a week's worth of wages left in the post office and a few pounds in her purse. The trip to Cork had cost almost nothing, and the Warringtons hadn't let her put her hand in her pocket for anything, so the only things she'd bought were a new bottle of lilac ink, some more writing paper, some cakes and chocolates for the children in the hospital and a bunch of flowers for the Warringtons' house on the day she went home. They in turn had given her a beautiful engraved fountain pen and made her promise to write often, now they knew the letters would no longer go astray.

But after that money was gone, there would be no more wages.

So where could she go? What could she do? Even if she had enough left to get back to Cork, she didn't think she should. The Warringtons' kind offer of accommodation was timed for September, and she could hardly take them up on it unless they got the funding for the new teaching job. She couldn't go back with nothing in her pocket and no way of earning anything and demand they look after her.

'Grace? What are you doing just standing here?'

It was Charlie McKenna.

She tried to smile at him. 'I don't know what I'm doing, to be honest, Charlie.'

'Aren't you going to go into the house?'

'No, Charlie. I don't think I'll ever be setting foot in that house again.' She couldn't believe she'd said those words, but they were true; she knew it as they came out of her mouth. There was no going back.

He stood looking at her for a long moment, then nodded and reached down to take her bag. He straightened and linked her arm. 'Well, at least come and have a cup of tea and a bowl of soup, Gracie, while you think about it,' he said. 'I have something in the house to show you, and besides, it's as well not to be making a big decision on an empty stomach.'

As soon as he'd said it, she realised how hungry she was, and she walked gratefully at his side down the street, past the post office to his little house. Declan had left his copybook open on the table, and she smiled to see it. Every character he'd written was legible; there was no longer any fear of him not passing the exam when it came.

'Is this what you wanted to show me? It's wonderful how well he's doing.'

'He is doing well, thanks to you, Gracie, but no, that's not what I meant. But I want to get you fed first – you look pale and famished.' He served her up a bowl of carrot and parsnip soup from the big saucepan on the range, cut her a slice of bread and buttered it, made her a cup of tea and sat down opposite her, watching her as she ate.

'So what happened just now, between you and your sister?' he asked, as soon as she'd got the soup and bread into herself and felt a little stronger.

She tried to keep her voice calm as she answered him. 'I've lost my job, Charlie. She's replaced me with a man called Francis Sheehan, and he's lodging in the house and…' She was going to tell him about all her parents' things being burnt, but the words stuck in her throat. She swallowed. 'I just had to get out of there. I couldn't bear it.'

He reached for her hand and patted it, his kindly face crinkled with concern but also encouragement. 'Maybe it's for the best, Gracie. You deserve a life, one of your own. You're like your parents, God be good to them, and Maurice was a grand lad too, if a bit quiet and reclusive, but I don't know where that sister of yours was got. She is poison. Get away from her, girleen. However you do it, get away.'

'But to where, Charlie?'

'There's a place for you here, Gracie, while you decide, and all the food you can eat and tea to drink. The back bedroom, 'tis all yours, and nobody would put in or out on you.'

'I couldn't ask you to…' Grace was overwhelmed by his generosity.

'Ara, Gracie, *a stór*, you didn't ask me. I offered.'

'I couldn't impose like that…' Tears filled her eyes.

'Will you hoult your whist, girleen?' He patted her hand again. 'Your father was a wonderful friend to me, and your mother as well, so 'twould be my pleasure to help you out. We'll be the talk of the place, but sure every last man Jack of us in this village knows what the *cailleach* is like, so the only mystery is how you stuck her so long. Now' – he stood up from the table – 'maybe this will help take your mind off things.'

He went to his sack, hanging from the nail in the wall, and extracted a small flat parcel.

She took it from him in surprise. 'What is it, a book?' There were a lot of the pink American stamps stuck all over the parcel, and her name and address were written on it, but in a different hand, more flowery than that of Richard Lewis.

'No point in guessing, Gracie. Open it and find out.' Charlie picked up her bag and headed for the hall door. 'I'll take this up to your room for you and find you some sheets and a pillow and few bits, and I'll send Declan over to the schoolhouse later on for a box of anything you've left behind.'

'Oh please, don't send Declan there.' The thought of making that gentle, nervous boy ask Agnes for anything struck fear into her heart. 'I'll do it myself.'

He turned to wink at her before he carried on up the stairs. 'He's a lot stronger than he used to be, Gracie. I'd say he's able for your sister's tongue now.'

While he was gone, Grace cut the string with the knife he'd handed to her and unwrapped the parcel. Inside was indeed a book, with a plain brown paper cover on it, on which was written *For your friend Tilly, from Richard's sister, Sarah*. Amazed, she looked inside the paper cover; it was titled *The Well of Loneliness*, by someone called Radclyffe Hall. What a strange present across the ocean, from one young woman to another she had never met. What was behind it? Tilly wasn't much of a reader, so Grace wasn't sure she'd like it, but she'd pass it on.

She thought for a moment that was all there was in the parcel, but when she peeped inside the book, taking care not to crease the spine – she hated if someone read a new book before her – the usual envelope was tucked inside. Delighted, she shook it out from between the leaves and opened it.

Dear Miss Fitzgerald,

My sister thinks your friend Tilly will enjoy this book. I have no idea why, but Sarah says she has a friend who loves it, and she thinks Tilly sounds just like her.

Grace grinned. It was hard to imagine there was another girl like Tilly anywhere in the world. She hoped she'd described her properly in the letter and that Sarah hadn't got the wrong idea; Sarah was hardly likely to be friends with a down-at-heel farming girl. The daughter of a wealthy rancher, perhaps, with herds of cattle and horses.

I have thought long and hard about your story, and it seems to me that you should report your sister and that priest to the cops, though I understand if you are reluctant to do so. It's hard when it's family, I'm sure.

He was right. There was no chance of her ever reporting her own sister to Sergeant Keane, and she wasn't sure yet how culpable the canon was.

I think it's most unfair that due to your sister's behavior, you have been deprived of a visit to England. Nathan tells me that Sister Kenny has returned to Australia, but he still believes she will be in Detroit in a year or two. Meanwhile, perhaps you will benefit from a visit to Warm Springs here in Georgia.

Grace chuckled at the absurdity of this offer, even though her heart was warmed by his extreme kindness. It was almost comical how on one level, she and this boy knew so much about each other, yet Richard Lewis obviously hadn't a clue what 'having no money' really meant. In his world, it probably meant you couldn't afford a second house, or a yacht.

I have to say, I feel personally responsible for your difficulties, for advising you to open your own account and move your savings. I realize if I'd never said anything, your sister's scheme would have gone unnoticed for much longer, but it's very hard when a rift happens in a family, and it must be very painful for you. And perhaps telling you about Sister Kenny was just a way of creating further disappointment in your life.

In fact, telling her about Sister Kenny had worked out beautifully. And she wasn't sorry she'd found out the truth about her wages. Yet he was right in some ways. Life would be so much easier if she hadn't found out about the money. She wouldn't be out of a job and a place to live, her parents' belongings would still be in the spare room, and the little children of Knocknashee would still be happy. Francis Sheehan, by the look of him, was clearly a dull, sour man, cut from the same cloth as her sister, who seemed delighted with him, and she dreaded him raising his hand to her beloved pupils.

So partly in order to make amends for meddling in your life with such terrible consequences, I would like to offer you this ticket from Cork to New York, first class of course, so you will have a comfortable bedroom and stewards to help you with your luggage and whatever else you need.

What? No. Not possible… Her mind reeling, she peered into the envelope. Inside was a thick creamy piece of card.

A ticket to America.

First class.

After she'd recovered her breath, she returned to the letter, reading on in growing astonishment.

I hope you won't feel that I'm putting too much pressure on you, Miss Fitzgerald, but Nunez's editor at The Capital *thinks this would be a very interesting way to complete our story about the bottle, and the newspaper will pay all your expenses at Warm Springs. So please don't see this as charity. You are clearly a strong and independent young woman, and nothing could be further from my mind. On the contrary, you would be doing us all a great favor.*

If you are willing, I can pick you up in New York on June 17th, and I will accompany you to Georgia. You can come and stay on the island for a week, and let Nunez take a picture of you where your bottle came ashore, and meet Sarah, and Nathan too if he can get away from work for a short while, and then I and my sister will drive you straight to Warm Springs and bring you back to your ship after your month of treatment.

Yours sincerely,

Richard Lewis.

PS Would you mind sending me a telegram to the post office on East Beach, St. Simons, just a simple yes or no, because a letter might take weeks, or get lost, and the newspaper has to plan for the feature.

CHAPTER 23

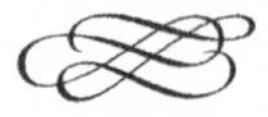

'Of course you must go.' Tilly was adamant. 'You must send the telegram immediately, as soon as the post office opens tomorrow. Have you the money for it? I can help.'

'It's fine. I have some in my account. But across the ocean, Tilly? To meet total strangers?'

They were sitting at the McKennas' kitchen table, together with Declan and Charlie. Up until now, only Charlie had known about her American letters, and even he knew very little about the boy writing them. She wanted to tell these three dear friends together and get their advice. At Grace's request, Declan had bicycled all the way to Tilly's farm to fetch her, and Tilly had followed him home, riding her pony, Ned, who was tied up outside.

'Do you think he's a good person?' asked Declan, his hair falling over his face.

'I think he is. Listen to the sorts of things he says...' She read out some portions of the letters to them, the descriptive bits, nothing too personal, as Charlie sat shaking his head in amazement.

'I think Tilly's right, Gracie. He sounds fine, and you should go. Your father would have loved to hear about this, so he would. When we were *garsúns*, he used to always be dreaming about America. He had a brother, Con, who went to Chicago back along, oh, I'd say 'twas fifty years ago now. I don't know what ever became of him, but Eddie was fascinated with the place. He might have gone himself, only he had his eye on your mother and she would never leave.'

Grace never knew that. There was so much about her parents she didn't know, and Agnes had never been willing to discuss them at all.

'To America? Really?' she asked, grasping at any chance to talk about them now that she had nothing else left of them.

'Oh, he'd have gone fine, so he would. But your mammy was as much a part of this place as the mountains, and about as movable.' He chuckled.

'But if she'd agreed, they'd have gone?'

'In a heartbeat. Sure Eddie was forever going on about Philadelphia and Chicago and Boston. He knew all about them places, reading all about them and all. But Kathleen took not a tack of notice of him, and he gave up in the finish.'

Eddie and Kathleen Fitzgerald. Even to hear their names spoken aloud was lovely.

'Yes, your daddy would be glad to have you meet a real American, so he would. You should go.'

'But first class...' she felt so overwhelmed. 'Isn't it too much to accept?'

'Sure he obviously has so much money he doesn't know what to do with it, and of course he should share it around,' Tilly was decisive in this as she was in everything. She'd picked up quite a lot of Alfie's notions about socialism and was all for taking money off the rich and giving it to the poor. The Spanish Civil War was over, but Alfie was now in Paris with a bunch of communists and writing letters about terrible stories coming out of Germany. 'Besides, he says it's not charity, it's for the newspaper.'

'Maybe he's just saying that to be nice...'

'I think you should go, for your health, Grace,' said Declan, looking at her with melancholy eyes from under his long hair. 'We'll miss you, though.'

'Of course we'll miss her,' Tilly said, 'but she'll be back. And even if you take this job in Cork, we'll all visit each other then, won't we?'

Grace had told them about the Warringtons as well, that maybe she'd be at college and teaching at the hospital in September if all went according to plan. 'Of course we will. Lizzie said the other spare room, the one upstairs, can be used if I want anyone to visit, and I want all of you to come when you can. I just wish I could have every child from Knocknashee visit me as well... Oh, the poor things. I'll have to write each of them a note.'

'You do that, and I'll deliver them for you,' said Charlie. 'And now, Grace, you've asked our advice, and we're all agreed you should go, so as Tilly says, you get over to Nancy first thing and send that telegram. Now how about a cup of tea?'

'I'll make it.' Declan rose to his feet.

'There's a warm brack in the oven,' she said to him as he brought mugs and milk to the table. 'I threw it in while you went for Tilly and Charlie was out doing the garden.'

'I thought I smelled something baking, but I didn't dare to hope.' Charlie rubbed his hands in glee as Declan placed the tin with the hot glazed brack on the table and brought the butter dish. 'I love a bit of brack. Now wasn't it a good idea of mine to bring you here to live.'

After everyone had eaten and declared it was the best brack they'd ever tasted – even Tilly, whose mother was such a fine baker, asked for the recipe – it was time for bed.

Grace followed Tilly out, where Tilly untied Ned from the lamp-post outside Charlie's door.

'I'm so glad you're not living with Agnes any more. It's so great to be able to just see you face to face and not have to be exchanging letters,' Tilly said, unknotting the reins.

'I know. I wish I could get out to you like I used to do as well.' Grace sighed, remembering when she was a child, before the polio, running up the steep rocky hill to Tilly's farm, beyond the graveyard where her parents were buried. 'Oh, hold on, I have something for you.'

She went back inside and came out with the book. 'I never heard of it, but Richard's sister, Sarah, thought you might like it? I've no idea why?' She handed it over.

Tilly looked as perplexed as she was. 'Thanks, though I think she might be confusing me with you. You're the one for the books, Grace.' She popped the small book in her pocket. 'What if I came with the trap one of the days next week, and you could come out to the farm that way? You could even stay overnight – Mam would love it.'

Grace smiled, basking in the warmth of their friendship once more. 'I'd love that too.'

'So that's settled then. Good night, Grace!'

Grace watched in awe as her friend launched herself on Ned's bare back – she didn't bother with a saddle, just reins – like the cowboys you'd see at the pictures, lithe as anything. What must it be like, she wondered, to be that agile?

* * *

SHE HAD NEVER SENT a telegram in her life, but Nancy O'Flaherty was very helpful and handed her a sheet to fill out with what she wanted to say.

'How much per word?' Grace asked, before she set pen to paper.

'Ah, don't worry your head, Miss Fitz, send as many words as you need. Sure it's next to nothing to send a telegram,' Nancy reassured her.

Grace strongly suspected the postmistress was lying and was planning to pay for it herself. She probably had heard the whole story of Grace leaving the schoolhouse and moving in with Charlie by now and wanted to show she approved.

Grace kept the telegram as short as she could. *YES*, she wrote, and handed the sheet over the counter.

Nancy glanced at it with an amused expression. 'Are you certain, Grace? Will they know what you mean, or who you are? You haven't even put your name to it.'

'It's fine, thank you. They'll know who I am and what I mean.'

'I suppose whoever it is wouldn't be getting that many telegrams from Knocknashee,' agreed Nancy as she sent it off. 'Anything else, Miss Fitz?'

'Just to post this.' She handed over the letter she'd written to the Warringtons, using the new pen they'd given her when she was leaving and the lilac ink and paper she'd bought in Cork. She had asked them to put her up for two days while she got organised for the boat trip. 'And I'll need to take out the rest of my wages from my account. I can't save any of it this time around, I'm afraid.'

To her delight there was more in the account than she expected. The department paid two weeks in arrears, so they'd owed her for the last two weeks she'd done before Easter. If she was very careful with her money, maybe she'd have enough to get by.

* * *

A TELEGRAM CAME BACK from Richard Lewis the same day, thanking her in ten words for agreeing to the visit.

She tried to keep herself busy for the next few days while she waited for the Warringtons' reply.

It was strange having no job and no Agnes to keep her tied up with an endless list of tasks, but she coached Declan for his exam every day, though he hardly needed it any more, and took over the cooking and cleaning in return for her bed and board, which Charlie refused to take any money for.

She wasn't sure of herself in the kitchen, but Charlie and Declan seemed to think she was a French cordon bleu chef or something; they polished off every morsel and were effusive in their praise. It was such a pleasure after cooking for Agnes, who had never offered a word of appreciation but was quick to point out if the shepherd's pie was too salty or if the potatoes were not mashed smoothly enough.

She saw Tilly nearly every day, including an overnight stay from which she was sent away with a huge basket of eggs and honey and cake, all from the farm, some of which she planned to bring to the Warringtons because she knew, like Charlie, they would refuse to take any money for helping her. Tilly said she hadn't had time to look at

Sarah's book yet because the sheep were lambing, but she promised to have it read soon and let Grace know what she thought of it. Grace secretly suspected she never would.

She didn't see Agnes once.

Declan had insisted on going over on the Monday with a large wooden box to gather Grace's things, and he came back looking a bit shook but still standing at least; he refused to say anything about what was said.

So at least she had her colourful crocheted bedspread and her books, as well as her mother's pictures, which Charlie promised to keep for her while she was away gallivanting. There was an old wardrobe in her room that smelled of mothballs and a chest of drawers for her meagre clothing collection. She stacked the books on the low windowsill and hung the pictures on the wall. It was small but it was cosy, and most importantly it was under a different roof to Agnes.

The following Sunday was the first day she would see her sister again, at Mass, and she wondered how it would feel, or if Agnes would even acknowledge her.

As she walked through the town with Declan and Charlie, one on each side of her, she tried to take her mind off the coming meeting by thinking about the Sunday lunch she was going to serve. She'd got some pork chops from Carroll's butchers on Saturday and planned to fry them with onions and serve them with a nice applesauce made from the cooking apples that Charlie had in his pantry. There were several large Bramley apple trees out the Geata Bán road, and everyone took apples from them in the autumn and kept them wrapped in paper so they could use them all year until the trees were laden with fruit again. She had some left-over boiled potatoes from yesterday that she'd roll in melted goose fat, and then she'd roast them in the oven to go with the meat...

They passed through the church gate and up the path, and then down the aisle, and there was Agnes in her pale-blue coat, sitting rigidly right at the front. Grace prayed with all her heart that her sister would not look around and see her.

The three of them took a pew nearer the back. She hoped it might be Father Iggy today, but as Mikey rang the bell as the altar boy, the canon came out through the sacristy door in his vestments.

After a stern glance around the church, he turned his back to the congregation and started speaking the Tridentine Mass in Latin in his whispery voice. Like all the rest of the congregation, Grace knew the responses to the prayers by heart.

On and on he went, and it seemed even longer than it normally was. He added extra Gregorian chants, sung by himself, and everyone mumbled along, though in truth they had no idea what he was saying.

When it came to the homily, though, he switched to Irish, and with mounting horror, Grace realised she was the subject of it. He spoke of indecent behaviour, of people in the parish living in situations that were thoroughly reprehensible, single women living under the same roof as men to whom they were not related, causing scandal and bringing shame. He spoke of showing a good example to young people, of respecting the memory of those who went before, of letting families down by behaving in such a wanton manner, especially when the young woman involved had been responsible for the souls of so many young children in the town.

Her cheeks burnt as she felt the eyes of her neighbours upon her. Declan flushed and went to stand, but Charlie leant over and placed a hand on his leg, shaking his head slightly.

After what felt like an interminably long diatribe, the priest reverted to Latin and finished the Mass. She wanted to die as she went up to receive, fearing he would refuse her but not daring to risk not going up either. He gave her communion, thankfully, but not without a withering look. She kept her head down as she walked back to her seat, and as she passed her sister, Agnes glanced at her for a split second with a small, cold smile. It had all been planned.

Out in the churchyard did she imagine everyone glancing their way? Some people gave her a sympathetic smile or an encouraging nod, but most people scurried home, not wishing to get involved in either side of what was clearly after becoming a feud between Grace and the Church.

'I'm going to speak to him,' Declan was fuming. 'He had no right making a show of Grace and us like that.' Grace had never seen him like that.

His father placed his hand on his shoulder. 'We'll do no such thing, Declan. Come on away home now, *a garsún*, and leave him at it…'

'But Da, how can you say that? After the way he treated us, after everything?' Declan was hurt and confused as much as livid.

'Because I know that auld priest of old, Declan, and I know we can't win against him,' Charlie murmured as he led Grace and Declan away. 'We're doing all right, we've a nice little place, and I've the job and everything. And Gracie is on her way soon – she's out of the clutches of the *cailleach*.'

'Ah, Da, you can't let it go…'

'Declan, *a mhic,* listen to me, will you, for the love of God. He need only snap his fingers and we lose everything. Don't rile him. You have to learn to pick your fights in this life, and don't be foolish enough to pick ones you haven't a hope in hell of winning.'

'So we let him destroy us again, is that it?' Declan demanded, shaking his father's hand off his shoulder.

The look of sheer sorrow on Charlie's face made Grace link the older man's arm and squeeze it.

'We just have to make the best of what we have now. We'll make a good life, you and me, but we can't go to war with yer man above. That won't end well for us – trust me, Declan, it won't. Nobody can take on the Church and win.'

CHAPTER 24

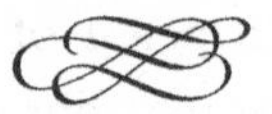

It was Friday, but both Warringtons had taken the day off in her honour, and they'd had a farewell lunch in the grand Imperial Hotel in Cork. She was all packed to take the boat that evening, in a couple of hours. She closed the lid of the enormous case resting on the bed.

When she'd arrived on Monday, Lizzie had laughed at the smallness of her brown battered suitcase and had insisted on lending her this huge one. Grace pointed out that she hadn't enough to fill it, but Lizzie said she knew that and that was why they were going to spend Friday out shopping for clothes.

Refusing to listen to Grace's protests, the doctor's wife had bought her a whole wardrobe of lovely light dresses, because Richard Lewis had said Georgia was so much hotter than Ireland. She also insisted on a bathing costume for Warm Springs, which Grace wasn't sure was necessary but Lizzie said just to be sure, as well as a new coat, several hats... Grace couldn't stop her. There was nothing much to be done about her shoes because of the calliper, but apart from that, she was going to look more elegant than she'd ever done in her life.

Her right leg had stiffened up again during her time in Knocknashee, even though she'd done her best to warm it with a hot water bottle, but the few days of treatment Lizzie gave her helped a lot, and she was more mobile again now. Hugh told her that in first class, she should be able to have hot baths as many times a day as she wished, and there might even be a nurse who could help her with the exercises.

She pulled the heavy leather case to the floor and turned it up on its side to do the straps so it would be ready to be lifted out to the car. Her heart pounded as she fixed one buckle after another. This journey was going to be terrifying, but wonderful...

There was a knock at the front door, and she glanced out of the window to see a telegram boy, in his uniform and bright buttons, on the step. Moments later Hugh's heavy feet crossed the hall as he went to answer it.

'Telegram for a Dr Warrington, sir.'

'Thank you, that's me.' The door closed, and she heard him return to the kitchen, then a murmur of voices as he spoke with his wife.

A few minutes later, there was a tap on her door. She pulled the last strap tight and went to open it. Hugh stood there, and unusually for him, he looked serious. 'Will you come into the kitchen, Grace?' he asked.

In the kitchen Lizzie stood with her back to the range, looking as solemn as her husband.

Grace's stomach turned over. 'What is it? Is everything all right?'

'Oh, Grace,' murmured Lizzie, her eyes full of tears. 'I'm not sure we should tell you this...'

'Tell me *what*?'

Hugh put his hand on Grace's shoulder, facing her. 'We've had a telegram from Dr Ryan in Knocknashee...' His eyes that were normally crinkled in laughter were dark with worry, and she could see the inner turmoil he was experiencing.

'What's happened?' Her mind raced in horror. Had something happened to Tilly? Charlie? Declan?

'I'm afraid your sister, Agnes, has had a stroke.'

Grace felt a sound like water rushing in her ears. 'Oh, good God... Are you sure?' That day she'd left the house before Easter, she'd thought Agnes was having an attack or something, but it was only rage. 'Sometimes she has these turns?' She knew from the doctor's expression she was grasping at straws.

Hugh shook his head, confirming her worst fears. 'She's alive but is almost paralysed and unable to speak.'

'Oh no, oh no...please God...' Images flooded through her mind. America. Peach trees. The packed suitcase. Richard Lewis... Agnes, alone and unable to move, with no one to care for her...

'We seriously thought of not telling you, Grace,' said Lizzie. 'We were so worried if you knew, you might think you had to go home.'

'I do have to go home.' The dawning certainty made her feel ill. There was nobody else. Maurice was a priest and too far away. It would have to be her.

'You don't have to, you really don't,' begged Lizzie. 'Nobody would blame you if you don't go back. Oh, I knew we shouldn't have told her, Hugh...'

'You had to tell me,' said Grace firmly. 'How could you not? She's my sister.'

Lizzie grabbed her hand as if she could physically restrain her from going back to Knocknashee. 'But everyone knows the kind of person she is, Grace. She is undeserving of your care and compassion...'

Grace hugged her in return but then stepped back, shaking her head. 'And that's exactly why I have to go, Lizzie. There's no one else in the world who cares for Agnes one little bit. She has driven everyone away. She is all alone in the world, apart from me.'

Hugh spoke then. 'But a stroke like this is catastrophic. She won't get better, Grace. You are her next of kin, I know, but you should not have to sacrifice your whole life and future for someone who has been nothing but cruel to you.'

'Despite everything, she took me in when I left here. She gave me a home.'

'Only so she could exploit you.'

'Even when she took away my job, she didn't throw me out. I left of my own accord.'

'Because she burnt your parents' things. That was one of the cruellest things I've ever heard. Nobody would blame you even a little bit if you decided to let her fend for herself.'

'How can she fend for herself? She will have no wages now, nothing to pay anyone to look after her. I'll get back my old job as assistant at the school – I'll make sure the canon employs me.' Her heart raced; she was finding it hard to breathe.

Hugh started pacing the kitchen, as he always did when agitated. 'You don't need to do this, Grace. I can write back to Dr Ryan, say you've already left for America and that when you get back, you're under my orders to stay here in Cork, undergoing further treatment, and as a result, you are not in a position to care for her. Nobody would question it – it's the truth.'

'I need to think…' was all Grace could manage. She had to get out in the fresh air. She had to breathe.

Lizzie followed her to the door. 'Grace, you don't have to do anything you don't want to do. You owe her nothing.'

She walked down the steps out into the spring day. The bright sunshine seemed to mock her misery. Just when her life had finally begun, it was going to be stopped in its tracks.

Whatever Hugh and Lizzie said, she could see the faces of her parents in her mind. Agnes was their child, her sister. She couldn't abandon her…could she?

She envied people who could walk and walk for hours. She wished she could walk and walk, think this through, but she couldn't. Instead she headed for the nearest post office, one street away. Better not to think after all. Just do what had to be done and get on with it. She asked the postmistress for a telegram form and filled it out with the name and address.

'Make it short – it's going to be expensive,' the postmistress warned, seeing the address in America.

She closed her eyes to think about what she wanted to say. Or if she wanted to say anything at all. Instead she could just get on that boat...

She opened her eyes and wrote rapidly before she could change her mind. *Agnes had stroke. Can't come. Sorry.*

CHAPTER 25

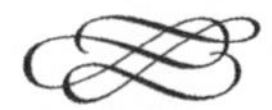

KNOCKNASHEE, DINGLE

June 1939

Grace waited for the canon at the sacristy door. This was going to have to happen. This would have to be sorted for once and for all.

She didn't want to defy this man. He had a reputation and was feared. If Canon Rafferty had an opinion on what a member of the congregation should do, regardless of their feelings on the matter, it inevitably went the priest's way.

But after six weeks of being back in Knocknashee, she'd decided she had to act. Enough was enough.

When she'd returned to mind Agnes, the school board – that is, the canon – had grudgingly given her back her job as assistant teacher, so she had the money to look after her sister. Francis Sheehan had moved up to be the head teacher. He was lodging elsewhere in the village now, in a bigger room now that he could afford it on his increased wages, so at least she didn't have to look at his dour face over breakfast.

His miserable face was the least of the problems, though. It hadn't taken him very long to realise he had full authority over everyone, children and parents, as 'the Master', and he started to go further even than Agnes had done, beating and roaring from one end of the day to the next. When Grace objected, he tore down the map from the wall in the juniors' room and forbade her from teaching the juniors history or geography, or about anything beyond the small confines of where they were born. He said it was getting in the way of them learning their letters and numbers, which was all they needed to know. Even the tin whistles and the piano were banned.

Then this Friday just gone, he'd overstepped the mark entirely. He'd done more than use the strap; he'd thrown Janie O'Shea against the wall. And when one of the boys intervened, he'd punched him in the face and made his nose bleed. The man had to go.

Thirty minutes after Mass ended, the canon eventually emerged, his long soutane, down to his ankles, swishing as he descended into the churchyard.

She stepped forward. 'Canon, I wonder if I might have a word?'

He stopped to look at her in surprise. His wispy hair poked out the side of the four-winged biretta he wore on his head.

'Grace, shouldn't you be at home doing your Christian duty in caring for your sister?' he asked in his whispering tone. 'Poor Agnes, she mustn't be left alone...'

'I know that, Canon, and Teresa, Mrs O'Flaherty's oldest, is sitting with her as she does when I'm working. Perhaps you would like to drop in and see her yourself one of the days?'

She couldn't help saying it. Since Agnes's stroke, the canon hadn't come to see her once. It was as if now that Grace's wages were no longer being spent on him, he had no use for the poor deluded schoolmistress, who was now not even that but a shell of a woman.

Agnes had recovered very little movement since her stroke. Her left arm was useless, and her right hand trembled so much, she had to be fed soup from a spoon and milk through a straw.

Her speech had come back a little, but it was almost impossible to understand unless you knew her well. Sometimes Grace thought the stroke had softened her; sometimes she wasn't so sure. That glint in Agnes's eye could be as much hatred as gratitude.

'It is my curate's job to visit the ssssick,' whispered the canon. He always spoke so quietly, he was hard to hear, but the callousness was loud enough.

'Father O'Riordan has visited my sister every day, that's true, but I thought you and Agnes were special friends, Canon Rafferty.'

The priest fixed her with a hard stare. His dark-blue eyes were rheumy and watery, and his eyebrows, though scant, were long and hung over his eyes, 'Well, Grace,' he answered slowly, and she hated the condescending way he said her name, as if she were eleven still. 'Let me remind you, in case you have forgotten, "by insolence comes nothing but strife." The Book of Proverbs.'

'I didn't mean to be insolent, Father, but it's important I have a word with you in private.' She hated the pleading sound that had crept into in her voice the moment he'd quoted the Bible at her. It was born out of years of subservience to this man. She had to be stronger; she had to stay calm.

He hesitated, still annoyed, but then turned back towards the church. He held the door of the sacristy open, gesturing she should enter ahead of him, then followed her in.

They stood there, facing each other.

'What is on your mind, child?' he whispered.

'I want to be promoted to the position of head teacher in the autumn term, Canon Rafferty, instead of Mr Sheehan.'

She'd practiced this very short speech over and over, but preparing and saying these words to this intimidating man were two totally different things, and her stomach twisted in fright as they came out of her mouth.

The canon looked at her in utter amazement. 'Well, Grace, with all due respect, Knocknashee National School has a perfectly good head teacher in Mr Sheehan, who is older than you are, and as a man, he commands greater respect. He is also fully qualified. So I think it would be best to leave him where he is, don't you?'

'I don't, Canon Rafferty, and I urge you to change your mind. Mr Sheehan is not suitable for the job of teacher at all. The first thing I would do as headmistress would be to ask for his resignation. He is brutal to the children. He threw a girl against the wall and punched a boy so his nose bled –'

'I'm sure Mr Sheehan had his reasons.' He tried to usher her out of the sacristy, as if she was a hysterical female and he was not going to waste any more of his time with her.

'I know about the money, Canon.' She stood firm, keeping her voice steady. She couldn't believe she was doing this, but she was.

'I beg your pardon?' He scowled at her.

'I found a chequebook by accident a long time ago, purporting to be for the school board but with the stubs to all sorts of hotels written in my sister's hand, though it took a while for me to work out what was happening.'

She didn't mention she'd recently had a word with the curate, who as deputy head of the board was able to tell her there was no separate account for the board, only the one for the school.

Canon Rafferty went pale. 'How dare you go snooping! I know nothing about what you're saying!'

'Maybe I should not have been snooping, Canon, but nor should you have been spending my money on wine and dinners out and ice cream in Ballyferriter.'

'Ice cream? Ballyferriter?' He pretended astonishment. 'What on earth are you on about?'

'When I came back to my position as assistant teacher, I searched further, and I've now seen the paying-in book for that account in the filing cabinet, Canon Rafferty. My sister kept everything very neatly, and the exact amount of my wages went in there every two weeks, nothing else, and you were a named signatory as well as my sister.'

He was paler than ever; his lips too were almost white. 'I know nothing about this. Of course I am a signatory on the school board account, but your sister managed it…'

'I want to tell you, Canon Rafferty, that though my sister is neither mobile nor continent, she is capable of a little speech, and she was able to tell me the school board doesn't have its own account. Agnes is no longer your ally, Canon. She knows who her friends are.'

This was not true; Agnes had said nothing about it. But Grace didn't care about telling the priest a lie in order to protect the curate. It served this entitled, evil man right for never visiting her sister once in all the time since she'd had a stroke. He had no way of knowing if Grace was telling him the truth, and he knew it. He opened and closed his mouth several times, but no sound came out; it would have been comical were it not so serious.

'You two have been stealing from me, Canon Rafferty, claiming the money was being saved for my future, but it never was. Now the best way out of this is with the minimum of fuss. So I'll expect a letter confirming my appointment as headmistress in September, after which I will ask Mr Sheehan to resign, a decision you will endorse as chairman, and if he refuses, I will dismiss him with immediate effect. I will teach all the children until another teacher can be found.'

'You have no right whatsoever to come in here demanding –' he began again, but with less conviction now.

'Or, alternatively, Canon, we can discuss this with the Department of Education, Sergeant Keane and the bishop. All of whom would be interested to know what exactly has been going on.'

He swallowed. But said nothing. A heavy silence hung between them. Grace found she was actually enjoying this.

'Do we have a bargain, Canon? My position in return for my silence on the matter of your financial...doings?'

He refused to meet her eye or utter a word, but a single nod of the head gave her all she needed.

CHAPTER 26

One month later, she sat in the kitchen with a hot jar pressed against her leg before trying to exercise it. She had more time to do this now that school was finished for the summer, despite the difficulty of minding Agnes.

It wasn't ideal. The jar was a ceramic thing meant for warming beds, but the hip bath upstairs was too small to be any good, even if the difficulty of carrying up the number of kettles needed was worth the effort. The hope she'd enjoyed at the hospital, that maybe she could be a bit more mobile, was dissipating, but she hated to be lazy and not try anything, so she kept on with the jar and tried to keep moving her toes.

Tilly had suggested coming up to the farm and using the much bigger tin bath they had there, which could be placed in front of the range and was much easier to keep topped up, but she couldn't put her friend to the trouble of fetching her every day in the trap, even if either of them could have spared the time.

Teresa was happy to drop in for a couple of hours every day, and Father Iggy was also very helpful. But there was only so much one could demand of one's friends, so she assured Tilly there was no problem, she could use the jar, it did the trick.

She was interrupted from her exercises by a gentle knock on the front door. Hastily refitting her steel, she got to her feet and hobbled down the hall.

Declan stood there, his piercing blue eyes uncertain but hopeful.

'Hello, Declan, have you a letter for me?' Since he'd passed his post office examination with flying colours, Nancy O'Flaherty had taken the young man on as a part-time postman, dividing Charlie's round, which had grown far too large and busy for him. Getting out and about and having to meet people every day seemed to have made Declan even stronger in himself. He often pushed his dark silky hair away from his face these days instead of hiding behind it, and he was happy to make eye contact now with anyone except the canon.

'I...I...ah...no, it was more I had an idea and thought you might like it. I've rigged up a hot water heating thing that seems to work, and I was thinking if you don't mind, I could bring it over and make you a proper bath house in your backyard. Tilly said you needed a big bath, like, and she had a cattle trough she said would be ideal, not like a small tin bath.' He flushed deep crimson as he spoke, as if the suggestion was somehow improper, and the silky dark hair flopped forward again, hiding his face.

She stared at him in amazement, and it took her a moment to find her voice. 'A bath house? For me?'

'Well, yeah, I hope you don't mind...'

'Ah, Declan, you didn't have to go to all that trouble for me?'

'It wasn't a big job, sure.' He gave her a ghost of a smile, pushing his hair out of his face again. 'Will you come and see it anyway? And if you like it, I can move it over to your place and build a little bath house around it.'

Intrigued, she limped with him up the street and past the post office to the postman's cottage, and sure enough, there in the long narrow yard behind the house, in the open air, stood a cattle trough, cleaned and scrubbed like new. It was placed against the kitchen wall, and a big tank, wrapped in wool and bound with bailer twine, stood squatly beside it.

'So how does it work, Declan?' she asked. It looked a very unlikely contraption.

'Turn that tap and you'll see.' His hair had flopped down again.

She gingerly turned the circular tap near the bottom of the tank, from which came a tube that rested over the side of the trough. Within a few moments, piping-hot water gushed out, steaming in the air, making her gasp.

'How did you do it?' She was amazed.

'Ah, it's boring…' He shrugged.

'Tell me – I'm really interested.'

He looked sideways at her to see if she was serious, that she really wanted to listen to something he could tell her, then concluded she was in earnest and said softly, 'Well, I got some copper and made a tank with a combustion chamber, and then I put a coil of pipe into the combustion chamber, where I fed water from the bottom of the heater into the coil. A tube runs from the coil up the flue, and then I connected that to the hot outlet pipe. The water gets hot in the coil fairly fast and then heats the tank, and I wrapped it in wool to keep it from cooling too fast.'

'Declan, that's brilliant! And how did you know how to do it?' She couldn't help thinking his intelligence was wasted on a post round. Not that Charlie McKenna was stupid, but he'd not stayed at school past twelve, so he hadn't had much of an education.

He swallowed. 'I used to work in a big house, up the country, and they had one, more elaborate than this. It was always breaking down, and the man that used to fix it showed me how. I thought I could make a smaller version here. It will do the job for your leg, I thought.'

Grace knew from Charlie that as well as spending his time in an industrial school and doing lessons, the boys there were sent to work on local farms and businesses, ostensibly to give them some training, but they never saw a penny of their wages.

'Well, I think that's amazing,' she said as she turned off the tap. 'But would you not want it for yourself?' She knew there was running cold water in the McKenna house and a big range in the kitchen, but there was no back boiler on the stove to heat water, and father and son washed under the freezing tap in the back yard.

'Ah no, we're grand as we are.' He blushed again. 'So will I make a start this afternoon, so? I'll have to make a little house for it at the back of your kitchen. I'll put a timber floor in it and paint it white inside so it will be nice, and when I'm done, Tilly says she'll bring Ned down with the cart to take the trough and the tank across, and then it will be ready to go for you.'

She recalled the relief from pain she'd felt in the deep bath of the Warringtons' house and wondered if, through Declan's hard work and ingenuity, the same effect could be achieved here. How amazing if it could.

'Well, I think this might be the nicest thing anyone has ever done for me, Declan, thank you.' Her own voice was choked now.

He gave her another hint of a smile and pushed back his hair, revealing his face again. 'You're welcome, Grace. I hope it helps.'

CHAPTER 27

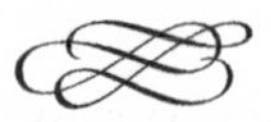

ST SIMONS ISLAND

ctober 1939

Dear Mr Lewis,

I want to thank you again properly, and at much greater length, after that telegram and then my very short letter. I was in such shock and misery at the time, I couldn't bring myself to say much. But my life has improved so much thanks to you, Mr Lewis, that I'm eager to tell you all about it.

Before I start, thank you for writing back and saying you understood, and that there was no need to reimburse you for the ticket – how generous you are! It was so kind after all the trouble you went to for me.

When I was unable to take you up on your offer to visit Georgia, I was very distressed; I thought my life had ended. But your advice about Sister Kenny and your advice about my wages have both turned out for the best, and I have escaped my prison after all.

As you know, my sister had a stroke. She is very incapacitated and needs constant care, but I have a lot of help with her, a lovely girl called Teresa O'Flaherty, so I am not trapped. Teresa is engaged to be married, though, to a man from Annascaul. That's a long way away, so I'll have to find someone else after she marries. The reason I can afford to pay Teresa is because I'm now the headmistress of Knocknashee National School.

You advised me to go to the 'cops' – we call them the guards – about my sister and Canon Rafferty, but in the end, it wasn't necessary. I just let the canon know that I knew all about it, and he caved in at once. And so now I am the headmistress and I run the school to my own satisfaction.

I got rid of a dreadful teacher called Francis Sheehan, and I have a lovely new assistant teacher now – his name is Declan McKenna. He is gentle and clever and everything you could want in a schoolmaster, and the children love him.

You might think this strange, but Declan was a postman before he started here. I knew he had a grá *to teach. It was only a dream, but then I discovered he knew so much about science – he's amazing at maths as well – so I thought, why not? The canon didn't like it, but the curate backed me to the hilt, and to be honest, there wasn't much the canon could do about it, given what I know about him.*

Mr Lewis, this brings me to another very important thing I have to thank you for, and that is for telling me about Sister Kenny.

As you suggested, I did ask Dr Warrington what he thought of her, and he said the current science was against it but his wife had seen her in London and was fascinated. We tried out her ideas together, and my leg felt so much better afterwards.

There was no way of continuing the treatment in Knocknashee, and I was going backwards, but then – and this is how I found out he was a genius at science – Declan McKenna built me a hot water bath house in my back garden. You see, I'd told my friend Tilly about the treatment – I'm sorry, she hasn't read your sister's book yet; she keeps promising she will when the summer is over, as it's a very busy time for farmers and she's on her own – and she asked Declan to do it, and he did.

So every day, and sometimes twice, I fill this enormous bath right up. To be honest it's a cattle trough – I nearly didn't tell you that because it sounds so mad – but it's perfect, and no trace of cattle in it, and the ache in my leg disappears. I do the exercises Mrs Warrington taught me to stretch and manipulate the muscles and to create new movement memory, and I'm sure I'm getting better every day.

Charlie says if it carries on like this, he might be able to get me up on a bike, and Declan says he will fix one up for me. Generations of Knocknashee postmen have had bikes, and one of the outhouses behind Nancy O'Flaherty's post office is what Charlie calls 'a study of two-wheeled locomotion through the ages', so there's plenty of parts. I don't think it will ever happen, of course, but I love just the idea of being able to ride a bicycle. In the hospital it was a dream I had over and over, that I could cycle a bike down a hill on a summer's day, the wind in my face... I'd say it's a wonderful feeling. Charlie says, though, I won't really know what it's like until I've felt the sweat out through my back from cycling up the other side, and I have to admit I've never had a dream about that bit.

I do sometimes feel restless to travel around and see other places, I suppose. I still try to imagine Georgia, but all I can see is a map and the page of a book. I doubt I'll ever see it in my lifetime now, but Tilly would probably say there is no doubt there are people in Georgia thinking the same thing about never having gone anywhere. National school teachers in Australia are probably not fizzing with the excitement of their lives either. They probably walk to school every morning and think, Oh, look, there's another boring old kangaroo, *while I'd give my eye teeth to see one in real life. But you probably think I'm just rawmeising on, that's a word we use for talking a load of old rubbish, and I don't blame you, I am rambling...*

I do love where I am, though, and am usually quite content. I know it is lucky to see anything and live anywhere at all. I was teaching the children about the solar system recently, and it occurred to me how incredibly unlikely it is to even be born at all. Stars and galaxies and more planets than we can even count, and yet here we are.

Now that's probably quite enough from me.

I don't know what strange providence brought us together, Mr Lewis, a letter in a whiskey bottle crossing the ocean, but you have certainly been the perfect answer to that mad letter I sent to St Jude.

You've helped me find my purpose in life, and I only hope I could do the same for you someday, but in the meantime, be aware that I'm wishing you the very best.

Yours with gratitude,

Grace

Then, in very small letters to save starting another sheet, she'd added a postscript.

PS I enclose a photo...

Richard, who had been reading while lounging in a rocking chair on the porch, sat up with a start and a sharp intake of breath.

...that I had taken when I went to Dingle to see a show called Cullen's Celtic Cabaret. Just to let you know, the picture is in black and white, but I have dark-red hair. I tried to tidy my hair up for the photo, but it has a mind of its own, and the sea wind was blowing, so apologies for that. Perhaps I should have kept my hat on; in hindsight I should have, but it's too late now. I don't have any other to send you. G.

Even before he'd finished reading about it, he was searching for it. The envelope lay torn open and empty. He shook out the three pages of the letter, but nothing fluttered out. He stood and searched under the cushions of the rocking chair, down the back of it, all around on the porch. Nothing, nowhere. Had it slipped through a crack? Had she forgotten to put it in? It was beyond frustrating. He checked the envelope again...

And there it was! He'd missed it the first time because it was so small, a two-inch square of white card caught under one of the flaps, almost invisible. He turned it over eagerly. A black-and-white photo of a girl sitting on a bench by the water, her face in profile, her hair adrift in the wind.

He stared in disbelief. So this was what Grace Fitzgerald looked like?

It was so far from the many ways in which he'd imagined her. Not a poor, twisted cripple with a face drawn in pain. Not the blue-eyed, flaxen-haired girl he was trying to write a song about. Not the woman he walked with on the shore in his dreams, the one whose face he couldn't see. All of those images dissolved to mist, and this solid picture rose up and took their place.

This was her, at last. The real Grace Fitzgerald. And she was amazingly beautiful.

* * *

JACOB NUNEZ READ Grace's words with an amused expression. He was a dark, slender man, with horn-rimmed spectacles and thick, dark, wavy hair. He and Richard were having a beer together in the King and Prince Resort overlooking the beach.

He handed the letter back to Richard. 'Interesting girl. What on earth was that about the canon and the cops?'

'I can't tell you, I'm afraid. She swore me to secrecy.'

'Shame. Maybe fictionalise it for a magazine, then – no names, no pack drill. Let's see this picture?'

Richard reddened slightly but extracted his wallet and took out the photo of Grace.

'Very pretty,' said Jacob as he handed the photo back, a small smile playing around his lips.

'She is.' Richard replaced it in his wallet.

'She certainly makes up for Miranda breaking your heart.'

Richard laughed and rolled his eyes. He'd recently received a wedding invitation, on very fancy card. *Mr and Mrs Theobald Logan are pleased to invite Richard Lewis to the marriage of their daughter Miss Miranda Logan and Mr. Algernon Smythe.*

'For a start, Jacob, Miranda hasn't broken my heart – I'm looking forward to her wedding. And Grace Fitzgerald can hardly be my girl – she is on the opposite side of the ocean. We just write and we're honest.'

'A much-underrated quality in a relationship, honesty. Which is why I love your sister. She's very direct.'

'That's one way of putting it,' said Richard, thinking Sarah could be a bit too darned direct at times. Like the time she'd dropped him in it about not wanting to be a banker.

Jacob grinned. 'She's got a good heart, Richard, and I'm crazy about her, but yes, she's got a wild streak, and I'm worried marriage and kids will be too sedate for her.'

'You're thinking of proposing?' He was startled; he hadn't realised it had come to that.

'What do you think?' Jacob looked him straight in the eyes, and Richard hesitated and felt himself flush before answering.

'It's not what I think, it's what she thinks, I suppose. But Jacob, you do know my parents will cut her off. You will have to provide for her in the way she's used to being provided for, and on a newspaper photographer's wage...'

'I know, I know...' Jacob sighed, folding his arms and glancing through the long glass windows towards the ocean, where the last glow of the setting sun gilded the water. 'I know I'd have to settle down and earn a proper living. My uncle is a jeweller in Manhattan, and he keeps asking me to join the business – he has no children of his own.'

'Well then?'

He shook his head. 'No, I can't settle down just yet. The war has started, Richard, though you'd hardly know it. I've been talking to my editor. They've agreed to send me over.' He lit a cigarette and took a sip of his beer, looking at Richard over the rim of his glass.

'Oh...' This was even more startling news than the suggestion that Jacob might propose to Sarah. 'But...' He felt oddly deflated. Selfishly he wanted to say *What about me?* The two of them had been working so well together. 'Sorry, I mean, congratulations I think. Hope you don't get shot at over there. Do war photographers get killed much?'

'I'll try not to get killed, but I'm not going to ask your sister to wait for me. I'll tell her how I feel before I go, but I can't ask her to marry me while my whole life is up in the air. Although who knows? It might be over by Christmas.'

'If it isn't, and America joins, I suppose we'll have to do what we can.' He was beginning to feel like a spare part, with everyone on the move. 'My two buddies, Chip and Albie, they've applied to transfer to the Navy. Maybe I'll do that too.'

Jacob looked surprised. 'Is that what you want?'

'Chip thinks it's probably best to get in before the draft. And if my country turns out to need me, I won't be found wanting.' The words sounded grandiose and a bit naive, but he realised as he said them that he meant them. Everyone seemed to be getting ready for this thing. Only Nathan was scathing about it; when he'd visited Richard in June, he'd remarked that 'wars were thought up by old men and fought by young ones, and doctors like me are left to pick up the pieces, literally.'

'Well, that's a shame.' Jacob flicked ash into the ashtray with a slight smile. 'I was hoping you'd want to join me on my travels – my editor did ask if you were interested. I told him you were a spoiled rich kid dabbling in the arts who likes his creature comforts but that I'd sound you out on the off chance...'

Richard reached over to punch him playfully on the arm, laughing, his heart lifting, suddenly feeling like he had a proper place in the world after all. 'I hope you didn't say all that garbage to him!'

'I did, and it's not garbage. But I also said I couldn't imagine a better man to have on the road with me, that you were brave and steadfast and stuck to your principles, even though it had you in trouble with your family...'

* * *

LATER, after a long evening planning the route they would take to Europe, Richard read Grace's letter again by the light of the oil lamp next to his bed.

You've helped me find my purpose in life, and I only wish I could do the same for you someday.

But hadn't she done that already? It was only after reading the letter she'd sent to St Jude that he'd decided to stick up for himself with his family and demand to make his own way in life. He'd never finished that damn song, but now it looked as if another avenue was opening up to him, one where he could use his skills as a writer to make an actual difference in the world.

Jacob had suggested that maybe they could stop in Ireland on the way, see what Ireland was planning to do in the war.

Richard already knew the answer to that one. 'Grace says that Ireland will never join with England if there is a war anyway, because Ireland and England have been at war themselves for so long.'

'Is that so? Well, we won't bother with Ireland then,' Jacob had said carelessly, before exploding with laughter at Richard's expression. 'Well, OK then, we *might*.'

Smiling, Richard rolled over to put the letter on his side table. The photograph was there, leaning up against a book. He propped his head on his hand, staring at it. She was looking out to sea with wide expressive eyes, as if she could see all the way to America. All the way to him.

CHAPTER 28

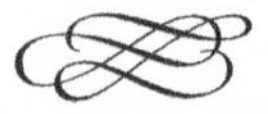

KNOCKNASHEE, DINGLE

ctober 1939

GRACE TIDIED her room after the day's activities, getting ready for the next day's learning.

The classroom was still. It was hard to imagine that all day long, the sounds of children's happy voices filled the dry, dusty space. She wiped the board, closed the damper on the pot-bellied stove – there was a slight chill in the air, though the day was sunny and bright – and mopped up an ink spill on Mikey's desk.

Satisfied the room was tidy, she got the artwork ready to go for tomorrow. The children loved Fridays because it was art day now and they could mix up the powder to make poster paints and paint pictures that Grace would peg on a line across the classroom to dry, as her mother had done. Agnes hadn't approved of wasting money on such things, but Grace had bought several tubs from Mr Delaney, who came around twice a year with boxes of copybooks and pencils and other school supplies.

Tomorrow they would draw and paint leaves. The trees in the yard were just beginning to turn, so they'd go foraging first and identify them, measure them and then trace or rub them. She was looking forward to it herself. She had always loved painting.

She sat at her desk, making out a spelling test for the older children, when she looked up at the sound of a tap on the door. 'Dad was wondering did you want to come over for your tea, as you have Teresa until six?'

'I would, Declan, but I'm meeting Tilly on the strand, our last picnic on the beach before it gets too cold.' She smiled as she stacked the children's exercise books in her basket.

She would correct these books later at home, in the sitting room, which she had turned into a bedroom for Agnes. There was a warm fire always, and fresh wallpaper on the walls, and new trinkets to replace the ones her sister had destroyed. She thought Agnes liked it well enough, because she didn't complain. In the evenings, Grace would keep her company, first sitting and marking the children's books, then maybe reading aloud. Sometimes she would play the piano or put a record on her parents' old gramophone, and those were the times she felt that the glint in her sister's eye had turned more to gratitude than spite. But she still couldn't be sure.

'I'll see you tomorrow, then, Grace. I'll be taking my lot out down the strand myself to teach them about the rocks, if it doesn't rain.' He laughed. 'They're refusing to believe me that any rock in Ireland could be over a billion years old.'

It was amazing how Declan had come on in confidence. She let him teach the older children because they were easier to manage – particularly after they'd been through her hands – and readier to learn about the things he could teach them, advanced maths and science and how to fix things.

After following him out and waving him off, she locked up the school, dropped the basket off in her house, checked in with Teresa that everything was OK, then made her way out to the strand at Trá na n-Aingeal, popping in to Bríd Butler's sweetshop on the way to buy a quarter pound of toffee for her and Tilly's dessert. She'd never forget the favour Bríd had done her, telling her about Agnes and the canon's ice cream trysts in Ballyferriter. If it wasn't for that hint, she might never have figured things out.

'I'll throw in a few liquorices too for you Miss Fitz, I know you like them.' Bríd was always generous.

IT WAS one of those days that looked warmer from inside than it was outside, and she was glad of her new woollen coat and hat.

At the entrance to the strand, Ned the pony stood grazing, his halter tied to the branch of a tree. Grace gave him a pat and thought for a moment there was something different about him, but she wasn't sure what so she just carried on.

Tilly was waiting for her, sitting on the flat rock at the mouth of the cave under the statue of Our Lady, where Grace had found the Paddy Whiskey bottle. They had met here every few days since last July, after Tilly insisted on teaching her to swim. Grace had been afraid at first, but the sea was warmer than she imagined, and the sensation of swimming was wonderful; she could move so easily in the buoyant salty water, the same as any other person. It was almost as good for her leg as the hot bath, and it was wonderful that the bathing costume Lizzie had bought her could be put to good use.

'Tilly.' She waved as her friend looked up and shielded her eyes from the sun.

'It's beautiful, I hope you brought your swimming costume, else we're skinny dipping.' Tilly leaned up on one elbow as she joined her on the rock.

'Of course I did.' Grace laughed.

TILLY LAID OUT THE PICNIC, and they tucked into the brown soda bread, spread with home-made butter and blackberry jam, and a bottle of tea to share, and then they got changed in the cave and went for their dip, because the sea on the west of Ireland stayed warm for much longer than the land.

Tilly made a little fire of driftwood afterwards, to make sure Grace didn't get too cold now that she was out, and wrapped her in a blanket and massaged her leg the way Sister Kenny said it should be done. Then Grace put her coat and hat and calliper back on, and they had an apple tart with the top of the milk in a little jar Tilly had brought for dessert, and the last of the tea, still warm. It was delicious.

Afterwards, they sat gazing out at the calm sea, the sun lowering and turning it gold. Tilly wore trousers and a handknit jumper, and her hair was still in the short style. Grace pulled out Bríd's toffees and they both ate two, even though they were full to the brim, and then Tilly lit up one of her precious Sweet Aftons. Grace had never smoked, but Tilly loved her cigarettes and blew out the plume in a long thin bluish line, hand shielding her eyes from the bright sun.

'So, what next?' Tilly asked, enjoying her cigarette.

'In life? I don't know, really. How about you?'

'Ah, Marion has written to say she is expecting a baby. Mam's delighted to have one related to her, though I can't say it fills me with any great joy. Six children to care for already… What in the name of God was she thinking?'

'I doubt she was.' Grace smiled, and Tilly laughed and flicked the butt of her cigarette onto the rocks.

'Come on, let's go skip a few stones.'

Tilly strolled towards the shore, bending to pick up the flattest stones, and then skipped them across the water, much more elegantly than the clumsy way Grace had tossed in the Paddy Whiskey bottle at this very spot. 'There is a way, you know, of not getting pregnant,' she remarked as Grace joined her.

Grace looked in surprise at her friend. What was she talking about? Everything Grace knew about that whole side of life, she'd learnt from Tilly. Her parents had died before she'd needed to know what were called the 'facts of life', and Agnes was hardly going to sit her down and tell her.

She'd thought she was dying when she got her first period in the hospital, until one of the nurses explained what was happening. But they didn't go into any details about the connection between that monthly annoyance and the making of a baby. Tilly had laughed when Grace came home and Tilly discovered that she had no clue, and filled her in. Mary O'Hare had the whole thing drilled into her daughters for fear they'd be caught out with a baby before marriage.

Mrs O'Hare was unusual, though; nobody ever spoke about such matters as far as Grace could see. People got married, babies arrived, and that was all about it.

'Do I want to hear this?' Grace asked doubtfully.

'I don't know, do you?'

'Well, it won't be any use to me either way, so probably not.'

'Don't talk nonsense, Grace,' said Tilly, looking cross, the way she always did if Grace put herself down. 'It's me that has no use of it, not you. I'm not ever going to be in the position of trying or not trying, having six and then going mad and having seven and then eight – I bet Marion goes again...'

'But do you never want a baby at all?' Grace had tried to put her own *grá* for children of her own out of her head a long time ago. But it still made her sad sometimes.

'Well, I'd need a fella for that, wouldn't I? And that's the very scenario I'm trying to avoid, so no.'

'We'll be a pair of old spinsters together so.' Grace chuckled.

'How bad,' Tilly replied, skimming another stone and crowing with delight when she got ten skips. 'You know,' she said, when she'd finished congratulating herself, 'I read that book?'

'Which book?'

'That one your friend's sister sent me from America.'

'Oh, that...' Grace was amazed. 'Well, when I get his next letter, I'll write back and tell him what you thought of it. So, what did you think of it?'

'It was OK,' said Tilly shortly. 'Now, I need to get back to the farm. Daisy needs milking.' She ran to the mouth of the cave and returned with the blanket over her arm, carrying the basket she'd brought the bread and tart in that now tinkled with the empty bottles of tea and milk.

Together they picked their way across the shore and reached the entrance to the strand and Ned. 'I didn't bring the trap today. The wheel is busted, and I'm waiting on Declan to come fix it,' said Tilly, who normally gave Grace a lift home now that there was no problem with them being seen in the village together. The canon would glare at Tilly if he spotted her, but he was clearly afraid to say a word, especially if she was with Grace, whom he was horribly smarmy to these days; it made them giggle.

'That's all right. My leg is so much better, it's no problem to walk,' and it was true, she was so much more agile than she used to be.

Tilly untied Ned's halter and stood smiling at her. 'Do you like Ned's new saddle? Well, not new exactly, it's probably ancient, but it's still fine. I bought it in the mart last week. Very unusual. It's American, like a cowboy would use, and you can lean back in it, so it's comfortable for long journeys. What do you think?'

So that's what was different about Ned today; he was wearing a saddle.

'I think it's lovely, Tilly. It certainly looks more comfortable than riding bareback,' said Grace, stroking the saddle, which felt very soft; it had a high padded back.

Tilly laughed as she let down the huge stirrups, which were clearly made for big boots and which dangled on wide, soft leathers. 'It's not for me, Grace, it's for you.'

'Me?' The idea of her leaping onto a pony was madness. 'Oh, Tilly, it's a lovely thought, but I couldn't possibly…'

Her old friend sighed in mild exasperation, the way she always did if Grace expressed any anxiety about her latest madcap scheme. 'Listen, Grace, there was a time when you couldn't possibly go to the cabaret, but you did, and you couldn't possibly dance, but you did, and then you couldn't possibly stand up to your sister, God help her, or the canon, but you did, and in July you couldn't possibly swim, but now look at you. You've done so much. And Grace, you can do this too. I know Ned isn't a bicycle, so you're not going to be whizzing downhill with the wind in your hair – he's a bit old for that. But if you'd let me help you onto this stone here, and then while I hold him, you can stand on your good left leg and we can get the right one over – I'm sure you're flexible enough to do that now.'

She wasn't so sure, but Tilly as usual was right. It took a few goes, but Ned was very patient, and eventually she was up. She'd never been on a horse before, and she felt very high, but the saddle was easy to sit in. Tilly laid the blanket over her knees and led Ned by the halter while carrying the basket with her other hand, so there was no danger.

As they strolled back to the town at a slow, slightly bumpy pace, Grace drank in the beautiful countryside, the mountains turning rusty with autumn heather, the green rocky hill of Knocknashee, the ancient graveyard where her parents were buried, and to her left the ocean stretching all the way to America, benign and twinkling and flat. The gulls wheeled and cawed around the fishermen sailing home, seeking guts, as the less aggressive razorbills and kittiwakes waited for their chance.

Was a letter already on its way to her, flying across that vast expanse of waves?

'Miss Fitz, Miss Fitz!' chorused a little gang of children, led by Mikey O'Shea and Aisling Walsh, gathering around her as Tilly led her up the cobbled street of the town. 'Miss Fitz, you look like a queen from a picture book!'

It made Grace laugh, and Tilly laughed too. But with such a lot of love and lightness around her, and sitting up so high and just being led along, it was hard not to feel a bit like a queen – even one of such a small place as Knocknashee.

THE END

If you enjoyed this novel and I sincerely hope that you did, I would really appreciate a review. They help us authors more than you know.

The second book in the series, Yesterday's Paper will be published later in 2024, but you can pre-order the ebook here Yesterday's Paper, and it will land on your device on publication day!

If you would like to join my reader's club pop over to www.jeangrainger.com to sign up. It's 100% free and always will be, and I'll send you a free full length novel to download as a welcome gift.

In the meantime, you might enjoy getting stuck into another of my series. The Aisling Series.

Here's a sneak preview!

For All the World

Chapter 1

DUBLIN, IRELAND, JANUARY 1917

PETER

He felt it as much as heard it. The deafening pounding of stamping feet on the wooden floor of the Gaiety Theatre, the rapturous applause that never wavered in intensity as the entire cast took their second encore, and then got even louder and warmer as the other actors slipped back into the wings, leaving only Peter and the actor playing Macbeth standing side by side on stage, their arms held out to the audience.

It was intoxicating, the waves of sheer love coming from the full house, the calls of admiration ringing down from the gods. He couldn't believe he'd actually pulled it off, playing a leading role at only seventeen years of age.

He'd been seven when he'd first sneaked into the Abbey in the shadow of a lady's dress. He was small for his age, and she'd had so many hoops and such a large bustle, the doorman never spotted him scuttling past on his knees. It was the opening night of John Millington Synge's *Playboy of the Western World*, and there was all kind of commotion because of a reference to Pegeen Mike, the girl of the place, being in her nightie, which sent the ladies and gentlemen of the audience into a right spin altogether. Little Peter had watched, enthralled, as the audience rioted and the Dublin Metropolitan Police had to be called.

He sneaked into lots of shows after that, and though none of them were quite so eventful, he learnt to love the theatre.

By the time he was eight, he was running errands for the stage manager, Mr Griffin, fetching and carrying in return for watching the shows for free. Mr Griffin gave him the odd penny, and the regular cast adopted him as their mascot and let him come backstage. He made himself useful, listening to them say their lines and correcting them if they went wrong. He wasn't much good at the books – he'd left school too young – but he had an incredible gift for recall. If he heard a poem spoken, or a prayer or a song, he could remember it straight off, not a bother in the wide world. And if he heard an actor read their part just once, then he'd know it by heart, better than them. Not only that, he could mimic the exact way they said the words – the women's voices just as well as the men – which made everyone laugh.

Mimicking people was why he'd left school before he'd learnt much of anything. He'd gone to a little national school up on North King Street, St Michael's, where there were no desks and forty children in each class in the room. The brothers who taught there were cruel, and one day one of them caught him imitating Brother Constantin to amuse his friends. The brother picked him up by the hair and dangled him until he cried – he was only seven – and then asked him why he was crying. Peter shouted at him, 'Because you're hurting me, ya big thick eejit!' And he got a beating for being cheeky, and so he never went back after that.

He spent the next years trying to help his mother, giving her the few secret pennies he earned at the theatre to buy bread when his father had drunk his wages down the pub, like he always did. He begged shops for half-rotten vegetables, ran to the pawnbroker and the money lender, trying to keep the show afloat. At last he turned ten and was old enough to get a proper paid job as a messenger boy at the Guinness brewery, where his father worked.

Peter liked his job. He started at five in the morning and finished on the dot of one; another messenger took over then. It meant he got to meet all kinds of people and knew the city like the back of his hand. And it gave him the rest of the day to hang around the Gaiety Theatre. As he grew older, he even got to be on stage, carrying a spear or a pitchfork if a crowd of soldiers or angry peasants were needed, and for that he was paid sixpence, which also went secretly to his mother.

A week ago he'd had his first real break. The actor who played the porter in *Macbeth* had gotten too much into character and was so drunk he could hardly stand up. The director, Louis O'Hare, had heard Peter mimicking the porter's lines, and the next minute, he was being dressed in the porter's costume. He was rigid with fright, but he tried out the piece of advice he'd heard given to the cast by Arthur Shields, Dublin's best-known actor, who had popped in one day to see how rehearsals were going. Like Arthur said to do, he breathed deeply in and out, and the nerves left his body with every exhale.

When he walked out on stage, any remaining fear he'd had just melted away. He wasn't Peter Cullen playing a drunken porter. He *was* the drunken porter. O'Hare was so pleased with his performance that the original actor was relegated to being Peter's understudy and sat in the wings sulking for the rest of the run.

Until tonight, when a different actor had let Louis O'Hare down.

Christine Kemp, who acted Lady Macbeth so brilliantly, that afternoon lost a baby she didn't even know she was carrying and was in the hospital haemorrhaging half to death apparently. He'd heard the women gossiping before they shut the door on his flapping ears. He'd been sad to hear it; Christine was lovely, and sometimes if she got flowers, she gave him one to take home to his ma. Everyone was mad about her. But the show must go on. Except Christine's understudy, who had never once been called upon, had disappeared for a last night of passion with her soldier boyfriend, who was being shipped out to France tomorrow. Peter was sent out to search every pub and place she might be, but he returned alone with only fifteen minutes to spare until the curtain went up.

'I'm so, so sorry, Mr O'Hare. I can't find her.' He was nearly in tears of disappointment himself. This was the night his siblings were coming to see him play the comic porter. The tickets were two shillings each, but Mr Griffin had given him four free tickets on the proviso he didn't say a word. Even cast members didn't get free tickets when the show sold out, and this one had filled the theatre every night. And now they had no leading lady.

Instead of howling and tearing his hair out, Louis O'Hare looked Peter up and down. 'You know this whole play backwards, don't you?'

'Yes, Mr –'

'Millicent!' barked the director over his shoulder at the make-up girl. 'Take Peter here and dress him up as Lady M, and tell Joe he's back on as the porter.'

'Mr O'Hare!' Peter was horrified. What would his brother and three sisters think if he pranced around up there in women's clothing? 'Mr O'Hare, I can't! I'm a boy!'

But Louis O'Hare was a man with his back to the wall. It was the last night of the show, and he needed the ticket money to turn a decent profit. 'Don't matter a rattlin' damn if you're a gorilla. You're doing it. Besides, all the female parts were played by boys back in Shakespeare's time, when women weren't allowed. I've heard you imitate Christine – you have her to a T. Now off you go to the dressing rooms. I'll make it worth your while if you don't make a dog's dinner of it. There's a good lad.'

The strange thing was, even though he was a boy, as soon as he set foot on the stage, he changed into Lady Macbeth, every bit as much as he'd been the comic porter. And the applause...on and on and on. The theatre in all its forms was a drug, and he was addicted. This was what he would do for the rest of his life.

* * *

LATER, after the whole cast had congratulated him – they knew as actors what a hard thing he had done, to play someone of the opposite sex with such conviction – he sat and gazed into the mirror, wiping the greasepaint from his face.

He was in Christine Kemp's dressing room, and it wasn't the cramped cupboard he'd had to put up with when playing the porter. Here the mirror had the bulbs all around it, like he was a proper star. The golden wig was hanging carefully on the hook – Millicent in costumes told him she'd batter him if it got a tangle – the scarlet and gold velvet dress so wretchedly uncomfortable that he wondered if women really wore such garments was draped over the back of a chair, and Lady Macbeth's stiff white ruff was in its box.

It was taking him a while to come back to himself, but with each wipe of the cotton cloth, Lady Macbeth disappeared and seventeen-year-old Peter Cullen came back into view: floppy blond hair and navy-blue eyes, a symmetrical face, a dusting of freckles over his nose, straight brown eyebrows, a delicate but square jaw. He suspected it was because he could pass as a girl that Louis O'Hare had risked giving him the part. Without the ruff, his Adam's apple showed, but that was the only sign of his manliness. He didn't care. He was surrounded by big strong fellas all day, who just cursed and fought and drank, and he had no desire whatsoever to emulate them. He wasn't puny himself, far from it – he was lithe and athletic – but he still had some growing and filling out to do. His beard, before Millicent shaved it off, had been soft and fair; it would coarsen in time.

Anyway, he was glad he looked nothing like his father, a swarthy man, strong from a lifetime of rolling Guinness barrels in the brewery. Kit Cullen was handsome in his own way, but Peter hated him, and so he was happy when Ma said Peter took after her brother, Anthony, who died of scarlatina when he was twelve. Same cupid's-bow lips, she said.

Peter had no idea what that meant, so he asked Kathleen, his older sister, and she explained. He wasn't sure having bow-shaped lips was a good thing at first, but it seemed it was. Women liked it anyway; he'd discovered that. His pouting mouth drew their attention. The girls in the canteen and the laundry would tease him when he came delivering messages from the bosses at the brewery, calling him their lover boy, offering to kiss him, saying how they'd like to take him home.

One old woman who worked in the tannery, with thread-veined cheeks and hands like sandpaper, told him that if she had him, she'd put him in a glass case and throw sugar lumps at him. He'd told his ma and Kathleen this, and they'd howled laughing, explaining it meant she thought he was nice. But he thought it sounded daft.

He was relieved May wasn't here tonight. They'd been walking out, nothing serious. She was a nice enough girl. She'd come to the theatre when he was playing the porter and waited at the stage door to get his autograph; somehow it had ended up with him offering to walk her home.

She was too middle class for him. It turned out she lived in Ranelagh in a lovely red-bricked double-fronted house with a garden out the back, and she told him her father was high up in the bank and her mother from a big farm down the country, so he decided not to tell her about his own background; it would only shock the poor girl.

She was mad about the theatre, knew all the actors and was always talking about this production or that one. She said she'd been in a few productions, amateur, but her parents didn't approve.

The theatre had widened his vocabulary and given him a range of accents to choose from. His fellow actors were all what his father would call toffs, from places like Rathmines and Ranelagh. The fella playing Macbeth was English but lived in Seapoint, and Duncan and Banquo were from Dún Laoghaire, which was fierce posh. So he'd let May believe he was from somewhere like that, and now he was stuck with the lie.

Luckily there was a drive once a year by the wives of the Guinness bosses; they brought in all the clothes that didn't fit or were too worn for their husbands and sons and let the workers take what they wanted. This spring he'd found a pair of black trousers and a smart white shirt that were nearly new, and Kathleen took them to work with her and had them washed and pressed with one of the laundry's heavy irons. He'd even found a pair of proper shoes, a little big for him but fine with two pairs of socks. So he was able to look respectable when he took May out for a cup of tea or a walk in the park.

And so far he had managed to avoid being introduced to her parents, who might ask more searching questions, and he'd make sure to finish with her before she found out where he was really from.

As he finished changing into his one set of good clothes, which he now wore to the theatre instead of his workman's clothes and hobnailed boots, the dressing room door burst open and his sisters, Maggie, Connie and Kathleen, came running in, followed by his older brother, Eamonn. The girls were bubbling and laughing with excitement.

'Holy Moses, Peter, was it really you?' Eight-year-old Connie's eyes were shining with wonder at it all. 'We was lookin' for ya in the porter's dressin' room, and the man said you was in here, and he said not to say, but it was you playin' that woman. I swear I never knew it was you! I couldn't believe it when he said you was playin' a mot.'

'Shh, don't be tellin' anyone. I wouldn't normally be doin' it, but our lead actress is sick, and I had every line of the play off by heart, so Mr O'Hare – he's the director – he made me do it at the last minute. And it's good you didn't know it was me.' He glanced at Eamonn apologetically as he buttoned up his white shirt. 'I'm not plannin' to make a career of playin' women, just so you know, and maybe better to not say anything about it at work. Wouldn't want Da findin' out.'

Kit Cullen already thought theatre people were all 'pansies' and had shown no interest in coming to see Peter playing the comic porter. He'd forbidden Peter's mam to go either, and she was so downtrodden, she hadn't dared defy him. God knew how Kit would react if he found out his son had been playing a woman.

'Ah, it's grand, Peter,' Eamonn said, with a wave of his hand. 'I never copped it was you, so I'm sure no one else did either, so don't be worryin' about that. C'mere to me, I hated all that stuff in school. Remember Jonesy tryin' to teach me poems and all that? Couldn't get outta there fast enough. But you were somethin' else up there, and whoever they thought ya were, they all were glued to ya.'

Peter grinned at Eamonn fondly. His brother's strong working-class Dublin accent was incongruous in these sumptuous surroundings, but he had made the effort to come and was doing his best not to mind that his brother had played a woman up there on the stage. Eamonn took after their father, but only in his looks. When it came to personality, Kit was surly and often drunk and communicated mostly with his fists or slurred nonsense. But Eamonn, who was a couple of years older than Peter but had stayed at school a while longer, was a great laugh and could rattle off stories nineteen to the dozen with a cigarette hanging out of his mouth.

'And you were amazin', even if you were havin' to act being a lady – that must have been really hard,' fourteen-year-old Maggie added, hugging him. 'Like, I never knew yer wan was you, but when she was goin' on about the blood on her hands, "Out spot," I was on the edge of me seat, I swear.' Her china-blue eyes and copper curls made her look fairly theatrical herself, Peter thought.

'Lady Macbeth was desperate altogether, wasn't she?' piped up Connie. 'Poor auld Macbeth, ya'd feel sorry for him, wouldn't ya?' She was so sweet, with her blond pigtails and her best frock on, a faded blue one that had been Kathleen's and then Maggie's.

'Ye would not! The big eejit, believin' all that rubbish outta them witches, and his mate Banquo after tellin' him not to trust them, but he wouldn't listen 'cause he was dyin' to be the king.' Maggie's mad mop of curls was loose; their mother would have a fit if she saw her out without a hat. 'He was just a greedy bas –'

'Maggie Cullen!' Kathleen gasped, ever the older sister. 'Do *not* use that language in here.'

Maggie giggled. Their ma would wallop her for cursing, but all the women in the button factory where she worked said desperate things, and Maggie picked it up like a sponge.

'And you're not supposed to say the name of that play in a theatre anyway. You're supposed to call it "the Scottish Play", 'cause it's cursed and terrible things happen to people who say that word...' Peter spoke in a spooky voice that frightened Connie and made Eamonn laugh.

The door flew open again, and this time it was Mr Griffin, the stage manager. He was fat, with a huge bushy moustache and a shiny bald head. He could be snappy, but Peter knew he had a heart of gold under the gruff interior, and tonight he was beaming as he handed Peter a brown envelope out of the pile he was carrying.

'Your wages. Three weeks as the porter and an extra bonus for playing Lady M. It was a mad idea, but you did great. Well done, son. You pulled it off, and no one noticed you were a young fella. Louis had to rush off to the hospital to see poor Christine – we're hoping she'll pull round. There's a great lady doctor there, Kathleen Lynn. Anyway, he wants you to know you really pulled his fat out of the fire this time, Peter, and when we audition for *Hamlet,* you're to show up and he'll find you a part.'

'Thanks, Mr Griffin.' Peter was almost dizzy with delight. Visions of playing the Dane himself danced through his mind...

'Maybe he's got you pegged as Ophelia,' joked the stage manager, before he rushed off to deliver the other envelopes, leaving Peter smiling ruefully. It wasn't the dream to be playing women, but he was on stage and he was acting and that was all that mattered.

'Well, go on...open it,' Eamonn urged, and Peter realised the eyes of all his siblings were fixed on the envelope. He'd been so excited about O'Hare's offer to join the troupe that he'd forgotten about the money. And in fact he had no idea what to expect. When he'd been told to play the porter, no one had mentioned wages. Lady Macbeth had come out of the blue. What did actors earn anyway? Did they make a good living?

Money was always tight in their house, and the Cullen family lived week to week, even though everyone except Connie and Ma worked. These days Eamonn rolled barrels with Da in the Guinness brewery, Maggie worked in the button factory and Kathleen as a seamstress in Arnotts in town. But Kit Cullen still threw his own wages down his neck in the form of the very stuff he spent the week slaving to make, and any of his children's wages he could get his hands on as well.

Peter felt the envelope before he opened it – no coins, which he found strange. He eased the gummed flap of the envelope open, reached in and felt paper. His heart sank. He hoped it wasn't a cheque – only rich people had a bank account – but more likely it was an IOU; he knew well Louis O'Hare was big on owing money to people. He extracted the rectangle of paper. It was a ten-pound note.

'Ten pounds? For three weeks' work?' Kathleen was astonished. 'That's not right surely?'

'Maybe it's a mistake?' Peter said, as amazed as his siblings. He got nine shillings a week as a messenger boy, which was less than two pounds a month, so could he really have earned so much in three weeks? Is that what the theatre paid, for doing something that wasn't hard work for him at all?

'Don't say a word, even if it is,' Maggie said wisely. 'Wait till you see if he asks ya for it back.'

'Yeah, maybe I'll do that.' It was wonderful to have so much to give to Ma. She could squirrel it away and use it all for herself and her children, unlike all the other wages coming into the house from Eamonn and the girls, which her husband bullied out of her. He felt an urge to celebrate first, though.

'Will we go for a wan and wan?' He grinned at them.

The suggestion made his younger sisters squeal with delight, but Kathleen looked cautious. As the oldest daughter, she carried the burdens of the family on her shoulders.

'We shouldn't. The gas man is callin' Thursday and Da emptied the meter, so we need all the money we can get...'

'Ah, Ka.' Eamonn put his arm around his older sister. 'It's only a few chips and a bit of fish. We can surely do that after Peter's big night, so will we let him enjoy himself?'

'All right, but three between the five of us, right?' Kathleen smiled and raised an eyebrow.

As they set off for Burdocks, the fish and chip near Christ Church Cathedral, his siblings chattered on and on about the money and the play, but Peter tuned them out. He was an actor, a proper paid actor. It was incredible. Nobody he knew was anything like that. Everyone was a docker or a cooper or a driver or something like that, but he was an actor. And not only that, he was making proper money – money his da need never know about. Things were looking up for the Cullen household.

Chapter 2
PETER

The five of them crept up the tenement stairs in the dark, avoiding the rotten floorboards that made it a treacherous climb. Their rooms on the third floor of Number 11 Henrietta Street were all they could afford, and those rooms were leaky and cold and miserable. Peter tried not to rub his elbows on the walls. They were painted with Raddle's red and Ricket's blue, which killed the germs, they said, but your clothes were destroyed if you rubbed it, and he wanted to keep his one good shirt clean.

It was hard to believe the grand Georgian townhouses of Henrietta Street were once home to Dublin's elite, toffee-nosed lords and ladies who thought of Dublin as the second city of the British Empire. Traces of old magnificence still remained: large and wide front doors, brass boot scrapers set in the granite steps, decorative fanlights, intricate coving and ceiling roses, sweeping staircases with elaborately decorated banisters. But these days Henrietta Street housed Dublin's poorest of the poor, broken men and beaten-down women squashed into every room like sardines, their shoeless children dressed in rags and living on bread and watered-down porridge.

His mother did her best for them all, feeding them better than most, washing and scrubbing, hanging out her family's laundry to dry on the wires that crisscrossed the street, anchored in the brickwork by five-inch nails. But with only one toilet and one tap in each house, shared between all the families who lived there, it was a struggle, and the pervasive smell of human waste assailed Peter's nostrils as he climbed to the third floor. A hundred people in a house meant for one family could make for terrible smells.

Eamonn, who had gone ahead, stopped and turned, shushing the chattering girls with his finger to his lips. Lying across the stairs, the stink of porter strong off him, was Larry Maguire, their father's most hated neighbour. And that was saying something, because Kit Cullen hated everyone.

Larry was fond of a drop, as they said, but that wasn't why Peter's father despised him. The reason was, Larry regularly mocked Kit Cullen's claims that he had fought in the Post Office last year with Pearse and Connolly and the rest of the men who signed the Proclamation of Independence, declaring Ireland to be free of the old enemy. The valiant rebels fought for over a week, and the British hammered them back, and everyone feared there'd be nothing left of the city by the time it was done. Peter and Eamonn couldn't get to work. Henrietta Street was on the north side of the Liffey, same side as the Post Office, where most of the fierce fighting took place, and at any time, they might have had to evacuate. Ma made them stay inside – well, Peter and the girls. Eamonn slipped out when Bridie Cullen wasn't looking.

Peter's father had turned up four days after the fighting began, claiming all sorts of heroics. Nobody believed him, but fearing his meaty fists, they kept silent. Only Larry Maguire was brave – or rather drunk – enough to jeer him, telling everyone Kit Cullen was in the back room of O'Donnell's pub out in Drimnagh for three days and nights during the Rising that saw the city in flames.

'Is it not a great wonder,' Larry was heard to remark often and at great volume in the halls of the house, 'how the English were draggin' every last man jack of the Volunteers in for questioning, but they never so much as raised an eyebrow at our brave Kit, and he such a hero for old Ireland? 'Tis for all the world like a miracle, so it is, and aren't we lucky such a bright star of a free Ireland is still here to tell the tale?'

Larry had two enormous brothers who could batter Kit Cullen in three seconds flat if he challenged Larry to a fight, so Kit pretended to laugh it off as the ravings of a drunkard and took out his bad temper on his family instead, doling out even more insults and digs than usual to poor Bridie and his children.

Peter sighed as Eamonn stepped carefully over Larry, trying not to wake him. This was so stupid, such a Neanderthal way of going on. Getting plastered, battering people, working like a dog for a bite in your mouth and to pay the rent to a landlord who enjoyed fine port and a feather bed in the leafy suburbs of Dublin, well away from the inner city. If only people used their brains and not their fists, or guns for that matter, things would be so much better. He longed to get out, get away from here. He loved his ma and Eamonn and the girls, but he wasn't like them, he knew that. They couldn't see a life beyond this place, this poverty. They believed it was all they deserved. Peter didn't necessarily believe he deserved better, but he was determined to get it anyway.

He would be eighteen in the summer, and he'd been giving his ma all his wages since he was ten, but as he followed Eamonn over Larry's snoring body and turned back to lift little Connie across with Kathleen's help as well as give a hand to Maggie, he decided for the first time in his life to tell his mother a lie. He'd say he was sure Mr Griffin had made a mistake and only meant to give him a one-pound note, not a tenner, so he would have to give him back the rest. And then he'd use the other nine pounds to do something different for himself. He didn't know what the future held for him yet, but it didn't involve staying in the tenements and drinking himself into a stupor every night, that was for sure.

Eamonn eased the door of their rooms open; it was really just one big room of the original house divided into three by thin partitions. The living room, if you could call it that, was where they cooked and ate, and also where he and Eamonn shared a settle bed that was pulled out at night and folded away during the day. The second space was their parents' bedroom, and the last, which was tiny, had a double bed the three girls shared. Despite his ma's best efforts, the whole place smelled of damp and body odour.

Peter's heart sank as he entered the living area. It was after midnight and he just wanted to sleep – he had to be up at half past four for work – but his father was still awake, sitting on the settle that his sons needed to sleep on, dressed only in his vest and trousers, his braces hanging down and his forearms on his knees. He didn't look up as they entered. The gas lamp was lit, and there was a bottle of stout on the table next to an empty glass.

The girls slipped away into their room, all their happy chatter and good spirits evaporating into a scared silence.

Eamonn approached Kit the way you might stalk a wild animal, cautiously, making no sudden movements. And Kit Cullen was like an animal, thought Peter. He was hairy like an ape, and his shoulders and arms were huge.

'We might just pull out the settle there, Da…' Eamonn said quietly.

Kit didn't move.

Peter and his brother exchanged a look. This could go any way. Kit could just stand up and go into his own bed, and they'd pray not to hear the animal sounds of him forcing himself on their mother through the thin partition. Or he could try to pick a fight and batter them. Or he could be all bonhomie, demanding his sons drink with him and listen to endless rambling and entirely fictitious stories of his great bravery in the face of the English. If he got started on his hatred for England, they'd be there until it was time to go to work.

'Da?' Eamonn tried again. Their father sat with his fists clenched in his lap.

Peter tried then, leaning down to speak. 'Da?' He hated how meek his voice sounded, but he knew the slightest intonation that displeased Kit could result in carnage.

This time his father looked up, and his hard, unblinking eyes were full of hate. 'Tell me, Peter…' His voice was gravelly, menacing, but not slurred, so he hadn't taken much drink, not enough to slow him down. 'Tell me what made ya think that ya could make a show of me like that?'

Peter glanced at Eamonn in alarm. 'What? I don't –'

The next thing he knew, he was pinned to the inside of the door, his pressed and washed shirt in a ball in Kit's fist, his father's scarlet face inches from his.

'Shamin' me on purpose, was it?' Spittle landed on Peter's cheek, the horrible stench of his father's breath turning his stomach. 'Makin' a fool of me, dressin' up like some kind of a faggot, so the whole place can burst their arses laughing when Larry Maguire goes shouting up and down the halls about Kit Cullen's young fella prancing the boards painted up like a tart?'

The sweat of fear poured from Peter, running down his back. Larry... He should have thought of Larry. The theatre bar was one of the few places left that hadn't barred the old drunk, and he often hailed Peter from his stool at the counter. 'Peter Cullen, son of the famous war hero! Ha, ha, ha!'

'Da, it wasn't like that...' he managed, but his father was pressing hard on his windpipe and he couldn't force any more words out. It was nearly impossible to breathe.

'Da, let him go!' Eamonn tried to intervene but got his father's elbow in his face, sending him reeling.

'Down the docks till this time, were ya?' roared Kit, jabbing Peter in the stomach with his fist as his right hand tightened even more around his son's throat. 'Got a few bob for that skinny little arse of yours, did ya?'

'We were at Burdocks chipper, Da,' Eamonn protested, scrambling back to his feet.

Kit ignored his older son and jabbed Peter in the stomach a second time. 'Or up in Monto? With the rest of the brassers?' He hocked a ball of phlegm and spat into Peter's face, and as Peter, winded and choked, tried in vain to take a breath, he could sense the foul globule sliding down his cheek and onto his chin. He started to think it was the last thing he would ever feel, because the lights in his brain were going out one by one...

'Kit!' His ma's voice cut faintly through the roaring in his head. He could see her; she was in her long nightdress, her hair loose.

'Stop it! Leave him alone! You're killing him!'

'That's right, defend yer little girl!'

'He's your son!'

'He's no son of mine.' With an evil grimace, Kit Cullen tightened his already deadly grip on Peter's windpipe and leant in closer, bright scarlet with rage. 'No son of mine is a nancy boy. No son of mine gives Larry Maguire a reason to make a laughing stock of me!' He drew back his meaty fist again, but this time Eamonn grabbed the heavy iron kettle off the top of the pot-bellied stove and swung it as hard as he could, catching Kit on the back of his head.

Bridie let out a shriek as Kit went down like a sack of spuds, and Peter slid weakly to the floor, gasping for breath. Eamonn dropped the kettle, the girls appeared, and all the Cullen family just stood and stared at their father, motionless on the threadbare carpet. He was face down but awkwardly twisted in the middle because his fat belly had forced his hips to roll to one side. A trickle of blood leaked down his neck from the back of his head.

'Is he dead?' asked Connie in a breathless little voice, and Bridie Cullen let out a wail of horror.

'What will we do, what will we do?' she groaned. She had fresh bruising on her face, Peter could see as his vision cleared. His father had obviously taken his rage out on her before he and the others got back from the theatre. This was all his fault for agreeing to play Lady Macbeth, and now his older brother would be hung for murder.

Eamonn knelt on the floor, his fingers on their father's neck, feeling for his pulse; the brewery had sent him to a first aid course last year. 'Stop crying, Ma. He'll live, worse luck.'

'But what will we do, what we will do?' she kept on asking, standing over him, wringing her hands. 'He was trying to kill Peter! He was trying to kill his own son.'

'I know, Ma. Kathleen, get somethin' to bandage his head. The cut's only shallow. If we wrap it tight, we'll stop the bleedin'. Maggie, clean that kettle. Wipe it and scrub every bit of blood off it. We'll tell him he was drunk and fell and hit the back of his head off the floor. With a bit of luck, he won't remember any of it. Connie, go back to bed and go to sleep. We never heard nothin' nor saw nothin', right?'

'But he was trying to kill Peter, his own son,' Ma kept repeating in a bewildered voice. 'Kit said he'd swing for him. I didn't believe him – he wouldn't kill his own son. But he did. He tried to kill him.'

Her husband stirred and groaned, and Bridie Cullen let out a terrified shriek. 'Oh God, what will we do!'

'Get Peter out of here, that's what we're going to do,' said Eamonn, getting to his feet after tying up their father's head wound with a piece of cloth Kathleen had ripped from her own skirt.

Peter pushed himself into a sitting position against the door. 'You want me to leave here?' His voice was hoarse, his windpipe so bruised.

Eamonn came to help him up. 'Yes, and not just the house. You have to get out of Dublin, Peter. He's tried to kill you once, and he'll try to kill you again. We have to tell him you've left the country – it's the only way.'

'But where will I go? It's the middle of the night. And I was going to audition for another part...'

'I know, but ya can't do that now unless you want to be dead. Ya have to get out of here, as far as you can go. Maybe that young wan of yours – May, is it? Hide out at her place till the mornin'.'

'Ah, Eamonn, I can't go running to her. She hardly knows me.'

'Well, you have to get out of here anyway. And listen, when you've got where you're going, send a message to me. Not here or at the brewery. Maybe send it to Kathleen in Arnotts. She'll see I get it. Tell me where you are, and I'll let ya know how things are goin' here. But go now, y'hear me?'

Peter knew his brother was right. He'd no idea what to do, where to go, but staying here wasn't an option. Never had he seen such murderous hate as was in Kit Cullen's eyes tonight. His father had intended to kill him, and he would try again, and if his mother or Eamonn tried to stop him, he'd kill them too.

His mind raced. He had the money Mr Griffin gave him in his pocket, a whole ten pounds, less the fish and chips. He'd already been thinking of moving on. But not like this, so fast, with no plans.

Where were his hobnailed work boots? He needed to pack a bag...

Kit Cullen moaned and started to push himself up before collapsing back again, muttering to himself.

'Peter, just go. Quick!' his mother begged him, tears running down her bruised face.

There was no time for him to pack; Kit was coming round too fast. He hugged Kathleen and Maggie briefly – 'Say goodbye to Connie for me' – and held his ma for a long second, whispering in her ear, 'I'll write.'

She clung to him, sobbing. 'Take care, Peter. Take care. Please God, we'll meet again in this world.'

Eamonn clapped him on the shoulder, and Kathleen tried to push his father's donkey jacket on him, but he shook his head. He wanted nothing of Kit Cullen's. His father groaned again, and his mother gasped and gave him a frightened shove towards the door.

In the hallway, he stepped over the still-unconscious Larry Maguire, the man who had started all this trouble, made his way cautiously down the rotting stairs and let himself out into the starry Dublin night.

IF YOU'D LIKE to read on just click this link:

For All The World - The Aisling Series - Book 1

GLOSSARY

Glossary

Irish Names Pronunciation Guide:

Siobhán - Shove-awn
Sinead - Shin-Ade
Diarmuid - Deer-Mud
Aisling - Ash-ling
Aoife -Ee-fah
Pádraig - Paw-drick
Seán - Shaun
Máire - Maw-rah
Bríd - Breed

Cnoc – hill (often anglicised to Knock)
The Sidhe – fairy people (Often anglicised to shee)
Cailleach – witch
Oiche Samhain – the Ancient Celtic festival of Samhain, now called Halloween.

Tóraíocht Dhairmada agus Grainne – The Pursuit of Diarmuid and Grainne – an Irish mythology story

Messages – an Irishism for groceries

Ologáning - complaining

Divil – Irishism for the devil but used playfully

Dia dhuit – literally God be with you – hello in Irish

De bhúr mbeatha – God be your life – Also hello in irish

Fláthúlach – generous

Naomh – Saint

Íde – the name of a female saint.

Poitín – illegal alcoholic drink

Naggin – a small bottle of alcohol.

Sleán = a spade with a blade on the end for cutting peat from the bog

Báinín – A while knitted sweater usually in a ornate pattern. Called Aran sweaters in English.

A brasser – a brass coin of small value (also a prostitute in Dublin)

Mamó – affectionate term for grandmother

Bob – a shilling - 12 old pennies

Roan - seal

Bothán – a small farm of poor land

Boreen – a small road –

Peist – a worm

Garsún – A boy/young man

Alanna – from Irish a leanbh, my baby. An endearment.

Scutting – mischief

Sugán – a kitchen chair with a hemp or rope seat. Make of timber.

Beál scoilte – talking too much, a gossip. Literally means, mouth escaping.

Trá – beach

Na nAingeal – the Angels.

Amadán – a stupid person

Hault your whist – be quiet

Girleen – young girl, anything with een on the end means small.

A stór – an endearment – my love.

Glic – clever like a fox – not book smart but instinctively so and possibly a bit sly but for survival purposes.

Scéoined – an anglicisation of the Irish word to be frightened of

Flúirseach – abundant, plentiful.

Bulls Eye – a black and while striped mint sweet/candy

Buíochas le Dia – thanks be to God.

Craythur – an Irish version of creature but meant kindly

Trína chéile – all mixed up

Piság - a superstition

Rawmeising – talking nonsense

Sceitimíní – excited chatter

Eejit – idiot

Geata Bán – white gate

Brack – a kind of Irish fruit cake where the fruit is soaked in tea.

Madrín rua – a fox

Slán – goodbye

Gobdaw – an ignorant person

Gallivanting – carefree travel

By dint of – by means of

Jaunt – a trip

Cailín – young girl

A mhic – my son

ABOUT THE AUTHOR

Jean Grainger is a USA Today bestselling Irish author. She writes historical and contemporary Irish fiction and her work has very flatteringly been compared to the late great Maeve Binchy.

She lives in a stone cottage in Cork with her lovely husband Diarmuid and the youngest two of her four children. The older two come home for a break when adulting gets too exhausting. There are a variety of animals there too, all led by two cute but clueless microdogs called Scrappy and Scoobi.

ALSO BY JEAN GRAINGER

The Tour Series

The Tour

Safe at the Edge of the World

The Story of Grenville King

The Homecoming of Bubbles O'Leary

Finding Billie Romano

Kayla's Trick

The Carmel Sheehan Story

Letters of Freedom

The Future's Not Ours To See

What Will Be

The Robinswood Story

What Once Was True

Return To Robinswood

Trials and Tribulations

The Star and the Shamrock Series

The Star and the Shamrock

The Emerald Horizon

The Hard Way Home

The World Starts Anew

The Queenstown Series

Last Port of Call

The West's Awake

The Harp and the Rose

Roaring Liberty

Standalone Books

So Much Owed

Shadow of a Century

Under Heaven's Shining Stars

Catriona's War

Sisters of the Southern Cross

The Kilteegan Bridge Series

The Trouble with Secrets

What Divides Us

More Harm Than Good

When Irish Eyes Are Lying

A Silent Understanding

The Mags Munroe Story

The Existential Worries of Mags Munroe

Growing Wild in the Shade

Each to their Own

Closer Than You Think

The Aisling Series

For All The World

A Beautiful Ferocity

Rivers of Wrath

The Gem of Ireland's Crown

Made in United States
North Haven, CT
20 July 2024